AN INTERLUDE IN BERLIN

AN INTERLUDE IN BERLIN

JEFFERSON FLANDERS

Munroe Hill Press
Lexington, Massachusetts

Cover design by Mick Wieland Design

ISBN-13: 978-0-9908675-6-2
eBook ISBN: 978-0-9908675-8-6

Munroe Hill Press
Lexington, Massachusetts

In memory of those who, by word and deed, brought down the Wall

Denn die einen sind im Dunkeln
Und die andern sind im Licht
Und man siehet die im Lichte
Die im Dunkeln sieht man nicht.

There are some who are in darkness
And the others are in light
And you see the ones in brightness
Those in darkness drop from sight.

— *"Mack the Knife," Bertolt Brecht*

A NOTE ON BERLIN, 1958

Berlin in the late 1950s was a city that had been shaped and transformed by the ebb and flow of history. It still bore the scars of the massive Allied bombing campaign during the waning months of the Second World War. Berliners remembered the dark days of spring 1945 when the Red Army sacked the city, looting and raping, killing anyone who resisted.

When the leaders of the victorious Grand Alliance met in Potsdam in the summer of 1945, they agreed to divide Germany into zones of occupation. Berlin, the capital of the vanquished Third Reich, located some 110 miles inside the Soviet Zone, was split into Russian, British, French, and American military sectors.

The awkward arrangement imposed upon the city—a Western island in a Communist sea—was to lead to conflict among the four occupying powers. As the Soviets established puppet governments in Eastern Europe, and the U.S. responded with the Marshall Plan to prop up the struggling democracies in the West, the battle lines of the Cold War formed and hardened.

In 1948, the Soviet leader Josef Stalin used the introduction by the Allies of a new currency (the Deutsche Mark) into West Berlin as a pretext to blockade rail, road, and water access to the city. Stalin calculated that this threat to the civilian population, which was dependent on imported food and fuel, would force the Allies to abandon the city. Instead, the United States and the United Kingdom responded by using three pre-approved air corridors to fly supplies into Berlin. The airlift was a success, and the Soviets lifted the blockade on land access in May 1949.

Later in 1949, the Federal Republic of Germany was established with Bonn as its capital and Konrad Adenauer as the first chancellor of the

West German government. In October, the Russians and their East German allies formed the German Democratic Republic and placed Walter Ulbricht and the Socialist Unity Party of Germany (*Sozialistische Einheitspartei Deutschlands*, or SED) in control. An attempt in 1951 by a United Nations special commission to hold free elections in Germany failed, doomed by Soviet intransigence.

Despite the creation of two Germanys, the Allies maintained that under international law the status of Berlin as an occupied area had not changed. British, French, and American troops remained in control of their sectors, and West Berlin was not included as part of the Federal Republic.

In the American sector, the top military leader (United States Commander, Berlin) shared responsibilities with the lead diplomatic official (the assistant chief of the U.S. Mission). From its offices in suburban Dahlem, the U.S. Mission was responsible for all State Department and United States Information Agency activities in Berlin, including RIAS (Radio in the American Sector) and Amerika Haus, a cultural center. The Central Intelligence Agency located its Berlin Operating Base across from the U.S. Headquarters on Clayallee (a street named after U.S. General Lucius Clay).

As a place where East and West intersected, Berlin became a unique *Treffpunkt*, a meeting point, and a city teeming with spies. Intelligence agencies recruited sources, placed penetration agents, and, when deemed necessary, took more direct action, including abductions and assassinations. Soviet leader Nikita Khrushchev called it a "swampland of espionage." In East Germany, the Ministry for State Security (*Ministerium für Staatssicherheit*), commonly known as the Stasi, was modeled after the Soviet KGB as the "shield and sword of the Party."

West Germany had its own spies. In the early 1950s, the CIA financed the Gehlen Organization, an intelligence group led by a former German general and staffed with those veterans of the Wehrmacht, Abwehr, and SS, who were deemed sufficiently denazified to work for the West. In 1956, it became the *Bundesnachrichtendienst*, or BND, the official agency tasked with foreign intelligence. The Federal Office for the Protection of the Constitution (*Bundesamt für Verfassungsschutz*, or BfV) was established to handle domestic security.

The stalemate over Berlin's status continued for more than fifteen years after the end of the Second World War. Travel between sectors was still possible, and some 50,000 East Berliners (called *Grenzgänger*, regular cross-border commuters) journeyed to the West to work every day.

However, it was a crime for East Germans to attempt to emigrate. Nonetheless, each month in 1958 some 7,500 East Germans had applied for asylum at the Marienfelde refugee center. Ulbricht feared that the loss of professionals, technicians, and other educated citizens could lead to the collapse of a functioning society. He pressured the Soviets to resolve the status of Berlin.

Khrushchev responded to Ulbricht's pleas in November 1958 with an ultimatum to the Allies based on alleged violations of the Potsdam Agreement. Khrushchev demanded that France, Britain, and the U.S. withdraw their troops from Berlin and accept a neutral, demilitarized city administered by the United Nations. If they didn't comply within six months, he threatened to sign a separate peace treaty with the GDR that would turn the question of access to the city over to the East Germans. The Allies quickly rejected Khrushchev's demands, vowing never to accept East German control over Berlin.

There wasn't immediate agreement within the Allied camp on how to deal with the Soviet ultimatum and its May 1959 deadline. Adenauer and the French prime minister, Charles de Gaulle, argued against any concessions. Great Britain's Harold Macmillan, who had advocated detente with the Russians, hoped for a compromise solution to the problem of Berlin and the question of German unity. The Eisenhower Administration pledged its support of a free Berlin, but privately an ailing Secretary of State, John Foster Dulles, questioned whether the U.S. might resolve or mitigate the nagging issue of Berlin through diplomacy.

Whether Khrushchev would precipitate a full-blown crisis by ceding control of East Berlin in May—a decision that could lead to a military confrontation or perhaps even war—remained an open question.

PART ONE

ONE

It was the Russian, the silent stranger in the corner, who frightened Christa.

Her nerves were already on edge. She had been deeply troubled when Kruger had shifted the weekly meeting, their *Treff*, from a smoky workers' pub near the Friedrichstrasse Station to the Ministry of State Security compound in Lichtenberg. She worried about the change in location—the Stasi facilities located between Ruschestrasse and Magdalenenstrasse had a sinister and dark reputation, a bleak place where bad things happened, things that East Berliners knew better than to discuss, even with their closest friends.

When she arrived at the gray, forbidding main building that housed Stasi headquarters, Kruger had greeted her coldly and ushered her through a series of linoleum-floored corridors to a cramped room. It was cold and bare with a concrete floor and it smelled of disinfectant, and she knew it was a place meant for interrogations. Kruger motioned for her to sit on a wood chair placed in the center of the room in front of a small table. She knew Gerta, the dour Stasi officer already in the room, but the grizzled older man sitting in the corner was a stranger.

Kruger introduced the man as Comrade Mikhail, and he briefly nodded to her but did not speak. Christa immediately tensed, concerned: Mikhail was a Russian name. Who was he? Why was he there in the room with them? It was bad enough to be entangled with the Stasi—any contact with the Soviets represented even graver dangers.

Was it something to do with Konrad? Could her brother be the reason the Russian had joined her debriefing? Had Konrad said something to his captors at Hohenschönhausen, the Stasi prison, that had attracted the attention of the still and quiet man in the corner of the room?

She rejected the idea—Konrad was too young, too insignificant, to be of interest. It had to be something else.

She felt confident she could handle Kruger and Gerta. She had been dealing with them for quite some time now, ever since she began her double life as an informer. They were nasty, but all too familiar—she knew well their types.

She glanced over at Kruger, the Stasi officer who had first recruited her to inform when she joined the Volkstheater troupe. He was an insecure bully, an ambitious and officious young bureaucrat on the make. She hated the way he looked at her, staring at her breasts, licking his lips. Fortunately, he hadn't tried anything, hadn't made any advances. Perhaps that would come later.

His drab colleague, Gerta, reminded Christa of a frustrated teacher from her school days, Frau Blau, a cheerless woman who had enjoyed enforcing the rules to make her students miserable. Gerta resented Christa with the pinched jealousy of the plain. She would welcome any chance to punish Christa for her youth and good looks.

Kruger and Gerta pulled up chairs and sat behind the table. The Russian remained in the corner, watching, silent. Christa felt her hands perspiring, and she felt slightly sick to her stomach. She told herself to stay calm.

"Your report," Kruger said, adopting an officious tone.

She began slowly, offering up the latest Volkstheater gossip. She didn't understand why the petty quarrels and shifting romances of a few mediocre actors and actresses had anything to do with state security—most theater people ignored politics—but she gave her handlers what they wanted. They had Konrad, and that meant she would cooperate.

She had always been very careful in what she told them, never inventing or fabricating, offering just enough information for them to fashion the official reports they had to file. She fought the temptation to settle any scores. After all, she didn't know who else might be informing, and she assumed that her Stasi handlers would check whatever she told them against the reports of any other informants in the company.

"Any subversive comments of late?" Gerta asked. "What of Manfred Walther? He has expressed anti-state sentiments in the past."

"You'll be happy to hear that Manfred recently praised Comrade Ulbricht's leadership of the Party in front of the entire company," Christa said. She had warned Manfred of troubling rumors about his political reliability, and she had encouraged him to make a public show of his loyalty. The actor had taken her advice to heart and Christa believed she now had made at least one friend in the company, one ally.

"Do your colleagues suspect that you're informing?" Kruger asked. "What you have reported is of little value. Are they suspicious of you? Are they hiding their views?"

"They don't suspect," she said. "There has been little political discussion. We're all very caught up in rehearsing for Comrade Simonov's play, *The Russian Question*."

She glanced over at the man in the corner. He sat there impassively, a glass of tea cradled in his hands, his eyes partially hidden behind rimless glasses. He had the high cheekbones of a Slav, and she guessed that he was in his sixties, or perhaps older, judging from the deep creases on his face and his thinning gray hair. Christa didn't know what to make of him, and his continued silence. The way he stared at her without desire or emotion unnerved her, for it was rare for a man to show no interest in her.

Why was he there?

As if he could read Christa's mind, just then the man stirred. "I would like to speak with Fräulein Schiller now," he said, speaking German with a pronounced Russian accent. "Alone."

Kruger and Gerta exchanged a look. It was clear to Christa that the Stasi officers were afraid of the Russian. They rose to their feet to leave.

Kruger glared at her as he left the room. Christa wondered whether Kruger resented that he was being excluded from whatever conversation the Russian wanted to have with her. It was absurd that he would blame Christa—she had no control over the situation—but Kruger was sensitive to any slight, real or imagined.

The Russian moved over to the table, occupying the seat Kruger had vacated. He placed his glass of tea on the tabletop in front of him. He waited until the door had closed behind Kruger before he spoke. He fixed his eyes on her.

"I will ask you a few questions. Do not lie to me."

He produced a slim black notebook from his coat jacket pocket and carefully opened it, thumbing through it until he found the page he wanted. He held a pencil in his left hand, ready to write.

"Why were you were dismissed from the Berliner Ensemble?" he asked.

Christa took a deep breath. She could feel her heart racing. It was a dangerous question. She wondered what her file said about her departure. What would Helene Weigel, the artistic director of the Ensemble, say about her if asked? "I was never told directly, but I believe it was because of my brother, Konrad. He had been detained by the authorities for some things that he said. He is young, and doesn't think before he speaks. That's all. He's no subversive."

"You doubt the judgment of State Security?"

"I'm his sister," she said. Her mouth felt horribly dry, and she shot a glance at the glass of tea on the tabletop. "I know Konrad. He sometimes says foolish things. He makes jokes that he shouldn't, but he doesn't mean anything by it. He's just a young man who likes to show off for his friends, to push against the boundaries of what is permitted."

"You are close to him." Again, it was a statement, not a question.

"He's all the family I have left in the world."

Comrade Mikhail consulted his notebook and nodded. "Your parents are dead. Your father, Franz von Schiller, a career military officer, fought for the Fascists in Spain. Decorated by Franco for bravery." He grunted. "Campaigns against the Poles and the French. And then von Stauffenberg's staff. Part of the militarists' scheme to assassinate Hitler. Like the other conspirators, executed when it failed. What do you think of the 20th of July plot? Of your father's role?"

"I was very young," she said. "I was sad, of course, at the time, to lose my father so suddenly. Now I see that he was no different than Hitler and the other war criminals."

"Even though your father and von Stauffenberg sought Hitler's death?" The Russian stared at her, his eyes alert, watchful, behind his thick lenses. "I think that you're lying to me. You secretly see him as a hero. He was not, of course. He and the general staff only turned on Hitler because he was losing the war. It's no surprise that his son harbors reactionary and subversive views."

She remained silent. The Russian was correct: she was proud of what her father had tried to do, but she knew better than ever to say so. Konrad felt the same way.

Comrade Mikhail took a sip of his tea. "Despite your family's past, there are ways that you could demonstrate your own loyalty to socialism, to the state. You must be ready to make sacrifices." He waited for her response.

"I'm eager to prove my loyalty," she said. She took another deep breath. Where was the conversation heading? Did he want to take her to bed? Was that the sacrifice he had in mind? Had she misread his interest in her? Perhaps he was no different than other men. "I'll do whatever you deem necessary."

He thumbed through his notebook again, pausing at a page and reading something. "Do you know Stefan Schmidt?"

"Everyone knows Herr Schmidt. He is a very fine director." She stopped, suddenly conscious of her mistake. Stefan Schmidt was the artistic director of the recently-established Neues Theater in West Berlin. He had been friends with Helene Weigel, although never a Party member. "Of course, I mean that in a technical sense only. They say he's been seduced by the whipped cream of the Ku'damm cafés."

"The whipped cream?" To Christa's surprise, the Russian seemed amused by her comment. "The whipped cream of the Ku'damm. Yes, that's clever." He cleared his throat. "Next week Schmidt will invite you to join his troupe. He will ask you to play the role of Miranda in a production of *The Tempest*. You will leave the Volkstheater and accept his offer."

"Isn't the Neues Theater in the British sector?"

He ignored her question. "Schmidt will arrange for you to stay with one of the actresses, at her flat, but you will return to the East once a week and report to Comrade Kruger."

"Am I to inform?" she asked.

He hesitated for a moment, studying her before he replied. "For now, become a valued member of Schmidt's troupe. Make friends." He wrote something in his notebook. "No lovers. No men. Tell anyone who asks that you have given up on romance for the time being."

"I understand."

"You may be approached by our adversaries, by Fascist counterintelligence officers. You must be prepared for this. Tell them that you're an actress, nothing more. This is your chance for a lead role in an important production. You're ambitious. You want nothing to do with politics. Refuse if they ask you to help with their counter-revolutionary propaganda."

"Why would they bother with me?"

"Your arrival at the Neues Theater will cause a stir. An actress from the Berliner Ensemble, from the German Democratic Republic. Their security men are trained to watch for the changes in routine, to investigate the uncommon. They will be curious."

"Aren't you afraid I might like it better there than here?" she asked. "The daughter of a war criminal?" She knew she was taking a chance, but Comrade Mikhail didn't appear disturbed by her outburst.

"We have your brother. You'll not stray too far."

She bowed her head slightly, acknowledging the point. As long as they had Konrad, they had the whip hand. She would do what they asked, and the Russian knew that.

"In any event, we will be watching you," he said. "We'll know if you waver, if you're also seduced by the whipped cream. We can, and will, find you whenever we care to. I say these things not to threaten you, but to inform you. We must have no misunderstandings." He paused, his brown eyes alert. "So do we have an understanding?"

"What about my brother?" she asked. "If I do what you ask, will you release him?"

"His case can be reconsidered. Your demonstration of loyalty to the state will count heavily, as will my recommendation."

He closed the notebook and returned it to his coat pocket. "Comrade Kruger will make the needed arrangements," he said. He rose to his feet and left the room without looking at her again. She realized that her strange audition was over, and that she must have passed scrutiny.

She didn't yet know why she had been selected to work in the West. Why the Neues Theater? It didn't make sense, but there had to be a reason, and she would eventually learn it. For now, it was enough to know that it was a chance to help Konrad, a chance she had to take.

* * *

The light was fading when she reached the street. The temperature had dropped several degrees, and she turned up the collar of her wool coat against the chill. She walked for a few blocks, ignoring the closed and sullen faces of the men and women around her, avoiding eye contact, until she saw a few trees and open space ahead of her—there was a small park tucked into the neighborhood.

She sat down on a battered wooden bench in the park and tried to collect her thoughts. She felt numb—both from the cold and from the fear that had followed her from the interrogation room. When she glanced around, she discovered that the park served as a courtyard for a Gothic building, a church, with twin towers. A small sign identified it: *Glaubenskirche*, Faith Church.

She was surprised to find a church so close to Stasi headquarters. She would have thought that the authorities would have razed it and scattered the congregation, or that they would have made it a government building. She had read that the Jacobins had converted a cathedral in Paris into the Pantheon, a holy place for the saints of their revolution.

Konrad would see the humor in it, the idea of a "Church of the GDR." Stained glass windows of Marx, Lenin, Ernst Thälmann, and Walter Ulbricht. Hymns replaced by the Internationale, and the banal songs that the Party had them sing about the glories of socialism. She smiled at that mental picture, and then, with the thought of her brother and his ironic grin, felt tears well up in her eyes.

She rummaged in her handbag and found the fading photograph, one edge jagged, a picture that she had carefully cut in half, that showed her and Konrad, smiles on their faces, their hair windswept and tousled, the North Sea to their back. She was twelve years old in the photo, and he was eight. The missing half of the photo had included their parents. She had cut the picture in two because her father had been wearing his uniform and she knew better than to carry around something so incriminating.

They had been happy that long summer. Her father had been home on a brief leave, and they had gone swimming and sailing and had picked wild blueberries and elderberries. They had picnicked by the sea. At night, they had clustered around the piano, her mother playing, and they had sung folk songs, many of them sentimental. They were innocent then—at least Christa and Konrad were. Her father never talked about the horrors of the Eastern Front, or of the monsters in Berlin leading his beloved Fatherland into madness and destruction.

That summer had been a lifetime ago. Now, her innocence long gone, she had few illusions left. She would do whatever it was that the Russian wanted her to do. She wanted Konrad freed, and cooperating was her best hope.

Then, once they were together again, she and Konrad would flee from the Krugers and Comrade Mikhails and they would not stop until they were far from Berlin.

She found herself silently praying that God would protect her and her brother—which was absurd, because she had seen too much in her short life to believe in a Superior Power, one that cared about what happened to her or anyone else. It was the nearness of the church that had confused her, and she finished her prayer abruptly, angry with herself for her weakness.

She would rely on herself, as she always had before. She would not make the mistake of placing her trust in anyone else, not with her brother's future at stake. And her own.

TWO

At Union Station, Mr. Johnson had welcomed Dillon home with a broad smile on his handsome mahogany face and with a firm handshake. The Piedmont had been thirty minutes late leaving Washington—the conductor said there were some problems with signals on the track—and Dillon was eager to stretch his legs after the long train ride.

He took a deep breath of the crisp late November air as they walked together to the Randolphs' wood-paneled Country Squire station wagon that Mr. Johnson had parked on the street across from the Charlottesville train station.

On the drive to his father's house, they made small talk. It was slow going—the streets were clogged with cars carrying fans on their way to the last game of the season for the University's beleaguered football team.

Dillon wondered what Mr. Johnson knew about his abrupt return to the United States. Mr. Johnson (the Randolphs had always called him by his surname) didn't ask, and Dillon didn't volunteer any details about the reasons for his sudden homecoming. Dillon suspected that his father had told Mr. Johnson something about the scandal, but he knew that the family's long-time driver and handyman would never say anything about it to him or anyone else.

They followed the winding, wooded road that led to the Randolphs' house, and Dillon found himself tensing. He didn't look forward to the strained conversation he knew he would have with his father.

When they pulled into the circular driveway, Dillon glanced up at the familiar red-brick facade and Palladian columns—he was back home. Some of John Custis Randolph's political rivals had mocked him for building a house that bore more than a passing resemblance to Monticello, Jefferson's famous mountain-top residence. Nonetheless, everyone in town, including those who privately sneered at what they considered ostentation on the part of John Custis, turned up for the annual Randolph holiday party, typically held on the Saturday before Christmas.

Dillon's father was waiting on the front porch. He wore a tweed coat and a Brooks Brother button-down shirt and regimental tie. He had noticeably aged since Dillon had last seen him—his hair had turned completely gray, and there were deeper lines in his face.

They had not discussed Dillon's hasty and ignominious departure from Canberra in any detail when Dillon had telephoned from San Francisco to relate the bad news. John Custis had asked a few pointed questions over the long-distance line, but had said little in reply—like the federal prosecutor he had once been, he kept things close to his vest. Dillon had no doubt that his father was disgusted by the situation, by the scandal, by his son's poor judgment. It didn't have to be said aloud.

"Glad to have you back home, Dillon," he said before they shook hands.

"I'm sorry it's under these circumstances, sir."

"Well, that can't be helped now, can it?"

They stood next to each other, awkwardly, on the front porch. Mr. Johnson had already commandeered Dillon's luggage and hurried into the house with it.

"You're not going to the game?" Dillon asked.

"To the ritual slaughter, you mean? Maryland has a much better squad, and we've had a particularly dismal season. No, it's too cold, and I'm not in the mood for sitting through another lop-sided loss."

When they entered the house, Lucy, his father's cook and housekeeper and Mr. Johnson's wife, emerged from the interior of the house to welcome Dillon home with a hug.

"It's been too long," she said. "I've been in the kitchen all morning. Lunch is ready for you in the dining room."

They sat across from each other. Lucy filled their glasses with sweet ice tea and served them their lunch—roasted chicken, green beans, sweet potatoes, and dinner rolls. His father waited until Lucy had left the room before he addressed Dillon's situation.

"I've spent the morning on the phone with Dan Reynolds," he began. "He was kind enough to hear me out. We go back a ways. Helped him more than once when I was on the Hill, before they made him an assistant secretary. I argued for a second chance for you, for an assignment where you could redeem yourself. Fortunately, he agreed that was what was necessary."

Dillon knew better than to say anything in return. He would wait and hear his father out before he responded.

His father fiddled with his napkin. "I would not normally intervene so directly," he said. "This was a special case. I didn't want to see you destroy a promising career over one stupid mistake. Reynolds felt the same way."

"Thank you," Dillon said. He felt his face flush with embarrassment. "I appreciate whatever you have done on my behalf."

"Don't thank me, yet. Wait until you've heard what's ahead for you. It looks like you'll be assigned to our mission in Berlin. Political attaché. Not ideal, in some ways, but it's a job on the front lines, and it's Europe. If you can keep your nose clean and show some initiative, this Berlin posting could repair some of the damage to your reputation." He paused, studying Dillon's face. "That's assuming that you've learned your lesson."

"I made a bad mistake, and I'm sorry for it. It won't happen again."

"For Christ's sake, Dillon, did she have to be married? If you were going to screw around, couldn't you have found an unattached girl? You've never had to look far for female companionship."

"We were both lonely." He shrugged, reluctant to share anything more with his father.

Dillon had spent a year at the consulate in Sydney before his transfer to the embassy in Canberra. He first encountered Lavinia Hughes at one of the Ambassador's cocktail parties a few months after his arrival. He had been attracted by the hint of sensuality under her poised reserve, and the way her lithe body moved in her silk dress. They had talked about poetry and literature—which her husband, Bill Hughes, an agricultural attaché—found boring. After Bill had abandoned them to compare notes with his British counterpart, Dillon had openly flirted with Lavinia, convinced that she wasn't taking him too seriously.

Two months later, when her husband had traveled to Brisbane for a week on official business, leaving her behind, Lavinia had invited Dillon to dinner, and then into her bed. They spent every night of that week together, but Dillon fully expected that their brief affair would end upon Bill Hughes' return.

He had been careful to keep it light, lending a sympathetic ear to her complaints about her lifeless marriage, but never suggesting that their time together would be anything more than a dalliance, a fling. He thought she understood, but he was proved wrong.

Three days after her husband's return from his trip, Lavinia had turned up at Dillon's doorstep lugging two suitcases and proclaiming her deep and abiding love for him. She breathlessly explained that she had asked Bill for a divorce—so that she could be free to make a fresh start with Dillon.

Dillon handled her protestations of love poorly—he was abrupt, dismissive, telling Lavinia that he didn't love her, and that she was mistaken in believing that he represented the solution to her marital problems. She had said nothing in return, but the tears streaming down her cheeks served as mute testimony to her hurt. Dillon called for a taxi to take Lavinia and her bags home, and was relieved when she left without protesting.

He tried not to dwell on what happened next—his confrontation with the Ambassador the following morning after Lavinia's botched suicide attempt, his rushed departure from Canberra, and the icy reception at State upon his return to Washington.

Dillon was brought back to the present by the sound of his father clearing his throat. "I take it the woman has patched things up with her husband?"

Dillon wondered how much John Custis had learned from his State

Department contacts. Did he know about Lavinia's attempt to take her own life? Had he learned of her stay in Sydney Hospital?

"I believe so, from what little I could learn in Washington. They weren't particularly forthcoming. Lavinia's husband has taken a leave. Out of sight, out of mind. Like my being sent back to the U.S. They're trying to hush things up."

"At least someone is thinking straight about this mess," his father said. "Had this woman left him, that would have put you in an even worse bind. If they keep their mouths shut this doesn't have to turn into something out of 'Peyton Place.' You don't want this story making the rounds." He rubbed his eyes. "Not that yours is the first nasty scandal in the annals of the diplomatic corps, nor will it be the last. But for your sake, it needs to be contained."

"I recognize that," Dillon said.

"Berlin offers a marvelous chance to atone for your slip-up. It's the center of attention these days. Ike has rejected the ultimatum by Khrushchev. We'll have to stand fast there, just like '48 with the Airlift." His eyes glistened. "Standing shoulder-to-shoulder with the Berlin Command would be something to be proud of, damn proud of."

Dillon looked down at his lunch plate. He had eaten very little, and he knew that Lucy would have her feelings hurt. It couldn't be helped—since he had learned about Lavinia's attempt to take her own life, he hadn't had much of an appetite.

"Your Uncle Leigh will stop by later," his father said. "He asked if he could spend some time with you today. A quiet chat. Too many people will be around at Thanksgiving."

"I'd like that."

"There's a silver lining in all this. You'll be able to put to good use the German you learned in Cologne." He hesitated, watching Dillon's face. "You should know that Reynolds initially offered a post in Bonn for you. I told him no, that you didn't want to be on the periphery, you wanted to be in the thick of things. A second chance. A chance to set things right."

* * *

Uncle Leigh arrived later that afternoon and spent thirty-five minutes closeted with John Custis in his study before the two of them emerged.

"If we could have a word in private," Leigh said to Dillon. "John says we can chat in his hideaway."

Dillon followed his uncle back into the study, closing the door behind them. He looked around quickly—the room hadn't changed since his last visit home. A wall of photos chronicled his father's days in Congress. Most featured John Custis Randolph shaking hands with the famous and near-famous. In the middle of the wall, occupying the place of honor, hung the photograph of his father with Franklin Delano Roosevelt in the Oval Office, both seated and smiling artificially for the camera. President Truman's photo was relegated to bottom row, reflecting John Custis' dismissive view of the former Senator from Missouri, the "accidental President."

On the writing desk, there was one photo in a standing silver frame, a picture of Dillon and his brother Wash, in his Marine uniform, after Wash's Quantico graduation ceremony. Wash had his arm draped over Dillon's shoulder, and they both gazed at the camera with broad grins.

Leigh picked up the framed photo and studied it for a long moment. "A terrible thing. To lose him so far from home. The folly of war. Old men sending young men off to die."

"Wash was doing his duty," Dillon said. "He was a Marine."

"I know. It still hurts to think of what could have been."

Dillon nodded. "It hurts every day."

Leigh coughed slightly, and looked over at Dillon. "Your father brought me up to speed on your status. Not all the gory details, but enough that I thought we might have a little private chat."

Leigh thought of himself as a country lawyer. He had been the anchor for Randolph & McFarlin, while his older brother was in Congress, making sure that the practice prospered and continued to be regarded as one of the most prestigious law firms in Charlottesville. He delighted in needling John Custis, arguing that the family could only afford one politician.

Dillon and Leigh had always been close—both second sons, both overshadowed by dynamic older brothers. When Dillon's mother had died when he was twelve, Leigh had looked after Dillon that summer, while John Custis dealt with his grief and anger by immersing himself in work. Leigh took Dillon camping, taught him how to play tennis, and had introduced him to Wordsworth, Shelley, and Keats. Dillon had learned "I Wandered Lonely as a Cloud" by heart that summer, and it somehow helped ease the pain over the loss of his mother.

"He told you that the plan is to assign me to Berlin?" Dillon asked.

"He did. That's a positive development. I'm sure that you know that you're a fortunate young man."

Dillon nodded in acknowledgment. He had no illusions about what would have happened without his father's intervention. He would have been quietly urged to resign, or he would have been banished to a consulate in Central Africa or Southeast Asia.

"I realize that," Dillon said. "It's a second chance, and those are hard to come by."

"That's a good reason for our talk. While it's a second chance, you have to assume that by the time you arrive, the grapevine will have worked its wonders. Everyone in Berlin will have heard some version of the Dillon Randolph story. Cad and seducer of a colleague's wife. Some may give you the benefit of the doubt, a few of your colleagues may envy you, but most will see you as a reckless libertine, a Don Juan on the prowl, and every move you make will be scrutinized."

"Not a pretty picture you paint, Uncle Leigh."

"A realistic picture, though. Assume that you'll be watched, by diplomatic security, by your chief of mission, and especially by the females. You should take things slowly, especially when socializing. You may find a bored wife or two eager for a roll in the hay. I'm sure you know the type. Run in the other direction. And I don't have to tell you that you must avoid even the slightest hint of impropriety."

"If you don't have to tell me, why are you telling me?"

"Because your father asked me to. Look, Dillon, this is quite awkward, but it needs to be said. If we take back the Presidency next year, then your father should be in line for an important role in the new Administration. We're due for a Democrat in the White House. It's likely that Dick Nixon will be the nominee, and he can be beaten."

"Not if Adlai runs again."

"The word is that he's had enough. There are other candidates—Jack Kennedy, Johnson, Humphrey, maybe Stuart Symington. Tricky Dick is no Ike—he's dark, grim. The country's ready for a change." His uncle contemplated the wall of photos for a moment. "My point is that if we win, and your father comes under consideration for a Cabinet position, we don't want there to be anything standing in the way. No hint of impropriety or scandal."

"No besmirching the Randolph family name? Is that it? You can tell my father not to worry. I'll only fuck the local talent."

"There's no need for vulgarity."

"Sorry," Dillon said. "I don't mean to take it out on you, Uncle Leigh. I'm disappointed in myself. But I do learn from my mistakes, and I won't make the same one again."

"No one expects you to become a monk. You're a healthy young man. But a little discretion will go a long way."

"I wouldn't make a very good monk," Dillon said. "But discretion will be the word."

"Have you been writing? Any new poems?"

"Not lately. A touch of writer's block. Maybe Berlin will change that."

Dillon wasn't naive; he knew that no matter how well he performed in Berlin, there would be doors closed to him. He had violated one of the unwritten rules of the Foreign Service—*Thou shall not covet thy colleague's wife*—and it was likely that the episode in Canberra would haunt him for the rest of his career.

On the long flight back to the United States, he had considered resigning. He had entered the Foreign Service at the urging of his father, and he knew what leaving it under a cloud would mean to their relationship. He did have other options. Dillon could pursue graduate work, and he knew he would be welcomed by the English Department at the University. In the end, he decided against it—he was damned if he was going to admit that he had failed.

He wouldn't leave the Foreign Service until he had proven to his father that he had made things right, that he had repaired his reputation. With that accomplished, he would feel free to make of his life whatever he damn well pleased.

* * *

Dillon found his college roommate, Charlie Woods, waiting for him in a booth at the Virginian. There were two empty beer glasses on the table in front of him. Charlie's ruddy face lit up with a smile when he spotted Dillon.

They shook hands, and Dillon slid into the seat across from his friend. Without being asked, a waiter arrived with a pitcher of beer and filled their glasses.

"I told him to be ready," Charlie said. "I figured you'd be thirsty."

"How are things? How is Molly? And Jane?"

"They're both fine. We couldn't find a babysitter, or we would have gone to the game."

"You didn't miss anything from what I heard on the radio. We lost, badly."

Charlie made a face. "So only one win this season. Duke. They're as sorry as us. I do hate constantly losing the last game of the season to Maryland."

"How are things with you?"

"Routine," Charlie said. He took a sip of his beer. "Not much going on. I've brought in some solid clients, so I think the partnership is within reach. Molly and I have our ups and downs. You heard the joke about the wife who goes to her doctor to complain about her bedroom problems?" Charlie grinned, and Dillon waved at him to continue. His friend loved to tell jokes, typically off-color ones.

"So the wife tells the doctor she's very concerned. 'Every time we're in bed and my husband climaxes, he gives out a Rebel yell.' The doctor reassures her, tells her that she shouldn't worry, what her husband is doing is unusual but completely natural. 'I don't see what the problem is,' he says. The wife shakes her head. 'The problem is,' she says, 'that damn yell wakes me up!'"

Dillon laughed and Charlie's grin widened. "You'll appreciate the joke more when you're hitched yourself, Dillon," he said. "It goes with the territory. But seriously, Molly has been good for me, and Jane is adorable, if I say so myself. Who knows, maybe we'll try for a boy." He took a longer sip of his beer. "Can you drop by tomorrow, after church?"

"Afraid not. I came home to see my father. To apologize." Dillon took a deep breath. "I got myself into a jam in Australia. Tangled up with a woman, there. She felt more for me than I did for her."

"That's a familiar story," Charlie said.

"A bit different this time. She had a husband. Then she decided she didn't want to stay married, and when I told her that *we* weren't going to work, she decided to turn our light romantic comedy into a near tragedy. Thank God they were able to pump her stomach at the hospital."

"That's bad, Dillon. Real bad. How are things with her now?"

"I don't really know. She's gone back to her husband, or so I was told. Of course, they recalled me to Washington in disgrace and if my father hadn't pulled strings, I'd be out on the street."

"What happens next?"

"I've been reassigned to the Berlin mission as a political officer. My father called in some debts. He and my Uncle Leigh hammered me about my bad judgment and irresponsibility."

"What about the posting to Berlin? A good thing?"

"I quite like the idea," Dillon said. "You can't get any closer to the heart of the matter, can you? It's a test for the country to see if we can stand up to the Russians. There's the added benefit that my father can brag that his son is on the front lines of the struggle against the godless Reds."

"That's not fair," Charlie said. "Lord knows your family has sacrificed enough. No one expects more. I don't think your father does. Sounds to me like he's trying to get you out of the mess you've created. And it is a mess, Dillon."

"I never said it wasn't."

"Put yourself in your father's shoes. He's lost one son, and now he's worried that you're derailing your career, to say nothing of the morality of the situation. It's adultery, whether or not her marriage was on the rocks."

"There's general agreement that I've been a bastard. Morally, that is. I don't have much of a defense. We were both lonely. But I never led her on, told her that I loved her. I'm blameless on that count."

Charlie waved his hand in dismissal. "I'm not standing in judgment, Dillon. I'm concerned about you on a more practical level. Fooling around with a married woman is a good way to get yourself killed. One jealous husband with a revolver. He wouldn't be blamed, you know. There's not a jury in Christendom that would convict him. You're the bad guy."

"Am I?"

"To the world, yes. And I know it takes two to tango, so whoever is between the sheets with you shares the blame. But there's some blame, and I'd be lying to you if I didn't say so."

"Well, this is the third lecture of the day on this topic. My father, my Uncle Leigh, and now my best friend. I get it. I'd be a fool to chase another married woman."

Charlie nodded, satisfied that he had done his duty as a friend. "Well, a change of scenery can't hurt. You'll be on the ramparts in Berlin. Lots of Cold War tension. Colorful."

"From what I gather, there's nothing colorful about Berlin, especially in the winter. I'll be freezing my ass off, worrying that the Russians are going to send their tanks across the border, while you're back here drinking beer."

Charlie raised his mug in a mock salute. "A poem, in the form of a toast. 'Here's to those who wish us well, and those that don't can go to hell.'"

THREE

Christa began the year 1959 at a raucous Silvester party hosted by Stefan Schmidt in his spacious Charlottenburg apartment.

Outfitted in a velvet smoking jacket with a shawl collar, Stefan circulated around the living room, greeting his guests—mostly actors and actresses from the Neues Theater, and a few stagehands favored by the director with an invitation to his New Year's Eve bash. Stefan filled the crystal flutes of his guests with Sekt and encouraged them to sample the assortment of canapés on a side table. His latest boyfriend, Fritzi, sat with Stefan's poodle Marlene on his lap and fed the dog scraps of veal sausage.

Christa enjoyed the party, taking in the tipsy chatter and latest theater gossip. She sat next to her flatmate, Liesl, and sang along as Milo played show tunes on Stefan's piano. They all laughed when Milo dedicated "Mack the Knife" to Christa and mugged his way through the song—her time with Bertolt Brecht and the Berliner Ensemble had made her a minor celebrity in West Berlin theater circles.

Stefan was in an expansive mood. His romance with Fritzi was in the honeymoon phase. And everyone in the company knew he had been delighted with the rehearsals for *The Tempest*. Christa had worked hard, wanting to prove herself, carrying the script with her all day and, whenever she was alone, reciting her lines from memory and checking to make sure she had them exactly. She preferred to practice her lines when she was walking to and from the theater—because she would be moving on the stage—and she got used to the strange looks of people passing by who must have imagined her a crazy woman for talking to herself.

Stefan was nothing like Brecht or Benno Besson or any of the directors at the Berliner Ensemble. He cared about aesthetics, about performance, not about class struggle or how theater could improve the lot of the proletariat. Christa couldn't imagine Stefan decorating the stage curtain with Picasso's dove of peace, as Brecht had, or agonizing over how best to portray workers on the stage. Ideological questions bored Stefan. Why he was cooperating with the Stasi was a mystery. Christa wondered what leverage they had over him. Stefan treated her carefully, gingerly, and she assumed that he had been instructed to handle her with *Samthandschuhen*, kid gloves, and to smooth her way with the company.

At midnight, Berlin welcomed the New Year with tolling church bells and a near-deafening barrage of fireworks. The explosions must have brought back unwelcome memories for older residents of the city, to the dark days when it was a war zone, even though Berlin had been at peace for nearly fifteen years. Milo and Fritzi joined in the celebration by lighting firecrackers and throwing them out the parlor windows. The guests toasted each other with their glasses of Sekt, wishing each other *Frohes Neues Jahr*. Liesl hugged Christa while Stefan kissed Fritzi and a thoroughly drunk Milo threw confetti into the air.

Christa looked around at Stefan's smiling guests and felt herself relaxing. It was certainly better than her last Silvester celebration—an evening she had spent in Prenzlauer Berg with one of her girlfriends, drinking glasses of Berliner Luft peppermint schnapps and ringing in the New York feeling depressed about Konrad, about her prospects at the Volkstheater, and about her life in general.

She felt welcomed by her colleagues. She had taken an immediate liking to Liesl, who had just turned twenty and recently joined the troupe and had never lived in a large city before. Stefan had arranged for them to share a small flat in Wilmersdorf.

Christa loved everything about the Neues Theater. It had been founded, and underwritten, by a reclusive industrialist from Bremen, an Anglophile who dreamed of exposing Berliners to Shakespeare's greatest works and was willing to pay handsomely to make that happen. He had purchased a turn-of-the-century red-brick building off the Ku'damm which had been an elementary school and a clever architect had transformed its auditorium into an elegant jewel of a theater. The rehearsal space and dressing rooms were well-lit and spacious, and the theater lobby—once the school's entrance hall—boasted a hand-painted tile floor and glittering crystal chandelier.

While the Neues Theater wasn't about to stage Ionesco or Beckett, Stefan hinted to those actors he was recruiting that the future might include some experimental productions, and in the meantime, who didn't want steady employment and a juicy Shakespearean role or two added to their resume?

She didn't understand why she had been infiltrated into the Neues Theater. What was Comrade Mikhail thinking? How did she fit into his plans, whatever they were? She was glad to be in the West, surrounded by people who cared about the theater, absorbed in interesting work, but she worried about what she didn't know.

Christa knew that she would have to please the Russian in the year ahead for there to be any hope of Konrad's release from prison. She would be ready when the time came, when they told her the real reason for her presence in the West. She wouldn't rest easy until that day.

* * *

A week later, on a Tuesday, she had arrived early at the Neues Theater when Stefan pulled her aside and handed her a sealed envelope. When he wouldn't look her in the eyes, Christa knew it had come from the East. Neither spoke. She was sure that they would never talk about their connection with the Stasi.

She left the theater and only opened the envelope when she reached the street. The unsigned note inside read: *Magdalenenstrasse 15.00 h.* She felt herself tensing at the invitation—she dreaded returning to Stasi headquarters. Since Christa had joined the Neues Theater, she had met several times with Kruger near the Friedrichstrasse Station, but never at the Ministry of Security compound. There hadn't been much to report, and Kruger had seemed bored by the whole exercise.

Christa placed the envelope and note in her handbag and headed to the S-Bahn station. On the ride to Lichtenberg, she tried not to worry about the upcoming meeting. To keep her mind off what lay ahead, she softly recited her lines from *The Tempest* to herself.

Kruger was waiting for her at the entrance to Stasi headquarters. He greeted her curtly, and accompanied her through the dark, narrow hallways to the same interrogation room where she had first met the Russian. He opened the heavy oak door for her, but didn't follow her inside.

Comrade Mikhail waited for her, already seated at the wooden table. A glass of tea sat in front of him. This time, there was another glass, which she assumed was meant for her. He motioned for her to take the chair across from him.

He began by encouraging her to try the tea, which she did—to be polite—and found warm and slightly sweet. Then he asked how she was faring at the Neues Theater. Did she like her fellow actors and actresses? Had they accepted her? She did not doubt that he had read Kruger's reports, and she figured he was probing to see if she would tell the same story.

"They have accepted me," she said. "I believe Stefan has insisted on it. The company is much different than the Berliner Ensemble. There's no sense of purpose. No commitment to the struggle." She paused, thinking. Had she contradicted anything that she had already told Kruger? No, she had been consistent.

"You admired Brecht," he said, making it a statement, not a question. "He fooled many impressionable people, but he was no hero. A bourgeois intellectual. Decadent. That he was given the Stalin Prize was a farce. He had an Austrian passport and a Swiss bank account—did you know that?"

She shook her head. "I did not know that, but I worked with him, and I believe his heart was in the right place."

"His heart?" The Russian frowned. "I went to see this Berliner Ensemble when it came to Moscow, after Brecht's death. His characters are cardboard. Contrived. Abstract. Would a man with heart write plays like that? Do you know Chekhov?"

"Of course. *The Cherry Orchard*. Long ago, I played Anya." It had been in a school production, but she wasn't going to tell Comrade Mikhail that. Better that he believe she had a deeper knowledge of Chekhov—a Russian playwright, after all—than she actually did.

"You were Anya? Now, that's a role for an actress." He sipped his tea. "Someday, we will produce a socialist playwright with the talent of Chekhov. One who understands real people, workers, peasants. That will be the day."

She stayed silent. There was a time when she would have argued with him about the virtues of the Berliner Ensemble, about the dream of a theater that could help redeem Germany from its dark past and create a new socialist order. She had been proud of being part of the artistic vanguard. She remembered what her closest friend in the company, Lena Eisfelder, had once said, that when people talked about their idea of heaven, no matter what their religious beliefs might be, it was a place of peace, equality, and love—the same vision of a world run by socialist principles. The Ensemble could play a part in achieving that vision. If Lena, a woman whose parents had perished in Dachau, could believe in the dream, then so could Christa. Or so she had thought.

After Konrad's arrest, and his imprisonment in Hohenschönhausen, it had all changed. Christa had been relegated to minor parts, and many in the troupe began to avoid her. She had lost friends—although now she recognized that they had never truly been her friends. Lena, at least, had stayed in touch, but even she had been reluctant to be seen in public together.

Christa had moved from disbelief, to anger, to resentment, and then, finally, to resignation. She had fallen from the summit, and there was no return. She had not lost her faith in a more just society, but she no longer believed it would ever be achieved in the German Democratic Republic. Konrad had been right, the regime would never accept reform. There would be no thaw, no change for the better. She could only bitterly regret that they hadn't left for the West when they had the chance.

"I have brought you here today for a reason," the Russian said. "It's time that you did more than parade around a stage in a costume. It's time you did something useful."

He laid two black-and-white photographs on the table before her. They both were of a blond man, handsome, with a square jaw and a lean frame. One showed him in long white trousers and a sweater, holding a tennis racquet. The other photo appeared to have been taken from a yearbook of some sort. Christa guessed that the man was in his late twenties.

"This is Dillon Randolph. An American, a diplomat."

Christa remained silent. She wondered why he had shown her the photographs of the American.

The Russian leaned forward, peering at her. "Randolph comes from a decadent, aristocratic family. Part of the ruling elite. His father operates in powerful circles in Washington. These are the very reactionaries who stand in the way of socialism around the world." He took his glasses off, and cleaned them with his handkerchief. He held them up to the light for a moment, inspecting them, before putting them back on. "The Americans have posted Randolph to their Berlin mission. Like many of the decadent bourgeois, he's a womanizer. He has been sent to Germany because of a scandal. He seduced a married woman, the wife of a fellow diplomat. His weakness presents us with an opportunity."

"What is it that you wish me to do?"

"We want you to meet this man."

"You wish me to meet him?" She thought she knew what the Russian wanted her to do, but she wanted to hear him say it.

He grunted. "Let's not mince words. We want you to take him to bed, to make him your lover."

"Why would I ever agree to do that?"

Comrade Mikhail stared at her for a long moment. "I've seen your file. There should be no moral objection on your part. You're no virgin. You've had many lovers. There are good reasons for you to agree. You want to help your brother. You hope to be restored to the Berliner Ensemble. Both of those ends can be achieved if you do as I ask."

"Why do you wish me to seduce him? To what end?"

"To our ends."

"Which are?" She could tell he didn't like her questions, but she needed to know what she would be getting herself into.

"It's simple. Once he's your lover, you will introduce him to some of your friends in the East. Then we will persuade him to assist us." The

Russian stared at her. "You said you would make sacrifices. Now is the time. If you have second thoughts, you must tell me now. There can be no turning back."

She had known there might be a price to pay for Konrad's freedom. It was degrading to be told she must go to bed with a strange man—to whore herself—but she couldn't let that dissuade her. She could sleep with the American—she would approach it like a new role. She would find something about him that appealed to her, and she would focus on that.

"I'm an actress," she said. "I can play this part."

"This is why you were instructed to take no new lovers. You had to be unattached for some time. Should they check." He stared at her. "You have not been with a man since I last saw you?"

"You know that I haven't," she said. "I'm sure your watchers have told you that." She assumed that Stefan was informing on her, and perhaps others at the Neues Theater. There was no way of knowing and it was better to presume that they all were.

"I wanted to hear that directly from you."

"I've had no lovers, and no one from their secret police has approached me."

Comrade Mikhail nodded, satisfied with her answer. "As soon as you become involved with Randolph that will change. If you're questioned about him, your story is simple. You're a woman who has fallen in love. You don't believe in politics—you care only about the stage and your new lover." He opened his notebook and consulted a page. "You say that you played Anya in *The Cherry Orchard*. Just as in the play, you can think of our own little production as involving an arrival and a departure."

"And an axe to take down the orchard at the end?" she asked, surprising herself—she remembered more of the play than she thought. She waited, wondering if she had gone too far.

"Clever," he said. "No, we do not wish to harm the American. He will have his own part to play. He will supply us with information that we need. He will do so willingly, because he will put love before duty."

"There is some danger involved," he said. "In such a mission, there always is. In convincing him that you love him, you may convince yourself. Then, you could do foolish things." He shrugged. "This must not happen. You must understand the possible consequences. For you. For your brother."

"It will not happen."

Comrade Mikhail reached inside a leather bag at his feet and produced a slim book. He handed it to her—the title was in English: *Cedar Creek*; the author, Dillon Randolph. "Read this," he said. "Randolph's a poet as well as a diplomat. It will help you understand him."

She held the book in her hands, wondering what it might tell her about him, this American she was supposed to seduce.

"I have something else for you," he said. He reached into the pocket of his suit jacket and retrieved an envelope. He handed it to her. "Open it."

Inside the envelope, she found a thick stack of $20 bills. Christa stared at the man, wondering if it was a test of some sort—why would he offer her dollars? A trap of some sort?

"This is American money," she said. "Why do you give it to me?"

"You must look your best," he said. "Buy some new clothes. Some nylons. Perfume. High heels. You must shine for him."

She placed the envelope in her handbag. She knew better than to object. The Russian was correct—she did need to look her best, if she was to attract Randolph's attention.

Comrade Mikhail rose to his feet. "For now, no more contact with Kruger. We will give you a phone number that you will use only in an emergency. We will meet only when I say. You will know we have sent a message to you, when someone gives you a book of Chekhov."

"Someone?" Christa stood up, following his lead. It was clear that the meeting was over, and she was being dismissed.

"It may be a stranger. It may be someone you already know. That doesn't matter. The Chekhov is your signal."

FOUR

Berlin remained shrouded in fog for much of Dillon's first few weeks in the city. Walking down the Kurfürstendamm, the famous shopping boulevard that everyone called the Ku'damm, he would be surprised by the sudden appearance of men and women in their heavy wool winter coats emerging like spectral apparitions from a curtain of January gray.

In the late afternoon, the boulevards and side streets remained relatively dark as the dense fog acted to diffuse the light of the gas street lamps. The damaged spire of the bombed-out Kaiser Wilhelm Memorial Church, the Gedächtniskirche, seemed particularly mysterious looming above passersby in the gray mist.

It snowed on the second Sunday of January. Dillon had attended services at St. George's Church on Preussenallee, and when he emerged from the church the sidewalks and streets were covered by a light carpet of snow. He wondered if they were in for a long winter.

The dismal weather had left him feeling slightly off-balance. He found it harder to orient himself to the geography of Berlin, to become familiar with neighborhoods and landmarks, to relate the streets and subway stops on his fold-out city map to their actual locations.

Before leaving for Germany, he had spent six weeks in Washington with the seasoned State Department veterans of the Office of German Affairs prepping for his job as political attaché. Harold Braun, who had been stationed in Bonn for several years, took the lead in briefing Dillon. A short, balding cynic, Braun had a nervous habit of rubbing his chin when he talked. He sketched out the political situation in Germany and in the city, describing the parties and personalities, and explaining what sorts of information Dillon should seek to gather.

Braun insisted that they speak German, even while conceding that nearly every politician or journalist that Dillon would encounter in Berlin would be fluent in English. He tasked Dillon with reading the major German dailies, which were several days old by the time they reached Washington, and would ask him to summarize what he had gleaned from the papers—in German.

"You speak like a westerner, a Rhinelander," Braun remarked. "They should have sent you to Bonn."

Dillon took that as praise, a rarity coming from the jaded Braun, who revealed little of his own beliefs. His analysis of the current situation was always clinical and precise.

"The Russians see West Berlin as a Trojan horse in the middle of East Germany," he told Dillon. "The standard of living in the Western sectors is much higher. They lose hands down when there's any comparison of systems. Their propaganda is heavy on how Nazis and militarists dominate the West German government. There's just enough truth involved to give it some bite."

"Didn't denazification eliminate the worst of the lot?"

Braun rubbed his chin, and Dillon tried not to be distracted by the tic. "Better in theory than in practice. The idea was to separate the wheat from the chaff. Except we quickly discovered that you need some of the chaff, the ex-Nazi Party members, to run the country. It's true that Willy Brandt spent the war in Norway, and Adenauer resisted the Nazis, was put in prison, lived in exile in Switzerland. But there were limits to the housecleaning. Adenauer's chief of staff, Hans Globke, was in the Nazi Party and helped write the Nuremberg Laws. They claim Adenauer defended keeping Globke in his government by saying you don't toss away dirty water when you don't have any that's clean."

"That plays into the Russian's hands, doesn't it?" Dillon asked. "They can argue that we're allying ourselves with the Nazis."

Braun shrugged. "No one has clean hands. Their bark is worse than their bite. They don't want a war over Berlin. Khrushchev sent a private note to Dick Nixon saying just that. What we can't tell is whether Khrushchev is truly master of his own house. Remember, he faced down a coup in '57. Jawing at us over Berlin is a way to throw some red meat to the hardliners in the Kremlin, and prove to the Chinese that he's willing to challenge the capitalists. Berlin lets him pick a quarrel, seek some concessions, bolster his tough-guy credentials."

"So the threats are saber-rattling on his part?"

"For the most part. I'm sure he worries that some hot-headed Red Army tank commander will start lobbing shells into West Berlin. Not that we could do much for our people there if they do decide to move against us. The truth is that our guys are so outnumbered that they could only offer token resistance. God forbid it ever comes to that. It'd be like the Alamo or Little Big Horn for Berlin Command."

"Anyone ever tell you that you don't paint a particularly inviting picture of Berlin?"

Braun laughed. "One other bit of advice," he said. "Keep the cowboys from the CIA at arm's length. They may try to recruit you for one of their hare-brained cloak-and-dagger schemes. If you're approached by them, politely decline."

"And if they wave the flag at me? Patriotic duty and all that."

"Tell them that you're on probation for all intents and purposes and can't afford any missteps. When they check that out, they'll find out that it's true, and they should leave you alone." Braun moved his right hand toward his chin, paused, and pulled it away.

Dillon winced at the reference to his past. While Braun had never asked about Canberra, and Dillon hadn't volunteered anything about his time in Australia, he figured that the scandal was no secret. He could only hope that over time people would forget, that the story would lose its shock value.

"I doubt they'll bother with me," Dillon said. "But if they do, I'll tell them that I'm trying to lose my Peck's Bad Boy reputation, and they should recruit elsewhere. Give someone else a chance to be a hero."

* * *

Dillon's reception at the U.S. Mission Berlin—USBER was the State Department's awkward acronym employed in cable dispatches—had been properly formal and reserved. He quickly realized that the senior diplomats there didn't quite know what to do with him—the Mission already had its full complement of political officers, and they apparently hadn't been consulted by the State Department hierarchy about Dillon's assignment to Berlin.

The assistant chief of the Mission, Harrison Phillips, suggested that Dillon spend time on a temporary basis familiarizing himself with the current state of Berlin's politics. "Write up whatever you find interesting," Phillips said. "Then we'll decide which desk will be a good home for you." He added that some of Dillon's insights could be incorporated into the summary cables that went to Bonn and Washington.

Dillon resolved to make the best of his very loose brief. He plunged into the life of the city, taking every opportunity to flee the depressingly Spartan offices of the Mission—housed in the U.S. Headquarters on Clayallee—for the boulevards and cafés of Charlottenburg and Wilmersdorf. Dillon also spent as little time as possible in his dreary first-floor bachelor's apartment that he occupied on a side street in Dahlem.

He concentrated on mastering the political ins-and-outs of Berlin. He read the newspapers religiously, even poring over the turgid *Neues Deutschland*, which dutifully parroted the SED Party line. Quinn Warren, the American liaison to Willy Brandt, the mayor of West Berlin, arranged for Dillon to interview several members of the Senat, the executive body governing the city. Whenever the opportunity arose, Dillon invited Western foreign correspondents to lunch in the restaurants near the offices of Reuters, BBC, Time, and other news organizations in Charlottenburg. He paid for the socializing out of his own pocket—Uncle Leigh had given him several thousand dollars in cash before he left for Germany—rather than expensing it through the Mission.

He wrote several reports on the political situation, relying heavily on the notes of his lunchtime conversations, and was rewarded by having a few of his observations added to one of Harrison Phillips' cables to Bonn. Nonetheless, Phillips didn't assign him to a specific desk—Dillon hoped for the Eastern Bloc desk—but instead asked him to pick up the duties of those political officers on vacation. "It will give you a sense of the entire operation," he said. "Quite valuable from a career perspective."

Dillon took that to mean that Phillips still hadn't figured out what to do with him. He wasn't going to complain—he enjoyed the freedom of his vague role, learning the diplomatic do's and don'ts from a cadre of experienced Foreign Service officers.

Later in his first month, he took a sightseeing bus tour of East Berlin, joining a handful of hardy British and American tourists visiting northern Germany in the winter. When the bus crossed into the Russian sector, Dillon was surprised by how many of the neighborhoods were still in ruins, with block-after-block of rubble and masonry piled high, in some cases making small hills.

They stopped to view the massive Soviet war memorial in Treptow Park, followed by a ride along the long rows of recently constructed cookie-cutter apartment buildings on Stalinallee. The tour passed through the vast expanse of Marx-Engels-Platz which the East Germans used for their mass rallies, and then drove past the Brandenburg Gate, where Dillon spotted a red flag flapping from the quadriga—the copper-colored chariot carrying the Goddess Victory drawn by four horses—that topped the iconic structure. They skirted the edge of Potsdamer Platz, where Dillon spotted the massive illuminated display board that flashed headlines from the West Berlin newspapers, before the bus returned them to the American sector.

His brief glimpse into life in East Berlin was sobering. The contrast with the prosperity in the Allied sectors was striking. Dillon better understood why many of the West Berliners he had met were so concerned about Khrushchev's ultimatum. Across the white painted lines that marked the sector boundaries, they could see what their future would be like if the West decided Berlin wasn't worth fighting for and withdrew from the city. Dillon doubted that would happen, but he also knew that the status of Berlin could easily become a bargaining chip in larger negotiations over disarmament in Europe. Berliners certainly knew it, too.

* * *

Dillon understood why his most of new colleagues kept their distance. He had arrived with two strikes against him: the mess in Canberra, and the top-down nature of his posting. Further, they had to wonder how much clout Dillon might have back in Washington.

He made friends elsewhere. He met a young British diplomat, Reggie Jamison, at a cocktail party and discovered that he also played tennis. Dillon was delighted when Reggie proved to be his equal on the court, and he arranged for them to play twice a week at the Berlin Command's indoor courts behind the U.S. Army Shopping Center in Dahlem.

Dillon was quietly pleased when Audrey Wingate had approached him about giving a talk at Amerika Haus, the cultural center in Berlin run by the USIA. Audrey, a petite blonde with a heart-shaped face, was earnest and disarmingly direct. The daughter of a wealthy Des Moines Chevrolet dealer, she had parlayed her Northwestern degree in art history and her serviceable German into a job at Amerika Haus assisting the director in promoting American music, art, and literature.

"It's not often that a published poet falls into our laps," she said. "An *American* poet. We're always looking for interesting speakers who can share something about our culture with the locals."

"You could do better. I'm not much of a public speaker."

"Nonsense. A friend of mine, Doris Ross, heard you read from *Cedar Creek* in Charlottesville just after its publication. She said you were marvelous."

Dillon vaguely remembered the event, held in Old Cabell Hall, and how he had calmed his nerves with a few nips from Charlie Woods' flask of brandy before his appearance on stage. He didn't remember much of the day—a blur to him now—only that he had told a few jokes, read some passages from his poem, and answered two or three questions from the surprisingly large audience of students and faculty members, most drawn from the English Department.

"She's too kind," he said. "The truth is that I stumbled through my talk."

"You're too modest. For our event, I'd like you to read from your poem and then talk about its background. And the importance of poetry in American life. The Reds are always promoting that horrid man Brecht, even though he's gone to the Workers' Paradise in the sky." She giggled. "We need to raise awareness of our poets and writers, show that we're not a bunch of Babbitts without culture."

"A reading?"

"And answering any questions from the audience."

"In English, I hope."

"Of course. You'd be surprised by how many Berliners speak excellent English. It's been nearly fifteen years that we've been here, more than enough time to learn."

"Had the Nazis won the war, do you think we'd be speaking German today in New York and Washington?"

She tossed her head. "I wouldn't be. I would hope that we'd be in the Appalachian Mountains fighting a guerrilla action against them. Like Gary Cooper in *For Whom the Bell Tolls*."

"Didn't the Gary Cooper character collaborate with the Spanish Communists?"

"I know that," she said. "It was just an example, even though I can't imagine Gary Cooper ever siding with the Reds." She narrowed her eyes. "You're evading my question, Dillon. Can I count on you for a reading at Amerika Haus?"

"I'll come and do the talk," he said. "Tell me. Have you read *Cedar Creek*?"

She gave him a smile that showed off her perfect, white teeth. "Not yet," she said. "But I'll know it forward and backward by the time of the event." She kept her eyes fixed on his face. "I've already ordered one hundred copies from your publisher in New York. Air freight. The books will arrive next week, just in time for your talk."

"That soon?" He was caught off guard. "What if I had said 'no'? What would you have done about the books?"

"I figured I could persuade you," she said. "The power of positive thinking. Not to be immodest, but when I set my mind to something, I don't often get a 'no.'"

* * *

Amerika Haus was located on Hardenbergstrasse, close by the Zoo Station, near a number of boxy International Style buildings designed and constructed after the war—the Berliner Bank, the chamber of commerce and industry, and the Bilka department store.

A long, rectangular structure with large glass windows, Amerika Haus greeted visitors with an open terrace facing the street. American and German flags fluttered on twin poles. Steel block letters spelled out the name of the center on a blue tile mural that was reminiscent of the Stars and Stripes. When Dillon arrived at the front entrance, he found Audrey waiting for him.

"What do you think?" she asked, waving toward the building. "Two years old. Quite modern."

"I'm partial to colonial red brick," he said. "So this wouldn't be my first architectural choice."

"The architect's a German. Bruno Grimmek. He worked with Albert Speer once, but all is forgiven today." She stepped back for a minute and looked him over appraisingly. "You're dressed for the part today. You look like a poet."

Dillon had decided to wear a light tweed jacket, a white shirt, and a thin dark tie, the same outfit he had worn to his poetry reading at the University. "It's my good luck jacket," he said.

He followed her into the building, past an exhibit of abstract paintings, to Amerika Haus' auditorium. It was a functional room, with a simple raised stage and a lectern, a hanging movie screen, and rows of chairs for the audience. Dillon glanced around, and to his surprise saw that all of the seats were filled, with a few people standing in the back.

Dillon waited by the side of the stage while Audrey stepped up to the lectern to make his introduction. He was impressed by her poise—she didn't seem rattled by the large crowd.

Audrey beckoned to him, and Dillon walked over to the lectern, strangely calm when he had expected to be nervous. He adjusted the microphone and took a deep breath. He began by explaining that he would read from *Cedar Creek*, then provide some context for the poem, before finishing with questions from the audience.

"I'll do my best to answer them," he said. "Listening to Miss Wingate's flattering introduction, you'd think that I was ready for poet laureate status. The truth is that I'm a young poet, one with much to learn."

He slowly opened his copy of the book and cleared his throat. He took a quick sip of water from the glass on the lectern, before he began reading the opening of the poem.

> *Do the ghosts at Cedar Creek rest uneasy?*
> *Do gray apparitions wonder at the cost?*
> *The dead and maimed, heart-sick and soul-weary*
> *Lost sons, lost fathers, lost brothers, Lost Cause*
>
> *Do the blue ghosts regret their ghastly victory?*
> *Burned barns, ruined crops, a harvest of blood*
> *Sheridan's killing machine the coming of the Lord?*
> *Thousands lie forever mute in the Shenandoah loam*

He stopped and looked up, pleased, and surprised, by the sustained applause that followed. He closed the book and stepped out in front of the lectern and talked about how he had been inspired to write *Cedar Creek* after reading Herman Melville's "Sheridan at Cedar Creek."

"Cedar Creek was a pivotal battle near the end of our Civil War. I hoped to write about how everything about it reflected the best, and the worst, of the cause that Virginians were fighting for. The figures in the poem—the Confederate General Ramseur, the Union mapmaker Jedediah Hotchkiss, the slave girl Amelia, the surgeon Thomas Fanning Wood—they're all real people caught up in that historic struggle."

He returned to the lectern and read another section of the poem, about General Philip Sheridan's famous ride on his big gelding Rienzi that rallied the Union troops and turned the tide of the battle. He stole a quick glance at the faces of those in the front row—they were listening intently. When he finished reading, he turned to Audrey, who had stationed herself to the right of the stage. "Why don't I take questions?"

She nodded, and Dillon called on a diminutive silver-haired woman who wore a knitted gray woolen scarf and a blue coat.

"Do you consider your poem to be anti-war?" she asked.

"I think it highlights the senselessness of much of war," Dillon said. "The waste. The lives ruined. But I don't think that it's anti-war. Sometimes you have to fight. As a diplomat, I would hope that would be the exception, rather than the rule. I should say that I don't consider pacifism a realistic response to armed aggression."

"Is it common for a diplomat to write poetry?" the woman asked.

"I wrote much of this poem before I was a diplomat," Dillon said. "But we have a tradition of American poets who write in their spare time. William Carlos Williams practiced medicine, Wallace Stevens was an insurance executive, Robert Frost, a poultry farmer. I'm in good company." He paused. "And your great poets had some interesting occupations—Schiller, a doctor and professor of philosophy; Hölderlin, a tutor; Mörike, a pastor."

A lean, older man with a deeply lined face and a goatee beard rose to his feet. Dillon recognized him with a nod, and the man cleared his throat before asking his question in lightly accented English. "Your poetry appears to be squarely in the traditionalist school. Do you worry that you're out of step with the Beat poets, like Gregory Corso and Allen Ginsburg?"

Dillon smiled at the question. "No, I don't worry about being out of step. My poetry is rooted in my country's history. My family has been in Virginia since our Revolution. A long time by American standards. My background is dramatically different than that of someone like Allen Ginsburg. I believe his mother was a Russian immigrant. He sees the country from a radically different perspective." Dillon paused for a moment. "I guess you could say I've found different things to howl about."

There was appreciative, knowing laughter from the audience.

"Mr. Randolph is hardly a howler," Audrey said. "We have time for a few more questions."

A young man in a black leather jacket and slicked-back dark hair raised his hand, and Dillon nodded to him. The man wore steel-rimmed spectacles, and had a prominent jaw. He stepped into the aisle, and looked around to his right and left before speaking.

"A truly great man of letters, Bertolt Brecht, said that the task of the poet was to change the world and free the people. I find none of that in your poetry. Why is that?" The man's tone was hostile.

"Herr Brecht believed poetry should serve political ends," Dillon replied. "That's not how I see it. At its best, poetry becomes a mirror held up to life. One of our poets, Robert Frost, says that poetry is a way of remembering what it would impoverish us to forget."

"Frost is a bourgeois poet." Dillon's questioner raised his voice, glancing around at the audience. "You're one, as well. And you're also an apologist for a puppet regime that refuses to accept a democratic, neutral, and free Berlin." There were hisses and whistling from some in the audience, and the young man raised his hand in an effort to silence them. "So my question is simple. Why do you Americans insist on backing the reactionaries in Bonn? Why not allow Berlin to become a demilitarized and free city?"

His question provoked more hissing and a few boos and catcalls. The young man stood his ground, remaining planted in the aisle, his arms crossed defiantly.

"I'm not here this afternoon to debate foreign policy," Dillon said. "But I'll give you a brief answer. Your mayor, Willy Brandt, says that Berlin belongs to a free Germany. We agree. So do a vast majority of Berliners. Less than two percent voted for the SED in the December city elections." There was a loud round of applause from the audience. Dillon spread his arms in a gesture of openness. "Can I answer any questions about poetry?"

The young man in the leather jacket wasn't done. "What is it like to write poetry in the age of McCarthy?" he asked with a smirk.

"I don't agree with the premise of your question. This isn't the age of McCarthy. Senator McCarthy was censured by our Senate for his behavior. He has since died. Yes, a few people in our government were considered security risks and lost their jobs, but there were no purges, no camps."

"I suppose you have a similar justification for the barbaric way you treat Negroes in your country."

"The position of the Negro is not what it should be," Dillon said. "It's better than it was. President Eisenhower has strongly supported efforts to integrate our schools, and he's signed a Civil Rights bill. We don't have a perfect society in the United States, but we have a functioning democracy and that allows us to change and improve things."

"Another questioner, please," Audrey said quickly before the man in the leather jacket could respond. He muttered something under his breath and made a show of stalking out of the auditorium.

Audrey pointed to a young woman in a stylish fuschia dress near the back of the room. She had chestnut hair and large blue-green eyes, and it registered on Dillon that she was very pretty.

The woman showed no signs of nervousness as she stood erect by her chair. "Mr. Randolph, I began reading *Cedar Creek* last night, and I could not sleep until I had finished it. You tell a fascinating story. I know very little about American history, but as a Berliner there was much in it that spoke to me. To my heart."

"Do you have a question?" Audrey asked, interrupting. She seemed somehow annoyed by the young German woman.

"I do," the woman said. "Mr. Randolph, now that you are in Berlin, have you thought of writing a poem about this city and its people, about our tragic history?"

"I doubt that I could do that story justice," Dillon said. "I'm a stranger, a newcomer, and I've a great deal to learn."

"But no stranger to heartache and longing and the shadows of history."

"That's quite poetic, Fräulein. Perhaps you should be the one writing it."

She smiled. "I'm an actress, not a poet. I prefer that others write my lines."

Audrey broke in, glancing at her watch. "We've come to the end of our time," she said. "I want to thank Dillon Randolph for sharing his poetry with us and for his fascinating commentary. I understand all of the copies of *Cedar Creek* we had on hand have been purchased. We hope to have more copies of his book here at Amerika Haus in a few weeks—they must be sent from New York. For those of you who did buy a copy, Mr. Randolph will be signing books in ten minutes time in the front lounge."

Dillon first escaped to the men's room, where he splashed water on his face and dried it with a clean towel. When he reached the lounge, he found Audrey and a queue of people clutching copies of *Cedar Creek* waiting for him.

Audrey apologized that she couldn't stay—there was a dinner party in Zehlendorf that she had to run to—and steered him to his place at a small table. "Thanks a million," she said. "I owe you."

Dillon spent fifteen minutes fielding compliments and signing books. He looked up, and the final person in the line was the attractive woman in the fuschia dress who had been his last questioner.

"Hello. My name is Christa Schiller," the woman said, extending her hand for Dillon to shake.

"Schiller like the poet?"

"Like the poet, but as I said, I'm an actress. With the Neues Theater."

"I wish my German were as good as your English," Dillon said. She had a beautiful voice, with the hint of a slight British accent when she spoke English.

"My mother insisted that we learn the King's English. I studied it for many years."

"How did you end up reading *Cedar Creek*?" he asked.

"I saw the posters for your talk, and it interested me," she said. "I bought the book and, as I said, stayed up reading it. You have a way with words.

As an actress, there are times when I struggle with poorly written lines, so it's marvelous to read something so lyrical."

"Thank you. Are you in a play now?"

"I am," she said. "*The Tempest*, at the Neues Theater. Not too far from here."

"Shakespeare? In English?"

"In German. It's an excellent translation."

"And what part do you play?" Dillon quickly glanced at her left hand. No rings—which meant that she probably wasn't engaged or married. He was attracted to her. It wasn't just her looks—there was something about her, her obvious intelligence, her sense of humor, that appealed to him.

"Miranda," she said, and then made a wry face. "The only female part in the play."

"I've been found out," he said. "I'll confess I've never seen a production of *The Tempest*." He held her gaze for a long moment. "I'd love to learn more about the play. Are you free for dinner?"

"Not tonight. We have a performance." She shrugged. "I have a very crowded schedule. That's the life of an actress when she has a show."

He wasn't ready to give up yet. "You must have one free evening?"

She hesitated, considering his question, and Dillon was relieved when she nodded. "Monday, I'm off."

"Great. Shall I pick you up at your place?"

She shook her head, and suggested that they meet at the Paris Bar, a restaurant on Kantstrasse, a few blocks from Amerika Haus. "Do you like French food?" she asked. "As you might imagine, that's what you get at the Paris Bar."

"Even bourgeois American poets like French food. Shall we meet at six?"

Dillon looked around and realized the room had cleared out and that they were alone. He offered to walk her to the front of the building, and when they reached the street it had begun to snow lightly, with delicate snowflakes floating down onto the streets and sidewalks and quickly melting. Dillon noticed the young man in the leather jacket was waiting for them. He stepped forward, peering at them through his spectacles.

"Does he pay you in dollars?" he asked Christa. "Whore."

"That's enough," Dillon said. "Leave us be."

"Get out of our city, then," the young man said. "We don't want you here."

Christa said something to the young man that Dillon couldn't make out. The man grunted and stepped closer to them. He reached out and suddenly grabbed Dillon by his upper arms, shoving him away. Dillon responded without thinking, pushing him back. The young man swung a fist wildly, and Dillon ducked and avoided the punch.

Then Dillon hit the man as hard as he could in the stomach. The man bent over from the punch and then toppled, falling onto the pavement.

"Bastard," the man said. He looked up at Dillon. "Fuck you. Fuck Americans."

Dillon and Christa stood in silence as the man scrambled to his feet. Holding his stomach, he backed away from them, and then shuffled away down the street.

"I'm sorry for this rudeness," Christa said. She studied Dillon for a moment. "You're a man of many talents, it appears."

"My father had us take boxing lessons. Didn't expect they would come in handy here."

They stood there in silence for a few moments. Christa removed her left glove and reached out with her bare hand and let the snow evaporate on it. She turned to Dillon. "I shall see you on Monday, then, Mr. Randolph," she said.

Before he could respond, she turned and walked away up Hardenbergstrasse in the direction of Zoo Station. He watched her, admiring her graceful stride, as she slipped between two newsboys hawking the afternoon paper and then disappeared from view behind a street stand selling currywurst.

He wondered if anything would come of their dinner date, whether they would connect. He thought that she was interested in him, and there was no question about her appeal for him. He liked the idea of having a girlfriend, certainly a girlfriend as intriguing and alluring as Christa Schiller. He would find out soon enough if a romance was (to borrow one of Uncle Leigh's favorite phrases) within the realm of possibility.

FIVE

The security officer for the U.S. Mission, Lars Swanson, had been on leave in the States when Dillon had first arrived in Berlin. A week after his return, Swanson had approached Dillon and asked him to join him in his office at the end of the corridor, steps from the Mission's exit, for an initial security briefing and interview.

"A get-to-know-you chat," Swanson explained when Dillon reluctantly settled into the uncomfortable wooden chair across from him. "I like to spend some time with everyone new when they join us, and give them the lay of the land."

Swanson was a compact man with crew-cut hair, a prominent Adam's apple, and a disconcerting habit of holding eye contact longer than most people would find comfortable. A buff-colored file with Dillon's name on it sat on the desk before him.

"First time in Berlin?" Swanson asked.

"It is. I spent a semester in Cologne as a student, but never made it here."

"How's your German?"

"It's coming back. The Berlin slang takes some getting used to. A bit different from what they teach in the classroom, and not what I was used to in Cologne. I read much better than I speak. I won't be discussing Heine or Rilke in German, but I can order in a beer garden."

Swanson kept his eyes trained on Dillon's. "I have no idea who Heine or Rilke are, but you'll find a lot of the Krauts speak some English. My

German's just okay. My parents spoke Swedish at home, and there are some shared words, so I had a head start."

Dillon decided not to explain who Heine or Rilke was—it would come across as patronizing, and he wanted to stay on Swanson's good side. He sensed that Swanson didn't like him—no doubt he saw Dillon as another snobbish Foreign Service officer with Washington connections who secretly dismissed those in the Mission who had gone to lesser-known state schools. It wasn't how Dillon saw things, but there was no way Swanson could know that.

"You'll find most of the Germans are all right. Some of them are a bit stand-offish, but for the most part, it's live and let live." Swanson didn't pause, and Dillon realized that he wasn't particularly interested in holding a conversation. "What's important to remember is that we're behind enemy lines here. The Russians have been testing us, stopping our convoys on the road from Helmstedt to Berlin, making them wait. Ever since Khrushchev's ultimatum they've been more aggressive. When you're in the Russian sector, you're protected by your diplomatic immunity. Most of the Volkspolizei understand that—they're not going to stop you and give you the Fifth Degree—and it's the same for the Red Army troops. On the other hand, you never know when they'll try to harass an American. Spend as little time in East Berlin as possible and if you do go, take someone along with you. Safety in numbers."

Swanson leaned back in his chair. "Any questions so far?"

Dillon shook his head. He hadn't learned anything new from Swanson, and he was impatient to get back to his work.

"This is a city of women," Swanson said. "Since the war, German men have been in short supply. It means it isn't hard to get laid. Some guys come here and start tomcatting all over the place. A mistake, unless you're eager for a bad case of the clap."

Dillon nodded. He knew better than to say anything.

"It's simple. Stay away from the streetwalkers. The Stasi recruits good-time girls to collect information from our enlisted men. There's even been an officer or two who have embarrassed themselves. Haven't had that problem with anyone from the Mission. I'd like to keep it that way."

Swanson stopped, folding his hands together. Dillon realized that he was expected to respond.

"Understood," he said.

"Let me know if you meet any local girls who are curious about your work. Even the nice ones. I'd like to be forewarned. I can run a quick background check on them, and make sure there's nothing to worry about."

"Will do," Dillon said, although he wasn't about to share anything about his romantic life with Swanson, or anyone else. The last thing in the world he needed were additional entries in his personnel file. He wondered whether Swanson gave the same talk to all new men arriving at the Mission, or whether Dillon had been singled out because of his past. It would be naive to think that Swanson hadn't been alerted about the episode in Canberra and told to keep an eye on Dillon.

"Berlin is crawling with spies," Swanson said. "They say the Brits have their largest overseas spy station here, and I wouldn't doubt that it's the same for CIA. And then there's Army Intelligence and *our* Germans—the BND—and *their* Germans, the Stasi. The Russians run their operations out of their complex at Karlshorst." He frowned. "You can hardly turn around without bumping into an agent. That's another thing you should watch out for. If you run into trouble, you know where to find me."

"Thanks," Dillon said. "Girls and spies. Got it. I plan to stay out of trouble."

"That's the ticket," Swanson said. "Do that, and we'll all be happy."

* * *

As the week wore on, Dillon found it hard not to dwell on his upcoming dinner date with Christa Schiller. He tried to keep busy. On Saturday, he played tennis with Reggie, and on Sunday, after church, caught "The Big Country," a Western with Gregory Peck and Jean Simmons, at the Outpost Theater (where the Army screened the latest Hollywood movies). Dillon spent some of Sunday night in the office, intent on catching up on his paperwork.

On Monday, he was restless all day, unable to concentrate on his work. He told himself it was absurd that he would be so distracted by the thought of seeing Christa again, but there was no denying that he was nervous and excited.

He left the Mission early, driving to Charlottenburg and finding a parking space near Savignyplatz, the pretty city park situated on both sides of Kantstrasse. He went for a long walk in the neighborhood, hoping to settle his nerves. At one point, he sat on a park bench and studied the people passing by, the stolid businessmen in their homburgs, the stylish young women in their high heels, the wide-eyed American servicemen, and students and artists, he supposed, wearing all-black clothing that seemed to have become the uniform for intellectuals throughout Europe.

The Paris Bar was already crowded when he arrived. He looked around the interior of the restaurant and was impressed—if most of the patrons weren't speaking in German, he would have sworn he was in a Left Bank bistro. The low-hung chandeliers, black-and-white checked tile floor, zinc bar, and framed Art Nouveau posters on the white-washed walls made him think of a small café he'd chanced upon in the Sixth Arrondissement. The authentic feel of the place made sense—the Paris Bar had been opened by a cook in the French army of occupation who had decided to stay in Berlin after his enlistment ended.

Dillon asked the waiter to sit him in a corner and he nursed a bourbon on the rocks while he waited for Christa. He checked his watch twice, surprised at how nervous he was. He wondered for a moment whether she would stand him up—she had seemed reluctant to agree to the dinner, and it wouldn't surprise him if she didn't show.

He tried not to stare at the front door. He checked his watch again. Christa was fifteen minutes late. But then, relieved, he saw her enter the restaurant and say something to the waiter. Dillon rose to his feet and waved to her.

"Very pleased to see you," he said, when she came over to his table. "I was afraid that you had changed your mind."

"Why would I do that? I told you that I would meet you here."

"You didn't seem fully convinced that it was a good idea," he said, feeling the blood rush to his face, and hoping that she didn't see that he was blushing. "Thought you might stand me up."

"And miss supper with Berlin's foremost diplomatic poet? Or should that be foremost poetic boxer?"

"Either will do."

"Before we go any further, I have a confession to make." She smiled. "You should know that I'm appearing with the Neues Theater company only by invitation of the director, Stefan Schmidt. I live in East Berlin. I hope that doesn't complicate matters."

"Why should it? I talk to East Berliners all the time."

"Some people see things in political terms. I'm not one of them, but I understand why they do."

"And I'm a diplomat, which means that I'm supposed to build bridges. From East to West, and West to East."

While she studied the menu, Dillon took note of the small things about her: her delicate silver drop earrings, the birthmark near the corner of her mouth, the light gray wool scarf draped around her neck. She looked up and brushed back a stray lock of hair from her face. A faint smile surfaced at the corners of her mouth. It was clear that she was aware of his scrutiny.

After their waiter had taken their order, Dillon asked her about the Neues Theater. Christa talked about how she enjoyed playing the role of Miranda in *The Tempest*, and how she hoped she would be chosen to play Beatrice in *Much Ado About Nothing*, the next scheduled production for the troupe. Shakespeare's women were clever and adventuresome, and Christa loved their independence.

"I'm so pleased that Stefan has chosen Shakespeare's comedies," she said. "People can come to the theater and laugh and lose themselves for a few hours. We have enough grimness these days." She tucked her hair behind her ear. "Of course, there will always be politics. That's why you're here in Berlin, isn't it?"

"In a way. I'm more like a foreign correspondent than a politician. I talk to lots of people, local officials, diplomats, journalists—anyone I can find—about the political situation. I take them to lunch and dinner on my expense account. I play tennis once a week with one of the British diplomats. Then I write reports about what I've learned."

"Are you sure you're not a spy?" she asked with a smile. "In the East, they constantly warn us about the imperialist spies. Don't you do the same thing? Collect secrets?"

"Nothing so exciting. Sometimes I think they could replace us and send translations of the local newspapers in place of the official reports. Save the taxpayers in Kansas and Idaho some money."

"I don't believe you."

"You're the one with the glamorous profession. The center of attention, and, I suspect the center of significant male attention."

She shook her head. "I've sworn off men for the time being. I don't care for the complications, the jealousy, the desire to control."

"Not all men are like that."

"Do you really think so?"

"I do. As a man."

"I don't. Most men seek to control their woman, some openly, some indirectly. And strong women resist. What do they call that in French, *la guerre des sexes*? For now, I don't wish that battle or the distraction of romance. I have the chance to make a name for myself, to be noticed. There are producers, directors, who come to the Neues Theater. Who knows, perhaps a talent scout from Hollywood."

"Would you like to go to Hollywood?"

"And become a movie star? I would be flattered to be asked, but I have no wish to leave Berlin. It's my home."

They continued to talk over dessert and coffee, and Dillon was disappointed when Christa declined a second cup. The waiter arrived with the check, and Dillon paid him with a stack of Deutsche Marks, leaving a generous tip.

"When can I see you again?" he asked.

"I don't know. I must ask myself whether that would be wise. Should I risk the distraction?"

"You've enjoyed this, haven't you? Our conversation?"

She tilted her head slightly, studying him. "I have."

"I would like to know more about you, and your life," Dillon said. "And for you to know me better. Perhaps I can change your mind about the war between the sexes, persuade you to call a truce. I'm a diplomat, after all."

"I'm very busy with the troupe."

"Why don't I come see your play? We can have dinner together afterward."

"You're quite persistent. Are all diplomats so relentless?"

"Only when it's a good cause."

She hesitated, considering, and then relented. "All right. Come see the play. Friday night. I'll leave a ticket in your name at the box office. Then perhaps dinner, but I make no promises. I may be tired after the performance. And you must understand that I do not wish to complicate my life."

"No complications," he said, in what he hoped was a carefree manner. "And I promise to keep it that way."

* * *

On Friday, Dillon arrived thirty minutes early at the Neues Theater for the performance of *The Tempest*. To his surprise, every seat in the theater was already occupied except for his—a hard wooden seat in the center of the tenth row marked by a small numbered brass plate.

He admired the nineteenth-century decor of the theater—walls painted light blue, a pressed-tin ceiling, and a handsome dark wood proscenium stage, with a shallow apron. The theater was filled, and Dillon was taken by how many parents had brought their children along.

When the curtain rose, the audience murmured in delight at the set with its Mediterranean painted backdrop of azure blue skies, white-washed villas, and a palm tree or two—it struck Dillon as an enticing sight on a chilly, gray evening.

He didn't have to wait long for Christa to appear—Miranda came on stage in the second scene, and Dillon found himself leaning forward, captivated. She was the picture of innocence as she learned from her father, Prospero, that he was the Duke of Milan, and they had been exiled to their tropical island because of the treachery of his brother, Antonio. Christa seemed younger, more vulnerable, perfect for the part of a teenage noblewoman. Her lips were painted a vivid crimson, and he found himself wondering what it would be like to kiss them.

Dillon was surprised by how well the essence of Shakespeare's play survived its translation into German. He had read *The Tempest* before, in college, but he had never seen it performed. While he found himself drawn in by Prospero's manipulation of people and events, he nevertheless waited impatiently for Christa's scenes. He was impressed by her range—scornful as she railed against the monster Caliban for trying to rape her, tender and passionate when she pledged her love to Prince Ferdinand, her suitor. She looked out over the audience when she recited the famous lines from the play about a brave new world, her face reflecting wonder and excitement.

At the end of the play, Prospero remained alone on the stage, dressed in his sorcerer's robes, imploring the audience by their applause to set him free from his island captivity. When they complied, he jauntily exited, and the audience continued to clap and cheer. The entire cast returned to the stage, holding hands. When Christa took her bow, she was rewarded by a roar of approval.

As the audience filed out of the auditorium, Dillon made his way to the front of the theater and found a side door that led backstage. He made his way to the dressing rooms, and told a young woman there that he was looking for Fräulein Schiller. She asked him to wait and went to find Christa.

Christa appeared a few minutes later, still in costume, but with the heavy stage makeup removed. She looked tired under the harsh backstage lights, and Dillon hoped that she wouldn't beg off dinner.

"You were marvelous," he said.

"Thank you," she said. "I'm vain, like most actresses, so I wanted to impress you."

"Would you care for dinner?" he asked.

"Some of us are going over to the Badewanne, the Bathtub," she said. "They usually play be-bop, which no one can dance to, but there's a swing band this week. Would you like to come along?"

She had known the answer before she asked the question, Dillon thought. He was disappointed that he wouldn't have her to himself, but he wasn't going to pass up the chance to spend time with her.

"I'll try not to step on your toes," he said.

* * *

They were joined on the short walk to the nightclub by Christa's flatmate, Liesl, and two actors, Jürgen, the handsome actor who had played Prince Ferdinand, and Hans, who had donned Prospero's sorcerer's robe in the play.

It was a young, noisy crowd jammed into the Bathtub. A four-piece band was playing "One O'Clock Jump" and the patrons were enjoying the music and the beer, served in large mugs. What passed for a dance floor was filled with young couples moving to the music.

They pulled two tables together, and Dillon made sure that he found a seat next to Christa. The room was too loud to have much of a conversation, but Dillon figured that they could talk when the band took a break.

Dillon recognized the first notes of "Stompin' at the Savoy," a Benny Goodman favorite, and turned to Christa. "May I have this dance?" he asked her.

They proved to be well-matched. Dillon liked the feel of her hand in his, and how she followed his lead as they moved together to the music. He was suddenly grateful that his father had forced him to take formal dance classes when he was a youngster in Charlottesville; later, in college, he had found it easy to master the latest dance steps.

When they returned to the tables, Liesl clapped her hands together in delight. "Very nice. You two look great, like you'd been dancing together for years."

Before Dillon could thank her for the compliment, Jürgen moved next to Christa. "My turn, dear Miranda," he said and took Christa by the hand and led her back onto the dance floor. Jürgen proved to be light on his feet, a natural dancer, but Dillon resolved not to say or do anything that would make Christa think that he was jealous.

"Jürgen has been with the Neues Theater since Stefan founded it," Liesl said, leaning in and speaking into Dillon's right ear. "He's from Munich. They say his family has money, that they are important people. He's been very nice to me, and to Christa. Not everyone has been so welcoming."

"You're new to the theater as well?" He copied her technique and spoke directly into her ear.

"I am. I joined only a month before Christa. Renate, the actress who plays Ariel, was very unhappy when Christa came to us. There's only one major female role in *The Tempest*, and Renate wanted it badly. In her mind, Christa stole the part from her." Liesl wrinkled her nose. "Renate isn't half the actress that Christa is, and she's a royal bitch to boot."

When Christa returned to the table, she sat next to Liesl, on the other side of Dillon. He was frustrated because he hadn't managed more than ten words with her. He finally got his chance when Liesl excused herself to go to the bathroom, while the band took a break. Dillon looked around the Bathtub but didn't see Jürgen and Hans. When he asked Christa where they were, she smiled.

"I asked Jürgen to make sure Hans got home early tonight," she said. "He's been fighting a cold, and we can't afford to lose Prospero for even one performance."

Dillon was pleased with Jürgen's departure, which left him alone with Christa. Was he competing with Jürgen for her affections? He hoped not. He couldn't tell whether she was interested in her fellow actor. He also wasn't sure where he stood. She had him off-balance, and it wasn't something Dillon had experienced with a woman before.

"I wanted to thank you," he told her. "I've been thinking about what you said at Amerika Haus—that I should write about Berlin. The longer I've been here, the more I find myself intrigued by the idea, by the contradictions, the tension between East and West. I've been jotting down images, ideas, a phrase here and there, in my journal."

Her face lit up. "That's marvelous. I'm flattered. When will you begin to write verses? Is that how you work?"

"I have to be patient. One day I'll wake up and look out the window and feel the strongest impulse to write. I can get lost in it then, spend hours. I have to wait for that moment. I can't force it."

"Perhaps I can be the first to read your Berlin poem."

"I'd like that."

The band started playing "Rock around the Clock," and the crowd began singing the lyrics. Christa smiled at him and shook her head. It was too loud to talk.

Liesl returned from the bathroom, and she pointed to her watch. "Time for us to go," she said in a loud voice. "There's a performance tomorrow, and we can't stay out too late."

They left the club together, and Dillon paused once they reached the sidewalk.

"When can I see you again?" he asked Christa.

She considered his question for a long moment. "You can call me at the theater," she said. "A good time to reach me is in the late afternoon. If that is convenient for you."

"I'll make it convenient."

She regarded him warily, and he realized that he must have responded too quickly. "You promised to keep things uncomplicated," she said. "I plan to hold you to that."

"I promise. Cross my heart. The story of Dillon and Christa will be an uncomplicated one."

"That's good." She leaned into him and, barely brushing his lips, kissed him. Christa stepped back, giving him an enigmatic smile. "Let's keep it that way."

SIX

After thirty days in Germany, Feliks Hawes had reached the reluctant but firm conclusion that he would never care for the gray city of Berlin or its inhabitants no matter how long he stayed there. On one of his brief calls to Anna in London, he had joked that neither his Polish nor English half could feel comfortable in what had been the capital city of the Thousand Year Reich.

"It's ancestral," he told her. "Too many battles against the Prussians. Too much bad history. It's hard to think of them as allies."

"My parents always said that you couldn't trust the Germans," Anna had replied. "They'd seen too much in Warsaw and Budapest. I worry about you in Berlin. Please be very careful."

Hawes only talked with his wife about his work in vague generalities, but Anna was no innocent—she knew that what he did for the Service could carry an element of danger, especially when he was overseas.

"I will be careful, my love. And trust me, I won't spend a minute longer here than I have to."

Hawes had not wanted the assignment in Berlin. He wouldn't have volunteered for it, but he hadn't been given much of a choice. On a chilly Tuesday morning in early February, he had been summoned for an audience with the director-general. Dick White had been appointed by the Prime Minister to lead the Secret Intelligence Service in April 1956, brought in from MI5 to reform the troubled agency after a series of public embarrassments, including accusations that the Service's Kim Philby had spied for the Russians. In turn, White had recruited Hawes from D Branch to join him at the Broadway Buildings, the headquarters of the SIS.

On that Tuesday, Hawes rode the ancient lift to the fourth floor and made his way down the dark corridor to the director-general's office. A matronly secretary ushered Hawes into the inner office, where he found White sitting behind a sizeable dark wood desk. A bank of four phones in different colors had been neatly arranged in front of him. Two of the phones were black, one green, and one white. Hawes suppressed a smile at the thought of what would happen if all four phones rang at once—it would be a scene out of a Laurel and Hardy short.

White rose to his feet and greeted him, waving Hawes into one of the leather chairs placed in front of the desk. Hawes took a quick glance around the room. Thick curtains covered the windows facing the street. Crowded floor-to-ceiling bookshelves occupied the wall opposite White.

"You look to be in fine fettle, Feliks," White began. "How is the vetting process going?"

"The longer we're at it, the better we'll get at it."

"How is it being received downstairs?"

Hawes didn't hesitate. "Grudging acceptance from my colleagues. Others have made it abundantly clear that they hate the concept, part and parcel."

White grimaced and shook his head, displeased. Many of the Service's powerful senior officials, known informally as the Robber Barons, had resisted the idea of "positive vetting." It was common knowledge that Whitehall had reluctantly approved the approach—the close scrutiny of the political and personal history of prospective SIS employees—only because of American pressure. The powers-that-be had rejected the use of polygraph tests, an added screening device employed extensively by the CIA, but had to agree to the vetting regime.

White had asked Hawes to monitor the progress of the program. As an outsider brought into the organization by another outsider, Hawes had been snubbed or ignored by many of the veteran officers. He was an outsider by reasons of birth, as well. His father had been an officer in the Polish army, murdered at Katyn Forest by the Soviets. He had taken his mother's family name, Hawes, after his father's death. Despite his Cambridge education and his service with the commandos, Hawes would never be considered "one of us" by the patricians in the Secret Service, and he knew it.

White cleared his throat. "I'd like to enlist your help in resolving a different matter, although it is somewhat related to the vetting." He explained that he was concerned about Berlin Station. "It's no secret that there have been a series of cock-ups there. Two years ago the Russians exposed the secret tunnel into East Berlin we had built with CIA to tap into their communications. Then, we began losing many of our penetration agents in Eastern Europe."

White explained that Terence Lecky, the head of R5, the counterintelligence arm of the Service, had been asked to investigate the situation. Lecky had failed to identify the source of the leaks, but he believed that they emanated from Berlin.

"I'd like you to review Lecky's final report," White said. "It lays out what little we know. Then, focus on Berlin and the officers posted there for vetting. You'll need to spend some time in the field. You'll communicate your progress to me alone. Nothing in writing. Nothing shared with the station chief."

"Has London been ruled out as a source of the leaks?" Hawes asked.

"We haven't ruled out anything," White said, annoyed by the question. "But the worst losses have been in East Germany. The Stasi and KGB have been rolling up not only our networks, but also those of the Americans and the West Germans. Berlin's the likely place for the traitor, or traitors."

"Traitors? Plural?"

"We can't rule out a cell. Not after Maclean and Philby and that lot."

"If I may ask a question?" Hawes waited until White silently nodded for him to continue. "Why not send one of the senior men? Someone familiar with Berlin and the men there? As the new boy, I'm at a disadvantage."

"On the contrary, I regard it as an advantage. It's why you're the right man for the job. You approach this with fresh eyes. No loyalties. No blind spots. You speak fluent German. You're no cowboy, but you can act decisively if the situation calls for it." White opened the briefing box on his desk and removed the documents piled on top. He glanced at them briefly. "As I've said, why don't you start with Lecky's findings?" He slid the papers across the desk to Hawes, who rose to his feet and retrieved them.

White consulted his watch, signaling that the interview was over. "I suspect you'll want to spend some time in the Registry," he said. "Look over the action reports, the operations in Germany that went bad. Check the backgrounds of our officers in Berlin. A top-to-bottom review. We don't need another scandal after Philby and Maclean. This must be handled discreetly. No public prosecution if we can help it. If you can figure out who is behind this, we'll want to discover the extent of the penetration and what has been compromised. That's the key."

"No prosecution? We would let the bastard go scot free?" Hawes didn't hide his disgust at the thought.

White frowned. "We must take the long view, Feliks. Most important is to root out any other penetration agents. Assess the damage to means and methods, and to personnel. What would a public trial and conviction accomplish, other than to further sully the reputation of the Service?"

Hawes had no illusions about the nature of the assignment. If he did surface the traitor, or traitors, White wanted him to contain the damage, to handle matters discreetly. No scandal, no written record, no public prosecution. Hawes was reporting directly to the director-general not only because it guaranteed there would be no leaks about the investigation, but also because it allowed Dick White the ability to distance himself from the situation. He would rely on Hawes to keep the secrets, and if things went awry, it would be Hawes who took the fall.

* * *

A few days after arriving in Berlin, Hawes rented a flat on the fourth floor of a nineteenth-century apartment building just south of the new

Hansa Quarter, near the Spree River. The building had survived the Allied air raids at the end of the war—the landlord, a portly man named Fritz, explained that one bomb had landed on the roof but had failed to detonate.

"The bomb fell during the day, so it was English," Fritz said. "The fuse didn't work. The bomb must have been made on a Friday, when the workers were eager to get to the pub, no?"

Hawes shrugged and silently accepted the keys for the flat from Fritz. He didn't want to get into a conversation with the man. The less he knew about Hawes, the better.

During the next week, Hawes set out to learn the city. He donned the rough clothing of a working man, purchased from a second-hand shop, and walked for hours in Berlin neighborhoods, stopping in rough pubs and drinking mugs of Molle, listening to the bar talk. He studied the patterns of traffic from the Allied sectors into East Berlin.

Once, he dressed as a businessman and took the S-Bahn elevated train into East Berlin. He carried a Danish passport in the name of Georg Henriksen, a Copenhagen dealer in antiques, an identity he had never used before. He stayed in the Soviet sector long enough to confirm that it was similar to what he had seen in Warsaw and Budapest after the Communists had seized power. There were the familiar drab streets, the empty store display windows, the long queues in front of bakeries and butcher shops, the shabby pedestrians, the aging street trams emitting loud squeaks as they rattled by. In the faces of East Berliners, he saw the same despondency he had encountered in Poland and Hungary—people who avoided eye contact and gave furtive sideways glances whenever they spied the ever-present uniformed police.

Only after he felt that had a sense of the city did he begin his inquiries at Berlin Station. The offices of the Secret Service had been situated in a two-story granite building near the massive Olympic Stadium in Westend. Hawes started with the obligatory interview of Robert Dawson, the head of station, but quickly realized that Dawson was a bit of a caretaker, promoted after Peter Lunn, the prior station head, had been moved to Bonn.

He kept his distance during the first formal interviews of Dawson's senior staff, careful to remain neutral and noncommittal. Hawes could tell that they disliked him for his bland officiousness, convinced that he was a typical counterintelligence bureaucrat, a plodder incapable of appreciating the realities of running agents and keeping them alive in the field.

He did not expect much to come from the interviews. Too many reliable operatives in the East had been arrested for their apprehensions to be chalked up to carelessness, incompetence, or the efficiency of East German counterintelligence, yet his questioning turned up nothing to suggest any pattern of betrayal. He slowly came to realize that the answers to his questions wouldn't be found in the British sector.

He needed to pursue contacts and sources in East Berlin who might be able to shed some light on the leaks coming from Berlin Station. That meant Hawes had to turn to the West Germans, to the Federal Intelligence Agency, the BND. He had one friend there, Einhardt Schlegel, whom Hawes had worked with in the past. Hawes regarded him as a man who could be trusted, one of the "new Germans" who had little if any connection to the Nazi regime.

When Einhardt was twelve, his father had been killed defending the Seelow Heights as a member of the Volkssturm, the cobbled-together militia of older Germans thrown against General Zhukov's battle-hardened Red Army veterans. Einhardt's mother had been gang-raped by Russian soldiers when Berlin fell, and she had committed suicide days later. Not surprisingly, Einhardt hated anything to do with Russia or Communism.

It proved harder to enlist Einhardt as an ally than Hawes had anticipated. He called the BND office in Berlin repeatedly over two days, before they finally spoke. The conversation was strained, with Hawes unwilling to share too much over the phone and forced to speak elliptically. Einhardt reluctantly agreed to meet him in the Tiergarten, near the statue of Queen Luise.

It was a logical rendezvous place, Hawes thought—once the hunting grounds of the electors of Brandenburg, the massive park with its long pathways and hidden nooks had numerous spots for clandestine meetings. He had read somewhere that nearly all of the Tiergarten's trees had been destroyed during the war, or cut down afterward by Berliners to heat their bone-cold flats; the young linden, Norway maple, oak, and plane trees he saw in the park—dubbed the "green lungs of

Berlin"—suggested that the efforts at reforestation were having an effect.

Hawes found Einhardt waiting for him on the designated bench, a copy of *Der Tagesspiegel* in one gloved hand, a paper cup of coffee in the other. He wore a scarf and light, brown coat that he had buttoned up to the collar.

Hawes nodded a greeting and sat down next to Einhardt. "I appreciate your meeting me here," he said.

"Cold enough that only the spies and queens are in the park," he said.

"We could have met at a café."

"Better here."

"I've come hat in hand," Hawes said. "I'm in Berlin on a difficult assignment where I could use some help. I thought of you."

"I'm flattered." Einhardt didn't look at Hawes—he scanned the pathway in both directions, alert for interlopers. "How might I be of help?"

"We've had leaks in Berlin. We've been plagued by them. I've been sent to try to find the source. I hoped you might be able to help me solve the puzzle."

"I have a great regard for you, Feliks. But I must tell you that I don't feel the same about your people in Berlin." Einhardt waved his hand dismissively. "They are simply not reliable. Thoroughly penetrated by the opposition. If you must involve them in this investigation of yours, I will have to be very cautious in what I share."

"No, they'll not be part of this. Nor London."

Einhardt raised his eyebrows.

"I shan't find what I'm looking for out at Olympic Stadium. Too easy for whoever is involved to go to ground and to wait me out."

"I agree. Your leaker will be cautious to a fault."

"No doubt. I've concluded that I must find a trail leading back to Berlin Station."

Einhardt shook his head. "That will be very, very difficult."

"That's why I'm asking for your help. You're running agents in the East. They might hear things."

"What sort of things?"

"I don't know. Loose talk. A Stasi officer who's had too much to drink bragging about how they've penetrated the British Secret Service. Someone we might squeeze or bribe. Let it be known that you'll pay handsomely for information in the hopes that there's a greedy bureaucrat in the Stasi who will sell us our traitor. I recognize that it's a long shot, but I can't see any other way. Not with the limited time I have."

"The best counterintelligence requires patience. You must wait for the patterns to emerge, for a mistake to be made. A break in routine. A sloppy brush pass or a poorly disguised dead drop. It takes time for that to happen. You know that."

"I do. Nevertheless, will you help?"

Einhardt stood up, impatient, ready to leave. "I'll see what I can turn up. But Feliks, don't get your hopes up. I fear that you're on a fool's errand."

* * *

Hawes agreed with Einhardt Schlegel that successful counterintelligence required patience, but he didn't discount the benefits of being lucky. And he regarded the arrival of Dawson's predecessor, Peter Lunn, on an unscheduled visit from Bonn, as a stroke of pure luck.

Hawes hoped that Lunn might remember something from his time in Berlin that could help him make some progress on the case. They met in Dawson's office, porcelain cups of tea before them. A man of slight build with a prominent nose and light blue eyes, Lunn had been the captain of the British ski team at the 1936 Olympics.

"You were in Vienna during the Hungarian uprising?" Lunn asked. He spoke softly, with a slight lisp.

"I was in Budapest at the beginning of the revolution, actually," Hawes replied. "Made it back to Vienna on Saturday, the 5th of November."

"A sad show. I distinctly remember that day, reading the dispatches. The Red Army rolled into the city, put an end to it. You had been seconded to work with the Yanks there?"

"I had. They needed someone who could speak Hungarian. A special assignment, on short notice. I'd been in Budapest before, after the war, so I fit the bill."

No doubt Lunn had checked with his colleagues in London about Hawes, and had received a mixed report. Hawes had a reputation for independence: he had argued against sending émigré agents into Poland and Czechoslovakia, and had made clear his disdain for the overheated "roll-back" rhetoric of the American-run Radio Free Europe. It did not help with the Robber Barons that Hawes was proven correct on both counts. The SIS agents inserted behind the Iron Curtain had been captured or killed, and after Poland and Hungary in 1956 the Americans had quietly conceded that their broadcasts had been inflammatory and misleading—no Allied armies of liberation were poised to support an uprising behind the Iron Curtain.

"Budapest had to be an interesting assignment," Lunn said. "More exciting than your task here, I'd imagine. Dick White called and told me you'd be poking around. No question we've had a string of bad luck."

"What do you think? Has the breach been here, in Berlin?"

"Impossible to say. Have you chatted with George Blake? During my time in Berlin, our best spy runner. He might have some ideas about the origin of the leaks. One of the few chaps who've spent any time in the Russian sector. Our policy is that SIS officers are prohibited from going to East Berlin, but Blake has a Soviet source that he meets over there."

"Who keeps track of that?" Hawes asked. "The spy runners and their agents?"

Lunn brightened. "That was one of my reforms when I arrived in Berlin. We established a card file of all the agents. Whenever there was a problem, the officer on duty could consult the card and see the contact details. Of course, we kept the cards under lock-and-key, and only senior men were cleared to see them."

Hawes thanked Lunn and promised to keep him informed of any progress. He decided to take Lunn's advice and meet with George Blake, one of the few Berlin Station officers he hadn't interviewed.

He found Blake at the end of the corridor, sharing an office with Giles Newton. Blake sported a closely-cropped dark beard, and he surveyed Hawes with alert, intelligent brown eyes.

"We've been expecting you," he said. "Giles and I have been feeling neglected."

"You're Dick White's boy." It was Newton. He was clean-shaven and fair-haired, from his looks, ex-military. "So to speak. I imagine that you see things from an MI5 perspective. A tad black-and-white if you ask me. It's different when you're running agents."

"Is that so?" Hawes asked. He gave them an easy smile.

"He's no Johnny-come-lately," Blake said sharply to Newton. "From what I've gathered, Hawes has been on loan for operations in Poland and Hungary."

"Didn't know that you'd mucked about in the field," Newton said to Hawes. "You understand, then, that it can get messy. The people you have to employ aren't upstanding citizens. Some bending of the rules at times."

"I take your point," Hawes said. "What do you think lies behind the blown agents?"

"Who knows?" Newton asked, shrugging. "Bad luck? Sloppy tradecraft? Leaks from Gehlen's organization?"

"I understand you find yourself on the other side of the border now and then." Hawes directed his comment to Blake. "Have you heard anything over there that gave you pause?"

Blake shook his head. "I give the KGB and Stasi a wide berth."

"I can't say I care for this," Newton said. "The job's hard enough without feeling that we're under the microscope. If there are questions about how we've handled matters, let's resolve them. In short order. Review the files. Call in the bloody auditors. But let us get back to our work."

"Am I getting in the way of your work?" Hawes asked mildly.

"Not directly," Newton said. "But no one wants to work under a cloud of suspicion."

"Of course, we have nothing to hide," Blake said. "That's what Giles is saying. Didn't care for exams as a schoolboy, and I don't like them now, but I think you'll find nothing in our operation to raise concerns."

Newton cleared his throat. "Pardon me, Hawes, but if you don't have any more questions for me, I'd like to head off to the Marlborough Club. Our Tuesday bridge game."

"Nothing else," Hawes said. "A few more questions for Blake. I'll stop by if I think of anything."

Newton retrieved his briefcase from a corner of the office, and moved toward the door before hesitating. "You don't play bridge by any chance, do you, Hawes? We're always looking for players."

"Can't say that I do."

After Newton's departure, Hawes turned to Blake with a slight smile. "I take it you don't play bridge?"

"Chess, actually. Giles is the bridge fanatic. He was a bit defensive, I know, but he's a fine chap. He took the loss of our agents hard. Hell, I don't blame you for asking questions. I'd put myself and Newton and a few others at the top of the list to vet. I don't envy you the task. By the way, I assume you know that I'm running a Russian."

"I'm aware of that."

"Code name Boris. A Soviet economic advisor. Which means I'm one of the few officers with a free pass to the Russian sector. All countenanced by London, mind you, although I imagine for someone in your role, in counterintelligence, that doesn't matter. It offers me the means and the opportunity to pass information."

"We also look for motive," Hawes said.

"Then I assume that you've researched my background, and you know that I've no love lost for the Communists. Being a POW in Korea will do that. And I can assure you that I wasn't brainwashed, although my memory's not what it once was. Shakespeare says 'Change places and, handy-dandy, which is the justice, which is the thief?' I will always remember who the thief is."

"You're one of the duty officers?" Hawes asked.

"At times I am, like the others with some seniority."

"Weekends? Nights?"

"I do my duty. My wife isn't too happy about it. Can I ask—does this line of questioning stem from something out of order?"

"Duty officers have access to the index of agents, the card file."

"That they do. But the index is rarely used."

"Quite right," Hawes said.

"You could review the register in Dawson's office," Blake said. "Duty officers sign it when they use the card file."

"The honor system?"

"You could say that, yes. But it comes down to trust, doesn't it? In the final equation. A man can be trusted, or he can't."

Hawes studied Blake for a moment. There was something about the man he didn't like, an underlying arrogance. "Newton had some thoughts about where the leaks might have originated. What do you think?"

"I'd bet on our German friends as the problem. I don't trust them. Half of them were Nazis. Too many willing to sell out for cash. The great strength and great weakness of capitalism—the quick buck. Or in this case, the quick Deutsche Mark."

Hawes thanked Blake for his time, and shook his hand. "If you think of anything that might be of help, I'd appreciate it if you gave me a call."

"Do you expect to be here in Berlin much longer?"

"I wish I knew," Hawes told him. "There are one or two leads I need to follow. You never know whether they will amount to anything. But hope springs eternal."

* * *

Hawes spent the weekend reviewing his notes from his interviews with the Berlin Station officers, hunting for clues, for something concrete. Nothing jumped out at him. George Blake had an unusual and potentially questionable past, but Hawes understood why London trusted him: if three years as a prisoner in North Korea didn't make a man an anti-Communist, it was hard to imagine what would. But there was no telling what had happened to Blake during his years of captivity, and he was the only MI6 officer with a reason to visit the Russian sector. Hawes had learned not take anyone's loyalty for granted. The world offered many temptations—personal, sexual, ideological—and the polished Oxbridge diplomat was just as likely a traitor as the left-leaning cipher clerk of working class origins.

He took a long walk along the winding banks of the Spree, hoping that something of significance, some overlooked connection, would surface from his subconscious, but that failed to work. He had to concede, ruefully, that he had nothing to show for his time in Berlin except for his concerns about the agent index and his dislike of George Blake and his barely-disguised air of superiority.

It was time to return to London. He missed Anna, and he wasn't doing the Service any good by dragging out an investigation that wasn't producing results. Sitting at the kitchen table, he began drafting his report—an admission of failure—in long-hand, to Dick White. He was startled when the phone suddenly rang—it was Einhardt Schlegel on the other end.

"I think I have something for you," Einhardt said. "Not quite what you said you were looking for, but with the right tailoring it's a coat that might fit."

"I'm quite interested. I was about to give up hope."

"Meet me where we talked last. Twenty minutes."

Einhardt wasn't about to say anything more on the telephone, no doubt assuming that the line was tapped by the East Germans or the Russians.

Once in the Tiergarten, Hawes circled the statue of Queen Luise twice, noting the bullet holes scarring its pedestal, before arriving at the same park bench. He sat down and smoked a cigarette while he waited for Einhardt, who joined him a few minutes later.

"There's someone you should meet," Einhardt began. "One of my sources. A Stasi officer. He has a very interesting story to tell. He has brought to my attention something out-of-the-ordinary. A honey trap operation being run against an American diplomat."

"That's hardly out-of-the-ordinary."

"No, it's not. But there's something different about it." Einhardt paused. "Before we proceed I must have your word that you will not reveal any of what I'm telling you to your people, here or in London. You can never identify my source—*der Eber*, the Boar—to anyone, not even your director-general."

"Those are hard terms."

"London Block is damn leaky. The slightest rainfall and water pours from that place. I fear that your headquarters is no better."

"Then you have my word that whatever you tell me stays between us. No reports to London."

Einhardt seemed satisfied with Hawes' response. "Then I will proceed. About this honey trap, our storyteller claims that a Russian, a KGB colonel, has assumed control over the operation."

"From Moscow?"

"So our asset says. And here's why I'm telling you this, why it could help with your investigation. They've placed the swallow, an actress, in the British sector, at a theater there near the Ku'damm. They're running the operation on your turf. So here is how I thought you could use this development. It's likely that they're relying on their source in your Berlin Station to warn them if they attract any attention. There's a connection. A link. Perhaps a way for you to find your leak."

"The target is an American diplomat. You haven't informed the CIA about this?"

Einhardt made a face. "They would barge in like cowboys, guns blazing, and shut down the operation. My source would be blown, and we would never know what the KGB was up to." Einhardt lit up another cigarette. "You've worked with the Americans before. In Hungary, I believe. You know how they operate."

"I do. And I appreciate that you've brought this to me. I see the possibilities. I will need to meet this storyteller of yours. Hear this tale from him."

Einhardt nodded. He had expected the request. "I can arrange that. But he'll want to meet you in the East. He rarely comes over here. It's frowned upon for Stasi officers. Far too many temptations."

Hawes didn't like the idea of crossing into the Russian sector. There was always the possibility of being stopped by the East German police and asked for papers. "I'd prefer to meet him here, in the British sector. Not at the Hilton. Some place more discreet." The rooftop of the recently opened Hilton Hotel was reputed to be the favorite meeting place for Western intelligence officers and the spies they handled. Hawes figured the rumors had been started by someone on the Hilton staff, looking to attract tourists who enjoyed Ian Fleming novels, with the hint of intrigue and derring-do.

"That will be a hard sell," Einhardt said.

"Do what you can," Hawes replied. "If you think it will help, I'm willing to pay for the meeting."

"That goes without saying, no matter where you meet. The Boar has the soul of a Swiss banker."

SEVEN

Dillon had never pursued a woman quite like Christa Schiller before. He found her fascinating and desirable, and he was intrigued by her quiet self-assurance. She didn't seem overly impressed with him, and that made her somehow all the more alluring. He felt as if he had begun to understand her, and he was frustrated by her elusiveness in his courtship of her.

When he had telephoned her at the Neues Theater to thank her for their evening together, she had been friendly enough on the phone, but she wouldn't commit to lunch or coffee later that week, explaining that she had a very busy schedule.

"Why don't you call me next week?" she asked. "I may have some free time then."

He found himself cursing after he hung up the telephone. He wasn't used to being put off, and he didn't know what to think or to do. He believed that she was attracted to him—from his perspective, she had sent clear signals at the Bathtub. Hadn't she danced with him, kissed him on the lips? Yet now she was hesitating.

He waited a full week before calling her again. She gently declined his offer of dinner or lunch, but—just when he was beginning to lose hope that she would see him again—agreed to meet him for coffee at the Café Kranzler the next afternoon.

Dillon arrived early and took a seat indoors to wait for her. When Christa didn't turn up on time, he remembered that she had been late to their supper at the Paris Bar. When, minutes later, he saw Christa crossing the room to join him, a smile on her face, he was reminded again of how lovely a she was and how much he desired her.

"So what has kept you busy these days?" she asked after they had ordered coffee.

"The boring work of a diplomat. Talking. Writing reports. More talking. They say diplomacy is the act of thinking twice before saying nothing. Now that the Russians have agreed to discuss Berlin in May in Geneva, we're drafting white papers right and left."

"Ah, the political situation. The so-called Berlin Crisis. What can Berliners do? It's impossible, so it's best just to ignore it. All you serious men with your speeches and conferences can deal with it."

"I wish we could ignore it," he said. "But who knows? Maybe we'll figure out a way for Comrade Khrushchev to save face and back down."

"In the meantime, I'll go to cafés and drink coffee. And to the museum and the theater and the cinema. No politics. I tell Liesl that she should stop reading the newspapers. It only makes her gloomy."

"And how has it been living with Liesl?"

Christa smiled. "She's very young. Everything is new and exciting for her. We get along quite well."

"And the Neues Theater?"

"We're playing to full houses. But, as you might expect, there's always some backstage drama. This week, Prospero and Caliban aren't on speaking terms." She laughed at the dismayed look on his face. "Hans thinks Otto is stepping on his lines, distracting the audience by moving around too much. They aren't getting along. Stefan is tearing his hair out over it. In the end, they'll calm down."

"And Miranda? How is she?"

She brightened. "She's fine."

"And happy?"

"For the most part. I count my blessings. Of course, there are some sad things, but I wouldn't burden you with them."

"It's no burden," he said. "If there is any way I could help, I'd like to."

"My helpful Ami. I wish you could."

"We won't know if I could or not unless you tell me what is making you sad."

"Some day, perhaps, we can talk about it. When I know you better. Not now."

He nodded, pleased that she had suggested that they would see each other in the future. "When you are ready, I'm here. I've been told that I'm a good listener."

"Is that what your American girls say?" she asked, now openly flirting with him, her mood suddenly changed, lighter. "They flatter you by saying that. But the truth is that men don't really listen, do they? They want us to believe that while they court us, but after they have made their conquest, they no longer need to pretend. Then when we talk, their minds are a million miles away, thinking about other things, important things, like whether Hertha can win its next match."

He grinned. "A damning indictment. I wouldn't be like that. Not with you."

"You're sure about that?"

"I'm sure." He kept his eyes fixed on her. "I just need a chance to prove that to you. Aren't you a little bit curious to see whether or not I can back up my promise?"

"Curiosity killed the cat," she said. She stood up, and before he could react she leaned in and kissed him softly on the lips. "You are a nice man, Dillon Randolph. I must be off for an appointment. I enjoyed this."

"When can I see you again?" He was dismayed that she was ready to leave. He felt a need to pin her down to their next meeting.

"Call me. Perhaps we can go to a concert. Or a museum. I love museums."

"A museum it is. I'll call tomorrow with some dates."

She laughed. "My persistent and relentless diplomat. Call with your dates, and we'll see. No promises."

He rose to his feet, ready to accompany her from the café, but she stopped him. "Finish your coffee," she said. "I'll find my way out."

After she had left, he sat alone at the table, confused, wondering why she continued to keep him at a distance. She had kissed him on the lips again—that had to mean that she was attracted to him—but she hadn't fully agreed to a museum date. What was holding her back? Was she conflicted about seeing him? Or did she enjoy playing hard-to-get?

It was the first time that Dillon had cared more for a woman than she did for him, and it was a disconcerting feeling. He had always been on the other side of the equation, never the jealous or possessive lover. Now he parsed everything she had said to him, every gesture. Now he was jealous, worried that Jürgen, the actor with the matinée idol looks who played Ferdinand to Christa's Miranda, was capitalizing on his daily contact with Christa to court her.

Dillon feared becoming a cliché: the infatuated suitor, unable to see how foolish he looked to those around him. Later, when he looked up the word "infatuated" in the office dictionary, he found that the definition of the original Latin root word, the verb *infatuare*, was "to make a fool of." He wondered whether he should try to find someone else. There were plenty of pretty Berliners who would be delighted to date a young American diplomat. But, he told himself ruefully, they wouldn't be Christa.

* * *

Dillon found that he was spending less and less time in his office at the Mission. While he had attended a few of the parties hosted by foreign diplomats, he had invented excuses when his colleagues had invited him to social events. He told himself that he hadn't come to Berlin to have cocktails and dinner with Americans. Moreover, wasn't he following his Uncle Leigh's advice and staying clear of the wives and daughters of Berlin's Little America, the tight-knit expat community in Dahlem?

He was leaving the Mission, on his way to his Thursday tennis match, when Audrey Wingate stopped him.

"I have an invitation for you, stranger," she said, moving closer to him. "You're going to join me for a night on the town. I'm not usually this forward, but you've become quite the man of mystery. You never seem to be around. They say that all work and no play makes Dillon a very dull boy, and we can't let that happen."

"I think it would help my career prospects to be thought of as a dull boy for a while."

"Nonsense," she said. "Meet me at Amerika Haus tomorrow night at six o'clock. I'll be very cross with you if you're a no show."

She escaped down the corridor before he could make an excuse. He told himself that getting out for a night wouldn't hurt. He wondered whether they could visit the Bathtub, where they might run into Christa and the actors from the Neues Theater, and then felt his face burn from the thought.

When Dillon arrived at Amerika Haus on Friday night, Audrey was waiting at the front entrance. She wore a brown beret, a tight-fitting black sweater, and her lips were painted a vivid red—Dillon decided that she would have fit in perfectly at a beatnik party in San Francisco or a gathering of French students on the Left Bank.

"What do you think?" she asked. "Audrey the artiste? Audrey Hepburn in *Love in the Afternoon* was my inspiration."

"Quite fetching," Dillon replied. While she made him think more of Doris Day than Audrey Hepburn, he had to admit that the outfit did wonders for her sex appeal.

"I promised to show you the town," she said. "Tonight you must let me guide you. This city has always been a bit *louche*. The Nazis sent many of the decadent types to the camps, but they say it was surprising how quickly the night life came back."

"From what I've gathered, some of the brownshirts were fairly decadent themselves."

"They were," she said and giggled. "I thought about taking you to Kelch, a bar where the men dress as women, but you'd stand out a bit much. There are lots of clubs like that. I find them more than a bit strange. I've never understood why a big, strong man would want to put on a dress and makeup. Instead, we're going to Remde's St. Pauli am Zoo. They've quite a risqué show, not only by American standards. *Arsch und Titten.*' Tits and ass.'"

"Audrey, I appreciate the offer, but why don't we go someplace for a quiet bite to eat? Maybe catch some jazz. There's a be-bop place called the Bathtub. We can sample Berliner decadence some other time."

She shook her head. "The Bathtub is much too tame. I thought about Ballhaus Resi. There are telephones and message chutes on the tables and the idea is that if you see someone you fancy, you invite them for a drink or a dance. But I decided against it. Too many of the German girls would be sending messages to my handsome American date."

"I'm sure you'd have invitations from all the men," he said. "A pretty American girl."

"Why the adjective? Isn't 'pretty girl' enough?"

"I guess because American females count for exotic in Berlin, and you know how men are. The lure of the unknown."

"How are they?"

"Curious, I suppose. If you've dated only Germans, you'd be curious about American girls."

"And vice versa?"

"The human condition, isn't it? We all want what we don't have."

Remde's St. Pauli was on the second floor of a building on Kantstrasse. The nightclub had been decorated in a maritime theme, with fishing nets, lifebuoys, diving suits, and harpoons hanging on dark blue walls, with a garish painting of several blonde mermaids proudly displaying their naked breasts. Dillon glanced around—most of the patrons were middle-aged local businessmen, their faces already red from drink, with a few couples at tables here and there.

Audrey whispered something to the head waiter, and he led them to a reserved table next to a small stage. He took their order and when he returned with their drinks, Audrey downed her schnapps in two gulps and asked him to bring another. Dillon nursed his beer—he could only hope that Audrey could handle her liquor, because she seemed intent on getting drunk.

She squeezed his arm. "Why don't you take that tie off? Loosen up and enjoy yourself, Dillon."

There were two fishing rods next to the table, each with an oversized hook covered in red velvet attached to a heavy line. She handed one of the poles to Dillon. "You'll need this," she said. "Who knows what you might catch?"

A pretty redhead in a polka-dot bikini and high heels sauntered over to the stage next to them. She waited until the barman turned on a recording—a suggestive tune heavy on horns, snare-drum, and cymbals—and began dancing on a nearby elevated platform. Dillon was impressed that she could keep her balance as she gyrated to the music. Her bump and grind routine wasn't very erotic, nor did her fake smile convince Dillon that she was enjoying herself.

Audrey surprised him by quickly grabbing her fishing rod. She extended it toward the girl, and managed to snare the velvet-covered hook on the strap of her bikini top. Audrey gave the pole a strong tug, and the top slid lower, exposing the redhead's breasts. The girl smiled and removed her top completely, leaving herself naked from the waist up. She kept dancing, moving closer to their table.

"Very nice," Audrey said, turning to Dillon with a grin. She raised her fishing rod in the air. "Should I try for the bottom piece?"

"Let's not," Dillon said. "It's chilly in here."

"You're a spoil-sport." Audrey fished around in her pocketbook and came up with a handful of Marks, which she scattered on the platform.

The girl danced for a few more minutes, and when the music stopped, retrieved her bikini top and collected the cash littering the small stage. She calmly stepped off the platform and walked away.

"Bet you don't have this back in Richmond," Audrey said. "I know there's nothing like it in Des Moines."

"The nightclubs in Richmond would never try," Dillon said. "The town fathers would shut them down in a heartbeat. Not that I'm all that familiar with the nightlife there."

"You don't have a Southern belle patiently waiting for you back in Richmond, do you? An engagement ring on her finger?"

"No such luck. I'm from Charlottesville, by the way. Richmond's a big city, and I live in the country."

"You're hardly a country boy," she said. "You may want people to see you that way, but you're a cosmopolitan at heart."

"We can't always see ourselves as others do, can we?"

"Ain't that the truth," she said. The drinks were beginning to take effect. Audrey was slurring her words noticeably. "They warned me about you. The other girls. Your reputation preceded you, you know. The Errol Flynn of the State Department. A bit of a tomcat. A dangerous man to be alone with. But maybe I want to be alone with you. Maybe I'm partial to Errol Flynn. A girl could do worse."

"People gossip," he said. "They repeat stories that aren't true."

"I'd like to find that out for myself. We have all night. I'm at your command." She gulped her drink. "If my girlfriends back home could see me now, they'd be shocked. A lady should never be so forward. Or so they say. But I say the hell with them."

Dillon glanced at his watch. "It's getting on. We should think about calling it a night."

"It's ironic, isn't it? I'm the one trying to seduce you, and you're the one resisting. Who would ever believe it?"

"You're a lovely girl," Dillon said. "A sweet girl. I'm not the right man for you."

"I'm not a girl, I'm a woman and I could be the right woman for you. If and when you're ready to settle down." She pressed her body against him. "If you'll give me a chance."

He moved away from her. "Audrey, I think that would be a very bad idea. Things will look different tomorrow in the light of day."

"Is it her? The actress you've been parading around with?" She didn't wait for his response. "It's hard to compete with the mysterious and exotic Christa Schiller. I know that I must seem bland and safe in comparison. But you don't really know me. If you were to give me a chance, I know I could change your mind."

"We've both had too much to drink," he said. "You've been a good friend. I'd like to keep it that way."

She began to cry, and Dillon took her by the arm and led her out of the nightclub. She didn't resist, choking back sobs. Outside he hailed a cab and bundled her into it, giving the driver her address. She held her handkerchief to her eyes, and she wouldn't look at him.

After she had left, Dillon thought about heading over to the Bathtub, and decided against it. He would call it a night and drive back to Dahlem. In the morning, he would call a florist in Charlottenburg and have a bouquet of flowers delivered to Audrey at Amerika Haus with a note thanking her for the night out. It would be awkward between them for a while, but he didn't think he'd lose her as a friend.

He told himself he had done the right thing for the right reasons. Even if Audrey had appealed to him—and she didn't—sleeping with her would have been a terrible mistake. No matter what she said, she would have expected a commitment from Dillon, one he wasn't willing to give. The last thing he needed was a scandal that would cement his reputation as a womanizer.

And then there was the question of Christa. His night out with Audrey had only confirmed for Dillon that Christa was the woman he wanted. He wasn't going to let anyone, or anything, get in the way of winning her. He would have to be patient, but he knew that she was worth the wait.

EIGHT

It took a full week before Einhardt could arrange the meeting between Hawes and his Stasi source—the Boar had flatly refused to cross into the British sector. Even the offer of a substantial payment would not budge him.

"I can see his point," Einhardt told Hawes. "A Stasi officer doesn't travel to the West unless he has a damn good reason, and his superiors have approved the visit. If he were to come over here, and be spotted by an informer, the consequences would be harsh. The cells in Hohenschönhausen aren't heated. He won't take the chance."

"Which means that I must assume the risk, then," Hawes said. "I'm not in Berlin under diplomatic cover. How confident are you that he won't turn his coat? Have me arrested once I set foot in the Russian sector? I don't fancy spending any time in that prison cell, either."

"He's been a reliable source for some time now. Almost two years. His reports have checked out. We've paid him handsomely, and his money sits in a bank on our side of the border." Einhardt paused for a moment, reflecting. "But can I guarantee that he's truly ours? In this business, you know that you can never be sure."

"If you were in my shoes, would you agree to a meeting over there?"

"I would. I don't think the Boar would be foolish enough to betray you. That would mean betraying me, and the BND. He's in quite deep with us. Signed receipts for the money he's taken. We have chapter-and-verse on the sensitive information he's given us, his betrayal of his colleagues. He must realize that we can retaliate for any double-cross."

"Unless the Stasi has been dangling him as bait all along."

"It's possible," Einhardt said. "I don't think so. We've been able to hurt them with what he's told us."

"Set up the meeting, then. Somewhere very close to the sector border."

Einhardt nodded and said that he would ask for a rendezvous near the Friedrichstrasse Station, just blocks inside East Berlin. The location might give Hawes some psychic comfort, but they both knew that the proximity to the border wouldn't matter if Einhardt's agent had decided on betrayal. Hawes would be immediately arrested, and never have a chance to make a run for it.

On the Friday morning of the meeting, Hawes found himself on edge. He tried not to think about what could go wrong. Hawes rode the U-Bahn to Friedrichstrasse Station, and took a deep breath before he left the subway car. He glanced around the platform area, alert for the dark blue uniforms of the Tropos, the East German transit police. He was confident that his Danish passport in the name of Georg Henriksen would pass any cursory scrutiny, but he doubted his alias would hold up under prolonged questioning.

Hawes had reached the station exit when a young Tropo near the door looked at him and motioned for him to stop. He walked over slowly to Hawes.

"Papers," he said, staring at Hawes.

"Of course," Hawes said and produced the passport. He could feel his heart pounding faster. He took a deep breath, hoping to calm himself.

The young officer studied the passport. "Georg Henriksen," he said. "Why are you here in East Berlin?"

Hawes tried to smile. "Business. Here to see about antiques. That's my trade."

The Tropo glanced at the passport again and then handed it back to Hawes. "You may go."

Hawes nodded and quickly made his way outside. His heart was still racing, and he stood still for a moment to catch his breath. He looked around, relieved to see that he hadn't attracted further attention. Once on the street, he tried to blend in, walking at the same pace as the Berliners around him. He doubled back twice and saw no sign of anyone tailing him. He was confident that he hadn't been followed from the station.

Hawes hadn't been in the field for several years, not since Budapest, and he had forgotten how it felt to be in hostile territory, the constant uneasiness, the heightening of the senses—he felt like he could see, and hear, and smell more acutely.

He realized that in his anxiety he was walking too fast. He didn't want to draw any attention to himself, so he slowed down.

The rendezvous had been set for one o'clock near the Admiralspalast, the Art Deco theater that had once housed a spa and brothel for Prussian officers, and now showed dreary Russian and East German films. Hawes arrived fifteen minutes early and circled the block. He didn't want to linger there, and he hoped that Einhardt's source would show up on time.

When Hawes strolled by the meeting place—a mailbox on the east side of Friedrichstrasse within sight of the Admiralspalast—there was a man in a light tan coat standing there. He had thinning hair, a pencil mustache, and a weak chin. He looked nothing like a wild boar, Hawes thought, more like a harried bookkeeper or a sales clerk. He wondered whether the code name reflected Einhardt's dry sense of humor.

Hawes approached the man and, using the agreed-upon recognition phrase, asked him whether there were any good hotels nearby.

"You're a visitor?" the man asked.

"I am."

"For how long a stay?"

"Three nights," Hawes said.

The man nodded when he heard the correct response. He was nervous—his hands trembled, and he avoided eye contact with Hawes.

"I agreed to be here only because of Einhardt. He says that you'll not report our meeting to your people. I insisted on this condition." He looked around. "Let us walk. We should keep moving."

The man started down the street, and Hawes fell in next to him. "I'm curious. Why did you insist on that as a condition?"

"It should be obvious. Your Berlin Station has been penetrated. Infiltrated. How do you think we've rolled up your agents?"

"I'm not part of Berlin Station," Hawes said. "I'm here from London."

"At least your German is half-decent. You sound like a friend of mine from Danzig."

Hawes checked his watch—he wanted to get to the Boar's story as soon as possible. It was the reason he had risked the trip to the East. "Tell me about the Russian operation."

"That's valuable information. Pay, and you can have it. Perhaps, in turn, the Amis will buy it from you. You've agreed to pay, haven't you?"

"I have," Hawes said. It worried him that the man's hands were still trembling, that he had remained so nervous. "The money is being deposited in your account in the Berliner Bank. We trust you won't do anything to draw attention to yourself, I hope. No spending sprees."

The man shook his head vigorously. "I'm not stupid. The money stays in the bank. When the time comes, when I come over, it will be there." He sighed. "Why did you need to meet me? I gave Einhardt a full and detailed report. That should have been enough."

"Paper," Hawes said. "Words on paper. I can't talk to a written report. What can I believe? What is fact and what is conjecture? I need to know the author. The creator of this story."

"Story?" The man was offended. "It's no story. I explained in the report. The Russian has been handling the girl, Christa Schiller, an actress. She's to seduce an American diplomat."

"This Russian is KGB? Not military intelligence?"

"Yes, he's KGB. As I noted in my report. The girl is seeing the diplomat, a man named Randolph." He licked his lips. "By now, he's probably riding her at every opportunity. I envy him, she's a quite tasty dish."

"Were you there when the Russian met with her?"

The man smiled proudly. "I was there."

"What is the goal of the operation?"

"I'm not privy to that. They rely on me to help her with her cover story. To keep the director of the Neues Theater in line. He's a degenerate, a queen, by the way."

"The name of the KGB officer?"

"He calls himself Comrade Mikhail." He coughed nervously. "I believe his name is Durov. That's what I've heard."

"Durov? You're sure that was the name?"

"That's what I heard." He slowed his pace, and then came to a stop. "No more meetings. I won't risk it. Not with the Russians involved."

"But you will report to Einhardt if you learn more."

The man didn't respond, at first, and then spoke. "I've given you enough that you can take it from here." He looked around, shifting his weight from foot to foot. "I've been thinking about my immediate future. I don't believe it lies here. Inform Einhardt of that."

"We'll be in touch," Hawes said.

The man grimaced. "I'm leaving. The underground station is just up the way. Tell Einhardt what I said."

* * *

Hawes made one brief call to London when he returned to the British sector, to arrange an appointment with Dick White for the following morning. Later that afternoon, he took a taxicab to Tempelhof and caught a Pan Am flight to Frankfurt. From there, he flew British Airways to Gatwick and reached London before nine o'clock. He called Anna from the airport, and then took a cab to their townhouse.

She clung to him for a long moment when he arrived at the front door.

"I have missed you each and every day," she said.

"It's been the same for me."

"I know that there are times when you must be away. That doesn't mean it's any easier when you are away. I worry."

"You needn't worry, Anna. I spend my days interviewing people and writing reports. I'm no more at risk than if I was at my desk here handling paperwork."

"You belong at home. You need to be here if we're going to make a baby."

"I know," he said. "This assignment will end. Don't worry, we'll have children. It can take time. Isn't that what the doctor said?"

"He could be wrong."

"I'll finish soon in Berlin," he said. "I'll be back, and we can pick up where we left off. Home every night."

It hadn't been easy for her, acclimating to life in England. Anna had shied away from socializing with other Hungarians, worried that she might encounter someone from Budapest who might recognize her as one of the girls from the Hotel Duna. Hawes had told her repeatedly that she had nothing to be ashamed of, that she had done what was needed to protect her family.

"You made the choice that you had to," he had said.

"You see it that way," she had responded. "If they knew, people would say that I was no more than a whore."

"They would be wrong." He cradled her in his arms as she began to weep. "No one has the right to judge you. I'm so lucky to have you as my wife. That's what matters. Since the day we've met, there's only been you."

89

"The same for me," she said. "Only you, Feliks. I just wish that there had never been anyone else."

"With any luck, most of them got what they deserved during the uprising." He had smiled at her. "We can't change the past. Believe it or not, I wouldn't want to, because if you hadn't been at the Hotel Duna, I never would have met you."

Three years earlier, Hawes had received a chilly response when he had first informed his immediate supervisor at MI5 that he planned to bring Anna to London and marry her. Duna girls had been employed by the AVH, the Hungarian secret police, to seduce Western visitors so they could be blackmailed—it was not surprising that Anna would be viewed with suspicion by British counterintelligence. Hawes had gone to Dick White to plead his case, and White had intervened with the Foreign Office, insisting that Anna be allowed into the England and pressing the bureaucracy to produce the necessary paperwork. It meant Hawes had been able to marry her within weeks of their leaving Budapest, and he would be forever grateful for White's timely assistance.

He'd shared very little with Anna about the maneuvering necessary to bring her to England or about the hard questions he had fielded from skeptical colleagues. He had shielded her from that ugliness, but she had to realize that her past would make some in MI5 wary of him—suspicion, if not guilt, through association. He didn't care. If that was the price for marrying her, he was more than willing to pay it.

In the morning, they had breakfast together before he left for London. Anna brushed tears away when she handed him his valise, which she had carefully repacked for him. He promised that he would call her more often, and that he would return as soon as humanly possible.

Hawes arrived thirty minutes early for his appointment with Dick White. He walked around the West End and timed his arrival at the Garrick Club so that he would meet the always punctual director-general at the front entrance at noon.

"How are you finding Berlin?" White asked, once they were sitting in the club's dark-paneled dining room.

"Chilly."

White nodded. "Chilly it is. I spent a few days in Berlin in '45. The Soviets were floating rumors that Hitler was still alive, and General Eisenhower asked me to look into it. The city was flat on its back, piles of rubble everywhere, dead bodies covered with lime. Ugly. The Russians took me to the ruins of the Chancellery, near the Führerbunker. We drank vodka to excess, and one of the senior Russian officers slapped down a pair of false teeth on the table and claimed they were Hitler's choppers. A joke, of course. Everything I saw convinced me that the evil little man was dead, and the Reds were spreading the rumors as a way to throw us off-balance."

As they ate lunch, Hawes briefed White on his progress—more accurately, on his relative lack of progress—in his investigation of Berlin Station.

"I think I may have a break in the case," Hawes said. "Unexpected, but heartening. It's why I came back to see you. I think it could help us surface the source of the leaks. I've focused on the senior men around Peter Lunn. When he was in Berlin, Lunn created file cards for all of the Station's agents. They're still using the system. When there's a problem, the duty officer can check the file card index, find the agent's handler, and contact him. Only the duty officers can access the cards."

"Do you have concerns about Lunn?"

"I don't question his loyalty, but I've always disliked the bureaucratic zeal to put everything in writing and store it. Never cared for central registries of agents."

"Can't be helped."

"Perhaps that's so. At least, the card file has let me narrow the list of likely candidates to the duty officers."

White raised his eyebrows. "You have more to go on than this, I hope."

"It's early days, but as I said, I've stumbled across something quite promising." He explained about the Stasi source and his tale of a honey pot trap aimed at a young American political attaché.

"An American diplomat." White frowned. "I fail to see how this helps us."

"With some luck, it could lead us to the leaker. Let's assume that our traitor can communicate with the KGB if and when there's a pressing need, an emergency. I plan to shake things up—double the girl, have her work for us. Then, I share this promising development with our leading candidate at Berlin Station, and see if word gets back to the Russians. If they shut down the operation, arrest the girl, then we've nailed the penetration agent."

"You have a leading candidate?"

When Hawes said the man's name, softly, he watched the director-general's face closely, but White displayed no emotion.

"I've heard the name in passing," he said. "I can't say I know the man to any degree. I assume that you'll want him left in place, for now. So you can test him."

"Until then, yes."

"And if the Russians don't respond to the leak about the girl?"

"I try with the next man on the list."

"Capital. That should flush him out. You'll continue to work independently, reporting directly to me. I'll authorize an advance for the necessary funds. Just hold onto the receipts so we can keep the chaps in Accounting happy. Do you need personnel? Reinforcements?"

"I'll employ freelancers. A local or two, if need be. Cut outs. No connection to the Service."

White looked pleased. Hawes knew that the weaker the link to the Broadway Building, the less there would be to explain if things went awry. The director-general had to worry that rumors of a botched investigation of the Berlin Station would reach unfriendly ears in Whitehall.

After finishing lunch, White led the way downstairs. They passed a handsome, dark-haired man whom Hawes vaguely recalled as an actor he'd seen in a film or two. White and the man exchanged nods.

"Rex Harrison," White explained. "Nice chap. Afraid his wife, Kay Kendall, the actress is quite ill."

He paused in the Garrick's foyer long enough to offer a few parting words of counsel. "Remember, Feliks, nothing in writing."

"You know me. I've never cared for paperwork."

"A necessary evil, but not necessary now. We want the slate to be kept clean."

"Clean it shall be," Hawes said. "Clean as the driven snow."

* * *

Hawes left the Garrick first, and walked briskly toward Leicester Square, enjoying the mild weather. He found a phone booth on the street near the underground station. When he dialed the number of the Danube, the phone was answered by a male voice. Hawes pushed Button A to continue the call, and asked for Viktor Toth.

In the background, Hawes heard the sound of glasses clinking and boisterous male voices, what you would expect around lunchtime in a London pub. Then someone picked up the receiver.

"It's been a while, Feliks." It was Viktor's distinctive, husky voice. "How are you? And Anna?"

"We're fine," Hawes said. "Sorry that I've been out of touch. I'm calling because I need your help."

"Whatever you need. For you, anything. You know that. Anything within reason."

Hawes laughed. "Which is it? Anything, or anything within reason?"

"Both. But I'd like to stay out of Brixton, if I could, so I hope you're not calling about a second-story job."

Hawes had long wondered whether Viktor had ties to the London underworld. Where had the remainder of the money for his pub come from? In Budapest, Viktor had fenced stolen goods during what he laughingly called his Robin Hood phase. Had he left that all behind?

Hawes wouldn't be surprised if Viktor had connections with some less than savory characters.

"Nothing like that," Hawes said. "I can promise that you won't have to worry about occupying a cell at Brixton. I hoped I could persuade you to lend a hand with a problem I've encountered in Berlin. It shouldn't take longer than a week or two."

There was a protracted silence, and Hawes thought momentarily that the telephone connection had been severed, but then Viktor finally responded.

"That's a shame. Berlin is filled with Germans."

"I've noticed that, Viktor."

"I'm a Jew. I don't care for Germans. In fact, I despise them. You must realize that. Can you blame me?"

"I'm not wild about them either, but this will be a quick job. I wouldn't ask unless it was necessary. I need someone who I can trust, someone without connections to my firm. We'll cover your expenses and then some. I'd greatly appreciate your lending a hand."

Viktor sighed. "When do you need me to come?"

Hawes told him, and there was another long pause.

"I'll have to make some arrangements," Viktor said. "The barman will steal me blind when I'm away, but I imagine it's all for a good cause. And you and I can be chummy with all the Jerries. Drink beer with them. Sing songs about Horst Wessel. Whatever it is the Nazis do these days."

"I wouldn't ask if I didn't need you, Viktor."

"I know that. That's why I'll be there. And you know that I find life to be absurd much of the time. This is one of those times. A Hungarian Jew helping Her Majesty's Secret Service handle some shady business in Berlin. Imagine that."

NINE

A sunny morning, the air soft and inviting with the promise of spring. Christa was in a good mood—tickets for *The Tempest* continued to sell well, and she looked forward to her date with Dillon at the art museum in Dahlem. Liesl had suggested they have breakfast, her treat, at the Café Schwan, her favorite place for coffee. She was eager to talk about exciting news—Stefan had offered her the role of Celia in the upcoming Neues Theater production of *As You Like It*.

"It's a first for me," she told Christa, after they had been served coffee and rolls. "I've finally graduated from bit roles. You're used to being the star, so it may seem silly to you that I'm so excited, but this is my first real role."

"It's not silly," Christa said. "I remember how over the moon I was when I got my first good part. It's just the start for you, Liesl. Once people see how good you are, other chances will come. That's how it was for me."

"Do you think so? I'm so happy. You'll be Rosalind, and I'll be Celia. We can help each other learn our lines. I just hope I'm up to it."

"You'll be wonderful," Christa said. "You're a natural. By the time we've finished rehearsals, it will feel like second nature to you."

Christa stretched out her legs, enjoying the aroma of coffee rising from the cup on the café table. She took a sip, savoring the rich, strong taste of the Arabica, a welcome change from the watered-down coffee served in East Berlin. She took a bite of her sweet breakfast roll. Christa sighed softly, contented, glancing around at the near-empty room. Pale sunlight cascaded through the café windows. Outside, people hurried by on mid-morning errands.

"I must be off," Liesl said. "Fritzi promised I could look through the costumes, pick out the dress I like most."

Christa watched through the window as her friend hurried up the street, her head held high, eager to get to the Neues Theater and take the next big step in her acting career. Christa was delighted for her—she remembered how excited she had been the first time she had the chance to play an important role.

At times, she felt almost like Liesl's older sister. When Christa had first begun rooming with her, she had wondered whether—like Stefan—Liesl might be working for the Stasi. It only took a few days for Christa to reject that notion—Liesl didn't seem capable of leading a double life. She was open and trusting, and a bit in awe of Christa. She had no guile.

Christa had turned away from the window when a middle-aged woman approached her table.

"You dropped this, Fräulein," she said loudly and handed Christa a paperback book. Christa took it from her and glanced at the title—Chekhov's *The Cherry Orchard*. When she looked up from the book, Christa realized it was Gerta standing before her. She was amused that the woman had been told to deliver the volume of Chekhov to her. Did Comrade Mikhail think that spy mumbo jumbo was necessary when a Stasi officer that Christa knew all too well was the messenger?

Perhaps Gerta felt the same way—judging from the disapproving look on her face, she clearly didn't like carrying messages to Christa. "You're expected at Magdalenenstrasse this afternoon," she said sourly. "Two o'clock. Make sure that you're not followed. Bring the book."

Christa stared at Gerta. "I'll be there."

"You live well here, don't you?" Gerta said, motioning to the coffee cup and roll on the café table. "Lazing about in the morning with coffee and strudel. Nightclubs and bars. Shopping at the KaDeWe."

"We perform six nights a week."

"Decadent plays for the bourgeois."

"Shakespeare is decadent?" Christa arched her eyebrows. "Would his plays be performed in Moscow if that were so? They are, you know."

Christa could see the resentment on Gerta's face, the pinched look of a woman who now hated her even more now that Christa could enjoy the small luxuries of life in the British sector that she couldn't. Gerta glared at her.

"Don't think that we don't know what you're up to," she said. "We see it all. We've watched while you've whored around the city with your American."

"I'm doing what I've been told to do," Christa said. "If you don't like that, then why don't you make an official complaint to Comrade Mikhail? Or I can inform him directly all about our little chat this afternoon."

"Tell him whatever you like," Gerta said. She remained standing in front of Christa, fists clenched, defiant. "Two o'clock. Don't be late."

"You've done your duty, delivered your message. I'll be there."

Gerta turned on her heel and left the café. Christa watched as she marched up the street, her shoulders hunched over, her cheap, shapeless overcoat an advertisement that she came from the East. If only Gerta would realize what they had in common, Christa thought—they were both prisoners of circumstance—but her envy and resentment would never let her see that truth.

* * *

This time, Christa wasn't as nervous when meeting with the Russian. She knew, more or less, where she stood with him. Now that she understood what was expected of her, she didn't feel the terrible uncertainty and dread she had when she had first encountered Comrade Mikhail. She would be careful in what she told him, but she didn't approach him with as much trepidation as she had—he needed her.

One of the Stasi officers stationed in the front lobby accompanied her to the same cramped interrogation room. The Russian was already there. He glanced at his watch.

"You're here on time," he said.

"Your message said two o'clock. I try to follow directions." She handed him the paperback volume of Chekov, and he accepted the book without comment. She noticed that there was a file folder on the table next to him. Was it her file? She wondered what might be in it, what the informers she had assumed were watching her had reported to the Stasi. She didn't think Stefan would say anything negative about her, but she had no way of knowing who else in the company might be reporting on her.

"Punctuality is good," he said. "At least one of your colleagues believes that you have been seduced by the easy life in the British sector. The whipped cream of the Ku'damm."

She felt her face burn. It had to be Gerta, retaliating for imagined slights. "You instructed me to fit in with the troupe. It's true that I have socialized with them, but I have not forgotten the terms under which I joined the Neues Theater."

"I was not concerned. You know better. Now, have you been questioned by BND officers?"

"I would assume that you know that. You told me that you're watching."

He remained silent, and Christa realized that there were limits to how closely they could follow her. Comrade Mikhail didn't want to admit it, and she reveled in her small victory.

"I've been ignored by their security," she told him. "Stefan has told the newspapers that I'm not political, that I'm first and foremost an actress, that my passion is reserved for the stage. But if the BND decides to interview me, I'm prepared."

"I have been reading the reports of Comrade Kruger," he said. "You claim that the American now pursues you with some ardor. Is that so?"

"It is," she said, careful not to say anything more. She wasn't as frightened of Comrade Mikhail as she had been before—her connection with Dillon was of some value to him, and she expected that the Russian would tread carefully with her. They needed her for whatever it was they had planned for the American, and as long as that was the case, she figured she would be well-treated.

He had picked her for the mission—that's how she thought of it, now—and she was proving him right. She had inserted herself into Dillon's life without raising any suspicion on his part that she was anything other than an ambitious young actress. And he was falling for her.

"What do you think of him? Of Mr. Dillon Randolph?"

"He's a very confident man," she said. "He's very sure of himself."

"Do you find him attractive?"

She shrugged. "What does it matter? He's a handsome man. Dynamic. He's used to having women fall at his feet." She paused. "He's arrogant. Accustomed to having his way. I've made him a little jealous. He believes that he has a rival for my affections."

"A rival? Who is that?"

"One of the actors, a friend, Jürgen. He is Prince Ferdinand, my suitor in *The Tempest*. I've asked him to play another role off-stage, that of my would-be lover. He understands that it's part of a game, a game of love."

"This actor has no feelings for you?"

"No, Jürgen has no interest in me."

"You're sure?"

She laughed. "Jürgen pines after Willi, the bartender at Kelch, a club on Pragerstrasse. Everyone wears a dress at Kelch."

"I see. Degenerates." He looked at her. "A good trick if it makes the American fall in love with you."

"He's falling for me," she said. "I can tell."

"Have you slept with him?"

"No," Christa said. "We agreed at the start, didn't we, that it's better that I play hard-to-get?"

Comrade Mikhail pursed his lips. "Within reason. He has pursued you long enough. Sleep with him." He rubbed his chin. "Give him a taste, one taste. Then withdraw. He'll want more."

"You're very sure about that."

"He is used to having the whip hand with his women. Keep him at some distance, make him feel that he has not completely won you. You must never allow him to believe that you care for him more than he cares for you. It must be an unequal attachment."

"He's not my first man," she said defensively. "I don't need to be told how to handle him." She didn't want to talk about Dillon with the Russian. She had been attracted to the American diplomat—she couldn't deny that he could be charming—but she had been careful to guard herself against becoming emotionally involved. The romance was a means to an end—freeing Konrad, and herself. In the past, she had slept with men she had felt little for. Dillon Randolph would be no different. She was playing a part, nothing more.

"One other thing," he said. "I know that you remain angry about the treatment of your brother," he said.

"I'm sad," she said. "Not angry."

"No, that is not so," he said with certainty. "You're angry. You hate those who have put him in prison, and who keep him there. Unfairly, in your eyes."

She was silent. His certainty bothered her, but he was correct about how she felt. She was angry, and she did hate the men persecuting Konrad. She would never admit that to him.

"We must use this righteous anger of yours," Comrade Mikhail said. "Let this young American of yours see it. You must tell him the tale of the injustice done to your brother. He will believe it, of course, because he has been fed their propaganda." The Russian brought the glass to his lips and took a sip of tea. "I've arranged for your brother to be brought from Hohenschönhausen to one of the cells in this compound, and you may visit him today, for thirty minutes." He carefully placed the glass on the table before him. "Some of my German colleagues believe that your brother should be sent to Bautzen, the prison the Fascists call the Yellow

Misery. I haven't agreed to this. We will keep him here where he will be more comfortable until you have done what we have asked."

* * *

Kruger brought her to another building in the complex, a concrete-block structure with bars on the windows. Inside, two guards in uniforms were waiting for her. They escorted her down a long corridor that smelled of disinfectant and came to a stop before a thick wood door.

One of the guards produced a key, opened the door, and motioned her inside. The room was smaller than she had expected, with two chairs and a solitary light bulb hanging from the ceiling. She waited alone, anxious, too excited to sit down. She had not seen Konrad for more than a year, and she prayed that his health had held up.

She heard a key turning in the lock, and the door opened. Konrad stepped into the room, and she gasped. He had lost weight, and he looked older, there were dark circles under his eyes and his skin had a mottled, gray look to it.

Konrad gave her a wan smile, and she hugged him, shocked at how thin and bony his body had become. She noticed faded greenish bruises around his jaw and mouth.

"What happened to your face?" she asked.

"A small disagreement," he said.

"Are you all right?"

"I'm fine," he said, but she didn't believe him. He coughed, and she could hear him wheezing as he gasped for breath. "I've had a devil of a time trying to shake this damn cough."

Konrad took in her expensive Western clothing and makeup. "Why are you dressed like that? You haven't married one of the Party shits, have you?"

"Of course not," she said. "I've been working in a theater in the British sector. Shakespeare. *The Tempest*. I'm playing Miranda. The authorities here have encouraged me."

"The authorities?" There was contempt in his voice. "What are you doing for them?"

"They think it's beneficial for the GDR to show that we have talented actors, trained by Brecht, as good as anyone in the West."

He coughed several times before he caught his breath and spoke. "You know the song: 'The Party is always right, and against lies and exploitation, he who insults life is stupid or bad.' That's me, I guess." He hummed a few bars of the SED anthem.

"Stop," she said. "It's not funny. Mocking them is what got you here in the first place."

"I have a counter-revolutionary sense of humor." He rubbed his eyes. "When they have eradicated that, what will be left of Konrad von Schiller?"

"Konrad Schiller," she said, correcting him.

"Maybe I'll be like Winston Smith," he said. "I'll learn to love Big Brother." He leaned forward and whispered in English: "If you want a picture of the future, imagine a boot stamping on a human face—forever."

"Stop. Please. You must not talk like this." She was conscious that she was hissing at him. Konrad loved to provoke, and he never seemed to consider the consequences of his recklessness. He had been like that since their father's death. She glanced around the room, wondering if there were hidden microphones picking up whatever they had to say to each other. Most likely, there were. "We're going to get you out of here."

"Christa, always the optimist. Always the good girl. How do you intend to accomplish that? A miracle?"

"I'm working on something," she said, giving a quick, reflexive glance over her shoulder. "If all goes well, you may be given another chance to demonstrate your loyalty to the state. Promise me that you won't say anything to provoke them. Not now. And once you're out, then perhaps we'll take a vacation together. Perhaps we can visit Werner."

"Werner?" Konrad asked, puzzled. Christa nodded slowly, and then her brother realized what she was trying to tell him—their friend Werner Tessler had defected to the West the summer before and was living in Stuttgart—and his face softened with hope. "I'd like that. Very much. Do you truly believe that we could?"

"I do," she said. "But, for now, you must be on your best behavior. They have promised to keep you here for the time being, instead of sending you back to Hohenschönhausen. Or Bautzen."

"Bautzen?" Konrad shook his head. "God forbid. Do you trust them?"

She shrugged. "How long has it been since we've seen each other?"

"A year."

"They brought you here so I could visit you," she said. "A demonstration of good faith. They didn't have to do that. You see, I can give them something they really want. I can't tell you anything more than that."

"What they want you to do," he said. "It's something nasty, isn't it?"

She didn't say anything at first, and tears welled in her eyes. Konrad had always been direct, quick to get at the heart of the matter. "It's ugly, yes," she said. "I won't lie to you. Ugly, but necessary. But I'm willing to do what they ask because it will get you out, and that's what matters."

Before Konrad could reply, she reached across the table with her right hand and gently touched the side of his face with her fingers. "Don't say anything," she said. "Trust me that I'm doing the right thing—for you, for us."

* * *

After leaving the Stasi compound, Christa found her way back to the Faith Church and the bench by the little courtyard. She sat for a few minutes, thinking about Konrad and all they had been through together. When she was a little girl, Konrad and Nala, their Pomeranian, had been Christa's audience for her impromptu performances in the attic of the Von Schiller's Berlin townhouse. She stepped upon a real stage for the first time during her school's Christmas play, when she was ten, and she had felt herself come alive as she had recited her lines. She had been so excited. There was something magical about slipping into a costume and becoming someone completely different.

In her teens, she feared she would never get the chance to act. A girl of her class was expected to marry well, to manage the affairs, large and small, of her husband's household, and to fill the nursery with sons and daughters. Christa chafed at the thought—there was no room for her acting in that future. A respectable married woman could never appear on the stage. So she quietly rejected the idea of a conventional marriage. She would not trade her dreams for the comfort, and restrictions, of domestic life.

After the war, the world had changed for the sons and daughters of the Prussian aristocracy, particularly for those, like Christa and her family, who found themselves in the Soviet Zone, stripped of power and privilege. Christa, at least, gained something: the chance to pursue her dream of acting for a career. Helped by her good looks and her expressive, resonant voice, she had quickly found a home with the Berliner Ensemble.

She dedicated herself to her craft, eager to learn from the actors and directors in the Ensemble. The troupe became a second family. She had felt accepted, welcomed, part of something larger, which was why it wounded her so deeply when she was banished after Konrad's troubles with the authorities. For a time, she had blamed him for her fall from grace, but came to realize that it was a dreadful, twisted system that would punish her for the imagined faults of her brother.

Her time with the Neues Theater had been liberating. No long, hectoring political speeches, no cardboard characters, no absurd plot twists so that the heroes of Scientific Socialism could triumph in the end. Just the clever words of Shakespeare, written hundreds of years before, words that still moved and delighted Berliners in the twentieth century. More than once she found herself smiling and telling herself "the play's the thing," the famous lines from *Hamlet*, because that was true now for her, the play became the focus of the company's efforts every night when the house lights were dimmed and the curtain rose.

She had become a better actress. Christa felt free to channel more of herself, of her fear and rage and her hopes and dreams, into her performances. She could sense that she was connecting with the audience crowded into the cramped theater, an audience eager to escape into the imagined world of Shakespeare's magical island.

She did not want to give up this newfound freedom. She would live up to her side of the bargain with the Russian. Then, she and Konrad would leave for the West and start over. It wouldn't be easy, but Christa knew that wherever they landed in Germany, there would be theater people, members of her guild, and there would be a place for her.

* * *

Hawes had delayed approaching the CIA about Dillon Randolph until he couldn't delay any longer. There was no getting around it—Randolph was an American, and Hawes knew he couldn't go any further unless he had cleared things with American intelligence.

He drove to Dahlem and parked on Foehrenweg, a dead-end street lined with trees, and found his way to the red-brick building that housed the CIA's Berlin Operating Base.

He had made an appointment to meet with Thomas Ryder, one of the liaison officers who handled SIS requests. After his credentials had been checked by the uniformed Army guard at the front of the building, Ryder came out to meet Hawes in the lobby, welcoming him with a firm handshake.

Hawes studied Ryder on their brief walk to his office. He wasn't one of the fair-haired, boyish Ivy Leaguers Hawes had encountered in his past dealings with the American intelligence agency. Ryder had black hair and dark brown eyes and from his coloring, Hawes would have guessed that he was of Mediterranean heritage, perhaps Italian or Greek.

"We heard you were in the city," Ryder said. "The word is that Berlin

Station has welcomed you like the town whore at the church picnic."
He glanced around the room. "It's clean, the room. We have the facility
swept for bugs every two weeks. So far they haven't found anything, no
microphones."

"Has it been a concern?" Hawes asked. "Bugs?"

"More microphones per capita in this city than anywhere else in the
world. You can't trust the phones, either, because the lines run through
East Berlin. We're doing what we can to wiretap them, too. The KGB has
told its spy runners to meet their sources outside, in a park or on the
street, to avoid our microphones."

"Somewhat tense in the field at the moment?"

"We know Karlshorst has been told to run operations to make us look
bad, to back up Khrushchev's claim that Berlin is a swampland of
espionage. They're spreading disinformation, nasty rumors that we're
preparing to leave and that when we do, the Berliners will feel so
betrayed that they'll attack American and British dependents on the way
out. Swarm Tempelhof and Tegel, block the departing flights."

"Any rumors of another blockade?"

"Not a blockade. For years we've heard that the Soviets have a
contingency plan to seal off their sector from the West, Operation
Chinese Wall. The Red Army closed the sector crossing points for a few
days during the uprising in July '53. Under Potsdam, they can't block our
access, but they could try to control the movement of their Germans.
It's not likely they'd try it. We'd have a field day with the propaganda. It
would be an admission that our system is better than theirs."

He rolled a swivel chair from behind a battered, gray steel desk so he
could sit facing Hawes. He found a pipe in his jacket pocket, and lit it,
producing a cloud of fragrant smoke.

"You'll find me a straight-shooter," he said. "Level with me, and we'll get
along fine." He gave Hawes a look of appraisal. "They say you took care
of a messy situation in Vienna back in '56."

"Is that what they say?"

"It is. I made a call back to Washington. Dulles trusts you. They say it

106

had something to do with dirty laundry. Our dirty laundry. Whatever it is that you did, Dulles is eternally grateful. A good friend to have."

"Sorry to disappoint," Hawes said. "I'm not on a first name basis with your director. But I'm always willing to help an ally."

"You knew Matthew Steele?"

"I did. From his OSS days."

"Steele has become somewhat of a legend," Ryder said. "The scuttlebutt is that he spotted Kim Philby as a security risk early on, before anyone else. Apparently he got sidetracked pursuing the man he thought was Philby's handler, a KGB officer named Yatov. Like Steele was Captain Ahab chasing Moby Dick."

"Never read the book, but I saw the movie with Gregory Peck. It's true Steele had a hunch about Yatov, and it didn't play out. He went with his intuition, which isn't a bad thing to do when you're hunting spies."

"Is that why you're in Berlin? To hunt spies?" Ryder took a puff on his pipe. "Does your intuition tell you that someone in your shop is leaking to the Reds? Is that why your colleagues are eager to see you on a plane back to London?"

"You have good sources," Hawes said. "That's about it. The long and short of it."

"For what it's worth, Bill Harvey, our head of station, poked around after the tunnel operation was blown but concluded that it was just bad luck."

"That could be," Hawes said. "I've been asked to take a second look."

"I don't envy you that," Ryder said. "I've seen enough of how your outfit works to know that you won't ever be allowed to take off the gloves. Not if it's one of your own." He hesitated. "Then again, you may surprise me. They say in Washington that you're different. Not one of the old boys."

"That's fair. I'm not one of the old boys."

"I'm part Chickasaw myself," Ryder said. "My grandmother on my mother's side. We're from Oklahoma. That means I don't immediately trust you white folks. Never have."

"And I'm part Polish, so you know that I don't trust Germans or Russians." Hawes glanced over to make sure the door was shut. "As it happens, I came to discuss a different matter. Somewhat sensitive. I've stumbled upon something that bears investigation, but there's a catch. It involves one of your diplomats."

"The other side up to no good?"

"They're using a girl as bait. An actress. Classic honey pot. It appears that it's working. I'd like to let it play out, see where it goes. The girl, a German, lives in our sector, so we can handle the surveillance."

"I take it that you don't want us interfering?"

Hawes didn't answer Ryder directly. "We're focused on watching the girl, for now. We may need to approach the target, the diplomat, at some point. I'll keep you apprised of progress. We may ask for your help at some point."

"I'd like that," Ryder said. "The special relationship in action." He puffed on his pipe. "What's the name of our star-crossed diplomat? Don't worry, we won't spook him. For now, we'll keep our distance."

Hawes told him, and Ryder nodded. "I know about him. The Congressman's son. Bit of a bad boy." He grinned. "He needs to be on his best behavior. Lots of people watching. Uncle Sam has something like fifteen intelligence units operating in Berlin if you count the military, the Army and Navy units. We're tripping over each other. It's a small town for Americans. Not many secrets stay secret. Not for long. You might want to remember that."

PART TWO

TEN

Dillon woke to the distant rumble of thunder. He rolled over in bed and checked the alarm clock on his nightstand: seven o'clock. Outside, it was raining, and the sky had turned slate gray, not the weather he would have chosen for his excursion with Christa to the picture galleries of the Dahlem Museum—the Gemäldegalerie—which was now temporarily housed in the building that had previously been the Asiatic Museum.

The streets glistened in the rain as he drove to Wilmersdorf. He kept the windshield wipers on, and by the time he reached Hohenzollerndamm, the main street near Christa's flat, rainwater had begun pooling in the gutters. The sidewalks were empty of pedestrians, and there were few other vehicles on the street.

Sheltered under a red umbrella, Christa waited for him in front of her turn-of-the-century apartment building. He pulled over by the curb and quickly exited the driver's seat so he could open the passenger door for her.

They made small talk during the twenty-minute return trip to Dahlem. The museum was on Arnimallee, near the Free University, and that prompted Dillon to ask Christa if she had taken any courses there, or at Humboldt University, in East Berlin.

She shook her head. "My uni was the Berliner Ensemble. I would have been bored sitting in stuffy classrooms, listening to a professor droning on with his lecture. It's not like that in the theater. You must engage with the material. You must throw yourself into the role."

"Like Marlon Brando and Montgomery Clift and the other Method actors?"

She was amused by his comment. "No, not like them. They have all fallen prey to Stanislavsky's emotionalism. Little discipline. Too psychological in their interpretation. Acting should serve the story, not the ego. It's not impersonation. You should only expose as much of the character as needed, and then through gesture."

Once inside the museum, Christa suggested they walk the main galleries and then finish by viewing the famous bust of Queen Nefertiti. "I saw her once on Museum Island when I was a young girl," she said. "I'm eager to see her again. We should save the best for last."

"How did she end up here?" Dillon asked.

"To the victors go the spoils. After the war, they divided up the collection. The West got the real prize, Queen Nefertiti, and lots of the Dutch Masters."

They took their time as they explored the museum, strolling from gallery to gallery. Dillon was impressed by its large collection of Rembrandts, especially the dark energy of the Dutch painter's *Samson and Delilah*, Samson asleep in Delilah's lap as she turns to offer the shears to a man behind her. Christa was drawn to a Manet painting, a soft pastoral scene of a woman sitting in a summer meadow, her skirt spread out around her.

When they entered the room with the bust of Queen Nefertiti, Christa sighed softly in pleasure, and made her way over to the sculpture. She studied it through its protective glass box.

"She's so serene, so elegant," Christa said. She glanced at the small plaque affixed to the pedestal. "It says the name Nefertiti means 'the beautiful one has come.' She lived more than three thousand years ago, and yet seems so alive. Look at her smile. At her lips. I wonder what she was thinking when she sat for the sculptor?"

"Maybe she was hungry, impatient for her lunch?"

She made a face and laughed. "Ach! You're the hungry one. Let's go for lunch."

Dillon grinned and nodded—he was hungry. They stopped at a small restaurant in Steglitz and had *Königsberger Klopse*, meatballs in white sauce, boiled potatoes, washing the meal down with beer.

"There's a reason Berliners are so eager for culture, for art, for music, for theater," she said. "It's the sign of civilization. It's the best of us. After all that happened, it shows the world that we're not all brutes."

"I don't know that the world will ever see Americans as cultured," he said. "Walt Disney and John Wayne and Coca-Cola and skyscrapers. That's not very impressive when matched up against what Europe has to offer. Da Vinci, Bach, Shakespeare."

"I've met one very cultured Ami, a poet."

"I hate to admit this, but I'm not your typical American. My fellow countrymen don't have much use for poets. Except maybe Robert Frost."

"What sort of poet is he?"

"A very popular one, which means the literary types sneer at him—they're jealous, of course. Frost's poetry is much more nuanced than he's given credit for. I have a sneaky suspicion that one hundred years from now people will still be reading him. I can't say the same for anyone else on the scene these days. Certainly not Allen Ginsburg." He rolled his eyes and was rewarded by Christa's laugh. "Perhaps Robert Lowell, a poet from Boston."

"Perhaps Dillon Randolph, a poet from Virginia?"

"You heard what that older man said at Amerika Haus—he was correct, I'm a traditionalist, out of step with the poetic times."

"You're too pessimistic. I like your poetry, and you're young. Who knows what you may write in the future? Perhaps a famous love poem."

"If you're going to write love poetry, it helps to be in love," he said. "Or at least to believe you're in love. There's a difference, you know."

She nodded. "I know that, all too well. And it's even harder to find *wahre Liebe*, true love. If it even exists."

* * *

Christa seemed preoccupied by something on the drive back to Wilmersdorf, and she said very little. Light drizzle continued to fall and gray clouds filled the sky. Dillon stopped his Ford Consul in front of her neo-Gothic apartment building. It was one of the Mietskaserne structures built in the late nineteenth century, with spacious front apartments for the more affluent and a rear courtyard that let light in for the tenants. She turned to him and smiled.

"Would you like to come up and have a cup of tea?" she asked. "We'd have the place to ourselves. Liesl is out this afternoon, visiting her mother in Potsdam."

Dillon found himself smiling—the invitation to join her in her flat, alone, suggested that he had finally passed some sort of test. Did it signal something more, a greater intimacy? Or would she continue to keep him at a safe distance?

"You're amused by something?" she asked.

"It's nothing. It's been a good day. An audience with Queen Nefertiti, and then lunch with Berlin's rising young star of the stage, Christa Schiller. And now, afternoon tea."

"Not yet," she said. "I'm on the top floor. You have five flights of stairs ahead of you."

Christa led the way up the winding staircase, turning to him once in encouragement and smiling at him. It was a long climb.

When they reached the fifth-floor landing, he could hear the drumming sound of the rain on the roof of her apartment.

"A nice rain," she said, looking up at the ceiling. "A gentle rain."

Once inside her flat, she latched the door and turned to him. "We can have our tea, but would you like to make love to me, first?" She took his hand in hers and, smiling, looked into his eyes.

"Do you even need to ask that question?"

He touched her hair and kissed her lips gently. She led him across the small living room to her bedroom. There, she unknotted his tie and unbuttoned his shirt, and ran her hands across his naked chest. When she unbuckled his belt and unzipped his trousers, Dillon felt himself growing hard. He peeled off the rest of his clothing as she stepped back and slipped out of her dress and let it fall to the floor. She moved to the bed, and he kissed her again. She pulled him closer, taking his right hand and guiding it to her breasts.

She sighed when their bodies joined and whispered something that he couldn't make out. He kissed her on the forehead and eyelids, and she embraced him with a growing urgency. They found a rhythm, the bedsprings creaking beneath them as the rain kept drumming on the roof above, and then she cried out and Dillon found himself responding with his own hoarse cry of pleasure.

Later, they lay side-by-side on her narrow bed. "That was lovely," she said, touching his lips with her fingertips for a moment. She stirred and climbed out of bed and donned his button-down shirt. Christa perched on the edge of the bed. She reached over to her night table and found a pack of cigarettes in the drawer. She lit one and took a long pull on the cigarette, letting the smoke fill her lungs, savoring the taste.

"I didn't know that you smoked," Dillon said. "Can I have a drag?"

"Sure." She handed him the cigarette, and he took a quick puff and handed it back to her. She propped herself up on one elbow.

"You're very fetching in my shirt."

"A strange word. Fetching. Doesn't it mean getting something?" She shrugged. "The shirt keeps me warm. And when you next wear it, you'll remember me."

"I won't need that to remember."

He glanced around her bedroom. There were few personal touches, no framed photographs or keepsakes, just a few books piled on the night table. Next to a volume of Chekov, he spotted a copy of *Cedar Creek*—he was surprised at how pleased he was at seeing his book there.

Dillon was struck by how similar her bedroom was to his in Dahlem, in Little America. He hadn't bothered to decorate. What was the point? He slept there, but he lived elsewhere, in his office at the Mission, at the Schöneberg City Hall (collecting gossip from his fellow diplomats and from German politicians), and in the restaurants, nightclubs, and cafés of the city.

Christa noted his quick survey of the room. "I travel light," she said. "Besides, I might not be here for very long."

"You're leaving?" he asked, trying to keep his voice level. He was dismayed at the thought.

"I'm committed to the Neues Theater for this season," she said. "Stefan may ask me back, or he may not. The reviewers seem to like me. Of course, there's always one or two who don't. And there are complications. Some people reject the idea of an actress from the East on the stage in the West."

"Have you thought of staying here, whether or not you're invited?"

"To cross to the West? To leave everything behind? Family. Friends. Career." She shook her head.

"But you can be free in the West."

"Freedom? That's an abstraction. My family and friends are what is real. And they're in the East."

Outside, the rain had increased in intensity, drumming down onto the slate roof above them. They took turns with the cigarette, smoking in silence, and then Christa spoke.

"I'll continue to act, no matter what the future brings. On stage, you create something new, every night. The stage lights make it hard to see the audience. You must rely on what you can hear—whether they sigh, or laugh, or hiss. Then, at the curtain call, you can see their faces, and if it's been a good performance they tell you with smiles and nods and sometimes even tears. It's like a drug, you know, and once you have a taste of it, you want it more." She stubbed out the cigarette in an ashtray on the night table. "When did you first write poetry?"

"When I was twelve years old. I used to ride at my grandfather's farm, and my favorite horse broke his leg and had to be put down. I wrote some pretty maudlin verses about it, but I found that somehow that writing the poem helped it hurt less. Then when I got a little older, I started writing love poetry, for all the obvious reasons."

"So you fell in love, then?" she asked, smiling, lying down next to him and running her hand slowly across his chest.

"I was in love with love."

"So how would you make love to your Virginia girls? Did you go parking with them, like I've seen in the American movies?"

"When I was younger, we'd drive to the far side of the campus, where there was a lover's lane. It was relatively innocent, because no 'good girl' was going to let you get very far. Not without an engagement ring."

"And the girls who were not so good?" she asked.

"When I got older, I found that they weren't too hard to find. Tamara Knight was my first, and I guess you could say she seduced me. She was two years older. I was quite eager to be introduced to the mysteries of love. I was sixteen, and I thought sex was the most wonderful thing ever invented. For a while, I was in love with lust. Then Tamara went after a friend of mine, and I had a rude awakening to that old saying, all's fair in love and war." He paused, shifting so he could draw her closer and encircle her with his arms. "And for you, Christa? Your first love?"

"The war made it different. When we should have been caught up in teenage romances, the boys were pulled into the Wehrmacht or Reichsmarine. Or worse, into the Gestapo, although I'm proud to say none of my friends ever joined them. There were few opportunities for me to have a serious boyfriend. When my family returned to Berlin, I became involved with a man. An actor, of course. Hendrik Forst. I didn't love Hendrik, but I was in such a hurry to catch up on all that I had missed out on, living far from Berlin."

"And since Hendrik?"

"Ah, you know how we are in the theater. Many little romances. Always some drama. Broken hearts that miraculously mend before the next performance."

"I wish all broken hearts healed like that," he said. "I learned otherwise in my last posting, in Australia. Caused a scandal, disappointed a lot of people. My father, particularly."

"What is he like? Your father?"

"He's formidable," Dillon said. "Demanding. My older brother Wash was his favorite. My father had big plans for him. Senator from Virginia some day. Perhaps more. Wash went off to war, to Korea, with the Marines, and didn't come back. A victim of the vanity of General MacArthur, stranded at Chosin, surrounded by the Chinese."

"I'm sorry," she said.

"My father took it very hard. Hell, we all did. When he looks at me, I know he's comparing me to Wash. I come up short. I'm not a natural leader, like Wash. I ended up in the Foreign Service because it seemed a way I could do something, prove that I could contribute."

She excused herself and disappeared into the bathroom and came out fully dressed. She handed him his shirt. "We must talk, now," she said, sitting on the edge of the bed. "Despite this afternoon, nothing changes. No complications."

"Despite this afternoon?" he asked, disappointed.

"Do you think you in some way possess me now? That you have some claim?" She had crossed her arms defensively, and her tone was sharp.

He was surprised by the sudden change in her mood. "No, I don't think any of that. I very much want to see you again."

"I need to think about it. About us. I never planned on this, you know. A romance. Sometimes your mind says one thing, and your body says something different."

"What about your heart?"

She shook her head. "My heart? We agreed that to keep this something light. You promised, didn't you?"

"I did," he said. "But that doesn't mean that I can't hope for something more. But it's up to you whether that ever happens."

On the drive back to Dahlem, he thought about Christa and his feelings toward her. He didn't understand her. After they had made love, she had seemed to welcome their pillow talk, but then had suddenly withdrawn, had pushed him away. He wasn't happy with that—he wanted her as his lover—but he would take it slowly, confident that in the end he could win her over.

* * *

"Sorry to say, I don't have much to share," Einhardt explained. "You'll see that our dossiers on the girl and the American are quite thin."

Hawes waited for him to continue. They sat together in the side room of an out-of-the-way café of Einhardt's choosing just off the Nollendorfplatz in Schöneberg. Hawes glanced around—the place was empty, and there was no danger that they would be overheard.

"Beggars can't be choosers," he replied. "Whatever you have will help."

Einhardt reached into a leather briefcase sitting at his feet and removed two folders. He handed one of them to Hawes.

"*Die Akte* on Dillon Randolph," he said. "He's been in Berlin for only a brief time, so it's largely gossip and hearsay. One public appearance—a talk on poetry at Amerika Haus. Rumors about a scandal in Australia. Randolph involved with a married woman. It's said his father, a former Congressman, pulled strings to get him sent here."

Hawes opened the file folder and briefly scanned the single document inside. There wasn't much to read. "It's puzzling. I don't know what the Soviets see in him. He's a bit reckless, for sure. Doubtful that he'll ever move up in the ranks in their Foreign Service, and he won't have access to classified information until he does. Unless his father is the target. Perhaps they hope to turn the son to get at the father?"

They exchanged folders—the girl's dossier included several documents and a photograph. Einhardt carefully returned Randolph's file to his briefcase before he spoke again. "As you can see, we have more on Christa Schiller—*von* Schiller until the war ended. Her father was Wehrmacht, one of the July 20th plotters with von Stauffenberg. Executed for his complicity. The family stayed in Warnemünde after the war, and then six years ago, after her mother's death, Fräulein von Schiller and her brother moved to Berlin."

Einhardt straightened his tie. Hawes had noticed that he paid close attention to how he looked—Einhardt was a bit of a dandy. "Christa Schiller turned up on our radar last fall when she joined the Neues Theater," he continued. "The director of the theater, Stefan Schmidt, may be working for the Stasi. He appears to live well beyond his means. The girl had once been in the Berliner Ensemble—Brecht's theater troupe—and the Neues Theater has been playing that up in their publicity."

"Brecht? Why would they tout that? Brecht was a Communist and a bit of a sod, from what I've heard."

"His name carries great weight in theater circles here. Landing an actress he trained is a coup for Schmidt."

Hawes held up the black-and-white photo from the file, a glamorous headshot. "She's quite attractive."

"That she is," Einhardt said. "The gossip is that she slept her way into the Berliner Ensemble."

"What does the Stasi hold over her?"

"A good question. We don't know." Einhardt shrugged. "They seem confident that she'll do what she's told, and that she won't bolt. It appears to be a straightforward sparrow operation. You know how it goes. She seduces the American, and then convinces him that she's in trouble. Only he can rescue her. If he bites, they get him to pass some relatively innocuous documents—say, a list of names and phone numbers from the U.S. Mission—and then, before he knows it, he's on the hook. They threaten to ruin him if he doesn't collect the sensitive information they want."

Hawes frowned. "Something doesn't add up. It's too crude. I don't think Randolph would fall for it."

"Who knows? Nothing ventured, nothing gained. Better men than him have been turned by a beautiful young woman. She is certainly something to look at, mind you. The Stasi specializes in compromising their targets sexually. It's not just dangling pretty girls as bait. They've sent handsome young men, Romeos they call them, to the West to pursue lonely secretaries in the government. The woman thinks she has found love everlasting, and is slowly persuaded to do whatever she's asked to—spy on her boss, pass along correspondence."

"There's something more here with Randolph," Hawes said. "I don't think it's simple blackmail."

"That may be. What do you propose to do, then?"

"Turn their operation to our purposes. I have a few ideas about how that might work."

"Since you contacted me, I've been very careful," Einhardt said. "I borrowed these files without signing for them. No need to call attention to the girl, or to Randolph. At this point, only you know the Boar's story. I can hold off on filing a report for a bit longer, but not forever. Once it's in circulation, there could be leaks. You must move quickly."

"How long?"

"I'm not sure. No more than a month."

"Could you forget about making a report?"

"That wouldn't be prudent," Einhardt said. "The day may come when the Boar defects. When he's debriefed, he'll tell them about the operation against Randolph. How do I explain that I didn't report it? It would raise questions about my loyalty."

"Then I guess you'll have to give your superiors the details at some point. The longer you can drag your heels, the better."

Einhardt shifted in his chair. "Your discussion with the Boar the other day has caused him great anxiety. He worries that you'll inadvertently expose him."

"I've never run an agent who wasn't anxious," Hawes said. "Paranoid. Afraid of his own shadow. He's no different."

"Except that he wants to come over to us, now. He says that he can't sleep for worry."

"What are you going to do?"

"Stall. Offer him more money. He's the best source I have from over there. I don't want to lose him."

"I'm willing to spend to keep the information flowing," Hawes said. "I'd like to make use of the Boar's closeness to the operation against Randolph. First, we need to turn the girl. Then I advertise that we've recruited her, but I only share the details with the officer I suspect of betraying us. The Boar tells us if word about her gets back. If it does, we know who is the traitor."

Einhardt nodded. "Clever. If nothing is passed, then you can eliminate one suspect and try the next." He rubbed his chin. "You don't even need to turn her, you know. Claiming that you have would be enough."

"Do you know George Blake?" Hawes asked. "One of ours at Berlin Station."

Einhardt shook his head. "By name only."

"There's something about him I don't like. Something not on the level. He's approved to work in the Soviet sector, so he could be up to mischief and we'd never know."

"I take it that he's your first target."

"He is," Hawes said. "I need your help on one other matter. Can you get me an identification card for a worker in East Berlin? Good enough to get past the Vopos?"

Einhardt nodded. "We collect hundreds of identity cards every day from the refugees. It's easy enough to alter them. I'll have to arrange for it to be done off the books."

"The name should be Viktor Keller. I'll send the photos to you by messenger."

"What do you use when you cross into the East? Not your English passport, I hope."

"No, I become a Danish dealer in antiques. Helpful to explain my accent when I speak German. Haven't had to show my passport yet."

"What about the girl?" Einhardt asked. "Do you want us to watch her?"

"No, that might raise suspicions. But you can't ignore her, either, because they would expect you to show some interest in her, particularly with her name in the newspapers. I'd suggest that you interview her at the theater. Keep it low-key. Nothing to unsettle her, just a way to show the flag."

Einhardt adjusted his necktie again. "I'll handle it myself, so there are no mistakes. Some of my colleagues might be tempted to show off in front of a pretty girl like her, question her more than once. You know how it goes."

Hawes thanked him, but Einhardt held up his hand to stop him. "I'll do what I can to help," he said. "I wish that you knew more. What are their intentions? The timing? Without that, I question whether your scheme will work."

"I agree," Hawes said. "I think we need to turn the girl. We also need the American to cooperate."

Einhardt rose to his feet, the briefcase in his hand. "You'll need more than your fair share of luck to pull this off, and time is not on your side. But they say you're a lucky one, Feliks. Let's hope they're right."

ELEVEN

Hawes had stationed himself by the Cosmopolitan's window so that he could watch the stream of passersby on the Ku'damm. He stirred his coffee with a spoon, and checked his watch. He was beginning to feel anxious, but then he spotted Viktor Toth sauntering up the sidewalk, suitcase in hand, hair slicked back, cigarette dangling from his lips.

Hawes found himself smiling—Viktor enjoyed playing the part of the slightly raffish tough guy of the American gangster movies, the charming rogue with street smarts.

Viktor approached the Cosmopolitan without hesitating, and then, after a quick side glance, continued walking up the street. Hawes sipped his coffee and waited. Five minutes later, Viktor returned, moving at a leisurely pace. He stopped momentarily in front of the restaurant's front window, studying the menu posted there, before entering by the front door.

Hawes kept his eyes on the sidewalk, watching the flow of pedestrians. He doubted that Viktor had picked up a tail at Tempelhof, but proper tradecraft demanded that he be certain before any contact. He didn't see any signs to suggest that Viktor had been followed.

Viktor glanced around the interior of the Cosmopolitan, spotted Hawes by the window, and came over to join him at the table. They shook hands. An elderly waiter appeared and poured a cup of coffee for Viktor.

"Sorry that I couldn't meet you at the airport," Hawes said after the waiter had left. "Every intelligence outfit in Berlin watches the arriving passengers and notes who is greeting them. My photo's been circulated by the Stasi, no doubt. Why blow your cover ninety seconds after you'd reached the arrivals area?"

Viktor grinned. "I'm glad to be a tourist. I'll consider this an all expenses paid vacation. I'm a bit disappointed. The guidebook I picked up said there's not much of a beach here."

"We're a ways from the sea. Lake Wannsee has some beaches, but it'll need to be a lot warmer before you start sunbathing."

They were comrades-in-arms more than friends, Hawes thought, members of the "band of brothers" who had been in Budapest during the October uprising. Viktor led the resistance fighters from the city's Eighth District, from the tough neighborhoods near the Keleti train station. He had helped Hawes escape from Budapest as the Red Army closed in, and when he surfaced in England in 1957, Hawes had lent him several hundred pounds, fully expecting that he would never be repaid. Then Viktor opened a pub in London, the Danube, and it had prospered, enough so that he was able to present Hawes with a cheque for the principal and interest some eighteen months later.

"How is Anna?" Viktor asked. He had settled into the chair opposite Hawes and stubbed out his cigarette in the ashtray.

"She's well."

"Enjoying life in England, is she?"

"She is, very much so. Thanks for asking."

"You two should stop by the Danube."

"We should."

"But you won't, will you? My place attracts too many people from Budapest, and Anna would feel uncomfortable around them. I understand."

Hawes didn't respond. Viktor was right—Anna didn't care to visit the Danube. It was a magnet for the exiles of Eastern Europe. Polish and Hungarian flags hung prominently on the walls next to the Union Jack. The red, white, and green Hungarian flag had a circular hole cut in its center—removing the hated hammer and sickle—just like the ones carried by the protesters in Budapest. Anna didn't want to encounter someone from her past, and Hawes didn't blame her. He didn't like the idea any better than she did.

"She's not the only one who did unpleasant things to survive," Viktor said. "We all did. Cut corners. Betrayed others. No one was clean. That's the nature of the system, what they make you do. You know that. Anna should know that."

"She wants to leave it all behind," Hawes said. "She dreads running into someone who might recognize her as a Duna girl. You understand. She's made a fresh start in England."

"I understand." Viktor lit a fresh cigarette and took a puff. "How goes it here?"

"It's tense. Khrushchev just announced that he's ready to sign a separate peace treaty with Ulbricht. A bluff, but it makes for great headlines and it rattles the Foreign Office types."

"Aren't there talks coming up in Geneva? In May?"

Hawes nodded. "That's why Khrushchev's talking tough. He's staking out his negotiating position."

"This diplomatic stuff is all fine and good," Viktor said. "But when you called, you said that you needed help. Off the books. A hint of some rough stuff."

"You read between the lines quite well."

"Before we go any further, remember that I won't work with Nazis."

"I assumed that. I would never ask you to. I hate the Nazis as much as I do the Reds. But there are Germans who didn't support Hitler. Not many of them, but a few. Adenauer. The mayor, Willy Brandt."

"But I doubt that you've asked them to help in this operation," Viktor said with a crooked smile.

"No, I haven't. Only one German. An intelligence officer I've worked with in the past. Trustworthy. Young enough to have missed the war."

"So exactly why am I here?" Viktor asked. "What do you want me to do?"

"For now, get to know the city as fast as you can. Then recruit two helpers. Hungarians living here. Or Poles. Tough chaps who hate the Reds and will do what they're told and can keep their mouths shut.

We'll keep their involvement circumscribed. Narrow. Follow this man. Watch this building." He handed Viktor a thick roll of Deutsche Marks. "You should be vague about your employer. If they conclude that it's the Americans, all the better."

"I take it that you can't use any of your own people."

"I can't. I'm afraid that it's come to that."

"Don't worry. It won't be hard to find Hungarians who fit the bill." Viktor dangled his cigarette between his lips. "Then what? What's going on that you need me and the other men?"

"I've stumbled onto a Russian operation. They're using a swallow, a young German actress. An American diplomat is the target. I'm not sure why, yet. For now, I need someone to keep an eye on them. Someone who can blend in. That's where you can prove helpful."

"I can do that," he said. He nonchalantly blew a smoke ring and grinned at Hawes. "That's a bit tamer, though, than I had imagined."

"It could get nasty. We'll have to wait and see."

"We've never talked about what happened in Vienna in '56, Feliks. Eva Nemeth told me, just before she left for Israel, that the Reds had killed Morris Rose. She didn't give me any details. What did happen? You were there."

Hawes gave a reluctant nod. He didn't like talking about what had turned into a failed operation. Morris Rose, an American defector living in Budapest and working for the KGB, had decided he wanted to return to the West. Hawes and a journalist from New York, a friend of Rose, had been tasked with getting him across the border to Austria. They had succeeded in doing so before their luck ran out.

"We were betrayed," Hawes said. "We had Eva and Rose tucked away for safekeeping in the Bristol Hotel. The Russians sent a team after Rose and they killed him before we could intervene. A black day. It was an American, a CIA officer, who tipped off the KGB." Hawes rubbed his eyes. "I blame myself. I let my guard down once we were across the border. They had to be desperate to eliminate Rose, because they burned their penetration agent in doing so."

"And what happened to him?"

Hawes paused, considering his response. "He took his own life when he realized that he had been exposed." Hawes looked out the window at the Berliners passing by. "Have you stayed in touch with Eva?"

"I heard from her a few months ago. A letter from Haifa. She's getting married to a doctor who emigrated from Argentina. Eva wants children. It seems she's putting Budapest behind her."

"And you, Viktor? Any regrets that you chose fair England instead of Israel?"

"I like cities. Big cities, so London suits me well." Viktor gave him another grin. "I like New York, as well, but I wore out my welcome there. As for the rest of Europe, I can't see living here. Not after what they've done to us, to the Jews." He paused. "There's a joke you can tell about any town or village in Central Europe. Poland, Hungary, Romania, it doesn't matter. The mayor calls in the police chief and tells him to round up all the Jews and the bicyclists. 'Why the bicyclists?' the police chief asks."

Hawes laughed. He was lucky to have Viktor's assistance on such short notice since he couldn't use anyone with any connection to British intelligence. It probably wasn't fair to ask Viktor to drop everything and take risks he didn't need to, but Hawes also knew there was a side of Viktor that craved action, that welcomed any chance to hit back at the Russians.

"We'll have you stay in my flat for now," Hawes said. "I have a place on the edge of the Hansa Quarter. And you need to get a passport photo. Your papers will be in the name of Viktor Keller."

"Keller? Clever. Hungarian but also German. What will you be doing?"

"Now that you're here, it's time for me to approach the diplomat, the target. See if he's willing and able to play a different part in this little drama. We'll need his cooperation for what I hope to accomplish."

"Do you think he has the nerve for this sort of thing?"

"I don't know. There's only one way to find out. We'll start down that road and see if he'll follow."

* * *

At lunch on Wednesday, Dillon stopped by the Kaufhaus des Westens, the KaDeWe department store, looking to buy some dress shirts. As he entered the ground floor, he bumped into Audrey Wingate. He hadn't seen her since their night out at Remde's St. Pauli. She hadn't acknowledged the flowers he sent, nor did she return the phone message he left for her at Amerika Haus. He had decided to leave well enough alone, and wait for her to make contact.

After an awkward moment of silence, Audrey spoke. "Thank you for the flowers, Dillon," she said. "I'm afraid that I humiliated myself at the nightclub. Far from my finest hour. I haven't felt like talking about it, which I'm sure you can appreciate."

"There's nothing to be embarrassed about," Dillon said.

"I only wish that were so. I said some things that I shouldn't have."

"Haven't we all, one time or another?"

"That's easy for you to say."

"I believe in clean slates. There's no reason for us to be strangers. Perhaps we can grab a cup of coffee sometime."

"No. I don't think so." Her face was flushed. "You made it clear that night how you see me."

"I see you as a friend."

"I don't particularly want to be your friend." Her voice was soft.

"I'm sorry you feel that way."

"Don't be so damn condescending."

Dillon shook his head, puzzled. "I don't mean to offend you, Audrey. I hope you don't feel that I misled you in any way."

"No, you didn't mislead me. I think I have a very good understanding of who you are. From what I hear, you're getting exactly what you want with your actress."

"That was beneath you, Audrey," Dillon said.

"It's the truth," she said, moving toward the door, ready to leave the store. "You just don't like hearing it."

* * *

The weather had turned for the better, and the sky over the city was a cloudless blue. There were no traces of the winter's constant brown haze, a product of the soft coal burned to keep the flats and buildings of Berlin warm.

Dillon jumped at the chance when Reggie Jamison telephoned and asked if he wanted to play tennis on the clay courts at the Rot-Weiss Tennis Club. Reggie had been eager to reciprocate for Dillon's arranging their indoor matches in Dahlem.

When Dillon arrived at the club in Grunewald, named for its red-and-white awnings, he found Jamison in conversation with a tall, distinguished middle-aged man in immaculate tennis whites. Jamison waved Dillon over and introduced him to his companion, Gottfried von Cramm.

"Reggie tells me that you are new to Berlin," von Cramm said. "Part of the American Mission. And you are a poet?"

"I'm guilty of that," Dillon said. "The poetry."

"I must take a trip to Marga Scholler's and find your books."

"Just the one. To be truthful, *Cedar Creek* is hardly a bestseller."

"But it's quite interesting," Reggie said. "They have copies at Amerika Haus."

"I'll stop by there," von Cramm said. "The next time you're here to play, perhaps I can persuade you and Reggie to share a Berliner Weisse or two and discuss poetry."

Reggie watched the German as he left the courts and headed to the clubhouse. "Von Cramm's a wonderful tennis player. Won two French national championships in the '30s, and almost won Wimbledon several times. A very brave man. When he refused to join the Nazi party, Himmler persecuted him on morals charges, for an affair they said he had with a Ukrainian Jewish actor. Then, during the war, von Cramm ended up on the Eastern Front where he won an Iron Cross. He survived and now he's married to Barbara Hutton, the Woolworth heiress."

"He fought in the Wehrmacht?"

"He fought for Germany, not the Nazis. I don't blame him for that, considering that the alternative would be a concentration camp."

Once on the court, Dillon inhaled deeply, enjoying the scent of the pine trees that surrounded the club. The clay surface was slower than Dahlem's painted concrete courts, and that helped Reggie, who didn't hit the ball as hard as Dillon, to extend rallies. Dillon found that he was breathing heavily. The sweat poured down his face and soaked his shirt.

Dillon double-faulted to lose his service game, and then recovered to win the next two, remembering to hit the ball sharply at an angle to either side and force Reggie to move from the center of the court. Reggie's return shots lacked pace, and several times he floated short lobs to the net that Dillon pounced upon and smashed for winners.

He looked over and noticed that a man in a beige suit was sitting on a nearby bench watching them. The man gave Reggie a wave and he acknowledged him with a nod. When they finished their set, Reggie brought Dillon over to the bench. They took clean towels from a wicker basket placed courtside and Dillon wiped his face.

The man in the suit walked over, and Reggie introduced him as Feliks Hawes, a new member of the British colony in Berlin.

"You're both relative newcomers," Reggie said.

"I've been here a month or so," Hawes said. "Temporary duty."

Reggie turned to Dillon. "Enjoyed the match tremendously. The clay helps slow things down, although I still came up short." He draped a towel around his neck. "I'd love to stay, but I'm expected for dinner. I believe that Feliks has a few questions about the ah, political situation in Berlin I thought you might be able to answer."

After Reggie said his good-byes, Dillon turned to Hawes. "You're with the British Mission?"

"No, I'm unattached at present. Based in London, here on a temporary assignment."

"The Foreign Office?"

Hawes gave him a thin smile. "In a manner of speaking. My branch of the government answers to the Foreign Secretary."

"I see," Dillon said. That meant Hawes was part of the British security apparatus. Dillon wondered why he wanted to talk.

"This meeting is not by chance," the Englishman said. "I asked Reggie and he was kind enough to make the introduction. There's a matter or two I'd like to discuss."

"Here? Now?" Dillon looked around the club. "Why don't you drop by the office? Say, eleven o'clock tomorrow. The Mission is on Clayallee, in the Headquarters building."

"I'd prefer to keep this informal if you don't mind."

"Okay," he said. "What's on your mind?"

"Christa Schiller."

Dillon didn't say anything for a long moment. "What about her?"

"How well do you know her?"

Dillon gave him a hard stare, immediately wary. "What business is it of yours?"

"We have concerns that she may be working for East German intelligence, for the Stasi. As a diplomat, you're a natural target."

"Shouldn't my security people worry about that? Assuming there's anything to worry about, which I doubt."

Hawes spread his arms wide, a gesture of apology. "I'm just doing my job. Miss Schiller lives in the British sector. We like to keep an eye on things. If you don't mind me asking, how did you happen to meet her?"

Dillon did mind, but he decided to answer. After all, he had nothing to hide, nor did Christa. "She came to a talk I gave at Amerika Haus about poetry." He shrugged. "I'm a poet on the side."

"A poet and a diplomat. An interesting combination."

"They told me I could contribute to the German-American cultural interchange by talking about my poetry."

"Excuse me, but the details in these things can matter. Did Miss Schiller approach you, or did you approach her?"

"She asked the last question from the audience, and then came up afterward to continue the conversation. I asked her to dinner."

"As any red-blooded chap would have."

"We had a marvelous dinner, and then she invited me to see her in a performance of *The Tempest* at the Neues Theater. She plays Miranda. That's it. No cloak-and-dagger."

"Are you lovers, then?"

Dillon flushed with anger. "That's none of your damn business."

"It is, actually. I'm trying to determine how far along in the recruitment process they believe that they are."

"Recruitment process? Absurd. Christa's an actress. Nothing more. Do you have anything concrete to prove otherwise? Any evidence?"

"Not yet," Hawes said. "You could help us with that. We could have a further discussion, confirm some things for us. Perhaps you could ask her a few questions about her past, delicately of course, that we can check out."

"No, I won't do that." Dillon fought back his anger. "I'm not going to spy on her. Nor am I going to let you poke around in my private life. Have you said anything to my security people?"

"I have not. We'd like to keep this quiet."

"There's nothing to keep quiet about." Dillon frowned. "Did Reggie know your reasons for wanting to talk to me?"

"I told him you knew a German national we had some questions about. That's all. He knows better than to ask too many questions. I'd appreciate it if you didn't say anything to him."

"I won't. As far as I'm concerned, there's nothing to say."

"We've not got off to the best start," Hawes said. "I recognize that this comes as a bit of a shock. I ask only two things. First, that you say nothing to Miss Schiller about this conversation. Second, that if you change your mind, that you feel free to contact me." He handed Dillon a business card. "As you can imagine, we need to keep an eye on the situation. Should we learn more, I'll be in touch."

"Let's hope not," Dillon said. "Someone has been feeding you faulty information. You're wrong. Dead wrong."

* * *

Hawes found Viktor in the kitchen when he returned to his flat on Flotowstrasse. A pot was simmering on the stove and tomatoes, onions, green peppers, and a clove of garlic sat on the cutting board. An open jar of red paprika powder was close to the stove. The aroma of fresh vegetables cooking filled the room.

"I'm making Lecsó," Viktor said. "My mother's recipe. Have a taste." He held out a wooden spoon for Hawes.

Hawes tried the stew and nodded in approval.

"You saw the American?" Viktor asked. "How did it go?"

"He didn't like what I had to say. I don't blame him. Who wants the security chaps digging into your personal life?"

"How much did you tell him?"

"Enough to get him thinking. Nothing too specific. Just that we had concerns about the girl, the actress. That we suspect that she's being controlled by the Stasi."

"Will he play ball with us?"

Hawes laughed. "You sound like a Yank."

"Why shouldn't I? I lived in New York. Will he cooperate?"

"Not yet. He was offended by the idea—spying on his girlfriend. I think he'll come around. We need to prove to him that she's not acting on her own. That's where you can help. At some point, she'll meet with her handlers. Most likely in the Russian sector. She has an excuse for crossing back and forth between sectors."

"Why wouldn't they meet with her in the West?"

"If our source in the East is telling us the truth, the man running the operation is KGB, and he won't want to expose himself over here. There's something else you should know. This Russian may be Mikhail Durov."

"Durov. He's the bastard who ordered Morris' execution." Viktor glared at Hawes. "When were you planning to tell me this? That it might be Durov?"

"When it made sense. It does now. I just learned it might be him the other day. I never expected to find Durov here. I'd been concentrating on one of our officers in Berlin, a man named George Blake. I suspect he may be the one leaking. I've been working on a way to test his loyalty."

"What do you know about him?"

"I've been through his personnel file a few times. He's arrogant. A colorful past. Father an Egyptian Jew with the surname Behar, and an English passport. Blake changes his name by poll deed. During the war, he fights with the Dutch resistance. Then a stint in Naval Intelligence before joining SIS. Learns Russian and then posted to South Korea. Captured by the North Koreans when they invade in 1950. Three years as a POW, treated roughly, but eventually exchanged and returns to Britain as a bit of a hero."

Viktor shook his head. "The Reds had him for three years? Didn't anyone think he might have been turned? Brainwashed?"

"They don't think that way. Blake's a friendly sort. Married to one of the secretaries at the Service. They assumed that he was a good chap. 'For he's a jolly good fellow, so say all of us.' If the Russians or Chinese turned him when he was a prisoner, it wouldn't have been through brainwashing. They would have given him special treatment. Gentle persuasion."

Viktor snorted. "When the secret police threw me in prison in Budapest, they didn't use gentle persuasion. When the bastards questioned me, they softened me up by putting me in the *stoika* position which they were taught by the KGB. You stand on your toes, your legs spread and your hands over your head and you lean against the wall with your fingertips. Two hours. They beat you with a hose if you fall down. That was their gentle persuasion."

"No evidence that Blake was mistreated. In any event, at least I know what's required next, whether we target Blake or Durov. We'll need photos of whomever the girl meets with. There's some risk. If she goes back to the East, and you're spotted by the Vopos when you're following her, you're going to need a story."

"Maybe I'm helping out a jealous buddy," Viktor said. "Following the girl because my friend suspects she's cheating on him, and I'm trying to get the proof."

"I can obtain a miniature camera for you," Hawes said. "Easier to conceal."

"No, I'd rather have a Kodak or a Regula in my pocket. God forbid I have to tell a story, but a snapshot camera makes me look a tourist, an amateur. If I get caught taking photos of the girl, I can argue my buddy wanted proof that she was cheating on him."

"Don't take any chances if you follow her into East Berlin. Make sure you're not being watched if you use the camera."

"Sure, boss," Viktor said. "Don't worry about me. It won't be my first time on the wrong side of the tracks."

TWELVE

The girl had been visibly nervous, looking around, checking over her shoulder, as she walked up Frankfurter Allee. Viktor had been careful to stay a block behind and to keep the brim of his flat cap jammed down so she couldn't see his face. He was on edge, wary, uneasy at being in East Berlin. He felt vulnerable and exposed walking on a main boulevard in Lichtenberg, so close to Stasi headquarters, a street with few other pedestrians and not much traffic.

It was clear that she had been worried about being followed from the moment she left her flat in Wilmersdorf that morning. She had carefully scanned the immediate vicinity when she emerged from her building, and Viktor had kept his distance as she made the walk to the Hohenzollernplatz U-Bahn station.

She was quite attractive—chestnut hair, long legs, and a lovely face. He could see why the Stasi had chosen her and how the American could have fallen hard for her. As he trailed her up the street, Viktor watched as a few young men walking by tried, and failed, to catch her eye. She ignored them all. He imagined that she was well practiced in rebuffing male advances.

Viktor had mixed feelings about following the girl onto the Underground heading east. He might catch her meeting her handlers in the Soviet sector, but going there would put himself at risk. He could pass as a laborer in his rough workingman's clothes, and he was confident that if the Vopos stopped him his identity card would hold up under scrutiny, although his excuse for carrying a camera was flimsy. He doubted his cover would survive for very long if he attracted the attention of the Stasi.

He took a deep breath and decided to follow her onto the train—Hawes was counting on him, and he didn't want to miss the opportunity of documenting any contact she had with the East German authorities. She took the train first to Alexanderplatz, and then switched to the U5. Viktor followed from thirty paces behind, and when she got off at the Magdalenenstrasse station, he silently counted to twenty before he exited the subway car. He waited on the platform for a minute or so and then climbed the steps to the street, and spotted her heading toward Frankfurter Allee.

When she stopped in front of the Ministry of State Security complex, Viktor decided to take a photo as she entered the main building. He positioned himself next to a thick street lamp pole, figuring that it would block the view of anyone to his south. He slipped the Kodak out of his coat pocket, and keeping it at belt level, pointed it in the direction of the girl and rapidly snapped four shots.

He pocketed the camera, convinced that he had not been seen in the forty or fifty seconds it took to snap the photos. He exhaled and leaned against the lamp pole for a moment, and then was startled by a gruff voice calling out something in German from over his shoulder.

"You. What are you doing here?" It was a burly police officer in the gray-green uniform of the Volkspolizei, eyeing him suspiciously.

Viktor stepped away from the pole. He took a deep breath before he responded and managed a grin. "A bit tired, sir. Out too late last night, too much beer. You know how that is."

"Your papers."

Viktor reached into his coat pocket for the identity card and handed it to the man. "I've been helpful to Colonel Müller in the past," he said, deciding to brazen his way through. He had picked a common surname, certain that there had to be several Müllers employed by the Stasi. He stood up straight, hoping to appear confident. "Just finished meeting with him. Do you know the Colonel? They say he's close to Comrade Mielke." Viktor gestured toward the Ministry of Security compound and winked, hoping that his mention of Erich Mielke, the feared Stasi chief, would impress the policeman.

"You're not a German," the Vopo said, looking at the card.

"I came here six years ago," Viktor said. "Construction work. And a few other things. If you like, we can go across the street, and you can ask Colonel Müller about this. I'm sure he'll set you straight."

Viktor counted on the policeman's reluctance to get involved in Stasi matters. There was no way of knowing how Colonel Müller might react—why take the risk? Viktor studied the man's face, looking for signs of doubt or hesitation. He could feel himself tense up. Would his bluff be called?

The Vopo handed him his identity card. "Move on, then," he said. "No loitering."

Viktor nodded and reached into his pocket for a packet of cheap Club cigarettes. He offered one to the officer, who shook his head. Viktor put a cigarette between his lips and calmly lit up before he strolled off. He didn't look back, and he walked slowly, as if he didn't have a care in the world. He could feel his hands trembling, and he jammed them into his coat pockets.

When Viktor reached the Magdalenenstrasse station, he felt for the rectangular metal camera case in his right coat pocket, wondering if the snapshots of the girl would be any good. He certainly hoped so. Despite what he had told Hawes, he wasn't sure that he could summon the nerve to follow her into the East again.

* * *

The Russian didn't wait very long before asking her the question, the one Christa knew that he would ask, and the one only she could answer. They had sat down across from each other in the now-familiar barren Stasi interrogation room, glasses of tea in from of them.

"You have slept with him?"

"I have," she said, lowering her voice, knowing that she was blushing. She wondered what would happen if she told him she wanted to quit, that she no longer had the heart for continuing the deception. She wasn't going to do that, not with Konrad's freedom in the balance.

"Very good. Now keep him unsettled. Don't let him feel secure." He studied her. "Remember that you're playing a role. You have deceived him. You must continue to lie to him. You must not become confused about your relationship with him."

"I'm not confused," she told him, and wondered if it was true. She had found herself thinking about Dillon, about their time together. If things had been different, she could imagine him as her boyfriend, her lover. He was handsome and intelligent and he had a keen sense of humor. There were things she didn't like about him—his arrogance, his poorly disguised jealousy—but he was falling in love with her and he made her feel wanted and that counted for a lot.

The Russian consulted his small black notebook. "Continue to make use of your friend Jürgen. Keep him in the picture, so that the American has a reason to feel jealous."

Christa suppressed a smile. It had been her idea, after all, to have Jürgen pretend to be a rival for her affections.

"We're prepared to move to the next act of this little play of ours." Comrade Mikhail shifted in his chair. "It is time for you to share with the American the injustice of your brother's prosecution and his imprisonment. How hard it has been for you. He must see how Konrad's persecution—and you should call it that—pains you. Then, you must ask him for help."

"I think it is too soon for that," she said. "We should wait. The longer we're together, the more he'll trust me."

The Russian was displeased. He scowled at her. "No, you'll do as I say. Asking him now will bind him even closer to you."

He rose to his feet and walked over to the door, opening it and motioning to someone Christa couldn't see. A lanky, keen-eyed man entered the room, and pulled another chair to the table. He and Comrade Mikhail sat down facing her. She guessed that the man was in his mid-thirties. He had dark hair, a high forehead, and a youthful face.

"This is Comrade Lothar," Comrade Mikhail said. "A trusted colleague. He has been briefed. You may speak openly in front of him."

Christa nodded at the man and remained silent.

"It is also time to tell the American you've found someone in the East who can help your brother," Comrade Mikhail continued. "You will bring Randolph to meet Comrade Lothar, here in our sector."

"I don't know," she said. She felt her throat tightening. "I think it's too soon to ask. It will make him suspicious."

"You can persuade him." The Russian stared at her, challenging her to disagree with him.

Christ knew better than to contradict him.

"We'll be there to help," Lothar said. He had a pleasant voice, and she could tell that he was an educated man. "Does he love you?"

"He loves the Christa I have fashioned," she said.

"Then he should want to make that Christa happy. Ask him to cross into East Berlin and meet with me."

"And what do I tell him about who you are?"

"That I'm a man with connections. A fixer."

"What if he refuses?" she asked.

"He will not. He's a man in love, as you say."

Christa looked away from him, eager to end the interview. What would happen after she convinced Dillon to come to the East and meet with Lothar? How would they entangle him in whatever evil business awaited? She had known that this day would come—that she would be asked to betray him—but it had been abstract before, not real. She didn't want to know what they had planned. She didn't want to add to the guilt she already felt.

* * *

Christa was two blocks from the Stasi compound, on her way to the S-Bahn, when she heard her name being called aloud. She turned to see

Comrade Lothar striding toward her, a smile on his face. She stopped and waited for him, wondering why he had followed her.

"A brief word," Lothar said when he reached her.

She regarded him warily. "What is it, comrade?"

"I'm sympathetic to your situation," he said. "I know this has been abrupt. But it is all for a good cause."

"Is that so?"

"We wouldn't ask you to do these things if it were not so. If you help us, you help your brother."

"I've done everything Comrade Mikhail has asked me to." She met his eyes. "Do you doubt me? Does he doubt me?"

Lothar raised his hands slightly in a conciliatory gesture. "You're also a woman. You must have some feelings for the American. It can be confusing."

"As I told Comrade Mikhail, I'm not confused," she said. "I've slept with him because I had to. He has no call on my emotions or my loyalty."

"That's as it should be," Lothar said. "There should be no mistake about that."

"There isn't," she said softly. "Nor will there be."

"There's another reason for you to cooperate. I've read your father's dossier. You should know that he ordered his men to do many shameful things during the war, things that no honorable officer would ever countenance. Crimes against humanity. You can make amends for your father's war crimes by what you do now."

"I will be late for my performance," she said. Christa didn't trust herself to say anything more. Did Lothar think she felt any guilt over what her father might have done during the war? Franz von Schiller at least had tried to stop Hitler, and had paid for his resistance with his life. And was the regime that Lothar served any better than the Nazis? She saw little difference.

She turned to leave, and Lothar stepped back to let her go.

"We're counting on you," he said. "Don't disappoint us."

* * *

Dillon had been annoyed and dismayed when Feliks Hawes telephoned him at the U.S. Mission. He was convinced that Christa was who she appeared to be, and that their romance was no different than any other springtime love affair. Dillon couldn't think of anything she had said or done that would suggest she was controlled by the Stasi. He had hoped that he wouldn't hear from the Englishman again.

Hawes didn't waste any time on the phone. He explained that it was urgent that they speak again, on the matter they had touched upon at the tennis club. Dillon reluctantly agreed to meet him in the Schöneberg Rudolph-Wild-Park, next to the Schöneberg City Hall, that afternoon.

Dillon followed the directions Hawes had given him. He walked past the park fountain until he reached the statue of a golden deer perched on a stone pedestal. He kept on, leaving the park, and then waited five minutes before doubling back. Hawes was waiting for him on a park bench, his jacket slung over his shoulder.

"You're clean," Hawes said as a greeting.

"Excuse me?"

"You haven't been followed. Clean from the S-Bahn station to here."

"I wasn't aware that I was being watched."

"My lads are good," Hawes said. "You should never know they are there. But you wouldn't see the Stasi, either, if they had decided to follow you. We would."

"Is there a reason for all the cloak-and-dagger?" Dillon asked. "Or do you enjoy playing adolescent spy games? You should know that I could care less if it was Beria was following me. I'm a diplomat. Period."

"Beria's dead," Hawes said. "By all accounts, shot in the back of the head by General Pavel Batitsky. And there are good reasons that the two of us aren't seen together."

"You said you wanted to continue our conversation. Against my better judgment, I'm here."

"I brought something for you to see," Hawes said. "It involves Miss Schiller."

"What about her?"

Hawes held out a large manila envelope, and Dillon reluctantly accepted it.

"Photographs," Hawes said. "Quite recent. Taken in East Berlin. Two of her entering the Ministry of State Security." He paused. "I wish there was an innocent explanation for her presence there. It's not a place anyone visits without a damn good reason."

Dillon took the photos from the envelope, glanced at them, and handed them back to Hawes. "These don't prove anything. Some people aren't happy that she's performing in West Berlin. Who knows? Maybe the Stasi wanted to question her about it."

"That may be. But the more logical explanation is that Miss Schiller is reporting to them, that she is under their control."

"And you think that she was sent after me? To seduce me? I don't buy it. Christa has been the reluctant one in our relationship. Concerned that a boyfriend would get in the way of her career. I've been the one chasing her."

"Perhaps she was reluctant. Perhaps it started innocently. But today, it looks quite different. She's answering to the Stasi, or the Russians, or both." Hawes waved his hand dismissively. "She may have grown to care for you, but that doesn't mean that she can resist them."

"Are we having this conversation because you want me to break it off with her?"

"No, actually, I don't want you to end it. Not yet. We'd like some answers. Who's behind this operation? What's the goal? Why now?"

"You want me to stay silent? To not ask her about these photos? This whole thing is lousy."

"There's some risk in allowing this to play out," Hawes said. "For you, and for your career. For the girl, too. If she is being coerced by the Stasi, we may be able to offer her a way out."

"What about my security people? Shouldn't they be briefed on this?"

Hawes didn't respond for a long moment. "I'd rather not involve them. Too many cooks, you see. I've discussed your situation with the CIA, so American security has been alerted. Just not your security staff at the Mission."

"Isn't ending it with her the safe bet?"

"You don't strike me as a 'safe bet' sort. If you walk away, the Russians will blame Christa for their failure. I don't think you want that. They can make it very hard for her."

"If I decide to work with you, if you're correct about Christa, then when do I confront her?"

"You don't. We wait until it's clear what they want. She'll do the asking. A favor, just at the edge of legality. Typically something small. Using your influence at the consulate. Perhaps something in the black market. The idea is to take small steps until you're compromised, and then they'll have you."

"I need to think about this."

Hawes studied his face, wondering whether he should say more. He shook his head. "Call me when you decide. Or when she decides it for you."

* * *

A large black car with U.S. Forces license plates, a Buick, occupied the parking space directly in front of Hawes' apartment building on

Flotowstrasse. Two men in dark suits wearing sunglasses stood by the vehicle, making no attempt to disguise that they were waiting for someone. Hawes knew they were there for him.

When Hawes approached them, he recognized that the shorter of the two was Thomas Ryder, the CIA officer.

"Why don't you get into the car," Ryder said. "We can talk there."

Hawes thought about refusing but decided he might as well see what Ryder wanted. The longer they stayed on the street, the more questions his neighbors might have.

Hawes sat in the back seat, next to Ryder. "You could have phoned Berlin Station and asked for a meeting," he said. "I don't appreciate having my cover compromised. How did you find me here?"

Ryder ignored the question. "There seem to be a lot of people very curious about what you are up to. I've been asked by colleagues of yours in Berlin Station whether you're working with us. I guess that's because of your connection with us back in '56."

"What have you told them?"

"The truth. That you're not working with us. That I have no idea what it is that you're doing." Ryder paused. "You were going to keep me in the loop."

"There hasn't been anything to report. Nothing of significance, at least."

"I don't like being kept in the dark. What have you learned about the operation against Randolph?"

"It's still in the initial stages. There's no question that the girl is under their control. She just visited Stasi headquarters. I've confronted Randolph about her involvement. He senses that it's true, but he doesn't want to admit it yet. His pride's been wounded. In the end, I think he'll cooperate."

"We don't want to be embarrassed," Ryder said. "Not in our own ballpark. Not with one of our diplomats at the center of a Soviet op. Put yourself in my shoes. How would London feel about it if the roles were reversed?"

"Fair enough." Hawes met Ryder's eyes. "You'll be the first to know if anything of substance develops. You have my word on that. But we don't know where this is headed. Until we do, I'd like to keep it simple. Just you and me."

"My counterpart in the BND has inquired about you, as well. The Germans are curious."

"There's no need to involve them."

"I agree. Their man in charge of counterintelligence, Heinz Felfe, is particularly unappetizing. A Nazi and SS officer, recruited after the war by General Gehlen. We believe that he's part of the clique within the BND that has no love for us. Unfortunately, Gehlen trusts Felfe."

"Do you think Felfe's leaking to the Soviets?"

"We know the KGB has targeted those with a grudge against us for recruitment. Like men from Dresden. The firebombing in '45 didn't leave you or us with many friends in Saxony. Dresden is Felfe's hometown, by the way. I don't tell the BND anything I don't want the Reds to know."

Hawes didn't say anything in response. He wasn't about to tell Ryder about the exception he had made for Einhardt Schlegel. He trusted his German friend to keep his secrets.

Ryder opened the car door and stepped out, motioning Hawes to follow him. They stood together on the sidewalk. "We'll keep our distance for the moment," Ryder said. "But you'll keep me up-to-date on progress. No surprises. Nothing unilateral. Nothing heroic."

"No surprises. That's fair enough. One other thing. I'm not filing reports to London. Nothing about this situation in writing. I'd appreciate it if you'd do the same. No mention of Randolph or the girl."

Ryder frowned. "I won't send anything to Washington, but I need something in writing on the record. I'll keep it in my safe. You've been at this for a while. You understand. Just in case there's a rainy day. I don't plan on getting wet."

THIRTEEN

On Thursday, Dillon and Christa lunched in the Savoy Hotel's restaurant. He had chosen the Savoy because he figured Christa would like being seen in the dining room there. It was a favorite spot for actors, directors, and other theater people—the Berlin Opera made its home in the Theater des Westens, just across Fasanenstrasse.

Dillon arrived first and politely rejected the table the maître'd offered him—it was too close to the entrance to the restaurant. They settled on a table against the far wall where Dillon could see anyone entering the dining room.

Christa showed up slightly late and gave him a long kiss on the lips before she settled in the chair next to him. Anyone watching them would conclude that they were lovers, Dillon thought, and yet he felt she was holding back, not letting him get too close.

Dillon didn't believe that she was working for the Stasi. Like all security types, Hawes suffered from free-floating paranoia. He might have better manners than his American counterparts, but at his core he was overly suspicious, imagining plots where there weren't any. Men like Hawes found it hard to trust others, for whatever reason. They were naturally on guard. In contrast, the Foreign Service attracted compromisers, people who looked to smooth over conflict, to build trust.

They ordered drinks—Dillon, a Pilsener beer; Christa, a glass of Rhine wine—and he was pleased that she seemed relaxed and happy to be with him.

"How are things at work?" she asked.

"It goes well. Back home, President Eisenhower gave a speech on television about Berlin. It will be in the papers here tomorrow. He announced that the U.S. would not back down because of threats by the Soviets, that we wouldn't retreat an inch."

"You're pleased with this speech?"

"Every American diplomat in Berlin and Bonn is pleased. The Soviets know that Ike is tough as nails. A former general. He won't be bullied."

"You call him Ike?'"

"It's his nickname."

"Do you like Ike?" she asked, teasing him, and Dillon had to laugh.

"I like Ike, even if he's a Republican and I'm a Democrat. Keep that a secret, will you?"

"I'm good at keeping secrets."

He was about to respond when Dillon heard his name called. He turned to find Audrey Wingate standing by their table, her face flushed, a lock of her hair slightly askew. He had not seen her since their awkward encounter at the KaDeWe.

"I spotted you two and decided to stop by," Audrey said. "So this is the mysterious actress?" She glanced over at Christa. "The girl who asked the questions at your talk at Amerika Haus?"

She was slurring her words slightly, and Dillon could smell the alcohol on her breath. He rose to his feet and quickly introduced Christa, who stayed seated, a faint smile on her face.

Audrey turned to Christa. "I hope you have the full picture about Dillon." She giggled. "He's quite the lady killer. Has he told you why he was posted to Berlin? What exactly he did in Australia to get exiled here? He was quite the bad boy. I'll bet that he hasn't shared that. A somewhat sordid story, in fact."

"Pardon me," Christa said. "I don't mean to be rude, but how does this concern you?"

"Are you trying to make a scene?" Dillon asked Audrey. He moved to restrain her with a gentle hand on her elbow, but she angrily pulled her arm away.

"Don't touch me," she said. "I'm just setting the record straight. I'm warning her for her own good."

"My own good?" Christa arched her eyebrows. "I find that difficult to believe, Miss Wingate. Do you sincerely care about my well-being? How could that be? You don't know me, and I don't know you."

"You should listen to me. You might learn something about Dillon Randolph. Has he written love poems for you? Keep them in a safe place. You can read them after he's discarded you. That's how he operates."

Christa remained calm. "Have you been discarded, Miss Wingate? Or merely rejected?"

"This isn't the time or place to have this conversation," Dillon said.

Audrey kept her eyes on Christa. "Dillon's been slumming since he arrived in Berlin. Do you think you're the only tramp that he's had?"

"So you have been rejected, then," Christa said.

"Audrey, please, let's stop this," Dillon said. "I think you've had too much to drink."

"No, I haven't slept with him," Audrey said, ignoring Dillon. "You have the advantage there, Miss Schiller, but from what I gather you're quite liberal with your affections."

"That's enough, Audrey," Dillon said sharply. Two German businessmen in expensive gray suits at a nearby table were staring at them. Dillon hoped they hadn't overheard the argument, but it looked like they had.

"I've slept with Dillon," Christa said. "I'm not embarrassed or ashamed about that." She shrugged. "A man and a woman who are attracted to each other, a natural thing to go to bed. As to being discarded, I don't accept your premise. I make no exclusive claims on Dillon, nor do I accept any. When it ends, it ends. And I do know what happened in Australia. It's sad when a woman tries to live through another, through her children or her man. She must live for herself, first. Is that how you live, Miss Wingate? For yourself?"

Audrey glared at her. "I warned you. You don't want to listen. You've made your bed, and now you must lie in it."

"You seem quite worried about beds," Christa said. "Could it be that yours is empty?"

Audrey flushed red and cursed under her breath. She spun on her heel and left the dining room, stumbling as she crossed into the nearby lobby.

Dillon returned to his seat. Christa turned to him with a look of amusement. "How is it that you have made her so jealous?"

"I'm sorry," he said. "I had no idea she would go on like that. There's never been anything between us."

"Jealousy can make people do strange things."

"It can. Haven't you ever been jealous?"

"Not over a man. Over losing a role I wanted to another actress, yes. You don't have to worry about me ever acting like her. We've had a good time, in and out of bed. But I will not throw myself off the top of the Funkturm if it ends. We're not children playing at love."

Dillon raised his hands slightly. "As for me, while I'm not overly jealous, I'd prefer not to have another man in the picture. Not while we're together. I wouldn't date anyone else, either, despite what Audrey claimed. In fact, since I've been in Berlin you're the only woman I've seen romantically."

"And Australia? I didn't want to admit to her that I didn't know about it."

"A stupid mistake. One I regret. I became involved with a married woman. A brief affair. She wanted more than I could give her, and it ended badly."

Christa took a delicate puff of her cigarette. "I don't let things drag out. When we're finished, it's over. *Kaputt.* It's better that way. Clean. No dramatics."

"An actress who swears off dramatics," Dillon said. "You're quite something, Christa Schiller."

"And you're quite something, Dillon Randolph." She leaned closer to him and lowered her voice. "Please get us a room. The second floor, if you can. That's where Garbo used to stay."

"A room?"

"Yes," she said.

"What about lunch?"

"Forget about lunch. I want you to make love to me. Since I've been cast as the naive ingénue who falls prey to her wicked seducer, I might as well live up to the role."

* * *

He watched her as she slept, her naked body curled up under the sheets, her face in repose, her breathing easy and relaxed. She looked much younger with her tousled hair, and for a moment Dillon imagined her as the little girl she had once been. He wondered about her childhood. From what he had gathered, it had been a privileged one. Her parents must have doted on her, and she no doubt had felt secure and cherished. The war and its aftermath must have been a shock for a teenage girl unaccustomed to hardship and deprivation.

Did that explain what she was so elusive? Did she learn in the hard years after the war ended to keep her distance? To mask her emotions? They didn't share the closeness he would have expected after sleeping together. She would only go so far, let him see only so much, and then she would withdraw.

Dillon worried that he was getting in over his head. He thought about her too often. He knew better than to press his luck with her. He had to be careful not to reveal his feelings, to scare her off. At the same time, he knew himself. Was part of the intensity of his attraction to Christa that the object of his desire seemed just out of reach? That he hadn't truly won her? In turn, would a less mysterious, less elusive, Christa bore him? It was different with her, he told himself. He couldn't imagine becoming restless—she was too clever, too alluring, too desirable. And yet it had happened with other lovers in the past.

He touched her hair gently, tenderly, careful not to wake her. He would let her sleep for a while longer. It was quiet in the hotel during the mid-afternoon. There was a little more time before she would have to get up and leave for the Neues Theater to prepare for her performance that evening. Dillon would watch over her until then.

*　*　*

Just when he had concluded that Feliks Hawes was completely wrong about Christa, that the Englishman's suspicions were unfounded, Dillon's confidence in his understanding of the situation was shaken by a strange encounter.

A day after his lunch with Christa at the Savoy, Dillon received a telephone call from a man speaking accented English, who identified himself as Vladimir Zavatsky of Tass, the Soviet news agency. Dillon knew that many of the Tass correspondents reported to the KGB or the GRU, Russian military intelligence.

"I'm calling to arrange an interview," Zavatsky said. "To discuss your views on the current political situation."

"Try our press attaché," Dillon said. "I don't give interviews."

"We can have our chat totally off-the-record. Nothing for attribution."

"Abernathy handles the press. You should give him a call."

"They say you're not a traditional diplomat. I'm not a traditional journalist. I assure you that a conversation would be of great mutual benefit."

"You seem quite confident of that."

"I promise it will be worth your time," Zavatsky said. "I understand that you like the Paris Bar. Five o'clock?"

"Why should I accept your invitation?" Dillon asked.

"Out of curiosity. And because I will pay for the drinks."

Dillon laughed. He was curious—while he had met a few East German officials, he hadn't had any contact with Russians. "Okay. Five o'clock."

At the Paris Bar, one of the waiters guided Dillon to a table where a graying, middle-aged man wearing half-glasses was studying the menu. Vladimir Zavatsky removed the glasses and introduced himself, inviting Dillon to join him at the table.

"You'd think we were in Paris, not Berlin," Zavatsky said. "On the whole, a much more congenial place. Paris, that is."

"You're familiar with Paris?" Dillon asked.

"I am. And London. One advantage of being a journalist."

Dillon didn't say what he was thinking—that the odds of Zavatsky actually being a journalist were very slim.

Zavatsky put his menu down, ready to order. "I understand that you're not only a diplomat, but a poet, Mr. Randolph."

"I've written some poetry."

"I've read it," Zavatsky said. "*Cedar Creek.* Much more to my tastes than your Beat poets. We Russians love poetry, you know. It's a spiritual experience for us, now that we no longer have the church."

"As long as the poet is approved by the Party. What about Pasternak?"

"There's a saying in Moscow—I haven't read Pasternak, but I condemn him. I've been away from the capital for many years, away from literary circles. During the trials in the thirties, they say that Stalin was given an executioner's list which had Pasternak's name on it. Stalin crossed it off, saying that the cloud dweller should not be touched."

"But Khrushchev has not let the cloud dweller keep the Nobel, has he?"

"Pasternak declined the prize. His choice."

155

"Only because if Pasternak went to Sweden to accept the Nobel, he would not be allowed to return to Russia."

Zavatsky shrugged. "Awarding him the prize was a provocation, a propaganda stunt. That was clear to us, and it became clear to Pasternak."

Their waiter appeared before them and Zavatsky patted his stomach. "I'm very hungry," he said, and proceeded to order a glass of red wine and the Pot-au-feu. Dillon settled for a glass of beer.

After the waiter had left, Zavatsky cleared his throat. "We've gotten off on the wrong foot," he said. "That was not my intention. You're a diplomat. Can you see things from our perspective? Take the situation in Berlin and Germany today. Would you have us accept a rearmed and unified Germany? After the millions and millions of our countrymen the Germans killed, to say nothing of what they did to the Jews? In our shoes, would you trust them? How many of them secretly long for the Fourth Reich?"

Dillon shook his head. "Adenauer's a democrat."

"Adenauer has Nazis throughout his government. He's an old man. Who will follow him? Not all Americans are as trusting as you. Your former Treasury Secretary Morgenthau wanted to make Germany a country of small farms. Remove the manufacturing, the industry, so that they couldn't build weapons again."

"Morgenthau's plan was too draconian. Too punitive. Why repeat the mistakes of Versailles?"

The waiter returned with their order. Dillon watched with fascination as Zavatsky consumed his beef stew in rapid bites, cramming French bread into his mouth after every bite, and then washing it down with the wine. It didn't take him more than five minutes to finish his meal.

"Quite good," the Russian said, dabbing at his mouth with the napkin. "As to the political situation in Germany, I believe Wall Street concluded that it would be easier to sell Coca-Cola all over the world if Russia had to worry about the threat of the Wehrmacht marching again." Zavatsky considered his glass of wine and took a final sip. "There are men in both of our countries who seek peace, and those who seek confrontation. It has been that way since the dawn of time, has it not? The party of war, and the party of peace?"

"A simplification," Dillon said.

"But perhaps a useful simplification. These factions exert influence on both of our governments. Your president must heed the concerns of United Fruit, and of General Motors, and of the Pentagon and the CIA. Our leader must consider the reaction of the Politburo, of our military commanders, of those who guard the security of the state. Is it so different? Things are not always what they seem. Some who we see as our adversaries are, in fact, our friends."

"I'm not sure that I follow you."

"I wish you no harm, Mr. Randolph. Nor your country. I believe in peaceful coexistence. I hope that you would feel free to call me when you have questions."

"What sort of questions?"

"All types of questions. What am I, Zavatsky, hearing from the Ulbricht government? From our diplomats? Or other questions that you might have. As you widen your circle here in Berlin, you may find yourself wondering about who you can trust. Friends, colleagues, perhaps even lovers. Who is trustworthy?"

Dillon didn't know how to respond. The idea that he would turn to Vladimir Zavatsky over the question of who to trust was laughable. And yet the Russian seemed to be serious.

"I'll keep that in mind," he managed to say.

"As a poet, you know about love. Yes? How dangerous it can be. How dangerous women can be. The Sirens. Ulysses tied to the mast so he would not be seduced by their song."

"Berlin is quite a ways from the sea," Dillon said.

"But Berlin is a city filled with women, like the Sirens."

Zavatsky consulted his watch and rose to his feet. "I'll settle the bill on my way out. Perhaps we can chat another time? I can get to

Charlottenburg quickly by the S-Bahn, and I do enjoy visiting the Zoo. We must stay in touch, Mr. Randolph. For our mutual benefit."

* * *

After Zavatsky's abrupt departure, Dillon sat at the table and thought about their bizarre conversation. Was Zavatsky trying to send some sort of message? Was he warning Dillon about Christa? That was how Dillon interpreted his comments about the Sirens. But why would the Russian warn him in such a convoluted way? It didn't make sense. Dillon was puzzled, and there was only one person he could talk to about his strange encounter with Zavatsky.

The barman let Dillon use the telephone at the front of the restaurant, and Dillon dialed the number Hawes had given him. Hawes answered on the fourth ring. Dillon explained that he wanted to talk, privately.

"Can you meet at the Café Kranzler?" Hawes said. "Thirty minutes. Find a seat outside. I'll come to you."

Dillon finished his beer and then walked the few blocks down Kantstrasse and Johannistalerstrasse, through sidewalks crowded with theater-goers, shoppers, and tourists, until he reached the entrance of the famous café on the Ku'damm. He sat down at one of the outdoor terrace tables and ordered a coffee.

A thin man wearing a shabby brown suit and scuffed brown shoes came over to the table. He balanced a coffee cup on a saucer in his right hand, and a cigarette dangled loosely from his lips. He sat down across from Dillon. The man reminded Dillon of John Garfield, the actor, with his dark hair and intense brown eyes.

"You are Mr. Randolph," the man said, a statement rather than a question. His English was accented, with a touch of Eastern Europe. "I'm Viktor, a friend and colleague of Mr. Hawes."

"Where is Mr. Hawes?"

"Feliks will be along shortly."

"You work for him?"

"In a way." He grinned. "At present, I'm helping him as a favor." Viktor stirred his coffee with a small spoon and then took a sip. He blew a smoke ring and watched it float away before turning back to Dillon. "Are you a Yankees fan by any chance?"

"I don't pay much attention to baseball," Dillon said. "I guess that I'm not your typical American."

"When I lived in New York I went to a Yankees game once. Saw Joe DiMaggio play once. The Yankee Clipper." Viktor hesitated. "Do you know why they call him that? What is a clipper?"

"It was a ship. A very fast sailing ship."

"Thank you," Viktor said. "DiMaggio did run smoothly, like a ship at sea."

"When did you leave New York?"

"After the war. I ran into some trouble with the police—New York's Finest—and I didn't think it would be wise to stay. Then I did something stupid. I went back to Hungary. When the Reds took over, it was too late to get out. I couldn't leave until '56. That's when I first met Hawes."

"In England?"

"No, we met in Budapest, during the uprising. Mutual friends. Feliks is quite solid. Not like the typical British university toff. He has guts—that comes from his Polish father—and he'll do what he has to without second-guessing himself."

"That's quite an endorsement."

"Ah, here is Feliks, now," Viktor said. "Time for me to play sentry." He rose to his feet, and Hawes slipped into his vacated chair.

"You wished to talk," Hawes said.

"Some things have happened that have made me wonder."

"About your actress?"

"Indirectly, but yes."

"What's happened?"

"A Tass correspondent named Zavatsky approached me. I'd bet my paycheck that he's KGB. At first, I thought he simply was sounding me out, hoping to cultivate me. But then our conversation took a strange turn. He offered to help me determine who in my circle was trustworthy."

"Strange, indeed."

"He mentioned lovers. That could only be Christa. Why would he warn me about her?"

"A mystery," Hawes conceded. "Is that all?"

"I've been cursing you for a week for making me suspect her. And now I'm here, which means my subconscious is telling me something. So the question is, what should I do?"

"Work with us. With your assistance, we can get to the bottom of this."

"How? What is it that you want me to do? Specifically?"

"Continue to see Miss Schiller, as if nothing has changed," Hawes said. "That may not be easy. You can't let on that you suspect her. Can you do that?"

"I can do that," Dillon said. "As long as we can resolve this quickly."

"You must not tell anyone about this. Not your best friend. Not your family. Especially no one at the Mission. We can't risk word getting back to the Stasi."

"What happens now? What do you plan to do?"

"Now we place some gentle pressure on Miss Schiller," Hawes said. "We'll have some assistance from a German friend of mine. We can't ignore her, you see, or we'd make the other side suspicious, and that wouldn't do. Not at all."

"I want to know the truth about her."

Hawes nodded. "I believe that you shall. Quite soon. If I had to hazard a guess, they won't wait much longer before they have her begin to compromise you in some way."

* * *

There was a light knock at the door of the dressing room. Before Christa could respond, Stefan Schmidt poked his head in, a look of worry on his face.

"Someone here for you," he said. "A man from the government. The BND."

"He asked for me?" She felt a chill. Comrade Mikhail had warned her that she might face questioning by the West German authorities. She took a few deep breaths to calm herself.

"He asked for you specifically." Stefan grimaced. "He's waiting for you in the theater. It's empty for now. I thought it was best that you talked to him where you'll have some privacy there."

Christa found a young man in a trench coat sitting in the first row of the theater. He rose to his feet and opened his wallet to show Christa his credentials, an official-looking card with his photo affixed, but closed it before she could read his name.

He motioned for Christa to sit in one of the empty seats. He stood with his back against the stage front, facing her, and she knew that he wanted her to feel intimidated by the positioning.

"This won't take long," the man said. "Just a few questions."

"I'm not political," she said quickly. "I don't care about all that. I'm an actress."

"The newspapers say that you're an excellent one." He adjusted his necktie so that it fell straight down his shirt front. "This is a routine interview. Since you're from the Soviet sector, it's prudent for us to have a brief chat. You understand that, even if you're not political?"

She nodded. "Yes, of course."

He produced a small notebook and pen and asked for her full name and address. Christa gave him the details on her Wilmersdorf apartment.

"You're staying with Fräulein Wengler? A fellow actress?"

"With Liesl, yes. It's easier than crossing back and forth every day. It can be a long day, with rehearsals and performances."

"It's come to our attention that you're seeing an American. One of their diplomats. Your boyfriend?"

"We're friends. Dillon Randolph. We met at a poetry reading. Nothing political."

"You seem concerned about politics, Fräulein."

"Isn't that why you're here? Making sure that I'm not a Red spy?"

The man smiled. "Are you?"

"Of course not."

"What about your family? Your parents?"

"My mother and father are dead. You could say politics killed them. So I have good reasons for staying clear of all of that. I'm an actress, pure and simple."

The BND man closed his notepad. He pulled on the cuff of his right sleeve, then his left. "I'm sorry about your parents." He paused, and reached into his coat pocket and found a business card, handing it to her. She glanced at it, noting that there was no proper name on it, just the word *Bundesnachrichtendienst*, and a local phone number.

"Should you decide you like life in Charlottenburg better than the East, please call this number," he said. "Ask for Einhardt. We can help. We will help. You would make some people very angry if you decided to stay in the West, and you would need to be protected."

"I have no desire to leave. I won't be calling."

"The day may come. Keep the card."

He nodded to her and left the theater through the main aisle. She remained in her seat, wondering whether she had convinced the man that she was what Christa claimed to be—an apolitical actress.

Stefan came over, his face a study in anxiety, one eyelid twitching. "What did he want? Did he ask about me?"

"A routine interview. I told him I wasn't political, nor a Red, and he seemed satisfied with my answers."

"Nonetheless, very disturbing," Stefan said. "I don't want them snooping around. It will disturb the other actors and God forbid the general public hears about it."

She didn't say what she wanted to, that Stefan was worried only about himself and whatever secrets he hoped to protect. "I must go to the East," she said to him. "I'll return in time for the performance, but I must report this."

Stefan grimaced. "I don't want to know about that. Go if you must. As far as I'm concerned, you're visiting your family. An emergency."

Christa hurried to the S-Bahn. She waited until she reached the Friedrichstrasse Station to dial the phone number she had been given for emergencies, and she quickly arranged a meeting with Kruger. She made her way to the street and walked around the block twice, making sure that she wasn't being followed.

Kruger waited for her outside the worker's pub. Christa explained that she didn't want to smell of smoke when she returned to the Neues Theater, and asked that they talk outside.

"What's the problem?" he asked. She could tell that he was annoyed.

"A man from the BND came by to question me," she said. "I wanted you to know, so that you could inform Comrade Mikhail."

"You could have waited. This is no emergency."

"The interview made me anxious. I thought it should be reported immediately."

"We don't want you to feel anxious," he said. "Why don't we find a nicer place and have a drink or two and discuss it further?"

"I have a performance," she said. She began walking back toward the station. He fell into step with her. "I must return to the theater."

"Why don't we meet after? Come back, and we can have that drink. I know a very cozy place."

He tried to take her hand, but she jerked it away from him. "What would Comrade Mikhail think of this?" she asked. "When I see him, he's curious about everything that has happened. Everything. What if I were to tell him everything? About your invitation?"

"That would be unwise," Kruger said. Christa could hear the anger and resentment in his voice. "You're high and mighty now, but when this is over, and the Russian goes back to Moscow, you'll need friends. You'd do well to remember that."

FOURTEEN

April arrived with soft breezes and weak sunlight. Dillon noticed vibrant spring flowers—daffodils, crocuses, irises, and tulips—were blossoming in the parks, and the linden and plane trees lining the city's streets were turning green. Berliners abandoned their fur hats and heavy coats for lighter clothing, and proprietors of cafés, restaurants, and beer gardens set chairs and tables outdoors for customers eager to luxuriate in the warmer weather.

Christa had left a message that she would meet Dillon at the fairgrounds in Charlottenburg; they planned to have dinner in the restaurant at the top of the Funkturm, the steel radio tower that dominated the Berlin skyline to the west.

Dillon parked his Ford in the fairgrounds lot and walked over to the base of the Funkturm to wait for Christa. The battleship gray steel superstructure of the radio tower reminded him of the Eiffel Tower. The locals had dubbed it *Langer Lulatsch*, the Lanky Lad.

Christa arrived ten minutes late and Dillon wagged his finger at her in mock dismay—he enjoyed teasing her about her habitual tardiness. She smiled and waved at him in response. She wore a light teal-blue dress with a flower pattern and had pinned up her chestnut hair, and Dillon was struck again by her long-limbed beauty. It didn't seem possible that she could betray him. He still held out the hope that Hawes was mistaken, that despite her visit to the Stasi headquarters, Christa wasn't being used by the East German security apparatus.

She kissed him on the lips when she arrived at the entrance to the radio tower. They took the lift past the restaurant level all the way to the observation deck near the top of the Funkturm.

There was a surprisingly stiff breeze on the platform. Christa took Dillon's hand and they moved to the edge of the deck, where there were panoramic views of Berlin and the surrounding suburbs. She pointed out the broken-off spire of the Kaiser Wilhelm Memorial Church, still visible in the fading twilight, and the fourteen-stories of the new Hilton Hotel. They walked over to the northern side of the platform and located the Olympic Stadium, a large white saucer in the near distance, and Le Corbusier's Unité d'Habitation apartment building on the edge of Grunewald Forest, which Christa explained had been praised by architectural critics but hadn't been as well received by its tenants.

"A penny for your thoughts," he said.

"Only a penny?"

Dillon reached into his trouser pocket and retrieved a one mark coin. "Would one hundred pfennig be more to your liking?"

She took the coin from him and placed in lightly in her left palm and then slowly made a fist.

"So. My thoughts. I wonder what it would have been like to have been born in Charlottesville, Virginia. Like you. How different my life would have been."

"Perhaps we would have been sweethearts. You would have been my date for the senior prom."

"The prom?"

"It's a school dance. You would have been voted Prom Queen. And then we would have both gone off to college."

"Now it is your turn," she said. "What are your thoughts?"

"My thoughts? On a night like tonight, I wish I could say the hell with it. My job, I mean. What am I accomplishing here? All stupid talk and writing boring reports that no one in Bonn or Washington reads. My job is to create a paper blizzard."

"And what would you prefer to do?"

"I'd like to write, but I don't want to scrape by as a starving artist. I could teach. That's what poets do today, they become college professors."

"And would that make you happy? It seems such a quiet life."

"Happier, I think. There would be a cost. It'd start World War Three at home. My father would be furious with me, in his restrained way. He believes that the Randolphs are meant to serve the country, preferably. With my older brother gone, I'm the last best hope for that."

He told her more about Wash, about how his older brother had been a natural leader, how his contemporaries gravitated to him, and how Dillon had looked up to him.

"Was he a poet, like you?"

"Hardly. Wash could never sit still long enough to write. He used to tease me about being artistic and introspective and that if I wasn't careful I'd end up in a Paris café wearing a beret and chain-smoking Gauloises."

"Instead, you've ended up in Berlin as a diplomat."

"That I have. And you're my compensation for missing out on the mademoiselles of the Left Bank."

"French women are too moody," she said.

"Unlike the stoic Germans?"

She gave him a mock scowl. "I'm the exception that proves the rule. A dramatic Berliner."

The light was fading fast now as the sun set. They watched in silence as it dropped below the horizon. As darkness arrived, the street lamps came on in the city and they could see the lights illuminating some of the larger buildings clustered near the Zoo Station.

"You can see how different it is between East and West," she said. "Bright lights everywhere here, and dimmed ones over there. The lights were bright all across the city when I was young. For a time, until things went badly in the war and the blackouts started. No need to make it easy for the Lancasters. The British bombed at night, when they couldn't really see their targets." She shivered. "May we go to dinner, now?"

Dillon had the head waiter place them at a table next to a structural column, where they couldn't be overheard. He ordered a bottle of white wine and they drank and made small talk until their waiter brought the special dish for the day, pan-fried trout, potatoes, and white asparagus.

"I like it when you talk about your family," she said. "To really know someone, to know who they are, you need to know their family, their past."

"We haven't talked much about yours."

She nodded. "That's true. There's only my brother, Konrad."

"When do I get to meet him?"

Dillon was surprised to see her eyes fill with tears. He took her hand, hoping to comfort her. "What's wrong?"

"I'm sorry." She wiped her cheeks with her free hand. "You can't meet him. Konrad's in prison, in the East."

"A prisoner?"

She looked around, clearly concerned that they might be overheard. She lowered her voice, and Dillon had to lean forward to hear her.

"Konrad is serving a sentence for subversion against the state. He was overheard mocking Ulbricht and the government. I begged him to apologize, to be contrite, but he refused. He can be so stubborn."

"He's in prison because of a joke?"

"A not very good joke. He said the only problem with calling the country the GDR was that it wasn't German, or democratic, or a republic." She sighed. "In hindsight, I know we should have never stayed in the Soviet sector. It's my fault. I didn't want to give up my career at the Berliner Ensemble. Konrad would never leave without me. So we stayed. My ambition kept him trapped in a place where it was just a matter of time before he got in deep trouble."

"You're not responsible for that," Dillon said. "Don't be so hard on yourself."

"I knew better. I kept hoping that it could be smoothed over. When it wasn't, there were consequences. My so-called friends stopped talking to me, and then I was told that there wasn't room in the Berliner Ensemble for me. An irony. When my career no longer was a reason to stay, we couldn't leave."

She picked at the food on her plate. "My brother has always been a free spirit. He never liked authority or rules. I told him a hundred times that he had to take care, but he wouldn't listen." She frowned. "We lost my father during the war. Was it growing up without him? Perhaps. I don't know. Konrad poked at those above him—his teachers, his bosses. His friends were the outcasts, always the ones breaking the rules and getting into trouble. Then he was arrested and tried, if you can call that mockery of justice a trial."

"How long is his sentence?"

"Five years. After he went to prison, things were very hard for me, professionally. At the Volkstheater, I acted in horrid propaganda plays that only ignorant Party members could stomach. A million miles from Shakespeare. I'm so very fortunate to have been invited by the Neues Theater to perform in the West. It's a fresh start for me."

"I'm sorry about your brother," Dillon said. "It must be very hard."

"There's still hope. He's alive."

"I wish I could help."

"It's my problem, not yours. But thank you for offering."

After dinner, he drove her back to her apartment in Wilmersdorf. They spoke very little on drive, both lost in their own thoughts. Christa invited Dillon for tea, explaining that Liesl was out with friends and wouldn't return until very late.

Once they were in her flat, she put the tea kettle on the stove and motioned for Dillon to sit at the kitchen table.

"I want you to make love to me," she said. "But first, there is something I want to ask."

"A gentleman could hardly refuse that offer."

"I've been thinking," she said. "About Konrad. I don't want you to feel that you must do anything. There may be a way for you to help."

"I'd like to help, if I can," he said, keeping his voice neutral. He tensed, realizing that she was about to ask him for something.

"There are businessmen who purchase expensive items in the West—Swiss watches, jewelry, nylons—and bring them into the Russian sector. They sell them on the black market there for a profit. There is the risk, of course, of getting caught by the Vopos." She looked down. "There is a man involved in this trade who is known for making arrangements. He says that it could be possible to arrange for Konrad's release. In exchange, there is something he wants. I would need your help."

"My help? How?"

"Your automobile. It has U.S. Forces plates. The Vopos don't stop and search a diplomat's car." She saw the look on his face and spoke more rapidly. "It would only be once or twice. Lothar says two trips would be enough."

"Lothar?"

"The man who arranges things. He is a *Schieber*, a black market guy. He says that he can get Konrad out."

He wasn't sure what to say. He was dismayed because Hawes had been right—she was asking him to do something illicit, something compromising. He tried to read her face, to figure out if she was telling him the truth about her brother. She seemed genuinely distressed, her eyes glistening with emotion. Then again, Christa was an actress, as Hawes had reminded him, capable of playing many parts.

"You know what would happen if I was caught smuggling?" he asked.

"You would be in trouble." She looked away for a moment, her voice breaking slightly.

"I'd be fired, sent back to the States in disgrace. It'd be a catastrophe. I'd be lucky to avoid criminal charges."

"It is too much to ask," she said.

"I haven't said 'no' yet."

"I don't deserve you," she said. "That you would even consider doing this. The risk to your career."

"By now, you must know how I feel about you."

"Does that mean you will help?"

He kissed her hard on the lips in answer, pulling her to him with a sudden, almost desperate urgency, suddenly frantically needing to possess her. She responded by leading him into her bedroom.

They undressed hurriedly. She lay on the bed, naked, and he turned her over onto her stomach, and entered her from behind, putting his hands on her shoulders and pressing her down into the mattress. He surprised himself by his own aggression, his desire to dominate, to treat her roughly. Was it because of her betrayal of their love? Or his? For they were both guilty of deception now—both keeping secrets, both holding back, both lying.

He grew excited as he thrust into her, and the bed creaked from his body pounding into her. Then he climaxed with a long gasp of pleasure. He rolled away from her and lay on his back.

She looked over at him, puzzled. "Why so different tonight?" she asked quietly.

"So you won't forget me," he said. "To show you a side of me you don't know."

She didn't respond, but left the bed and went to her closet and found a faded blue kimono that she donned. She came back to sit next to him on the bed.

"You've never talked about your mother," she said. "Why is that?"

"I hardly knew her," he said. "I was very young when she died. What's there to say? My father didn't remarry and so it was the two of us."

"That must have been very hard. A small boy with no mother. You have no memories of her?"

"Not enough," he said.

"I'm sorry for you. What is there beside family? It is the one good thing to hold onto, no matter what happens."

He took a deep breath. "That is why I will help you. With your brother. Two trips."

"You're sure? Truly?"

"I'm sure. I'll need some insurance, though. I'll leave a letter in my desk drawer before each trip explaining what we're doing. If it goes bad, it will be clear that we were trying to free a political prisoner, not looking to get rich. Not that it will matter much if we're caught."

"We won't get caught."

"I wish I could be so confident," he said. "It will be very bad for us both if you're wrong."

"I'll contact Lothar tomorrow," she said. "He'll want to meet you. Lothar's a very cautious man." She kissed him on his lips. "I'm so happy. To save Konrad from them. I had given up hope, and now you have given it back to me."

* * *

In the morning, Dillon telephoned Hawes and asked for a meeting as soon as possible. He didn't give the Englishman any explanation for his request, and Hawes didn't ask for one. Hawes suggested that they rendezvous at the Kurbel Kino, a cinema located on Giesebrechtstrasse, a side street between the Ku'damm and Kantstrasse.

Dillon purchased a ticket from the bored cashier at the entrance to the Kurbel and, as Hawes had instructed, took a seat in the last row of the near-empty cinema. He watched fifteen minutes of newsreels—a giant Khrushchev looming above on the screen, followed by a giant Adenauer—before Hawes slipped into the seat next to him.

Hawes suggested that they move to the lobby, where they took seats in a corner. The Kurbel's usher, a skinny teenager, dozed by the front entrance. Dillon surveyed the movie posters that decorated the walls—he recognized only one of the actors depicted, Hildegard Knef.

Hawes waited for Dillon to broach the subject they both knew they were there to discuss.

"You were right," Dillon said glumly. "She did what you said she would do. Her brother's in prison, or so she says. Charges of subversion. After hearing the story, I agreed to help her to get him out."

"What sort of help?"

"Smuggling. She claims that if we do this, there's a fixer who can arrange for Konrad to be freed. I'm to make two trips in my car."

"A diplomat plunging into the black market. That will certainly put you under their control. All to free her brother. If he is actually imprisoned."

"I don't know whether to believe that part of the story."

"She's an actress. She knows how to manufacture emotion. That's her stock in trade, you see. Convincing the audience to suspend disbelief. And you're hardly an objective observer by now, are you?"

"It would explain why she hasn't defected to the West. She won't leave her brother behind."

"Or she's a true believer helping to build a socialist worker's paradise and quite willing to lie to do so. Or she's bought-and-paid for. We don't know her motivation."

"I think it's time to alert my security people," Dillon said. "Christa may work in the British sector, but I'm an American diplomat."

"I'd rather that you not alert them. I'll inform the CIA. They've agreed to let me handle this, to allow it to develop further. So you're covered—you needn't worry about the State Department security chaps."

"It's no worry for me. It seems that it's a worry for you." Dillon could see that Hawes was sizing him up. It was clear that the Englishman didn't want other intelligence officers involved.

"I'd prefer to keep this simple. There is the danger of too many cooks.

Any clumsy moves and there's the distinct possibility of scaring the Russians off."

"You might see that as a negative, but I see it as a positive. I don't want to be in the middle of this. I'm ready to walk away, to break it off with her." Even as he said it, Dillon knew it wasn't true. Christa had a hold on him. He didn't want to end it with her, even if that was the safe thing to do.

"All true. But end it now, and they'll bring Miss Schiller back to their sector. She'll face interrogation. It will not go well for her. They'll blame her. I don't think you want that to happen to her."

"What are you proposing?"

"Stay the course. Meet with this fixer. When they ask, break the rules. Give them something to blackmail you with. Then, we'll learn what they're really after."

"What about Christa?"

"The time may come when we need her help. For now, you should play the part of her lover. Nothing has changed. The romance continues."

"Nothing has changed? You can't be serious."

"I take your point," Hawes said. "I meant that Miss Schiller must believe that nothing has changed. We need to learn more. Her handler is a Russian, a senior officer in the KGB named Durov. Mikhail Durov. We don't know why he has come to Berlin, and why you're a target. If you play along, at some point we may get the answers to our questions."

"May?"

"In my line of work, it's rare when we see things clearly. Do you know the passage in Corinthians about seeing through a glass, darkly? We may never be sure. Not completely." Hawes glanced around the lobby. The usher was now fast asleep. He turned back to Dillon. "When this is over, you'll get a letter of commendation from Her Majesty's government. That should do you quite nicely in Washington. Wonders for your career. And that won't hurt, will it?"

* * *

Hawes had a busy afternoon, holding separate impromptu meetings with Viktor and Einhardt Schlegel.

He began with Viktor, sharing what he had learned from Dillon Randolph.

"There's something going on that I don't understand," Hawes said. "Why on earth would Zavatsky approach Randolph and warn him?"

"I agree that it's strange," Viktor said. "Could it be some sort of test? Do they want to make sure he's so in love with her that he'll ignore a warning?"

Hawes shook his head. "And risk compromising the entire operation? No, I think Zavatsky wants Durov to fail. Some sort of internal rivalry. Zavatsky told Randolph he believes in peaceful coexistence. We know Mikhail Durov doesn't." Hawes ran his hand through his hair, thinking. "I believe that we have a choice. We can focus on George Blake or on Mikhail Durov. One or the other. We can test Blake, tell him we've turned the girl, and see if the word gets back to the Russians. If it does, they'll shut down the operation, and we'll at least know for certain that Blake is the traitor. But we'll lose Durov and any chance of figuring out what they're up to."

"Wouldn't you be the hero?" Viktor asked. "Unmasking Blake? They'll pin medals on you back in London."

"What if we could get Durov? Trap him? Expose the operation, its goals. I regard that as a greater victory."

"So how do you accomplish that? What's your plan?"

"We must turn the girl. She can tell us what they're planning to do. Then, we focus on Durov. We try to recruit him, bring him to the West. If he defects, he'll give us Blake and any other KGB penetration agents."

"Recruit Durov? Are you mad?" Viktor shook his head. "He'll never break faith with them. I'd bet my last pound on that. Or my last dollar. If he survived the purges, if he survived Stalin, I can't see him abandoning his comrades now."

"I have some ideas on how we might persuade him. I need to work more on that. But even if Durov won't bite, we can create the illusion that he's considering defection. Poison his reputation with Moscow Center."

"I don't think it will work," Viktor said flatly. "I have to ask you something. No offense?"

"None taken."

"Why don't we just kill the bastard? Flush him out into the open. We have the advantage of surprise. He wouldn't expect it. Payback for Morris, and who knows how many others."

"What are we left with, then? One dead Bolshevik. We don't learn the identity of the penetration agents in Berlin. We learn nothing about the reasons for the operation against Randolph."

"He'll never tell us anything," Viktor said. "He'll go to his grave first. I know his type well. So do you."

"I do," Hawes said. "But there's more than one way to skin a cat, and even an uncooperative and silent Durov could prove of great value."

"A shame," Viktor said. "I'd vote for silencing him permanently."

"Ah, but there isn't any voting. This isn't a democracy." Hawes slapped Viktor on the back. "Remember that we work for a monarch. We take the Queen's shilling, after all."

"You take the Queen's shilling," Viktor said. "I work for Feliks Hawes. I'm following your lead, so we'll do it your way."

Later in the day, over coffee with Einhardt in a shabby, poorly-lit café near Ernst-Reuter-Platz, Hawes faced skepticism from the BND agent when he gave him the outlines of his crude plan.

Einhardt shook his head. "I don't like this shift in approach. I'd rather we focus on Blake. I don't think that you can get to Durov. He won't talk. He won't defect. Nor will his masters in Moscow believe that he ever entertained the notion. They'll see through it. Chess is their national sport, you know. Not cricket."

"And cricket players aren't particularly devious. I'm counting on that, Einhardt. We can assume that the Russians have been told that I'm here investigating the leaks from Berlin Station. Now it emerges that I've been sent to Berlin for a different purpose, to arrange the defection of Mikhail Durov. And there's an extensive dossier to back up that story."

"Will they believe that in Moscow?"

"Some will embrace it. Randolph was approached by Vladimir Zavatsky, a KGB officer working as a Tass correspondent, and warned about Christa Schiller. It appears that Zavatsky hopes to derail Durov's operation. I think he represents a moderate faction in Moscow that opposes the hardliners, the holdover Stalinists."

"Conjecture."

"Yes, conjecture. But if this faction exists, then they'll use what we've created to discredit Durov. It's leverage for them. Moscow Center is filled with suspicious men. This story should tie them up in knots. Has Durov betrayed them? Has he considered going over to British intelligence? Or is it a clumsy plot on our part?"

Einhardt gave him a rueful smile. "You know that deception operations are the hardest to pull off. There must be evidence. Concrete evidence. You must convince them that the *Spielmaterial*, the documents, the paperwork, is authentic. All of it."

"I'm the one handling his defection," Hawes said. "Many of the documents I can create myself. Reports to London. A fairly extensive dossier on my scheme to bring Durov over. A Swiss bank account in his name. There are a few things that you might help me with. I have a list."

"I'll look at your list. What I can do, I'll do. I can't promise anything, but I'll do my best."

"That's the spirit." Hawes grinned. "I can't ask for anything more."

"This course of action comes with a cost," Einhardt said. "In pursuing Durov, you may never expose the traitor at Berlin Station. In the end, you could be left with nothing of substance. Are you sure it's worth it?"

"Colonel Durov isn't in Berlin to recruit a junior American diplomat who can't keep his pants buttoned up. He's too senior for that. There has to be something more involved. Zavatsky's intervention has convinced me of that. Durov must be here for a broader purpose, and we should do whatever we can to frustrate it."

Hawes was pleased to see Einhardt nodding in agreement. The BND officer would be more willing to bend the rules, more willing to risk damaging his career, when a senior Soviet intelligence officer was the target. Einhardt hated the Reds, and when presented with the chance to hit them hard, he would take it. Hawes was no different, and he made no apologies for that.

PART THREE

FIFTEEN

Christa could tell from the look of distress on Stefan's face that something had gone wrong. When she had arrived at the Neues Theater that morning, he had silently beckoned her over and then motioned her to follow him. He unlocked the box office door and invited her to join him in the cramped space.

"We need some privacy," he said. He reached into his jacket pocket and retrieved an envelope, which he handed to her. "I hate passing you their messages. You're to read it immediately."

Christa tore open the envelope, retrieved the folded-over note inside, and quickly read it: *Bring your friend to the Café Trichter tomorrow. 10.00 h. Lothar.*

She stared at the note for a long moment, and then tore it into little pieces and dropped them into a nearby wastebasket.

"Are you all right?" Stefan asked, his handsome features wrinkled with concern. "You look quite pale."

Her mouth had gone dry, and she swallowed before she responded. "I'm fine," she said. "It's about something I have to do. Something I don't want to do."

She felt numb. If she brought Dillon with her to East Berlin, it would mean crossing a line. It would entangle him. She couldn't evade the significance of her betrayal: she would be trading Dillon's future for Konrad's. Once he was involved, once he did their bidding on her behalf, he would be compromised. It would be worth it, she told herself, if it saved Konrad. She could deal with the shame and the guilt she felt later.

She realized that Stefan was staring at her. "I will need to visit the East tomorrow," she said. "I hope to be back before the performance, but if I'm delayed...."

"Renate knows Miranda's lines," he said. "That's why we have understudies. I'll feel sorry for the audience if you aren't back in time, though. Renate will make a hash of it, play Miranda heroically, like one of Wagner's Valkyries. She doesn't seem to understand that *The Tempest* was written as a comedy."

"It can't be helped," she said. "Thank you for understanding."

Stefan coughed and shifted his weight, clearly uncomfortable. "We have not talked about the situation you find yourself in."

"We have not."

"Please, let me say this. I'll help you, if you want. You've made many friends in our little ensemble, and I count myself as one. If you need to leave Berlin, I can talk to a colleague, a fellow director, in Hamburg. With my recommendation, I know he'll find a place for you in his company. You're very talented, Christa, and you're a pleasure to work with. You have a remarkable presence when you're on stage. They'll love you there. 'One of Brecht's favorite actresses, now in the West.' I will make the call—just say the word."

"They have my brother," she said simply.

"Ah, I see. Their hold over me is different. I've been indiscreet in my personal life. They threatened to expose me, to ruin me."

"Why do you stay, Stefan? Why don't you go to Hamburg yourself?"

"Hamburg?" He snorted. "I'm a Berliner. If I could survive the war here, I can manage this. I'm no hero, you see, and that's my secret to surviving. I'll be their errand boy. I'll do just enough to keep them happy."

Christa had heard the rumors that Stefan had been protected throughout the war years by a mysterious lover, an older man, who was an influential official at the Reich Ministry of Public Enlightenment and Propaganda. This man had kept Stefan off the Gestapo's "pink list" of suspected homosexuals, and had made sure he wasn't sent to the Eastern Front. Stefan was indeed a survivor.

"I'm touched by your offer," she said.

He waved his hand in a gesture of dismissal. "I'm far from brave. They would never suspect I had anything to do with your leaving. Every month, thousands escape to the West." He took a deep sigh. "Forgive me, but what about your American? I've seen how he looks at you. I hope that it has nothing to do with them. It's authentic, a true affair of the heart, yes?"

She managed a smile. "Are you a romantic, Stefan? An affair of the heart? Nothing so serious. An interlude for us both."

"An interlude. I understand." He looked over at her. "If that is what it is."

She ignored his implication. "As for the Stasi, you need not worry about me. I'll be fine. I've done what they've asked, and it's almost over. Once my brother is out, everything changes. Then we can talk about Hamburg."

"You must be very careful, Christa," he said. "They're ruthless when they want something."

"And I have something they want," she said. "I can give it to them. As long as that remains the case, I can manage things. Just as you do."

* * *

There came a time in every operation where one moved from the theoretical to the practical, from the planning stage to execution, and Hawes recognized that time had come. He was satisfied that they had addressed all that needed to be done. He believed that his plan was realistic and took account of the unexpected. They were ready to move against Mikhail Durov.

Hawes waited until after the lunch hour to stop by London Block and seek out George Blake. He found Blake and Giles Newton hunched over a detailed map of Berlin that they had unfolded on a large table in their office. Blake looked up and acknowledged him with a nod.

Hawes was disappointed—he had hoped to catch Blake alone, by himself.

"I thought I should brief you on some developments," Hawes began. "Nothing in writing at this point."

"Hush hush, then," Newton said. "Understood."

"Have you made any progress on your investigation of the leaks?" Blake asked.

"No luck yet. But I've stumbled across something of extraordinary importance. Unexpected, to say the least. It's sensitive enough that I can't be too specific. In fact, I shouldn't be specific at all."

"Then why the visit?" Blake asked. "Telling us that you can't tell us is hardly sporting."

"I have a good reason." Hawes paused, glancing from one man to the other. "You and Newton handle the comrades. This unexpected development involves them, and I thought you deserved a heads-up. I'm hoping to bag a defector in the near future. My catch—let's call him Ivan—is very well-placed."

"Quite exciting," Newton said. "What does London say?"

"Only a select circle has been made privy. Keeping it close to the vest. Defections are chancy, at best, you know."

"You say Ivan is well-placed," Blake said. "A diplomat? Someone from the Embassy?"

"Even better," Hawes said. "Intelligence. He's quite senior, and he's no innocent. A true believer until Khrushchev gave his speech about Comrade Stalin's crimes. Ivan lived through the purges, understood the necessity to break eggs, but something about the speech rattled him. He began thinking, and that's always a dangerous thing. He's lost his faith, and he wants out." He looked directly at Blake. "Imagine what he can tell us. Operational details. Penetration agents. The crown jewels."

"That sounds quite promising," Blake said.

"More than promising," Newton said. "A breakthrough. A chance to smash their damn networks the way they've smashed ours."

"Are you sure you can't use an extra hand or two?" Blake asked. "You've not worked in Berlin before, have you? It's not like other places. Easier to find trouble, especially in the Russian sector, and harder to fix a cock-up. I wouldn't underestimate the Stasi. They may have more than their fair share of bully boys in leather coats, but they've some very clever lads as well. There's not much that goes on over there that they don't know about. I would hate to see you on the back foot. London would certainly be unhappy, even if you're the fair-haired man of the hour. Let us know what we can do. Avoid difficulties in the field."

Hawes shook his head. "Thanks. Don't need the help. Already have made the necessary arrangements. But you have my word that you'll both be involved once we have Ivan snug on our side of the border."

"The Americans," Blake began. He paused. "You're not dealing with them on this by any chance, are you? *Sotto voce?*"

"Why would you imagine that?"

"You worked with them in Hungary, didn't you?"

"A special project when I was in Five," Hawes said. "On loan, because I'd been in Budapest just after the war and picked up a Hungarian phrase or two."

"So you're collaborating with the Yanks on this defection?" Blake fixed his gaze on Hawes, who stared back at him, without flinching. "Are they the ones making the arrangements to bring the defector across?"

"You've read Orwell, haven't you, Blake? The best way to keep a secret is to keep it from yourself."

Blake cleared his throat. "We wouldn't appreciate learning that the Americans knew more about this operation than the home side. Might I take a look at the file on your defector? Never know what I might spot."

"Sorry, under wraps for now," Hawes said. "But once he comes across, all will be revealed."

"By the way, you know that congrats are in order, don't you?" Newton asked. He slapped Blake on the back. "George has been called back to London. A chance to hobnob with our Broadway betters, isn't that so, George?"

"He also serves who stands and waits," Blake said. "Yet I'm not eager to join the ranks of the pen pushers. I'll make a lousy desk warrior."

"What's on the docket for you?" Hawes asked. "Will you stay connected with Berlin Station?"

"Doesn't look like it," Blake said. "They've been vague about my next assignment."

"I'll stop by and look you up when I'm back in London. Maybe even with Ivan in tow. We can all have a cup of tea together and tell war stories about Berlin."

"I'd like that," Blake said. "Do look me up, Hawes."

Hawes nodded, all the while thinking about the significance of Blake's sudden transfer. He assumed that Dick White was behind it, acting on what Hawes had told him at the Garrick. Blake would no longer have access to sensitive information about Berlin operations. In London, he could be watched carefully for a time before being transferred to a peripheral job, one where he couldn't do any damage. White, an experienced bureaucrat, would prefer a discreet solution to the problems of the leaks in Berlin rather than a nasty scandal.

Blake's transfer also meant that White was willing to short circuit Hawes' investigation in Berlin—without consulting him. That was his prerogative as director-general, of course, and Hawes tried not to take it personally. White had made it clear that he didn't want an airing of the Service's dirty laundry. He had acted, quietly, to ensure that wouldn't happen. In one sense it didn't matter, because Hawes' target was now Mikhail Durov. And if Blake was indeed a Soviet penetration agent, he would undoubtedly warn them about a high-level defection in the offing before he left Berlin—which was just what Hawes wanted.

* * *

Hawes drove directly from the Olympic Stadium to the CIA building in Dahlem. Thomas Ryder met him at the front entrance and escorted him to his office.

"I'm glad to see you," Ryder said. "I was afraid you might have forgotten about us."

"No, I haven't forgotten. I'm here as promised to brief you on progress. Something's surfaced I didn't expect. There's a Russian running the operation, senior KGB. A man who knows where the proverbial bodies are buried. We think that we can turn him."

Ryder whistled. "Is that so? Does this songbird have a name?"

"Let's call him Ivan for now."

"What have you offered him in return?"

"The usual. Protection. A new life in the West."

"What can we do? Do you need men? Money?"

"I'm not here to take up a collection," Hawes said drily. "I just don't want you surprised. A little advance warning that you can pass on."

"Washington will have a great deal of interest. We'll want to kick the tires, so to speak, and make sure that he is the real deal."

"I understand. When the time comes, when we have him in hand, I'll want to involve you and your people. A trip to the States may be in order. I'll have that discussion with Allen Dulles."

"You'll have it? Not Dick White?"

"Dick won't object. Dulles knows who I am. He'll want to hear about Ivan from me, not second hand. I've kept this counter operation as airtight as possible. If it goes well, it will be a week before the Russians realize that they're short a comrade."

"How will you manage that?" Ryder asked.

"Ivan will board a train bound for Moscow. A vacation. Except he won't stay on the train."

"I see. You know, if this goes wrong, and the Reds figure out what you're up to, they're going to scream bloody murder. Even if you get Ivan out, they'll claim he was kidnapped. They'll protest, demand an interview. They may retaliate." Ryder raised his eyebrows. "There won't be any leaks from here. In all candor, it's been your outfit with the problem."

Hawes nodded. "True enough. No point in denying it. That's why I'm playing it so close to the vest."

"You know about Red Cap?"

"Your program to recruit defectors from the East bloc?"

"That's it. If you land this Russian, what do you think about making him part of Red Cap? A joint operation?"

"Which would be a feather in *your* cap, you could say." Hawes understood the deal that Ryder was proposing—he wanted the CIA to share in the credit for Mikhail Durov's defection and to have early access to whatever Durov would reveal. Because of Dillon Randolph's involvement, Ryder could make it difficult, if not impossible, for any plan Hawes designed to succeed.

"You should know that it's not set in stone that he will defect," Hawes said.

"We've stayed out of your way so far. You've had a clear field. We've cooperated. Turnabout is fair play."

If Durov did cross to the West, Hawes only wanted the names of the penetration agents in British intelligence. He was sure that George Blake would top the list. The Americans were welcome to squeeze more out of Durov after Hawes got what he wanted. At least Hawes didn't have to worry about the petty politics and professional jealousies that typically arose whenever there was an operation with the Americans. With nothing on paper in London, he could do as he saw fit.

"Fair enough," Hawes said. "If Ivan comes across, he becomes a joint asset. Officially."

* * *

Hawes was pleased with the start of Operation West Wind—the name he had settled on for the planned defection of Mikhail Durov. He would use it for the paperwork that would eventually find its way into the Broadway Registry and the files of the BND in Pullach.

Operation West Wind existed only in Hawes' mind and on paper. It could not become real until Durov was presented with a concrete choice, and that required a face-to-face conversation with the Russian.

When Hawes returned to his flat, he quickly briefed Viktor about his visits to London Block and the CIA's Berlin Operating Base.

"Blake has been recalled to London, but before he leaves, I'm confident that he will pass along what I told him today. The news of an upcoming defection should stir things up at Moscow Center. They have hundreds of officers in Berlin. They won't know whom to suspect."

"When will you leak Durov's name?" Viktor asked

"Not until after we've made our play for him. In the meantime, we've raised the level of concern in Moscow." He handed Viktor an itemized list of things they would need for the operation. "Let's turn to practical matters."

Viktor quickly scanned the paper. "Some of this will cost you," he said. "Finding the Makarovs on the black market should be easy. Lots of drunk Russians lose their pistols or sell them. The syringe and drugs will be harder. More expensive."

"You can have more money. We're not going to be penny wise and pound foolish on this. Can you scare up what we need?"

Viktor considered the question. "I'll find the equipment. Don't worry about that. Worry about the American. He's the key to this. What do you think of him? Does he have the balls to pull this off?"

"He wouldn't have been my first choice," Hawes said. "He's a romantic. A poet. A bit of a womanizer. Issues with his mother, perhaps? All of which explains why the Soviets would target him."

"You're ducking my question. Can he do what needs to be done?"

"We shall see. The Reds are counting on him thinking with his cock, or with his bourgeois heart. They clearly believe the girl can control him. They've misjudged him, in my opinion."

"Have they?"

"He's not one for lasting attachments. When it comes to the girls, I believe that Mr. Dillon Randolph is a bit of a cad."

"And the girl?"

"No mystery there," Hawes said. "Ten years ago in Berlin you could have your pick of most any attractive woman for a bar of chocolate or a few packs of cigarettes. If she's telling the truth about her brother, it's no different for Miss Schiller. She's trading her virtue for his freedom."

"She's living in the British sector, now. She can defect at the drop of a hat."

"She won't sacrifice her brother. He's all that's left of her family."

"People do strange things," Viktor said. "Maybe she falls in love with hot water and clean sheets and good food. Maybe she falls in love with the American. With a man and a woman what starts as a game can end as something much more."

"It's a risk, of course. Durov knows that as well. He has someone in the troupe watching. Perhaps more than one. The girl will know the consequences of deviating from the script."

"Can you say the same for Randolph?"

"I'm watching," Hawes said. "Any signs that we're losing him, and I'll have a word with the State Department security people. He'll be on a plane back to the States sooner than you can say Jack Robinson."

SIXTEEN

Dillon remembered from his high school Latin class the story of Julius Caesar crossing the Rubicon with his Thirteenth Twin Legion, and how once across that shallow river—a move considered an act of treason by the Senate in Rome—there was no turning back. He felt that way about crossing into the so-called *Demokratischer Sektor* with Christa—once he did, they would have passed the point of no return in their relationship.

He didn't believe that he would be in any danger during his visit to East Berlin. Hawes had assured Dillon that he wouldn't be pressured by Christa's handlers until after he had compromised himself. For now, they would assess him, test his loyalties, determine how far and how fast they could push him—using his feelings for Christa as leverage.

There was no one in Berlin he could talk to about the situation he had found himself in, no one he could trust. Dillon decided to call his uncle in Virginia, even though he knew that he would have to be very careful in what he said over the phone. He called Leigh's law office on a Tuesday evening just after dinner—it would be early afternoon in Charlottesville. When his uncle answered the call, Dillon could hear the concern in his voice.

"I'm fine," Dillon told him. "I called for some advice."

"What sort of advice?"

"Remember when we read Walter Scott together? The lines that you had me learn by heart: 'So daring in love, and so dauntless in war, Have ye e'er heard of gallant like young Lochinvar?' Do you remember?"

"Of course I do. Daring in love, are we? Are you thinking of proposing to a young lady, Dillon?"

"Hardly. No, it's more the 'dauntless in war' part. There are times when it's not easy, here. Tough choices. Even for a junior political attaché. And I'm no Lochinvar."

Leigh laughed. "How could you be? 'There never was knight like the young Lochinvar.' But I'm sure you'll rise to the occasion, whatever it may be."

"You're more confident than I am. I'm not like Wash. I never wanted to ski the black diamond slopes."

"I know you, Dillon. You're more dauntless than you realize."

"Thanks, Uncle Leigh. Next time that I'm home, maybe we can talk about it."

"I'd like that."

"Please don't say anything to my father about this."

"As you wish, Dillon."

* * *

The sky was overcast when Dillon drove from Dahlem to Wilmersdorf the morning of their trip to East Berlin. When he collected Christa from in front of her flat, she asked him to wait before driving anywhere—they needed to talk first.

"If you're having second thoughts, I would understand," she said. "I'm asking a great deal. Are you sure that this is something you want to do?"

"I told you that I would help."

"I worry that you will hate me if anything goes wrong."

"I'll never hate you. And we haven't heard yet what's involved, what this guy Lothar wants us to do, so we can always walk away. There's nothing to go wrong yet." Dillon wondered—was her concern sincere, or was she making a calculated, but empty, gesture, sure that he would insist on going ahead?

She kissed him softly on the lips, and then sat back in the passenger seat. "Shall we go, then?"

He glanced over at her profile, marveling at her calm demeanor. There wasn't the slightest hint of anything amiss, and yet he knew that she was lying to him. He had come to accept Hawes' truth—Christa Schiller was working for the Stasi. She was about to deliver Dillon into the hands of his adversaries. Was it because of her brother? Or something else? Did she have any choice in the matter?

If the roles were somehow reversed, could he so calmly deceive her? In one sense, Dillon already had answered that question. He had remained silent, had not confronted her and given her the chance to explain. He was also lying, even if he could rationalize it as an act of self-preservation.

They drove through the checkpoint at Potsdamer Platz without a problem—the Vopos waved them through when they saw his blue license plates. Dillon found himself tensing at the sight of their uniforms, and he told himself to relax. He checked his rearview mirror, wondering about surveillance.

Christa must have sensed his anxiety because she gently touched his hand as it rested on the top of the gearshift. She had him turn onto Friedrichstrasse.

"I know this neighborhood well," she said as Dillon spied the bridge over the Spree ahead of them. "When I was first accepted into the Berliner Ensemble, it was a dream come true. I could not wait to arrive at the theater in the morning, to learn from Brecht. A great man, a decent man. I like to think that if he lived, things would have been different. He would have protected me. I believe that he would have been courageous on my behalf."

Christa had Dillon take a left onto Schiffbauerdamm, and then park the car around the corner from the Café Trichter. Inside, the dark-paneled room had large windows overlooking the Spree. The barman nodded to Christa and gave Dillon a long once-over. They ordered beers and took their mugs to a table near the front where they sat side-by-side.

"They know me here," she said. "This was Brecht's favorite place. He used to smoke his fat cigars in here and fill the place with smoke. Many of the younger actors would come to the Trichter after rehearsal and drink at the bar."

"I don't look much like a local. Will that be a problem?"

"They're used to foreigners coming to the theater, to work with Brecht."

Before Dillon could respond, a tall, dark-haired man dressed in a blue blazer, appeared in front of them. He had a prominent, straight nose, a high forehead, and an angular jaw.

"My name is Lothar," he said. "Welcome to the East." He bowed slightly to Dillon. "I'm glad that you agreed to meet with me, Herr Randolph."

As Lothar sat down across from them, a waiter appeared with a mug of beer and placed it in front of him on the table. Christa shifted her hand and placed it on top of Dillon's. "I've told my friend about you," she said, directing her gaze at Lothar. "About how you may be able to help my brother."

"That depends on whether you can help me." The man looked over at Dillon, appraising him. "I understand that you are with the U.S. Mission?"

"I am," Dillon said.

"And that is your Ford Consul parked outside? No problems at the checkpoint?"

"It is." Dillon found himself reluctant to give Lothar any details. He didn't want to say too much. "No problems at the checkpoint."

"That's good." Lothar drank from his mug. "There are expenses involved in these matters. Gifts to friends so that strings can be pulled. I will need to arrange for paperwork in advance. State Security runs by pieces of paper, like all bureaucracies, especially German ones. We need the paperwork that grants her brother a temporary bereavement leave. A death in the family—we'll say his mother, because even bureaucrats have a *Mutti*. These leaves are rare, but some are granted."

"Will that work?" Christa asked. "My mother's already gone, and I'm Konrad's only relative."

Lothar shrugged. "We'll have your brother in the American sector before anyone has a reason to check. We'll present the orders for the bereavement on a Sunday morning when there are junior men on duty. As soon as Konrad is out the door, you must drive him across the sector border in Herr Randolph's sedan."

"Who will present the orders?" Dillon asked.

"I'll accompany Christa. You'll wait nearby in your car. Once you're in the West, I'll make sure that the paperwork gets lost. There will be a record of Konrad Schiller being released, but the orders for bereavement will disappear. A small mystery. But Konrad is small fry—that's the term, yes?—and mistakes do happen, even in a socialist state guided by scientific principles."

"What do you want in exchange?" Dillon asked.

"To borrow the magic carpet you have parked outside." Lothar grinned. "Your license plates allow you to cross the sector border without being searched."

"I'm supposed to be in the Russian sector only on official business, and not by myself."

"Who will ever know? You have a ready-made excuse if you're questioned. Your romance has become more serious. You and your girlfriend have come to the East for you to meet her family. The course of true love."

"Christa said two trips."

"Yes, that is what I thought, but it may require three. My expenses will run higher than I had anticipated."

"What guarantee do we have that Konrad will be released?" Dillon asked. "I would agree to a third trip only after he has been freed and is across the border."

"You drive a hard bargain," Lothar said. "But an acceptable one."

"What is it that you want me to smuggle?"

"You're not smuggling. You're delivering goods. All you must do is drive. A man will bring you packages. You will place them in the boot of your car. He'll tell you where to make the delivery."

"How do we know that you will keep your end of the bargain?"

"What do they say—honor among thieves?"

Christa had remained silent throughout the conversation. She turned to Lothar and spoke. "We must know what is in the packages. And I drive a harder bargain than Dillon. One trip before Konrad goes free. The other two come after."

Lothar stared at her. "And what guarantee do I have that you will make the next two trips?"

"Honor among thieves."

"But you're an actress, not a thief." Lothar smiled, enjoying himself. "And I understand that you, Herr Randolph, are a poet."

"I am," Dillon said. "It appears that actresses are tougher negotiators than poets."

"That they are. I will agree to these terms, relying on your poet's honor." Lothar smiled again, baring his teeth. "My father was a poet and a playwright, among other things. Sadly, I did not inherit his talent with words. Instead, I must make my living in commerce, as a trader, procuring those things that people desperately want but are not easily available. So, in the end, I serve a necessary, if not particularly noble, function."

"When is the first trip?" Christa asked.

"I must make arrangements," Lothar said. "The magic carpet is the easy thing. Your brother's paperwork is a more delicate matter. I will contact you." He glanced over at Dillon, studying him for a moment. "Now I will incur expenses. In advance. I hope that you'll not change your mind."

"I won't change my mind," Dillon said. "Just make sure you can deliver what you've promised."

* * *

Dillon dropped off Christa at the Neues Theater and then drove straight to the U.S. Mission. When he telephoned Hawes, the Englishman suggested that they meet elsewhere in Dahlem, and he suggested a spot, outside the library at the Free University.

"You may have picked up a tail on your way back," Hawes explained. "Lots of open space at the University. We'll be able to spot any new friends you might have made."

Dillon arrived before Hawes, and found a place to sit on a short concrete wall outside the library which was located in the western wing of the Henry Ford Building, a gift from the American industrialist. Dillon looked around at the students walking around the nearby plaza—it could have been an American campus, except they were more formally-dressed, and many seemed older than the typical undergraduates he remembered from his college days.

When Hawes joined him at the wall, he nodded to Dillon. "Viktor assures me that no one has followed you," he said. "How was your reception in the East?"

"They want me to smuggle for them, using my diplomatic immunity."

Hawes listened intently, a pad and pencil at the ready to take notes, as Dillon recounted his trip to East Berlin and his meeting with the tall East German who went by the name of Lothar.

"He said his father was a poet and a playwright?" Hawes asked. "You're sure that's what he said?"

"He made a joke about not inheriting his father's talent."

Hawes sat in silence for a moment, absent-mindedly chewing on the end of his pencil.

"Why is this important?" Dillon asked. "Do you know who Lothar is?"

"From the description you've given, and from his comments about his father, I think your friendly black market smuggler may be Markus Wolf. He's high up in the Stasi. His father was a leading German playwright before Hitler. A Red, of course. We don't have any photographs of Wolf, just some sketchy descriptions."

"You told me that this was a Russian operation."

"It is. It must be very important to the Russians if they're involving Wolf. They trust him—he was raised in Moscow and speaks the language, one of the exiled Communists they brought back to run the country. Like Ulbricht."

"At least we're closer to figuring out what they're up to."

"Blackmail? Or something else. A provocation? Arresting you on charges of smuggling?"

"What would be the point of that?" Dillon asked.

"I'm not sure. Proof of the West's decadence? An attempt to wrong-foot your President before Geneva. They might hold you in jail as a bargaining chip."

"Not that much of a chip. My father is no longer in Congress, and we're Democrats. I don't think the Randolph name carries much weight in this Administration."

"I need to think this through," Hawes said. "Lothar's involvement is a complication. I expect that they'll move quickly now, to turn you, to put you in the bag. They trust Christa can persuade you. After all, you've crossed into the Russian sector with her, alone, violating protocol."

"How far do you plan to take this?"

"As far as we can, as fast as we can. Short of your arrest, of course. We won't let you do anything over there that they can hang on you. What would be ideal would be your meeting with Christa's control, the Russian. That's when we'll know what is really happening."

"And you are sure that this is worth it?"

"Worth the candle? I have no doubt. You strike me as a curious sort, Randolph. Don't you want to get to the bottom of all this?"

"I do," Dillon replied. "I just don't want to end up in an East German prison cell because of my curiosity."

* * *

Vladimir Zavatsky had twice called Dillon at the U.S. Mission and had left messages asking him to return his call. When Dillon reached him at the offices of Tass, Zavatsky skipped any small talk and asked to meet at the Berlin Zoo, in front of the Elephant House, in forty-five minutes. Dillon agreed, curious, wondering whether their meeting would prove as strange as their first encounter. Was Zavatsky's request somehow connected to the rendezvous with Lothar in East Berlin? Dillon decided that was unlikely. The call had to be a coincidence.

He telephoned Hawes and told him about Zavatsky's overture and asked whether there was any reason not to proceed with the meeting.

"Meet with him," Hawes said. "I don't think he's involved, but anything is possible. In any event, we'll keep an eye on the two of you. Make sure he doesn't bring along any muscle-bound comrades."

When he reached Hardenbergplatz, Dillon purchased a ticket to the zoo and entered through the Lion Gate. Along the pathway into the zoo, he passed a young family, the mother pushing a baby carriage, the father holding the hand of a little girl in a sun dress. A teenage girl flirted with an obviously smitten boy near the enclosure for the giraffes.

He found the Russian journalist waiting for him at the Elephant House, a natty fedora atop his head and a rolled up umbrella under his arm. Zavatsky had dark circles under his eyes, and he looked tired.

"Are we being watched by your security people, by any chance?" Dillon asked.

"There's no reason that we should be," Zavatsky said. "They know that I often visit the zoo. Unlike many of my colleagues, I can spend as much time in West Berlin as I care to. What is it that you say—rank has its privileges?"

"Isn't there a zoo in East Berlin, now?"

The Russian conceded the point with a shrug. "There is, the Tierpark. Ulbricht insists on matching the West. So he must have his own theaters, his own newspapers, his own zoo. But this is the better one."

He turned to study the elephants moving about in the fenced area in front of them. "They're fascinating creatures," he said. "Massive beasts, and yet so clever." He pointed to the closest elephant. "They call that one Shanti. The Germans are sentimental about these zoo animals. Shanti, the elephant. Schorsch, the polar bear. Knautschke, the hippo. Yet they're the same people who have twice set Europe aflame with war. Twice. Who put the Jews in the camps and burned them up. Who killed millions of my countrymen and women."

"Wasn't Hitler an art student, a painter? He loved art and yet was capable of ordering monstrous acts. I would think as a Marxist you would feel comfortable with such contradictions. The dialectic works that way, doesn't it?"

"We should save a discussion of the dialectic for another time." Zavatsky paused. "The elephant is the symbol of your country, yes?"

Dillon shook his head and laughed. "A symbol of the Republican Party, not of the country. I'm a Democrat."

"Of course. Your father, the former Congressman from Virginia. Yet the elephants run your country." Zavatsky motioned toward the largest elephant near them. "Elephants are powerful beasts. Nevertheless, they're slow to move and an angry attacker—such as a bear, shall we say—might be capable of striking at an elephant's throat. We must do what we can so that the bear and the elephant remain at peace, now that there are these terrible bombs. As a materialist, I do not believe heaven awaits us in the end. Thus, I fear these bombs. Thus, I savor every minute of every day. Thus, I come to the zoo. If these weapons are employed, all of that ends. As a materialist, I wish our existence to continue, not just for me, but for my family, and for the rhinos and giraffe and the elephants. Fair enough, yes?"

"Fair enough."

In the distance, there was the low rumble of thunder. Dillon glanced up and saw storm clouds gathering. A man in a tan jacket came walking toward them, a cigarette dangling from his lips. Dillon immediately recognized him—it was Viktor, Hawes' friend from the Café Kranzler. Dillon quickly looked back at Zavatsky.

"I asked you here because there's something you should know," Zavatsky said. "It involves the actress, Christa Schiller." He didn't wait for Dillon's response, but kept talking. "She has some associates who wish you harm. They control her. Keep your distance from her. Don't cross into our sector with her."

"Why are you warning me?"

Zavatsky shook his head. "I told you at the Paris Bar that I believe in peaceful coexistence. Those controlling Miss Schiller don't, nor do the men behind them. Any incident will strengthen the hands of those on both sides who prefer confrontation."

"Any incident?"

Zavatsky remained silent.

"Why should I believe you?" Dillon asked.

"Why should you not?" Zavatsky placed his fedora on his head. "Please heed my advice. Miss Schiller has been sent to entrap you."

There was more thunder, louder now, and the dark clouds had spread. It smelled of rain. Zavatsky unfurled his umbrella.

"She is, by all accounts, a lovely young woman," he said. "A shame that she has become the puppet of others." Zavatsky handed Dillon a business card. "Call me at this number, should you wish to talk further."

"Where does the phone ring? In Karlshorst?"

"At my flat. If I'm not there, and you need to talk, call my office and leave the time. I'll meet you here, in front of the Elephant House."

He nodded to Dillon, and raising his umbrella over his head, strode off in the direction of the main entrance, to the east. Viktor Toth, sitting on a nearby stone bench, glanced up from his newspaper and watched the Russian's progress.

Dillon waited a few minutes before leaving, and when he did, Toth was still sprawled out on the bench, studying his copy of the *Berliner Morgenpost*.

As Dillon headed back to the zoo entrance, two young men in black leather jackets stepped in front of him, blocking his way. He recognized the smaller of the two as the agitator who had challenged him at Amerika Haus.

"Time to teach you a lesson," the smaller man said. He wasn't wearing his steel-rimmed glasses and he squinted at Dillon.

As the men circled him, looking for an opening, Dillon put up his guard. The agitator moved closer, and Dillon turned slightly to face him. The larger man rushed Dillon, grabbing him by the arms. As Dillon wrestled with him, the agitator stepped in and threw a wild punch that bounced off Dillon's upper arm.

Out of the corner of his eye, Dillon caught movement—it was Viktor. In a moment, Viktor had thrown the agitator to the ground, and Dillon was able to push away the man tussling with him and break free.

Viktor stood next to Dillon. "Now the odds are even," Viktor said in German. "You will pay a price if you continue with this."

The two men exchanged glances and backed away.

"Fuck you," the agitator said, as he and his friend retreated up the pathway toward the center of the zoo.

Viktor glanced over at Dillon. "Are you okay?"

"I'm fine. I recognized one of them, the shorter man. He came to my poetry reading months ago, looking to stir things up. An agitator. Afterward, he took a swing at me, and I knocked him down. I think he was looking for payback."

"They weren't following the Russian," Viktor said. "He was clean when he arrived. They were after you."

"Tell Hawes what happened," Dillon said. "Tell him I think it was coincidental."

Viktor shook his head. "They were amateurs. If they'd been the Stasi, we'd have some bumps and bruises. Or worse."

SEVENTEEN

A week passed without incident. Christa proved hard to reach on the telephone, and when Dillon finally did talk to her, she seemed moody and distant. Lothar hadn't been in contact, she told him, and she made it clear she didn't want to talk about it. After a long silence, she reluctantly agreed to a dinner date, but the entire conversation left Dillon in a foul mood.

The following day, a breezy and sunny Thursday, Dillon had been headed to his car when Lars Swanson stopped him in the hall just short of the Mission entrance. The security officer wore a frown on his face, and he curtly asked Dillon to join him in his office.

Dillon reluctantly followed Swanson down the corridor to his office. He had deliberately avoided contact with Swanson in the past few weeks.

"Thought you might have gone AWOL," Swanson said once they were seated. "Been looking for you for a few days. You haven't been around the office."

"I've been busy. In fact, you caught me as I was leaving for a meeting in Schöneberg. What do you want to talk about?"

"We're not going to chat about whether the White Sox can beat the Yankees this season. We're going to talk about security."

Dillon made a show of checking his wristwatch. "Can we make it brief? I have an appointment at city hall."

"We'll take whatever time we need," Swanson said. "No more, no less." He made no attempt to hide his hostility.

"Is there some sort of problem?"

"I think I have you figured out, Randolph. We all know you have special pull in Washington. You don't think you have to follow the rules because you're protected by friends in high places. What's more, you're the type who gets a thrill out of breaking the rules. Like Marlon Brando. James Dean. A rebel without a cause."

"I get that you don't like me, Swanson. What does that have to do with anything?"

"The others may tip toe around you because your old man was in Congress, but I won't." Swanson's face had reddened in anger. "Christa Schiller, the Kraut actress you've been seeing. Ain't she from East Berlin?"

"What of it? She's living in the British sector, now."

"She's your girlfriend, isn't she? Didn't I warn you about the local talent?"

"I remember you warning me about streetwalkers."

"Your memory ain't so hot, then. I warned you to steer clear of security risks. I asked you to let me know whenever there might be a concern. A woman from East Berlin fits that bill, but you don't alert me, you don't say anything."

"She's an actress," Dillon said. "Not political. I hardly think she represents a major threat to NATO secrets."

"I can do without the sarcasm. Any woman with family in the East may be working for the Stasi, or the Russians. Considering your responsibilities at the Mission, you're a logical target. All of the political officers are."

"Did Audrey Wingate tell you about Christa?"

"How I found out shouldn't matter. What matters is that you didn't come to me and inform me of the relationship."

"I talk to lots of locals. Did you expect me to report every meeting, every conversation?"

"Do you fuck lots of locals, too?"

"That's way out of line." Dillon stood up, taken aback by Swanson's animosity. "I don't have to put up with this."

"Sit down," Swanson said. "You've admitted to a relationship with a woman who represents a risk to security. We have to resolve this."

Dillon slowly took his seat. He couldn't afford trouble with Swanson. "Let's say I accept your notion that Christa's a security risk, which I don't. Do you really think I'm going to whisper diplomatic secrets to her? Hand over sensitive documents? That's absurd."

"Who knows? Maybe. When men think with their little head instead of their big one, they do stupid stuff."

For a moment, Dillon wondered whether he should tell Swanson the truth about Christa, but immediately rejected the idea. Hawes had it right—the fewer people who knew, the better the chances of succeeding. "So is this a warning? An official warning?"

"We can make it official," Swanson said. "You don't want that, more bad marks on your report card. You have an opportunity to fix this. I expect you to do the smart thing. Break it off with her. Tell her you're feeling guilty about the girl waiting back home or that you've met another woman or that you've got the clap. It really doesn't matter, you just have to end it."

"Or what?"

"I go to the chief of mission, and then I write this up and send it to Bonn and Washington. It goes in your file. That would more or less shit can your career, from what I gather. With your reputation, they won't hesitate to yank you out of here."

Dillon looked at Swanson's flushed face and realized that he was going to have to lie. He needed to buy some time.

He covered his face with his hands, feigning anxiety. "I'll end it," he said. "I'm not going to jeopardize my future over a girl. She's not worth it. In exchange, I'd like your word that nothing goes into my file about this."

Swanson nodded. "You call it quits now, and this stays between us."

Dillon knew that Swanson was lying—the security officer would alert his superiors in Bonn and write something about Christa for the file. It would be another black mark, but if Dillon could help Hawes that wouldn't matter.

"I'll tell her tomorrow. We're supposed to have dinner." Dillon glanced over at Swanson, noting that, victorious, the security officer's face was less flushed. "I'll let her down easy. It's not the first time I've had to break something off." He paused. "In some ways, maybe it's for the best. It wasn't going anywhere, and I wouldn't want her to think that I was ready to be tied down."

"You're a cool customer, Randolph. But look on the bright side—you won't miss a beat. It's a city full of lonely women."

* * *

Dillon returned to his office and telephoned Hawes. They arranged to meet at Innsbrucker Platz in Schöneberg. Dillon waited twenty minutes for Hawes, flagging him down when he arrived and climbing into the passenger seat of Hawes' Volkswagen. They didn't talk until Hawes had driven to a side street and parked the car.

The Englishman wasn't surprised by Swanson's intervention. "I wondered how long it'd take before the girl turned up on their radar," he said. "People gossip. It's not like you've kept your romance a secret."

"Swanson demanded that I end it with her. Threatened to go to the head of our Mission if I didn't. I agreed to break it off when I saw her next. I figured that would buy us some time."

"This alters the timetable," Hawes said. "Accelerates it. You must tell Christa that we know she's working for the Stasi. Give her the chance to switch sides. We have little choice, now. Swanson is likely to start poking around."

"And if Christa refuses?"

"That would end the candy and flowers, wouldn't it? You'd wish her well and call it quits. That would make Swanson happy. We could all go on as if nothing had happened."

"As if nothing happened? I'm not a robot, Hawes. I do have feelings for her."

"I don't doubt that. But nothing too deep, those feelings."

"Don't you worry that I might have taken it to heart?"

"Tell me, then—are you prepared to make her an honest woman? Bring her back to the States as your wife and present her to family and friends? A German actress of dubious reputation? I'm sure that would do wonders for your career."

Dillon shook his head. "I just don't want it to end badly."

"Even though she was prepared to sell you to the Russians?"

"Who knows what she's been told to do? I'm sure they've held her brother over her head. Do what we say, and he'll get better treatment."

Hawes shrugged. "It doesn't matter, now. You have to confront her. Then, I must talk to her. There's no way around it."

"I'll need the photo of her entering Stasi headquarters," Dillon said. "She needs to believe that we know more than we really do."

* * *

It was a particularly beautiful afternoon—clear blue skies, sunlight, warm breezes. Dillon figured that anyone who worked in an office building had invented a reason to extend their lunch hour so they could bask in the sun and enjoy the glories of a vibrant spring day.

Perched on a stone bench, Dillon watched Christa as she approached Savignyplatz, marveling at her graceful walk. Christa stood out among those around her on Kantstrasse, in her charcoal skirt, light cream-colored blouse, and wool beret.

He had called and insisted that they meet, claiming that he had important news he wanted to share with her, in person. Dillon had dreaded the conversation that was to come. What if she denied everything? Or admitted it, but walked away? He wasn't sure that he was ready for that.

She smiled at him as she neared the bench and, for a moment, he couldn't believe that she was lying to him, that she was capable of betraying him, and then he remembered the images of her in front of Stasi headquarters and Hawes' cool certainty that she was controlled by East German intelligence.

What other secrets might she be hiding from him? Another lover? Another life, an existence that he knew nothing of, across the sector border?

"What is this news you have that is so important?" she asked, sitting down next to him, their legs touching.

"Have you heard more from Lothar?"

"I have not," she said, her smile vanishing.

"Christa, there is something I need to know."

"Why so serious? What is it?"

He lowered his voice. "I know that Lothar works for the Stasi. Are you working for them, too?"

"Don't be ridiculous. Why would you say that? Is this something your security people told you? The witch hunters?"

From his jacket pocket Dillon retrieved the photograph of her entering the Ministry of State Security building and handed it to her. She glanced at it quickly and made a face.

"Are you having me watched?" she asked. She looked down and away from him. "Are your witch hunters following me?"

"Why were you there? To meet Lothar? Or someone else?"

"I went there about Konrad. To convince them that he is innocent."

"That's very hard to believe, Christa. What about Lothar? Is he Stasi?"

"I don't know." She looked up at him solemnly.

Dillon found himself sighing. "Did they tell you to become my lover? That's what the witch hunters say. Was it all planned?"

She rose to her feet, her cheeks flushed. Dillon stood, as well, and grasped her by the arm so she couldn't leave. "What will happen when you tell the Stasi that it's over between us?" he asked. "And when they ask why?" He watched her face, sensing the hesitation, realizing that he was reaching her. "Why don't we sit down and finish this conversation? I don't want to see you hurt, Christa. I need you to tell me the truth. Don't you owe me that?"

She remained silent. He reached out to take her hand and she pulled it away from him.

"I believe that they're holding your brother over you," he said quietly. "I don't judge you for that. I believe that you've done what you felt necessary. It doesn't matter. I haven't stopped caring for you."

"What is there to say?" She looked down, avoiding his eyes.

"When did it start?"

He waited, aware that she was trying to decide what to say, how much to admit. They sat in silence until she spoke again.

"Last fall. First, they arranged for me to join the Neues Theater." She shot him a quick glance. "They told me that if I did what they asked, they would let Konrad go. I agreed. I didn't know you, then. It was the only way to help my brother. It's too easy to become cynical, when you live the way we do. You look around and see that the people who get ahead are the ones without scruples, the ones who show up for every Party meeting, who betray their friends—perhaps even their families."

She kept her head down, and he had to strain to hear her. "What is worse is that we have all become their lackeys, complicit in this system. You find yourself accepting what should never be accepted, accommodating them, going along. You tell yourself that you're only doing what you have to, what you must to get by, just like everyone else. It poisons everything. Whom can you trust? Your childhood friends? Your lover?

You can never be sure who is informing, who will guard your secrets, and who will trade them for their advantage."

Dillon reached over for her hand, and this time she let him take it. He pulled her close to him and embraced her, and she let her head rest on his shoulder. An older woman walking through the park made a wry face of commiseration at what she took to be a lover's quarrel.

"I'm sorry," Christa whispered to him.

"I understand."

"Do you understand?" she asked bitterly. "Do you know what it's like when they have such power over you, over your family?"

"I don't." He hesitated, and then asked the question he felt he had to ask. "Is there anyone else in your life? Over there? Do you belong to someone else?"

She shook her head. "No. There was just you."

He took a deep breath, aware that a great deal depended on what he had to ask her next. "I want to make things right. There's someone who can help us. He's English."

"He gave you the photographs?"

"He did. I don't trust my own security people, but I trust this man. He's intelligent and he listens. He's waiting nearby to talk to us. If you're willing."

"How long have you known?"

"Not long. I didn't believe until I saw the photographs." It was his turn to look away. "I have other questions. Personal ones."

Dillon could not read Christa's expression. He felt that she had retreated behind an impassive mask. "I would like to think we have something," he said. "We've been good together. But then I wonder if it's because you're a marvelous actress. Not just on stage. So I don't know."

"And would you believe me if I say I do care for you, Dillon? Or would you think that I'm just acting?"

"That's the curse of this, isn't it? We both wonder what's make-believe and what's real."

Her face betrayed nothing, and Dillon wondered what she was thinking. Had she grown to care for him? Was she ashamed of deceiving him? Or had she seen him as a means to an end? He told himself that he wanted to know the truth. But did he?

"I will meet with your Englishman," she said.

* * *

It took five minutes for them to walk to the antiques store on Grolmanstrasse where Hawes awaited them. Dillon figured that Viktor or another of Hawes' men had to be floating around somewhere nearby, making sure that they weren't followed.

A middle-aged woman in a tweed suit greeted them when they entered the first floor of the store. "He's waiting for you in the back, love," she said to Dillon with a light Scottish burr. "On the right."

They walked through the store, past dusty furniture, clocks, vases, and assorted bric-a-brac. In the back, Hawes had placed three wooden chairs in a corner and motioned for them to sit down. "We won't be disturbed. If Marjorie had set up shop on Keithstrasse, with the other antique dealers, she'd attract more customers. It's more of a hobby for her than a business." He turned to Christa. "Pleased to meet you, Miss Schiller."

She looked directly at Hawes. "So you're a British spy."

"Please sit," he said. "Would you like some tea? Marjorie will bring us some, if you like."

Christa remained standing. "You're a spy," she said. "True?"

"A spy catcher, actually."

"Do you believe that I'm one of those spies? That you've caught me?"

"No, I believe that you have been compelled to do the bidding of others."

"And now I must do your bidding?" Her tone was flat, resigned.

"We won't force you to do anything."

Dillon took her arm and guided her to the nearest chair. She sat down, and it seemed as if the fight had suddenly gone out of her.

"What would you have me do?" she asked.

"Answer some questions."

"To start. But then there will be more."

"Who have you been dealing with?" Hawes asked. "Lothar? Or a Russian?"

Dillon sat next to her, holding her hand, hoping that connection would bring her some comfort.

"Don't you already know?" she asked. "Are you checking? I answer to a Comrade Mikhail. They say he's from Moscow."

"Lothar. Is he Stasi?"

"No doubt. He's German." She turned to Dillon. "You said he could help."

"I believe that he can," Dillon said.

"You know what will happen to me and my brother if I'm found out by these men," she said, staring directly at Hawes. "You're part of this dirty business. You can have no illusions."

Hawes shifted in his chair and leaned forward. "Helping us is your best option, now, Miss Schiller. They must not learn that we know about the operation."

"You wish for them to continue with this? To entrap Dillon?"

"We need to know why Dillon has been singled out. Why is a senior officer from Moscow involved? Then, when we have those answers, we can extricate you both."

"What do you want me to do?" she asked.

"Do nothing for the moment. They will want Lothar to meet with Dillon again. You must tell us, in advance, about any meetings."

"How will you protect me? And my brother?"

"When it's over, we'll get you out of Berlin. We'll look to trade for your brother. Offer them an agent in exchange. Someone the Stasi wants back."

"All this you will do out of the goodness of your heart?"

"We're practical. We take care of those who help us. You can make things quite difficult for them, Miss Schiller. I should think that would be quite appealing."

"I will do what you ask," she said. She gave Hawes a bitter half-smile. "Just like them, you've written my part. I'll say your lines. I'm quite good at that."

* * *

Dillon found Audrey on the second floor of Amerika Haus, in a small cubbyhole near the director's office that held a desk and telephone. A poster advertising the Berlin appearance of the Dave Brubeck Quartet on their goodwill tour hung on the wall.

When she looked up from the desk, she gave him a defiant look. It was clear to Dillon that she knew why he was there—Swanson must have warned her in advance.

"My visit doesn't come as a surprise, does it," he said. It was a statement rather than a question.

She didn't flinch. "I have no idea what you're talking about."

"That's crap and you know it." He took a step closer and she shrank from him. "Did you think that your little stunt would endear you to me? Ratting to Swanson?"

"Why should I care if I endear myself to you? I could care less. I did what

I thought was right. Our security people needed to know that you were making a fool of yourself with your German tramp."

"Did you consider the consequences? What this could mean to my career?"

"Perhaps you should have thought about that before you chased after her. Did you stop and think about what involving yourself with an East German woman would mean for your country? For the Mission's security?"

"I didn't realize that you were tasked with guarding American virtue in Berlin. Is that really your excuse?"

"It's not an excuse."

"It sounds like it to me. I chose Christa over you, and this is your revenge. You've done a very, very stupid thing. You don't understand the damage you've done."

"I understand," she said, her mouth set.

"You think that you do. You're a spoiled girl who didn't get what she wanted, so she decided on revenge. I just pray that we can fix what you've done."

"I feel sorry for your actress," Audrey said. "Believe it or not, I feel sorry for her. You'll dump her in the end, if you haven't already, just like you did that poor woman in Canberra. You're a bastard, just like they said. I can only hope that some day a woman breaks your heart."

"Hope all that you want. Just keep your nose out of my business."

"Or what?"

"You'll be on a flight back to the States before you can turn around."

"As if you have the power to do that," she said, scornfully.

"Try me," Dillon said. "You'd be surprised by what I'm capable of."

EIGHTEEN

When Hawes broached the idea of meeting with Vladimir Zavatsky, Dillon immediately objected. He didn't want to do anything that might draw attention to Christa.

"He's KGB," Dillon said. "So is Christa's handler."

"But he warned you about Christa. He's trying to derail whatever mischief is planned. We have a mutual interest, I'd say."

"You can't be sure of that."

Hawes smiled. "Not unless I have a conversation with him."

"You've been the one arguing that we should keep our cards close to our chest."

"I have. But we're getting closer to playing those cards. Zavatsky may be able to help us understand what we're up against."

Dillon agreed to contact Zavatsky and arrange a meeting by the Elephant House the following afternoon. He and Hawes arrived at the zoo ten minutes early. When Zavatsky appeared, the Russian stopped for a moment, frowning, at the sight of Dillon's companion.

"You didn't say anything about another man coming." He looked over at Hawes warily.

Dillon adopted a conciliatory tone. "My apologies. This is Mr. Hawes."

"Why is he here?"

"I'll let him explain," Dillon said.

"Dillon has told me of his conversations with you. It appears that we share a common purpose, a desire to put an end to Mikhail Durov's current operation in Berlin."

"Let's not waste time, Mr. Hawes," Zavatsky said. "You're British. MI6?"

"I am."

"You wish to stop Durov? That is easily accomplished. Randolph must drop the girl."

"I have some ideas about that." Hawes turned to Dillon. "I think it's best if Mr. Zavatsky and I continue this chat by ourselves. In private."

Dillon stared at Hawes. "I'd like to stay."

"I don't think that would be wise. I'll explain later. Why don't you meet me at the cinema? Forty-five minutes."

Dillon nodded, grudgingly, and left. The two men stood in silence until he had disappeared up the pathway.

"You're correct that Dillon could end the affair. But that's a temporary solution. Stop this mischief, and the men behind it will try again. Better to expose Durov and his allies as dangerous incompetents. Discredit them in Moscow. Have them removed from whatever positions of power they occupy."

"How do you propose to accomplish that?"

"What if I provided you with evidence that Durov was negotiating with us to defect?"

Zavatsky snorted. "Preposterous. Who would believe that?"

"Others in the KGB have defected. When the time is right, we'll make Durov our guest. Only briefly. He may, no doubt, turn down our generous offer to join us in the West. But he'll have to explain why he met with me in Berlin, and the dossier documenting the numerous contacts with us that I'll give you."

Zavatsky looked over at the elephants. Two uniformed zoo workers had brought bales of hay, and the elephants had begun to feed, eagerly grasping the hay with their trunks and bringing it to their mouths to chew. "You cannot expect me to be directly involved in this."

"No, of course not. You do or say nothing until we provide you the evidence. Then you convey it to your superiors. The same information about this Operation West Wind will be shared with the Americans and with London. Your penetration agents will confirm the information that I give you. Then, those in your leadership that want peace can use this against Durov and his backers."

"Why should I trust you?" Zavatsky asked.

"I believe you find the prospects of a nuclear exchange with the Americans unthinkable. An incident in Berlin, a pretext for confrontation, would be very dangerous."

"I'll consider what you have said."

"No," Hawes said. "I need an answer now. If you won't collaborate with us on this, we'll go it alone. Milk what we can out of exposing Durov's plot. A propaganda victory. But I'd rather that his failure in Berlin benefits your more enlightened colleagues."

Zavatsky shook his head slowly. "Do you know what you're asking of me? The risk I must take?"

"If our roles were reversed, I might hesitate," Hawes said. "But I believe that I would act. In the interests of peace."

"If I help you, there are conditions. If your operation fails, I may be exposed. I accept that risk for myself, but I have a daughter, twelve years old, here with me in Berlin. You must promise me that you'll take her in."

"Her mother?"

"I'm a widower."

Hawes thought for a moment. "Does your daughter speak any English?"

"She does. We were in England together as a family for several years."

"What is her name?"

"Ludmila."

"It will not come to that, but if it does, we'll protect Ludmila."

"We agree on this, then."

"One more thing," Hawes said. "You'll need to arrange for the release of the girl's brother, Konrad Schiller. Only after Durov has been neutralized, of course."

"I don't like it," Zavatsky said. "To arrange that could further expose me. Is it necessary? I'm sure you can get the girl to cooperate without it. Is her brother of any consequence?"

"Could not the same be said of your daughter?" Hawes asked. "Of what consequence is she?"

Zavatsky grimaced. "You're right. I concede the point. I'll do what I can for the brother."

"You should have no contact with Randolph after today," Hawes said. "If we're successful, I'll meet you here to hand over the materials."

"And if you fail?"

"I imagine you'll read about an incident in the newspapers. Something quite messy."

Zavatsky sighed softly. "When I was a boy, in the winter we'd skate on the Voronezh when the river froze. In the spring, the ice would begin to melt. We'd go out on the river, on a dare, to see how far we could go. We were boys, foolhardy. More afraid of being seen as cowards than of falling in and drowning." He looked over at Hawes, his face drawn. "Now some in the Kremlin dare Chairman Khrushchev to go out on the ice. And in the West, it's the same. No one wants to seem weak."

"Let's keep them all off the thin ice, then," Hawes said. "Shall we?"

* * *

They met in the now-deserted lobby of the Kurbel Kino—the showing of the next film didn't start for hours. The chair by the entrance was empty, and there was no sign of the teenage usher. Dillon had waited impatiently for Hawes to arrive. He had been surprised when Hawes had asked him to leave the meeting with Zavatsky—he had hoped to learn more from the Russian about the nature of the operation targeting him, and more about Christa's role in it.

"I thought it best that I speak alone with Zavatsky," Hawes told Dillon. "Professional-to-professional. He does want to stop Durov. He has agreed to stay on the sidelines, while we sort things out."

"What did he tell you about the operation?"

"He repeated that you should end it with Christa. I don't think he's privy to the details of what Durov plans, or he's not about to share them with us. We'll have to uncover that ourselves."

"What next, then?" Dillon asked.

"I think it's time to knock them off-balance. This man Lothar's a cut-out—he stands in the way of our getting at Durov. We need to remove him from the picture. Christa must tell them that you're having second thoughts. There's something about Lothar you didn't like, that made you uneasy. He didn't seem trustworthy."

"Won't that make them suspicious?"

"On the contrary, they'll see your reluctance as quite natural. Agents often have second thoughts before they make a commitment. They need reassurance. It's a familiar pattern."

"I am reluctant," Dillon said. "That's the reality."

"That's also good," Hawes said. "Christa must insist that you'll only meet with the man who can guarantee Konrad's freedom. Not Lothar. Durov. We need him to show his cards."

"I'd like to spend as little time on the other side of the sector border as possible. Can't we meet here, in the British sector? It'd be safer for Christa. Safer for me."

"Durov would never come here. As long as they think she can deliver you, she's protected. For now, they need her. They'll want you in the East. Don't worry, we'll be nearby."

"Aren't we vulnerable over there?"

"To a certain extent, yes. That can work to our advantage. They won't expect a counter operation on their side of the border. The element of surprise."

"What if you've misjudged them? What if they're ready and waiting?"

"We've been very careful. That won't change. We'll vet any meeting place beforehand. If we see anything that gives us pause, you don't go."

"How far are you willing to go?" Dillon asked. "To protect us?"

"We'll do what's necessary. I've done some hard things in my time. So has Viktor."

"I guess my question is whether you're prepared to kill Durov."

Hawes raised his eyebrows. "We'll have failed miserably if that's our only choice. It won't be. I don't intend to fail."

* * *

They went together to talk it through with Christa. They met at an Italian restaurant in Wilmersdorf that had a private dining room.

Christa was nervous, jittery. She opened a package of cigarettes, and found some matches in her pocketbook. She lit a cigarette and took a quick puff and then exhaled. Hawes reached over and slid an ashtray across the table.

"The time has come, hasn't it?" she asked. "For my new lines."

"It has," Hawes said. "Dillon must meet with Comrade Mikhail. His full name is Mikhail Durov, by the way."

"How do you propose we do that?"

"Tell Durov that I won't deal with Lothar," Dillon said. "That I don't trust him. I see him as the middleman. If I'm going to risk my career, I need to meet with the principal, the man who can free your brother."

"He won't like that," Christa said, frowning. "He will be very angry."

"That can't be helped," Hawes said. "You'll tell Durov that you've come too far to give up now. You want your brother freed. You think there's a way to salvage the situation. You can convince Dillon that Lothar's contact is actually a corrupt official, a Russian advisor to Ulbricht's government. You suggest that Durov play the part of the Russian."

"I don't know," she said. She took a deep breath. "What if he refuses?"

"Then it's over," Hawes said. "We call it a day."

"Why must Dillon meet with him? With Durov?"

"A means to an end. It's the best way to learn what he wants. How Dillon's recruitment fits into the picture. Then I'll know how to proceed."

Christa took a long, nervous drag of her cigarette. "What about Konrad?"

"You can defect, now," Hawes said. "You don't have to deal with Durov or the Stasi ever again. But then I can't do anything about your brother."

"I see," she said. "There is a price. And if all goes as you have planned, can you protect us afterwards?"

"You'll need to leave Berlin. I think you could live in Frankfurt or Hamburg without fear of retribution."

"I don't know," she said. "If this goes wrong, it will cost me Konrad." She turned to Dillon, then, and held his gaze. "What do you think? Should I do this?"

Dillon didn't hesitate. "I would. If it were my brother, I would."

She remained silent for a long moment. She stubbed out her nearly-finished cigarette in the ashtray. "Tell me again what I must say."

* * *

The summons had been for lunch, which surprised Christa. Stefan had handed her the note when she first arrived at the theater, and he didn't say anything.

Christa followed the instructions in the note—taking the U-Bahn to Alexanderplatz and then crossing the wide, barren plaza to the drab restaurant they had chosen.

She had a hard time imagining the Russian anywhere but the cramped room at Stasi headquarters. In her mind, that was his natural environment, the dark place where he schemed and plotted and devised twisted ways to ruin people's lives.

When she entered the restaurant and saw Comrade Mikhail sitting at a far table, she took a deep breath. She told herself it was no different than a scene on stage—she would deliver the lines Hawes had written for her.

When she sat down across from him, he glared at her. "Comrade Lothar told me that you challenged him in front of the American. He's quite angry about it. Randolph had agreed to two trips before the release of your brother, and you insisted on one."

"Lothar pushed too hard. Randolph isn't stupid—I needed to prove that I would fight to protect him, or he would have been suspicious."

"Was that the reason?" he asked. "Or was it to get your brother out earlier?"

"In the American's eyes, isn't that my goal? Why wouldn't I want Konrad freed as soon as possible?"

"In the future, you must take your lead from Lothar."

"That won't work. Randolph didn't like Lothar. He doesn't trust him. He says it is too great a risk to take without guarantees that my brother will be released."

"Before, you were confident that he would do whatever you asked." It was an accusation. "What has happened?"

A waiter approached the table and the Russian made a gesture of dismissal. The man shrugged and backed away.

"He has fallen in love with me, but he's no fool. He doesn't like working through an intermediary, a middleman. He wants to meet with Lothar's principal." She hesitated, waiting, knowing that she had to be very careful with what she said. "I've been thinking. I could tell Dillon that Lothar's contact is a Russian. An advisor to the government. A corrupt one. The Americans think that you run things here, so he will believe that."

She watched his face, wondering how he would react to the lines Hawes had fed her, but to her surprise he showed no emotion.

"A corrupt advisor?"

"Perhaps you could play that part? You could meet with him." She tried to stay calm. If Comrade Mikhail rejected the idea, then many things would end—her relationship with Dillon, her time at the Neues Theater, her hopes of bringing Konrad to the West.

He frowned, skeptical. "He would take that risk? Meet with a Russian?"

"One with the power to free my brother? Yes, I can convince him. I am sure that I can."

He didn't respond, and Christa waited, knowing that she shouldn't say anything more. She needed to let him think it through. He would be suspicious of her motives, wary that she was trying to manipulate him on behalf of her brother.

"You will bring him to the East," he said. "Assure him that I can free your brother if he holds up his side of the bargain. I will meet with him. A place in Friedrichshain where we won't be disturbed. On May Day, when the city is preoccupied with the parades and rallies. An ideal day for our purposes."

"These smuggling trips. They're to compromise him, aren't they?"

"You will get your brother back. That's what matters to you, isn't it?"

"It is," she said. "And you promise to free him after the American does what you ask? After one trip?"

"He will be released, but he will remain in East Berlin. He will be watched. As will you."

She nodded, but didn't say anything. It was enough that Konrad would be freed. She was confident that she could find a way to get him to the West. There was Dillon's car—if he could smuggle items into the East, he could smuggle them out.

Comrade Mikhail rose from the table, and, without another word to her, walked out of the restaurant. He was angry with her, at losing control over the situation. She didn't care. She had accomplished her goal—a meeting between Dillon and the Russian.

She sat alone, thinking about her future, and that of her brother. Before, it had depended on a Russian spy. Now, an English one. But for the first time, she had begun to believe that there was a way out.

* * *

The phone was ringing in Hawes' flat when he returned from running some errands. When he picked it up, he heard Einhardt Schlegel's voice on the other end: "Fifteen minutes. The bridge." Then the line went dead. Hawes understood the message—Einhardt wanted to meet at the Moabiter Bridge, located within walking distance of his flat, around a bend in the Spree.

He looked out his window at the river. A pleasure boat was moving down the Spree at a leisurely pace, the couple aboard relaxing with wine glasses in their hands. A breeze moved through the willow trees along the riverbank.

He took his time on the way to the bridge. He found Einhardt standing on the pedestrian walkway near the middle of the bridge. They leaned over the railing of the bridge, two friends watching the Spree flow by, enjoying the late afternoon sun. Hawes glanced over at the nearby terrace of the Buchwald, a popular pastry shop, where patrons were enjoying ice cream and Baumkuchen cakes, the house specialty, along with coffee.

"I've made the arrangements that you requested," Einhardt said.

"Thank you."

"There's more to tell. It's not good. The Boar contacted me yesterday. He says the operation against Randolph is proceeding. They're going to frame Randolph for a crime. Arrest him on May Day—quite symbolic, of course—and refuse to turn him over to the Allies. No diplomatic immunity. They're going to make quite a show of it."

"A crime? Smuggling?"

"I'm not sure. The Boar won't tell me all that he knows until he's safely on our side of the border." He looked directly at Hawes. "What do you want me to do?"

"If he disappears, won't that alert Durov that something may be up?"

"I thought of that. We can buy some time. Have him call in sick. Violently ill. Can't make it into the office."

"Bring him across, then," Hawes said. "He has to tell us what he knows."

"Once I do that, I'll have to involve my superiors, and they'll want a full interrogation of Kruger. That's his name. Ralf Kruger. The protocol is to bring defectors to headquarters in Pullach."

"How long can you delay that?"

Einhardt scratched his chin, considering the question. "A day. Two days. I have a place where he can stay. Out of the way." He handed a slip of paper to Hawes. "Here's the address. It's in Wedding, in the French sector. He should be there by early afternoon. Why don't we meet there and debrief him together?"

Hawes nodded.

"You can stand down on this, Feliks," Einhardt said. "Remove the American from play, and they're left with nothing."

"And we lose any chance to hit Durov and the people behind him."

"I would take care, my friend. A lot can go wrong."

"I've never run an operation where that wasn't the case. I have a good feeling about this one. I want to play our hand out to the end."

NINETEEN

Christa awoke with a start, her heart racing, as she remembered the dream—a vivid nightmare that left her with a lingering and palpable sense of dread.

It took her a moment to realize where she was—in her narrow bed in the Wilmersdorf flat.

In her dream, it had been May Day and she and Dillon were driving in his Ford, on their way to the Friedrichshain address she had been given. Suddenly ahead of them, the Russian, Comrade Mikhail, appeared, standing in the street, blocking their way. His face was flushed red with anger. He had his hand up, the palm facing them, signaling them to stop.

Dillon had cursed and then accelerated the vehicle, and Christa had watched in horror as the car struck the Russian, tossing him into the air like a rag doll. But then, ahead of them a line of Vopos with machine guns had formed across the street. She begged Dillon to pull over, and he reluctantly brought the Ford to a stop.

Gerta, the Stasi officer, stepped out of the line of police and advanced on them. She brandished an ugly black pistol in her hand.

She demanded they get out of the car, staring directly at Christa all the while. "Or I will kill your brother."

Christa realized that Konrad was standing behind Gerta, his hands shackled, a dejected look on his face, and that Ralf Kruger waited steps away, holding another pair of handcuffs.

Dillon got out of the car first, and then Christa. They stood in front of the Ford, illuminated by its headlights.

Gerta smirked, triumphant. "We'll see how you do in Hohenschönhausen. We'll see if you're so snobby after the guards finish with you."

That was when Dillon rushed at her, and Christa heard gunshots and the sound of someone groaning, and she screamed, jolting herself out of sleep.

Her nightmare had felt so real. She breathed deeply, trying to bring her heart rate back to normal. It took several minutes to calm herself.

She lay on her back, now fully awake, staring at the ceiling. Was the nightmare some sort of premonition? Or just her subconscious at work, a reflection of her anxiety and trepidation about what lay ahead?

Could she back out now? Tell Dillon and the English intelligence officer that she had changed her mind, that the danger was too great? She would have a ready-made explanation for Comrade Mikhail—that Dillon had changed his mind, gone to his security people and they had insisted that he end his relationship with her. She would remind the Russian that she had warned them not to move too quickly, that she hadn't won his complete trust yet.

Christa knew she would be blamed for the collapse of Durov's plan. They would punish her. She would be removed from the Neues Theater company. Konrad would be sent back to Hohenschönhausen, and if Durov was feeling particularly vengeful, her brother might be transferred to Bautzen. She couldn't let that happen.

She peered out the window by her bed. In the moonlight she could see the empty street below. It was silent outside—no sounds of passing cars or any other noise. She tried closing her eyes, breathing slowly, keeping still, hoping to go back to sleep.

She knew that she had to go ahead with what Hawes had designed. There really wasn't any other course of action open.

* * *

It took twenty minutes of searching the neighborhood, but Hawes eventually found the address in Wedding on the slip of paper that Einhardt had given him. It was a nondescript, squat brick building that had seen better days. Paint was peeling from the front door. When he rang the bell, a pudgy, middle-aged woman in a floral house dress opened the door and stood facing him, her hands on her ample hips. She wore multiple bracelets of brass and silver on her wrists, and she had caked too much makeup on her face.

"What can I do for you?" she asked, the bracelets jangling as she moved her fleshy arms.

"I'm here for Einhardt."

She looked him up and down, studying him critically, taking his measure. "Not here for one of the girls?"

"Einhardt. I'm here for Einhardt."

Clearly disappointed with his answer, she led him into a garish salon with light green wallpaper and two matching emerald green couches. There were paintings of tigers, lions, and elephants on the walls. Einhardt Schlegel, a copy of *Der Tagesspiegel* in his hands, sat in a high-backed chair. He smiled when he saw Hawes.

The woman motioned to Einhardt. "Here he is," she said, and turned on her heel and left.

"Trude has a charming side," Einhardt said, folding up the newspaper. "Since you're not a paying customer, you won't get the chance to see it."

"Some safe house," Hawes said. "It's a knocking shop."

Einhardt conceded the obvious with another smile. "That it is. A fine place to hide our Stasi friend for a few days. Trude's girls can keep him occupied. Kruger is upstairs in one of the rooms. I've been waiting for you to arrive before I began to debrief him."

Hawes followed Einhardt up the narrow staircase, almost stumbling once on the worn carpet runner. They made their way down the dimly-lit hallway to the last room to the left.

Inside the room, Kruger lounged on his bed, reading a tattered copy of *Das Journal Capriccio*, a men's magazine, a pair of reading glasses propped up on his nose. He looked up at them and dropped the magazine onto the bed.

"You brought the Englishman," he said to Einhardt. "Very good."

Einhardt asked him how he was doing and Kruger grinned.

"I certainly can't complain about the hospitality here. If I'd known this palace of pleasure was waiting for me, I'd have come over years ago."

"I see the British remain interested," he said, glancing over at Hawes. "Good. What I have to tell you both is of great value and you have little time to spare if you wish to act on my information."

"Is that so?" Einhardt asked.

"Valuable enough to deserve a bonus."

"Don't be greedy and stupid. We've made a significant investment in you, Kruger. If you don't tell us whatever it is that you know, we'll send you on your way, now. You can head over to Marienfelde and take your chances with the other refugees."

"Can't blame me for looking out for myself. Who else will?"

Hawes spoke for the first time. "You told Einhardt that the Russians want to pin a crime on the American."

"That's how it looks to me. They've brought in another man from Moscow. First Directorate. An assassin. You can understand why I'm reluctant to say much more with a man like him around. But I think the plan is to eliminate the girl, and then to make it look like the American murdered her."

"They plan to kill the girl?" Hawes asked, stunned. "You're sure of this?"

"It's why I'm sitting here," Kruger said. "I told you that it was of great importance. They can claim that the American was a CIA agent, in East Berlin as part of a Fascist May Day plot to assassinate Ulbricht. Their story will be that the girl tried to stop him and Randolph killed her. They'll release photos. Her body. The American in handcuffs.

Evidence—weapons and explosives. And they'll find some poor souls to arrest who will confess to being part of the conspiracy."

"It's a wild tale." Einhardt shook his head. "Are you sure?"

Kruger shrugged. "I heard enough."

"What do they hope to accomplish?" Einhardt asked.

"Such an incident strengthens the hand of the hardliners in Moscow," Hawes said quietly. "They can pressure Khrushchev to abandon the talks in Geneva. Follow through on the ultimatum. Perhaps close off the sector border."

"I think that's the idea," Kruger said. "When the Americans demand Randolph's release, claiming diplomatic immunity, the East Germans will say he's a spy and a murderer and refuse. That will kill the talks in Geneva."

"When do they plan to do this?" Einhardt asked.

"May Day. They want it done in time to wreck Geneva."

"My colleague and I need to talk," Einhardt said. "Stay here. We may have more questions."

"I'm bored," Kruger said. "Can you ask Trude if one of the girls would like to keep me company?"

Einhardt shook his head in disgust, and they left the room. Downstairs, he motioned for Hawes to sit down in one of the high-backed chairs in the parlor.

"I don't know how much to believe of Kruger's story," Einhardt said. "But it seems quite risky to have Randolph and the girl meet with Durov."

"Risky, yes. But we can turn this to our advantage, catch them off guard. We can hit them hard, before they realize what is happening. We may have to leave the girl exposed for a short time, but we can keep Randolph clear of it."

"And the operative from the First Directorate?"

"He has to be neutralized first," Hawes said. "We'll be prepared."

"What about Kruger?"

"I think we can make greater use of his defection. He should be implicated in the double-cross, the betrayal of the operation against Randolph. Something concrete." Hawes paused, thinking. "Kill two birds with one stone. I've told the girl that the Germans would trade for her brother. Instead, why don't we have Kruger bring him out? Send him to the Stasi prison as Durov's errand boy, carrying orders for the release of Konrad Schiller. I assume you have people who can forge the paperwork."

Einhardt frowned. "We can arrange for that. What if they question the orders?"

"Kruger has to brazen his way through. He must show up at the prison at two o'clock on the dot and present the paperwork. Durov won't be a factor. We'll be dealing with him."

"And if Kruger fails? And they arrest him?"

"Kruger has to insist that he was only following Durov's orders. He has to stick to that story."

"You're sure you want to proceed with the rest of the plan?"

"I do," Hawes said briskly. "And now let's inform about Kruger about his new role."

When they returned to the bedroom, Kruger again tossed the magazine to the side. Einhardt closed the door behind them.

"Did you ask Trude?" Kruger asked.

Einhardt ignored him.

"You're not done," Hawes said curtly. "You have one more task."

"That wasn't the deal."

Hawes stared at him. "We set the terms. You'll go to the Stasi jail in Lichtenberg early on the morning of May Day. You'll present papers to the officer on duty releasing Konrad Schiller. You'll bring him to the British sector."

"Are you mad?" Kruger made a face. "Out of the question. I have defected. I can't go back. I won't go back."

"You will. You must do this first."

"Why should I stick my neck out on this? What's in it for me?"

"You get to be the hero," Einhardt said. "Stick it to the bastards on your way out. You'll have the proper paperwork. You're acting on the express orders of Colonel Durov who has ordered the release of the prisoner to your custody."

"No," Kruger said. "I won't do this."

"You will," Hawes said. "If you don't, we'll cut you loose and make sure your file ends up in the hands of your Stasi colleagues. You know how they deal with traitors. There will be no place for you to hide."

"Don't think of running," Einhardt said. "My men will watch this place. You won't get far."

"Bastard," Kruger said. "I should never have trusted you."

"Everything comes with a price. You want a new life with all the money you've hoarded in the Berliner Bank, you have to pay."

Kruger glared at them. "I won't forget this. What you've done."

"I wouldn't worry too much about that," Hawes said. "Worry more about putting on a convincing show for your Stasi comrades on May Day."

Once downstairs and back in the parlor, Hawes and Einhardt reviewed the sequence of the plan for May Day.

"Can you hide the girl for a day or two once we take Durov?" Hawes looked around the parlor. "Not here. One of your regular safe houses?"

"Why not? What's one more rule to break for my improper British friend? Then what, Feliks? What's the plan for her?"

"Once the dust settles, Hamburg or Frankfurt. She'll be too vulnerable in Berlin. Her Majesty's government will finance the transition. We'd appreciate your help with the paperwork, and in keeping an eye on her."

"Will this work?" Einhardt asked. "As much as I admire your ingenuity, there's a lot that can go awry."

"There always is. We may have to improvise. I readily concede that. But it's worth the gamble. Imagine the reaction in Moscow. The confusion. The entire operation against Randolph rolled up in one day. Everyone involved back on our side of the sector border. Questions about Durov's loyalty."

"If all goes well."

"What we have to do isn't complicated. On May Day, half of Berlin will be at the rallies in the Republic Square and Karl-Marx Plaza. The Vopos will be concentrated in the center of the city, not at the border near Friedrichshain where Durov has set the meeting. We won't be noticed. We'll be in and out before they know what hit them."

"I'll have Trude send a girl to Kruger now," Einhardt said. "We want him occupied. I've a fair amount to arrange. As you do."

* * *

Hawes wasn't surprised by his cool reception at the Olympic Stadium complex when he arrived there just after lunch. He knew that his continued presence in Berlin was an irritant, and that his SIS colleagues were eager to see him return to London. They wouldn't express their hostility overtly, not when he had the backing of the director-general, but they felt no need to make him feel particularly welcome.

In the hall on the way to Robert Dawson's office, the men he passed would barely meet his glance. The station chief's secretary looked as if she had swallowed something sour when she saw him, but she quickly ushered him into Dawson's presence.

After some small talk, Hawes asked Dawson if he could arrange for a secure line to London. Dawson started to say something and then stopped and motioned to the receiver on his desk.

"You're welcome to use my phone," he said. "It's got a scrambler device. There's static noise at times, and a bit of a lag, but it's serviceable."

Hawes thanked him, and Dawson rose from behind his desk. "Anything that I should know about?" he asked.

"Nothing of import."

"Right, then. I'll give you some privacy." He left the room without looking back, closing the door softly behind him.

Hawes had to wait five minutes on hold before Dick White could take the call.

"Are you are on a secure line?" White asked.

"So I'm told," Hawes said. "I wanted to give you a quick heads-up. Things are moving quite rapidly now. We're close to resolving matters here. A few odds and ends. Should be finished within days."

"Have you reached any conclusions?"

"No change in my views. The same prime candidate. I understand that you'll be hosting him in London for now."

"We thought it prudent," White said. "A change of scenery while you get things sorted out in Berlin. Did you turn up anything of note about his role there? His connections?"

"Nothing definitive. I'm working on something else." Hawes stopped, not sure how much he should say about his plans. "I'm trying to make a new friend for the firm. Someone who could clarify many things if he's willing to cross the border."

"And how probable is it that your new friend could shed some light on the leaks from Berlin Station?"

"Impossible to say. You know how it is. They can be set in their ways. I'd say a twenty percent probability."

White cleared his throat. "Better than zero, but that doesn't sound very promising."

"I'll have this resolved, one way or the other, within days."

"That's good. It's high time that you came home."

Dawson was waiting outside his office, and Hawes thanked him again. "It looks like I'm London-bound," Hawes said. "Only here for a few more days. I'm sure the director-general will have you review my report, not that there's anything new in it."

"A shame," Dawson said, although they both knew that wasn't the case.

TWENTY

May Day carried a special, ideological significance for Berliners. For years, the international workers' holiday had prompted rival celebrations in East and West Berlin, a chance for both sides to demonstrate how they supposedly guarded the interests of the common man.

Khrushchev's ultimatum over the status of the city had, in the words of Dillon's colleague Quinn Warren, "raised the ante." The major West German trade unions planned a "Freedom Day" rally in the Square of the Republic, within sight of the Brandenburg Gate. A huge sign with the slogan "Berlin remains free"—*BERLIN BLEIBT FREI*—had been erected there. The mayor, Willy Brandt, and the American trade union leader Walter Reuther, president of the AFL-CIO, were scheduled to speak. A huge crowd was expected to congregate in the square, and most of the diplomatic staff of the Mission had been assigned to attend the gathering.

In the Russian sector, the East Germans planned a massive military parade down Unter den Linden, imitating the traditional Soviet show of power in Red Square on May Day. It was a clear violation of the Four Power agreement barring Germans soldiers in uniform from parading through Berlin. The East Germans ignored the objections of the Western Allies, a reminder that they did as they pleased in East Berlin. And the Freie Deutsche Jugend, the East German youth group, was expected to turn out in greater force than usual to march by Amerika Haus, protesting the presence of the United States in Berlin and calling for a nuclear-free Central Europe.

Dillon wasn't concerned about missing the rally—if anyone from the

Mission noticed his absence and asked him about it later, he could always claim that he had been there somewhere in the vast crowd.

He spent the morning composing what he thought of as his "Get Out of Jail Free" letter. He took his time, choosing his words with care. In the letter, he explained that he and Christa were traveling to the Russian sector in the hopes of negotiating the release of her brother, a political prisoner in the East. He acknowledged that he was not authorized to embark on such a mission, but that "sometimes Americans had to take risks for freedom" (he smiled as he typed that last overblown phrase, recognizing that if things went awry it would make for good propaganda).

He signed and sealed the letter and put the envelope in the top drawer of his desk. He ate a hasty lunch of a ham and cheese sandwich and skipped a second cup of coffee—the caffeine would only make him even more jumpy.

On the drive to Wilmersdorf he switched on RIAS—Radio in the American Sector—and listened to jazz music, Ella Fitzgerald performing "April in Paris" with the Oscar Peterson trio. The announcer explained that Fitzgerald had appeared at the Free University the year before and the combo was back in Germany on tour. For now, at least, RIAS wasn't broadcasting any May Day rally news.

Christa was waiting on the street and she got into the passenger seat of his Ford without speaking.

"Are you okay?" Dillon asked.

"God, how I hate this," she said.

"It will be fine," Dillon said. "We just need to get through the next few hours. Hawes knows what he's doing. We just have to rely on him."

"I wish to make one stop on the way. In Charlottenburg."

On their way east, they passed crowds of Berliners headed toward Mitte and the rally. There were Berlin flags and banners with a black bear, the symbol of the city, flying everywhere. The advertising columns were plastered with posters for Freedom Day, covering up the routine ads for movies and upcoming performances.

He followed Christa's directions and negotiated their way through heavy traffic in Charlottenburg, heading north toward the Tiergarten. After they crossed the Landwehr Canal, she had him follow Kluckstrasse until it became Stauffenbergstrasse and then motioned for him to park in front of a number of large gray buildings.

"This is the Bendlerblock complex," she said quietly. "During the war, the headquarters for the high command of the armed forces."

They left the car, and he followed her through the gates of an imposing building, into an inner courtyard with cobblestones and several trees. In the middle of the courtyard, there was a bronze statue of a naked young man, his hands bound in front of him.

"A memorial for General von Stauffenberg and the others executed for the July 20th plot," Christa said. "They shot them here, in the courtyard." She turned to him. "My father among them."

Dillon nodded. Hawes had told him about Franz von Schiller.

She walked over and stood in front of the statue. "I was afraid to come here until today. If the Stasi ever learned that I had been here..."

"I'm glad that we came."

"My father was ashamed for the deal with the devil he and his fellow officers made. He was willing to risk all to set it right. I wish I had his courage, that I wasn't so afraid."

Dillon fought the urge to take her into his arms. They had not touched since he had confronted her at Savignyplatz, and Christa had kept her distance. He would wait for her.

"No," he said. "You're his daughter. Strong. Brave. You're doing the right thing." He glanced at his watch. "We must go, now."

Hawes and Viktor were waiting for them near the blue U-Bahn sign in front of the Schlesisches Tor station. They climbed into the back seat of the Ford. Hawes unfolded a city map and spread it out so Dillon could see. "The meeting place on Rigaer Strasse is damn close to Stasi headquarters," he said. "We have to move quickly. Durov should be alone—he has a reputation as a lone wolf. Please follow my lead, and this should go smoothly."

They crossed into the Russian sector at the Oberbaum Bridge. There was a single Vopo standing guard and he waved them past.

"I'll bet that all the coppers are at the march," Viktor said. "Thieves would have a field day, if there was anything worth stealing over here."

Hawes asked Dillon to pull the vehicle to the side of the street. He slowed the Ford and eased into a parking space in front of a solitary Trabant. There was ample room—few East Berliners in Friedrichshain owned private cars.

"Viktor and I will get out here," he said. "Give us five minutes to reach the meeting place on foot, and then drive over there."

Hawes turned to Christa, his face drawn and intense. "You must convince Comrade Mikhail to leave the flat and come down to the street. Tell him that Dillon has remained outside and he won't enter the building until he has met him, out in the open. Dillon should stand next to the car on the sidewalk, in plain view. Tell the Russian you're worried that he's going to bolt back to the American sector."

"That has the benefit of being true," Dillon said.

"It's plausible enough," she said.

"Now, I need you to listen carefully to this." Hawes paused. "There may be a man in the flat with Durov, another Russian. If he is there, and he comes down with you and Durov to the street, it's very important that you go first, that you're in the lead. Durov and the other Russian must be slightly behind you. If either of them take you by the arm as you leave the building, you must break free and run to the car. Do you understand?"

She nodded mutely.

"I don't like the sound of this," Dillon said. "We agreed that Christa would be protected. No rough stuff."

"She will be," Hawes said. "Viktor and I will be there, ready to detain the Russian. We just need to be prepared if he has anyone with him. It's time we had our chat with him."

"What if he resists?" Christa asked.

"We're also prepared for that. We can be very persuasive." He tapped Dillon on the shoulder. "Remember, wait five minutes before you drive to the address so we have time to get into position. If you don't see us near the entrance to the building, then keep driving. Head back to the British sector. Don't stop for anyone or anything."

"I wouldn't miss this for my life," Viktor said, grinning. "You'll be surprised at how quickly this goes. Trust me."

"That's exactly what we're doing, isn't it?" Dillon asked. "Trusting you."

* * *

They drove the last stretch through Friedrichshain in silence. Dillon found he was gripping the steering wheel so hard that his knuckles had turned white. He told himself to calm down.

Rigaer Strasse was clear of cars, and Dillon guided the Ford to a stop in front of the address Christa had been given. Dillon spotted Viktor loitering near the entrance to the building with a cigarette in his mouth and, just up the street, Hawes bending over to tie his shoe.

"They're here," he said. He glanced at his wristwatch. It was just before two o'clock.

"Before this starts, I want you to know that I'm sorry for deceiving you," she said. "It was wrong. I will have to live with that."

"We can talk about that later. You must focus, now. Do as Hawes asked, and don't take any chances."

"Time for my performance," she said. "Wish me luck." Before he could respond, Christa was striding purposefully toward the entrance of the apartment building.

Dillon fought against the urge to bolt from the car and follow her. He forced himself to sit still in the driver's seat for a minute or so and then slowly exit the car, and stand next to it on the sidewalk as Hawes had directed. He could feel his heart pounding, and he tried to breathe slowly, trying to calm himself.

He wondered what would happen upstairs. Would Durov be alone? Would Christa be able to convince him to come to the street? He worried that the longer it took, the more likely it would be that someone in the neighborhood would call the Vopos about an American automobile with diplomatic plates parked on the street.

Then, there was his deepest fear, one he didn't want to acknowledge—that Christa couldn't be trusted, that she was upstairs in the flat warning Durov, betraying him and Hawes and Viktor. He knew that couldn't be so, not after what she had just said—or could it? He rejected the thought.

He focused on the sweep hand of his watch, counting the seconds and minutes, wondering how it was going. Two minutes passed. He checked again. Five minutes. Surely, she had reached the designated flat, met with Durov and encouraged him to meet Dillon at the car. Six minutes. Dillon could feel the sweat soaking through the front of his shirt. Why was it taking so long? He noticed that Hawes and Viktor had moved to either side of the entrance of the building, standing with their backs to the wall so they couldn't be spotted from above.

Then, just as he was convinced that she had failed, the front door to the building swung open and Christa appeared with a stout man wearing a fedora accompanying her. Trailing behind them was a taller man, lean and fit. Viktor moved quickly with purpose toward the entryway, a pistol in his right hand hanging loosely by his side.

Dillon watched, fascinated, as Viktor came up from behind and then raised his arm. He pointed his pistol at the back of the lean man's head and fired it twice—the sound of the gun echoing loudly—and then the man collapsed and fell to the sidewalk. Dillon had seen soldiers killed by gunfire in newsreels during the Korean War, but he had never witnessed a shooting in person. It was deeply disturbing to watch—the sudden, brutal finality of it—even if Viktor's target had represented a clear danger to them all.

Surprised, Durov whirled around and grabbed Christa by the arm. Dillon acted on instinct, sprinting toward the man and tackling him from behind. He landed on top of the Russian, pinning him to the ground, and was struggling to keep him down when Hawes joined him. Hawes placed the barrel of his pistol at the base of Durov's neck, and said something to him in Russian.

Dillon caught a flash of silver out of the corner of his eye—Hawes had a syringe in his right hand. Hawes plunged the needle of the syringe into the Durov's exposed neck before he could protest. The Russian thrashed about for a few moments, and then went limp. Dillon let go of him and rose to his feet.

Viktor joined them and quickly searched the Russian, patting him down, and taking a pistol from his coat pocket. Hawes and Viktor lifted Durov by the arms and guided him toward the Ford.

Christa had stopped ten paces from the car, her hand covering her mouth, shocked by the sudden turn of events. Dillon quickly moved to her and placed his arm around her shoulder. He could feel her trembling.

"Open the back door," Hawes called over to him. Dillon left Christa and followed Hawes' instructions. She stood at the edge of the sidewalk, unmoving.

They placed Durov in the back seat, and Viktor climbed in next to him. The Russian slumped over. Viktor took his wrist and checked his pulse, and then nodded to Hawes.

"We need to go, now," Hawes said. He turned to Christa. She stared at him blankly, and he stepped closer to her, looking into her eyes. "Christa, listen to me. You must get away from here. Walk to the S-Bahn at Frankfurter Allee. Take the train to Zoo Station, and then go to the Paris Bar. The man who questioned you at the theater will be there. He'll take you to a safe place. Don't return to your flat. Don't contact anyone at the Neues Theater. Do you understand?"

She acknowledged him with a slight nod. Dillon reached out to touch her hand. "Are you all right?"

"I'm fine," she said. She glanced at the apartment building and then quickly looked away. Dillon saw that the dead Russian was in a sitting position with his back against the entryway, his head slumped over to one side.

Christa pulled her hand away from Dillon. "Time to go," Hawes said. She nodded and walked away, heading south down the street at a brisk pace. Dillon looked around—the nearby sidewalks remained empty. No one had ventured out from the neighboring flats to investigate the sound of gunfire. It didn't pay to be too curious in East Berlin.

"I'll drive," Hawes said, waving Dillon toward the passenger seat.

"Who was the other man?" Dillon asked, once they were in the Ford. "The man you shot?"

"A complication," Hawes said. "He had been sent from Moscow. We had no other option."

"The world's a better place for that," Viktor said from the back seat. "We simply did unto him before he did unto us."

"Where now?" Dillon asked.

"The safe house is in Kreuzberg," Hawes said. "Tucked away on a side street near the sector border with Friedrichshain. We'll have some privacy there with our honored guest."

"Did you know about the other man?" Dillon stared directly at Hawes. "The one who was shot? Did you know he would be here? Was I the target?"

"We knew. We were ready for him. You were not the target. Not today. Christa was. They wanted an incident on May Day—something shocking—that would scuttle the talks in Geneva. The idea was to pin it on you."

"You knew about this, and you didn't tell me?"

Hawes didn't take his eyes on the road. "Didn't learn about their scheme until yesterday." He hesitated. "We never would have let him get anywhere near you."

"But you let Christa walk into that building. You risked her life. You son-of-a-bitch."

"The girl's no innocent. She was willing to trade you for her brother. You shouldn't forget that."

"I don't," Dillon said. "But she agreed to help us, and you put her at grave risk."

"A calculated risk, and it's paid off." Hawes glanced over his shoulder at Durov, slumped over in the back seat. "Now he's going to face the consequences."

TWENTY-ONE

There were no signs of the Volkspolizei on the short drive through the near-deserted streets of Friedrichshain on their way to the safe house in Kreuzberg.

Hawes kept to the speed limit and avoided the main streets where any police might be stationed. Dillon checked his wristwatch—only fifteen minutes had elapsed since they had arrived at the meeting place.

Dillon wished that they had not left Christa behind in Friedrichshain, but he knew it was safer for her to find her own way back to the West. He could not relax until they had crossed the painted white line on the pavement that indicated the boundary between the Russian and American sectors. He looked over his shoulder into the back seat—Durov was slouched over, limp, still unconscious.

They passed quickly through the sector checkpoint—Hawes gave the bored Trapo on duty a nonchalant wave—and Dillon breathed easier when he saw the sign announcing that they were entering the American sector.

Hawes parked the sedan on a leafy side street in front of a three-story tenement. There was a vacant lot filled with rubble from a bombed-out building on one side. The Englishman turned to Dillon and handed him the car keys.

"It's your choice whether to come inside with us," he said. "Or you can go now to the Mission. I can meet you there, later."

"I want to know why," Dillon said. "I want to see this through to the end."

"Suit yourself."

Dillon left the car and waited on the sidewalk. A young man with a lean frame and stubble on his cheeks appeared in the doorway of the building. He cradled a Thompson submachine gun in his arms. Viktor walked over to him, and they had a brief conversation in Hungarian and then the man followed Viktor to the rear door of the sedan. The two of them carried Durov's limp body up the stairs and into the building.

Dillon and Hawes followed them up the stairs to the second floor. The flat was spacious, with high ceilings and wide windows looking out onto the street. There was a single armchair in the center of the room. Viktor propped up Durov in the chair. The younger man left the room and Dillon heard his footsteps as he descended the stairs.

"Miklós will stand guard at the front of the building," Viktor said. "Better safe than sorry."

Viktor stood next to the Russian, ready to restrain him if necessary. Dillon studied Durov—he was physically unimpressive, short, a heavily lined face, rimless glasses, iron gray hair. If you encountered him on the street, you would think he was someone's grandfather, although not a kindly one—there was something harsh in the face, even in repose.

Hawes glanced at his watch. "He should be coming around any moment now."

Dillon watched as the Russian slowly returned to consciousness, his face twitching slightly as he took longer breaths. His eyelids fluttered and then, finally, he opened his eyes.

"Ah, you're awake," Hawes said. "I apologize for the methods we were forced to employ. It's not pleasant to be drugged."

"Where am I? Who are you?"

"You're in Kreuzberg in the American sector, and I'm your host. For the moment."

"I don't know you." Durov glared at him, his fingers tightly gripping the arms of the chair, but he made no attempt to get up. "I demand to be released. You have no right to hold me. I'm a diplomat."

"You're no more a diplomat than I am," Hawes said, and then, switching to German, told him that he would be released after they had discussed some matters of importance.

"You're not Germans," Durov said in English. "You're Americans. CIA."

"What does it matter?" Hawes asked. "But to satisfy your curiosity, I'm from the British Secret Service. That is of minor importance. What matters, Colonel Durov, is that you have a difficult choice to make. To stay with us, or to go."

"You kidnapped me. There's no choice. Do you take me for a traitor? Never."

"You're here, nonetheless, and so I'll ask you to hear me out on one matter. When I'm finished, you can leave if you like. We won't attempt to stop you. I'm confident that you will conclude that it's in your best interest to stay."

Durov stared at Hawes but didn't speak.

"Would you like a spot of tea?" Hawes asked. Durov refused with a shake of his head. Viktor appeared with a tea kettle and mug and poured tea for Hawes, placing the mug on a side table.

Hawes picked up the tea mug and took a sip. "Very well," he said. "Let me explain why you're here. When we learned of your plans for Miss Schiller and Dillon Randolph, we thought we could turn them to our advantage. For the past month or so I've fashioned a story of a KGB colonel who's decided to defect to the West. I've hinted to the CIA, the Germans, and to my own service, that I had a big fish on the line. One who could expose Soviet spy networks in Germany and beyond. I could only reveal the identity of this official, however, when he was safely on our side of the border, ready for exfiltration."

Hawes stirred his tea. "I prepared an extensive file for Operation West Wind with notes from my meetings with this Russian—let us call him Mikhail—as he tantalized me with hints of the Stasi and KGB operations against us in Berlin. There are photos of Mikhail arriving at meetings in East Berlin, shot from a distance." Hawes rummaged in a leather briefcase, and removed a large buff-colored folder, tied with a black ribbon. "There's a poetic justice to this, as you shall see. This afternoon we will deliver a copy of these materials to Berlin Station, the BND, and the CIA. We know that you have agents in place, leaking to you, and we anticipate that within hours or so the news of Operation West Wind and this would-be defector—and his name—will be transmitted to Moscow Center. Perhaps even microfilm of the documents."

Hawes turned to Viktor with a slight smile on his face. "Why do you think Mikhail wishes to join us? To defect?"

Viktor returned the smile, playing along with Hawes. "He realized how corrupt and lousy the system is?"

"A noble motive, but that's not why Mikhail desires to defect. No, Mikhail has been caught up in an internal conspiracy at Moscow Center and now he has developed cold feet. He had thrown his lot in with the hardliners who want Chairman Khrushchev removed, and they had settled on a dangerous and risky course of action. An incident in Berlin, a shocking and brazen assault by the imperialists. Thus, the operation against the young American diplomat Dillon Randolph to frame him for the murder of an innocent actress—presented to the world as part of a CIA assassination plot against Comrade Ulbricht. An incident that would scuttle the negotiations in Geneva and prove that Khrushchev's softness toward the West makes him unsuitable to lead the Soviet Union."

"A fantasy," Durov said, his face reddening. "A fairy tale."

"But a fairy tale that our Mikhail quickly realized was a rash one, misguided, flawed. The scheme might not only bring down Khrushchev but also trigger a shooting war. And Mikhail had an attack of conscience. He didn't want to be responsible for initiating Armageddon. He wondered whether peaceful coexistence might offer a better future for the Mother Russia. He had seen enough of the West to know that it wasn't as described in *Pravda*, and he had been deeply disturbed by Khrushchev's Secret Speech and what it revealed about the depth and extent of Stalin's crimes. In short, he had second thoughts. It pushed Mikhail to the edge, enough so that he approached us—the British—for help. I happened to be the operative he made contact with. It's in the Operation West Wind dossier, along with the deal we agreed upon—the details of the operation against Dillon Randolph, an outline of the information you would share during your debriefing in England, a promise of safe harbor in the West."

"So now you make me this traitor." Durov spat on the floor. "Lies."

"Yes, lies. But believable lies. After all, you'll be ours on paper. A nice fat account at Bordier & Cie in Geneva with your name on it. I can produce the bank statement if you care to see it."

"Absurd. It will never work. They will not believe any of it."

"When they autopsy your colleague, the one we left behind in Friedrichshain, they'll find two slugs from a Makarov, which is the weapon you carry. In my report to London I'll be sure to mention that Comrade Mikhail had to kill a man to make his escape." Hawes handed his mug to Viktor. "When you do the sums, it looks very bad for you. The file, the photos, the bank account. Killing a colleague and sabotaging the May Day operation."

"What is it that you want?" Durov said. He bowed his head.

"The names of your penetration agents in Berlin. Especially in my service. The names of anyone we haven't uncovered in London working for Moscow Center. For disclosing that, you'll get the deal I've outlined. We'll protect you, resettle you."

"And the thirty pieces of silver?" Durov spoke softly, almost in a whisper. "Isn't that the reward?"

"Your situation is different. A matter of simple self-preservation. Go back, you're committing suicide. A defector who lost his nerve. They'll torture you and break you and make you confess to it all. But if you stay, you can have a life."

"I need time to think."

"There is no time," Hawes said, his voice hardening. "You must choose now."

"You would have me betray my comrades and my country."

"Your comrades? Won't they happily put a bullet in the back of your head because of this flimsy story I've concocted. Are those your comrades? You wish to remain under such a regime?"

"History is on our side," Durov said quietly. He seemed strangely detached, almost as if he had lost interest in their impromptu debate. "Your empire is dying. Unlike you, we understand the engine of history. Our system will win in the end. What may happen to me is immaterial. I have already done my part, made my contribution."

"On that we also differ," Hawes said. "What happens to the individual, to each one of us, has to matter. That's also in the Bible: 'But every hair of the hairs of your heads is numbered.' Even yours."

Durov grunted. "I feel sick. The drugs. I must use the toilet." He looked around the room and saw Dillon for the first time.

Hawes nodded to Viktor. "Assist him."

Viktor took Durov's right elbow and helped him to his feet. He patted Durov's clothing down, and then led him by the arm to the bathroom door.

"Leave the door unlocked," he told the Russian.

They sat in silence, waiting for Durov. Viktor refilled Hawes' mug with tea and poured himself a cup.

They heard the bathroom toilet flushing, immediately followed by a loud thud. Viktor quickly moved to the door and yanked it open. Durov lay on the floor in a heap. The bitter smell of almonds and something sour hung in the air.

Viktor turned Durov over and slapped his face. "Durov!" He slapped him again. Durov didn't move. He felt for the man's pulse and shook his head. "He's gone."

Hawes and Dillon stood at the threshold of the bathroom, looking down at Durov's body sprawled on the floor next to the toilet. Dillon found himself staring at the man's scuffed shoes—one of the soles had been patched. He didn't want to look at the Russian's face.

"I searched him," Viktor said defensively. "There was nothing on him."

"It's not your fault," Hawes said. "A false tooth, cyanide inside. After all that he had seen over the years, the purges, the executions, he wanted to decide how he was going to die. Not at the hands of the interrogators in the basement of the Lubyanka. Or dying alone in some obscure place as a defector, always looking over his shoulder, dreading a final visit from the Thirteenth Department."

Viktor grimaced. "He was a hard one. The old Bolshevik had the balls to quote the Bible to you. Thirty pieces of silver."

"He had the wrong reading for the day," Hawes said. "It should have been Romans. 'For the wages of sin is death.'"

Hawes sat down and lit a cigarette. He needed to think through the situation. Durov's defiant gesture had come as a surprise. Had he feared that he wasn't going to be released? Or had he simply hoped to avoid arrest, torture, and execution at the hands of his paranoid colleagues in the KGB? Perhaps he believed that taking his own life would thwart whatever Hawes hoped to accomplish with the fabricated defection story.

"He's wrong about that," Hawes said out loud.

"Who's wrong?" Dillon asked.

"Durov. Our scheme will still work. We can reach the same ends as we would with his defection. Everything remains in place to deceive Moscow Center."

"Except your defector is dead."

Hawes took a quick puff on his cigarette. "That's an inconvenient development, but not an insurmountable one. First, we'll return Durov to the Russian sector. Viktor, you'll need Miklós for this. Put the Makarov that you fired in Durov's coat pocket, and pour some beer on his clothing. Take him in my Volkswagen to the U-Bahn station at Schlesisches Tor. Put him on a train heading East. Then get back to the British sector as quickly as you can."

"That will raise questions about his death," Dillon said. "But what else does it accomplish?"

"I inform London that my prized defector has bolted, despondent, regretting his momentary seduction by the imperialists. I express fear that in his current state of mind he might harm himself."

"Clever." It was Viktor, nodding at the idea.

Hawes stood up and dropped the cigarette onto the floor and stepped on it. "Durov's near defection will feed the paranoia of the Second Chief Directorate, their counterintelligence officers. They know about the Red Cap program to lure their people to defect. They'll be scrambling, trying to ascertain what Durov may have told us."

"And the May Day operation will have been shut down," Dillon said. "No staged incident, no plot against Ulbricht, no pretext for the hardliners to pressure Khrushchev into a confrontation. No excuse to close the sector borders."

Hawes turned to Viktor. "No time to waste. I'll see you at my flat, later. Dillon and I will drive over there now."

"I must see Christa," Dillon said.

Hawes frowned. "Not now. The CIA will want to debrief you. You can't stay in Berlin, and I imagine they'll want you flown back to Washington."

"I won't leave Berlin until I've seen Christa," Dillon said.

"Fair enough," Hawes said. "We owe you that."

* * *

Christa went directly to the theater in Charlottenburg, where she found Stefan sitting at his desk, a stack of bills in front of him. She stood there for a moment, not quite sure how to begin the conversation.

"Is everything all right?" Stefan asked. "You look worried."

"I've done something that will make them very angry," she said. "I'll have to go away, leave Berlin. You must call them now and tell them that you suspect that I'm working with the Americans. That way they won't think you were involved in what has happened, and they won't retaliate against you."

"Don't worry about me."

"I do worry. You must call them. Today. You've been good to me, Stefan. I don't want you hurt. You must dissociate yourself from me."

Stefan nodded. "Thank you." He rose from the desk and hugged her. "Is there anything I can do for you?"

She kissed him on his cheek. "You're very sweet. Just take care of yourself and everyone in the company. That's all."

* * *

Christa climbed the stairs to her flat as fast as she could. At the landing on the fourth floor, she stopped for a moment, short of breath and her heart pounding.

She felt like she had slept-walk through the day, following the script the Englishman had written. Then, there had been the sudden shock of the killing of the stranger just a few feet from her, and the subway ride back to the British sector, all the while feeling dazed and frightened.

She fumbled with her key and opened the door, discovering Liesl at the kitchen table with a cup of tea and a plate of cookies.

"Sorry, I don't have time to talk," Christa said, hurrying to her bedroom. "Maybe later."

"What's the rush?" Liesl asked, following her to the bedroom door.

Christa found her suitcase and began filling it with clothing. Liesl stood in the doorway, a look of concern on her face.

"Is something wrong?" she asked.

"Things are fine," Christa said, continuing to pack the suitcase.

"Are you going somewhere? What about tonight's performance?"

Christa stopped packing, and turned to face Liesl. "I've told Stefan. I've been called away because of a family emergency. I'll be gone for a few days. I'll call when I know more."

"You've been crying."

"I'm upset." Christa wiped her tears away and gave Liesl a wan smile. "I'll be fine, don't worry."

"You'll make that bitch Renate happy. She's been dying to play Miranda. She won't be very good, but knowing her, she'll be bragging up and down the clubs on the Ku'damm about how her interpretation of the role is a refreshing change. From you, of course."

"It doesn't matter."

"Renate has been jealous of you from the day you arrived. She's always making snide comments about you and the Berliner Ensemble." Liesl made a face. "I hate that she's your understudy and that she gets to play Miranda."

"Don't let her bother you." Christa replied. "You've been a wonderful friend, Liesl. I'll never forget that."

Liesl studied her, concerned. "They will let you come back, won't you? The authorities in the East. You will come back?"

"Nothing has changed. Don't worry. I'll be back."

Christa hesitated at the door to the apartment. "Liesl, if anyone comes asking after me, please tell them I had to go home."

"Do you mean your Ami? I would have thought you would have told him. Have things cooled off between you two?"

She shook her head. "No, things are fine. I told Dillon." She felt uncomfortable lying to her friend. Things weren't fine, and she knew that she might never see Dillon again. "There may be others who might stop by looking for me. Let them know I'm in the East."

"Others?" Liesl was puzzled.

"Please just tell them that I'm away."

"Is everything okay?"

"I don't want to talk about it. Please, just do as I ask."

"I'll tell anyone who asks that you're in the East," she said. She kissed Christa quickly on both cheeks. "Just hurry back."

TWENTY-TWO

They drove directly from Kreuzberg to the Hansa Quarter. Hawes insisted that Dillon stay with him in his flat, concerned about his safety if he returned to Dahlem.

"The KBG station at Karlshorst will soon be in an uproar," he explained. "By nightfall, they realize they have a badly botched operation on their hands, and two of their own dead. They'll start looking for answers. You and the girl are the first people they'll want to get their hands on to find out what's happened. Or to hit back."

"Where is Christa? When can I see her?"

"For now, our German friends are keeping watch over her."

"Can I see her?"

"We'll arrange something for tomorrow." Hawes looked over at Dillon. "The CIA will want to debrief you. A man named Ryder. We've agreed on the story—you were assisting in a joint operation aimed at the defection of a high-ranking KGB field officer. Durov told Moscow that he was recruiting you. That gave him cover to meet with us and negotiate his defection. You crossed into the Russian sector on two occasions. No mention of Christa. No mention of Durov's actual aims."

"That's the story?"

"I can't mention your last minute heroics. Quite courageous. Tackling the Russian. But I will note that your assistance was vital to the operation, and that you should be commended, formally, in writing."

"I'm no hero."

"You did your part. You did it well. You could have walked away, and you didn't. That counts for something in my book."

* * *

They met in the late afternoon at the Zoo, this time near the lions.

Zavatsky waited by the protective fence, an amused look on his face. He spoke first. "Lions? Do we meet here as a reminder of Rule Britannia?"

"Just a break in routine," Hawes replied. "I've a man watching us to make sure that neither of us have been tailed."

"Let's walk over to the elephants, then," Zavatsky said. "My favorites."

They walked together, side-by-side, up the path to the Elephant House.

"You have news?" There were drops of sweat on Zavatsky's forehead.

"We've had an unexpected development," Hawes said. "The operation went smoothly, but Comrade Durov proved to be a spin bowler. He threw us a pitch we didn't expect."

"Except this is not playing cricket. What did he do?"

"He rejected the options I presented. He didn't defect—I always thought that was a long shot—but he also didn't walk back into East Berlin. He took his own life. A cyanide capsule. We had him cornered and that was his escape."

Zavatsky went pale. "Is this true? Or did Durov defect, and you hope to disguise this from us?"

"You'll have proof positive soon enough. His body should have been found by now. It will appear that he died of a heart attack en route to Lichtenberg on the U-Bahn." Hawes paused. "We'll stick to the plan. I'll share the Operation West Wind file with my colleagues. And I'll report that Durov seemed depressed, that he might be having second thoughts about defecting and that I worried that he might resort to something drastic. Later, his autopsy should pick up the cyanide."

Zavatsky stared at him, not yet convinced. "What of Randolph and the girl?"

"Both are safe. Randolph goes back to the States, and we'll move the girl out of Berlin. The resolution of this matter should prove helpful to you and your like-minded colleagues. The operation a failure, Durov discredited. It will give your Chairman more room to maneuver, perhaps even an opportunity to strike a deal."

"A victory for the dashing James Bond."

"I wouldn't know about that," Hawes said. "A partial victory, if that. I was sent here to find your penetration agent in our Berlin Station. I was unable to do that. I have my suspicions, but no hard evidence. He may still be there for all we know."

"Remember the story of Hercules cleansing the stables of King Augeas. He succeeded in a day, but the thousands of cattle there continued to produce dung. Even if you had found one of our sources in London Block, why would you think that we didn't have others?"

"You may," Hawes said. "We'll find them. It's just a matter of time."

Zavatsky shrugged. "Believe that if you like. What's important is that we don't allow the fanatics on either side to destroy everything." He looked toward the Elephant House. "Do you know that your bombers drove Simba the elephant mad? The explosions deranged him. He kept trumpeting in fear even after the air raids stopped. If there is a next time, there will be no worry about frightening the animals. They will all be dead, incinerated in a flash. Like us. And like the animals in your Regent's Zoo in London."

Hawes reached inside his jacket and produced an envelope. "Here are negatives of the Operation West Wind documents. I'd suggest only passing along a few of them. The corroboration will come from what your agents send to Moscow." He proffered the envelope to Zavatsky.

"If I take this, how do I know that you won't try to blackmail me?"

"You have my word."

"The word of an English spy."

"The word of an English patriot, given to a Russian patriot."

Zavatsky accepted the envelope and quickly placed it in his jacket pocket. "I take this from you only because it is necessary. Not because I have lost confidence in socialism. I have not. We have made great strides in the years since the Revolution. Capitalism has had centuries to develop—socialism has had less than fifty years. But the tide of history is with us. Our workers know the state will provide for them. Food, clothing, shelter, health care. They will not be discarded when they grow old and can no longer work. It may take another fifty years before it is clear to all that our system is superior to yours, but that day will come."

"I'll take the other side of that bet," Hawes said. "You should know that Durov made the same argument, and I think it's a losing one. Too many of us would rather have freedom." He paused, softening. "Fifty years from now, the loser buys the drinks at the Paris Bar."

"Done," Zavatsky said. "And if we're lucky enough to be around after all those years, I doubt we'll care who wins."

* * *

At the first light, Dillon got out of bed, exhausted from a night of fitful sleep. He studied his own reflection in the bathroom mirror as he shaved. He looked tired, drawn, and he knew he was still trying to come to grips with the events of the day before. As he knotted his tie, he thought about how his life had changed so dramatically in the space of one afternoon.

He found his journal in his inside coat pocket. He felt the need to scribble a few phrases. *This city is an island. Loyalties divided. Her distant eyes. Her distant lips. Betrayal or desertion?* He stopped, thinking of the look on Christa's face and her silence after the confrontation on Rigaer Strasse. She had retreated from him, masking her emotions.

He wasn't sure what came next. It was likely that he would have to return to the States, for further debriefing. Whether he would be allowed to resume his duties at the Mission was another matter. Then there was the question of his relationship with Christa—was there anything left to salvage? Could they repair the damage? Did she want to? Did he?

He found Viktor in the living room, already awake, sitting and smoking a cigarette, a submachine gun resting across his legs.

"Are you planning to go out?" Viktor asked. "I'll need to tag along. Hawes wants you covered at all times. Like a blanket."

"Is he around?"

"He went to talk to the Americans. He said he'd be back shortly."

"I'd like to take a walk along the river."

"Sure thing. I'll swap this Tommy gun for a pistol and we'll go."

When they passed through the lobby of the apartment building, Viktor stopped him at the entrance, insisting that he step outside first and check out the street. Dillon waited impatiently, convinced that Viktor was being needlessly cautious. He left the apartment building quickly once Viktor gave the all clear sign.

As Dillon walked along the curving bank of the river, Viktor trailed him by a few paces, keeping his hand in his right jacket pocket.

Dillon stopped and stared into the dark waters of the Spree, watching the ebb and flow of the current. It was Saturday, and there were already several pleasure boats on the river.

When they returned, Hawes was there waiting for them on the front steps of his building.

"Your own people are here to pick you up," he told Dillon. He waved toward a large American car, a Buick, parked further up the street. "They'll take you to see Christa, and then they'll start your debriefing. Viktor will bring your car over to Dahlem later. I'm afraid that we weren't able to free her brother."

"I don't understand."

"We took a run at liberating Konrad. There was only a skeleton crew at the Stasi jail because of May Day. We thought the appropriate paperwork presented by a Stasi officer in an appropriately arrogant manner would work. It didn't. Konrad had been moved back to Hohenschönhausen, out of our reach."

"You promised Christa you would trade for him."

"I told her we would try to trade for him. We'll wait a bit, and then see. No promises."

Dillon followed Hawes over to the Buick. A stocky man in an ill-fitting suit got out of the passenger seat, and Hawes introduced him as Thomas Ryder.

Dillon shook Hawes' hand, and climbed into the back seat of the Buick. The driver, a fit young man with a blond crew cut, kept his eyes forward.

"We'd like a brief sit down in Dahlem before you meet with Miss Schiller," Ryder said. "Thirty minutes or so. There are a few items we should discuss."

"As long as I see Christa today..."

"You will," Ryder said. "I promise you that."

* * *

They drove to Dahlem and the CIA's Berlin headquarters in silence. Ryder waited until they were in his office with the door shut before he spoke.

"Hawes has written a brief report about the operation. You get high marks for your role. I understand there will be a formal letter of thanks forthcoming from the British Foreign Office."

"I did very little," Dillon said.

"It's not in his report, of course, but Hawes says you tackled the Russian when things got nasty."

Dillon shrugged. "That's true. I'm no hero in this, though."

Ryder placed an unlit pipe in his mouth. "Hero or not, here's what you need to know. This was a joint operation, and we deliberately kept State out of it. The goal was Durov's defection, part of a program we call Red Cap. Your role was as a cover, an excuse for meeting with the Russian. To arrange his defection. It was just you and Hawes who went into the Soviet sector on May Day. Miss Schiller had no involvement. That's what the written record will show."

"I'm not sure I understand." Dillon was confused. Why was Hawes altering the account of what had happened?

"Let me explain. First, assume that the documents about Operation West Wind, which is what we're calling it, will find their way to Moscow Center. It's best for Miss Schiller's future if she's seen as a minor player. Unaware, unwitting. And after you see her today, cut off contact. No phone calls or letters. Not for quite some time, if ever."

"I'm not sure I can agree to that."

Ryder frowned. "The idea is to make you and Hawes the targets if Moscow decides on retaliation. That's why you won't be staying in Berlin, and why Hawes will return to London, pronto. The girl will be resettled in West Germany and will fade from view. Nothing to draw attention to her. As far as the Russians are concerned, she's just one of your many conquests."

"A lousy way to end things."

Ryder shrugged. "It's the best way. After we've explained matters to Phillips and the chief of Mission, we'll put you on the plane for Washington. Everything will be squared away before you leave."

"And the State Department security people? Swanson?"

"I'll take care of it. Swanson's got no reason to squawk. All's well that ends well."

"Did it end well?" Dillon asked.

"If you look at the big picture, it did. I can see where you'd have mixed feelings. A bit of a disruption to your professional and personal life. All for a good cause."

"If there's nothing else, I'd like to see Christa, now."

Ryder nodded. "We'll take you to the safe house after you've collected your belongings for the trip to the States. And checked in at the Mission."

"How is she doing?"

"She's not happy about what happened with her brother," Ryder said. "Can't say I blame her."

Two young CIA officers stood guard outside Dillon's apartment door while he packed. He found his small suitcase and filled it with a few shirts and trousers. He retrieved his journal from his desk drawer and placed it at the top of the suitcase.

They drove to the Mission and Dillon cleaned out his desk, making sure to rip up the letter he had typed explaining his trip to East Berlin.

Dillon found himself tensing as he entered Harrison Phillips' office where Ryder and Phillips awaited him.

"Mr. Ryder has filled me on your involvement with his agency," Phillips said to Dillon. "Somewhat irregular that I wasn't notified, or the Mission chief."

"Not uncommon in this type of operation," Ryder said. "We couldn't risk an inadvertent leak."

"I hold the appropriate clearances." Phillips said, pursing his lips. "There wouldn't have been any leaks from the Mission. I can assure you of that."

"It's no reflection on you or your staff," Ryder said. "A standard precaution."

"We're sorry to lose you to Washington," Phillips said to Dillon. "Always found your political analysis quite perceptive. First rate."

Dillon thanked him. "I'd like to stay in Berlin. Apparently, that's not in the cards."

* * *

They drove further west from Dahlem, passing a neighborhood with larger homes. The driver turned onto a private road and followed it for a half mile or so through the woods before they came to a gate. He hopped out of the car and opened the gate.

There was a villa at the end of a long driveway. Set in dense forest and with only the driveway for access, it was a defensible place, ideal for a safe house. Dillon wondered who had owned the property and buildings before German intelligence—a member of the Prussian aristocracy? Or perhaps a Nazi official.

They had Dillon wait for Christa in the villa's backyard. A tall hedge screened a well-kept garden from view. Above, Dillon could see that the sky was cloudless. In the distance, he spotted the white contrail of a jet against the blue. He looked down at a bed of roses, smelling their sweetness, and that of freshly-cut grass.

The back door of the villa opened and Christa appeared, wearing sunglasses and dressed in a long, linen dress. She walked over to him slowly and stopped a few paces from him, wary, guarded. Dillon was surprised at how nervous he felt. Confronted by her beauty, he realized that he still desired her, that he wanted nothing more in that moment than to kiss her lips.

"I'm so glad to see you," he said.

"They tried to get Konrad out," she said. Her tone was flat, resigned. "They failed. He'd been sent back to prison."

"Hawes told me."

"Durov ordered the transfer. I'm sure of that. He was angry at me. He never intended to release my brother."

"I'm sorry."

"How much did you know before we went to Friedrichshain?"

"Not much. Hawes kept me in the dark. Did they tell you what Durov had planned?"

She nodded and bowed her head. "Horrid. If that story is true."

"You doubt it?" he asked, surprised.

"Who knows? I know only what I've been told. They could be lying to me. To you."

"At least Durov is gone," Dillon said.

"Hard men," she said. "Both sides. They used us for their own ends. I agreed to betray you in exchange for my brother. You cooperated for your own reasons. To prove that you could be a hero, like your brother?"

"It wasn't like that."

"Over Brecht's desk there was a sign—*Die Wahrhiet ist konkret*. 'The truth is concrete.' I used to believe that, and now I don't. We all have our own truths, and they're not always concrete. That doesn't make them any less true." She turned to look at him, her eyes hidden by the dark glasses. "What's next? Can you stay in Berlin?"

"It looks like Washington for me. A debriefing. They won't let me come back to Berlin." He cleared his throat, nervous again. "After a few months, I think I can swing a visa for you to come visit. It's beautiful in the fall in Charlottesville."

She didn't respond, her head down.

"Say something, Christa," he said. "Please."

"I don't think that a visit would be wise."

"Could you take the dark glasses off?" Dillon asked. "I'd like to see your eyes." She complied, but still didn't look at him directly. "We'd need to start over," he said. "I'm not making any assumptions about how it would go."

She glanced back at the villa, evading his eyes. "We have lied to each other," she said evenly. "For me, from the start. For you, later. There would always be that."

"It wasn't all lies."

She turned to face him. "There's Konrad. I'll never abandon him. As long as there's a chance they can get him out, I must stay here, in Germany. Besides, what would I do in America? I'm an actress. I'd be miserable without the theater. And what of your career? I'm hardly the ideal woman for an ambitious young diplomat. The witch hunters would never trust you."

"I don't have to be a diplomat. There's teaching."

"The wife of the professor? Stuck in some small college town? Would I fit that life any better? The other women gossiping about me—Professor Randolph's strange bohemian wife. And perhaps I would again betray you, out of boredom or resentment, with another man. No, that would hardly do."

"At least you've thought about a future with me," he said. "Marriage. A family."

He was surprised to see that her eyes fill with tears. She blinked them away, and then slowly wiped her cheeks with her hand.

"I imagined playing that role," she said. "But I'm not the woman for it. I know myself, and I know that."

"What of love?"

"You're in love with love, Dillon. Are you ready to settle down? With one woman? Perhaps in ten years, but not now. There is more. My feelings. Do you know the Rilke poem, 'Woman in Love'?" She didn't wait for him to respond. "I think of the end of the poem, and I fear that if I went with you I would be destined to drown in *your* life, not mine. *Und zum Untergange in einem Andern bestimmt.* I do not wish that to happen, to be lost."

"Then what are we to do?"

"We go our separate ways."

He couldn't think of anything to say.

"Did you really believe it would last?" she asked, gently. "We had the time we had. That will have to be enough."

She looked off into the distance. "I think that I'll like Hamburg," she said. "Especially in the summer. It stays light outside until very late. People dine out after the theater on terraces where you can see the harbor."

"But the winters. It gets dark early."

"The winters will make me cherish the summers even more," she said, her eyes filling with tears. She took a step back. "Good bye, Dillon."

She left the garden with her head down, without looking at him again and without pausing.

He thought about going after her, somehow convincing her that she had to come with him, that they had a future together. Even as he considered it, he knew he wouldn't. She was right. They had the time they had and it would have to be enough.

TWENTY-THREE

Washington, July 1961

The air was thick and heavy when Hawes stepped out of the air-conditioning of the Willard Hotel lobby into a humid Washington morning. He took his suit jacket off and slung it over his shoulder. He cursed soundly—he knew he would sweat profusely on the walk to the State Department.

He thought about taking a taxicab there, but decided against it. At least he might get a bit of a breeze on his walk.

He found it wasn't much better in the lobby of the main State Department building—slightly cooler than outside but still uncomfortable. He removed his sunglasses and mopped his forehead with his handkerchief.

By the elevator bank, he saw Dillon Randolph waiting for him, looking calm and collected in a blue-and-white seersucker suit.

After they shook hands, Hawes complained about the humidity. "It's like being trapped in a bloody sauna."

"It takes some time to get used to it during the summer," Dillon said. "Lots of people abandon Washington on the weekend, head for Chesapeake Bay. I go home to Charlottesville, to the mountains, as often as I can."

"Lucky you."

"Rather than suffocating inside, why don't we take a walk? There's a park nearby. See if we can find some shade and a breeze or two."

They strolled a block or so to 21st Street and walked into the park and found an open bench. Dillon took off his jacket and arranged it over the edge of the bench. The park was cooler under the shady coverage of several mature elm and linden trees.

"An interesting piece of art," Hawes said, pointing toward a bronze statue of a discus thrower sitting in the center of the park. "Can't believe that the sculptor was a Yank."

"It's a copy of the Discobolus of Myron. A fairly recent gift from the Italian government. In appreciation for our help in recovering pieces of art that were stolen during the war." Dillon glanced over at him. "You said you wanted to catch up on the phone. What brings you to Washington?"

"Unfinished business from my time in Berlin. George Blake. I flew over to brief the CIA on what we've learned from Blake's interrogation. Not that they let me sit in on it. Not included in that club." He dabbed at his face with his handkerchief. "I've been sent to assure them that the new internal policies and procedures we've instituted will prevent another penetration agent like Blake."

"I assume that Blake's Draconian sentence was meant to send a message. Forty-two years in prison."

"Blake may have done more damage than Philby and Maclean combined, when all is said and done. It's clear now that he copied the names of our agents in East Germany from Peter Lunn's card file and passed them to the KGB."

"So he was the source of the leaks from your Berlin Station?"

"He was." Hawes gazed around the park. "It's lovely here. What do they have you doing at State, now?"

Dillon explained that he had been assigned to the Berlin Task Force, the State Department unit focused on policy matters concerning the city. "I'm what passes for an expert these days," he said. "I've been in the field, I speak German. It's true that I only lasted five months in Berlin on the ground, but I've been following all of the political developments closely. I've been back to Germany a few times. Frankfurt and Bonn, not

Berlin. Our security folks say no to the idea of me in Berlin. I've told them that's absurd, but they won't budge."

"Prudent," Hawes said. "After all, you were Durov's target. Considering how things shook out, I'd hazard the guess that you're on a list for possible retaliation. They lost two men—and you're still alive."

"Did Moscow buy the idea that Durov was considering defection?"

"I hope so. I'd like to think that we sowed the seeds of doubt, if not undermined their faith in the man. At the least, we muddied the waters. 'Confusion to our enemies.' Isn't that the old saying? At a minimum, we disrupted their May Day operation, and we caused some confusion." Hawes cleaned his sunglasses with his handkerchief, pausing before he spoke again. "This probably will be my last official trip to Washington. I'm leaving the Service. There's an opportunity to work for a chap I knew in the old days. Private security. Quite generous in the pay department."

"Private security? You won't miss the Service?"

"It's a young man's game, and I'm far from young. Twenty years in harness. These past few years, it's been particularly frustrating—trying to keep our retreat from empire from turning into a rout. Then there's my family, you see. Anna hates it when I travel, and she wants Nigel to recognize me when I appear at the front door."

"I didn't know you had a child," Dillon said.

Hawes' face lit up. "He's a year old now. Anna and I had begun to think that it wasn't in the cards, and then she finds herself pregnant. I was more than happy to buy a round for everyone at the club when Nigel made his appearance." Hawes looked at Dillon. "And you? A family?"

"Not yet. At the moment, I wouldn't make much of a husband. Not with the demands of the job and the hours I work. I've thought about it, especially since I lost my father six months ago. There had been talk of him joining the Administration, but he had to withdraw from consideration when he got sick."

"I'm sorry to hear that."

"He was very proud of my service in Berlin. The letter from your Foreign Office. It mattered to him that I had contributed."

They sat in silence for a long moment. Then, Hawes stirred and spoke. "I'm off to Germany next month. London wants me to stop by Berlin Station, review the new security procedures post-Blake. Locking the proverbial barn door after the horse has bolted. Any messages I can deliver?"

Dillon shook his head. "No messages."

"I read your book on the flight over," Hawes said. "Bought the last copy they had in Foyles. *The Island City*. A striking title."

Dillon didn't respond.

"Quite timely," Hawes said. "Your poem. Lovers in a divided city. Or perhaps they aren't lovers. You borrow from Catullus on that, don't you? *Odi et amo*. I love you and I hate you."

Dillon nodded. "Sometimes it's like that. When you get in deep enough, the emotions of love and hate aren't too far removed. I've had some time to think through what happened in Berlin. Distance helps. Some of what I've learned is reflected in the poem. I think I understand where I fit in, how I was manipulated." He raised his hand to stop Hawes from interrupting. "You and Durov fed small doses of poison to us. Mistrust. Suspicion. What is real? What is genuine? Always doubt in the back of your mind. There's no recovery from that."

"It was a bad situation. I'm sorry that you got caught up in it. Her, too."

Dillon hesitated. "What about Christa? Do you know how she is doing?"

"I occasionally check with a friend in German intelligence to make sure that she's all right. She's done well for herself—leading roles in several plays in Hamburg. A boyfriend or two. Nothing permanent."

"Her brother?"

"The East Germans turned down a trade."

"Have you spoken with her?"

"In the winter. I was in Germany and phoned her. She asked about you—whether you were still in the government. She seemed to think that you might be a college professor by now."

Dillon laughed. "No, I decided to remain at State. As long as I can contribute, do my part, I'll stay. With what's going on in the world, it doesn't quite seem like the time to beat a retreat to an ivory tower and write poetry."

"That may be so," Hawes said. "We all do what we can, for as long as we can." He put his sunglasses on, hiding his eyes. "When I read your poem, I wondered about the way things turned out. I may have misjudged you. The depth of your feelings."

"Is that an apology?"

"I did what was necessary. No apologies for that. But I wanted you to know that I'm not oblivious to the consequences. I wish it had ended differently."

"But it didn't," Dillon said. "Just one of those things. Some bruised feelings, but no permanent damage. And I have quite a tale to tell, some day. Quite a tale."

"And you did your part," Hawes said. "Like I told you in Berlin. In the end that counts for something. Perhaps everything."

TWENTY-FOUR

Berlin, August 12, 1961

Frank Sinatra was crooning "One for My Baby and One More for the Road" on the jukebox when Hawes entered Doyle's just before midnight. The place had filled up with American expats and servicemen drinking beer and enjoying themselves. At the bar, two men with crew cuts and short-sleeved shirts were loudly arguing over whether Roger Maris or Mickey Mantle would break Babe Ruth's home run record.

Thomas Ryder had invited Hawes to meet him at Doyle's, an after-hours place on a side street off the Ku'damm. Doyle's had been opened by a GI of Irish heritage who had fallen in love with a pretty Berliner and decided to stay in the city rather than return to South Boston. There were pennants of baseball teams pinned up behind the bar, photos of New York City and Boston on the walls, and a large framed movie poster of John Wayne in cowboy garb in a place of honor by the front door.

Hawes looked around for Ryder and didn't see him anywhere in the room. The barman poured a beer for him, and Hawes sat at the end of the bar to wait for the CIA officer.

Hawes had spent a frustrating day at the Berlin Station reviewing the tighter security procedures that had been established after the Blake fiasco. Now, only the station chief had unrestricted access to information about agents and sources. "Need to know" had belatedly become the watchword. Under the new procedures, night duty officers had to telephone a senior officer when they needed particulars about an agent.

Hawes doubted that this bureaucratic response would prove effective. The new by-the-book safeguards might prevent some leaks, but it didn't change the reality that there might be more traitors, more Blakes and Philbys, in the Service, and there was no mechanism in place to expose them. Yet when Dick White faced questioning at Whitehall, he could claim sweeping reforms had been instituted that addressed the problem. On paper, they had.

He felt a tug on his sleeve and looked up to find Ryder grinning at him. The American was dressed in a khaki suit.

"Let's find a corner," he said. "Bring your beer with you. Don't worry about paying, I run a tab here."

They settled in at a table tucked away in an alcove in the back of the bar.

"*Prost*," Ryder said, raising his glass.

"*Prost*," Hawes replied.

"Down the hatch," Ryder said, tilting his head back and drinking deeply.

"You've lost your pipe?"

"The doc made me give it up," he said. "I'm breathing a bit better, I think, but I miss it."

They finished two rounds before they turned to talking shop.

"Did you nail the bastard?" Ryder asked. "Blake. Personally, I mean. I wondered when I heard the news. Just after you showed up here, Blake was recalled to London. Did you blow the whistle on him then?"

"I suspected him," Hawes said. "Nothing I could point to. London didn't want to take any chances with leaving him here, I imagine. There wasn't a confirmation that he was a double agent until your people debriefed Sniper, the Polish defector, and he fingered Blake."

Ryder drank from his mug. "It stands to reason that Blake betrayed the tunnel. And the agents. Thank God we held back our best stuff. No offense, but after Maclean and Philby, we assumed that anything sensitive we shared with you might go straight to Moscow."

"No offense taken."

"At least the prison sentence for Blake was quite impressive. He'll be an old man before he gets out."

"I would have introduced him to the Lord High Executioner, if I had my druthers," Hawes said. "Bloody traitor, in every sense of the word. And it's our fault. We want the world to believe that James Bond is the quintessential British agent. Ian Fleming is quite the favorite son these days. It's a joke, of course. If people only knew the truth. It's a sick organization. For ten years, our mandarins sat in Boodle's and White's and sneered at your polygraph tests and loyalty oaths. We would never resort to such vulgar tactics. We never cleaned out the incompetents and the suspect. Do you know the talent spotter who sent us George Blake? The irony is delicious. Ian Fleming. And for the last few years, instead of focusing on the Reds, we've tried to salvage what's left of our empire."

"We have the same problem at the top," Ryder said. "They cover their asses. Look at the Bay of Pigs. Who screwed that up? Not Bill Harvey. Not the other guys in the field."

"Largely the White House, from what we hear."

"You hear right." Ryder glanced around. "What ever happened with Randolph? The diplomat?"

"I saw him earlier in the summer in Washington. He's assigned to the task force on Berlin."

"I figure you must have gone to bat for him, and Dulles must have whispered in someone's ear at State. I'd call that a damn good deed, Hawes. Not sure Randolph deserved it. The guys who can't keep their pants zipped up are a disaster waiting to happen. Security risks from the get go."

"I had him wrong," Hawes said. "He fell hard for the girl."

"Did he really?"

"He did. He's a poet, you know. Published a long poem about Berlin. The girl's in the poem, and you can't read it without seeing that he was torn up over the way it ended."

"I didn't take you for a reader of poetry."

"I'm not," Hawes said. "I made an exception."

They were interrupted by an athletic young man in a starched short-sleeve shirt who came over to their table.

"Sorry to bother you, sir," he said to Ryder. "I'm the watch officer tonight. I wouldn't bother you if it wasn't important. There's something strange going on at the sector border. Unusual activity. I thought you should know."

"What sort of activity?"

"We have reports that the Vopos and East German troops are massing at the sector border, stringing up barbed wire. Creating a barrier."

"Where are they doing this?"

"From what we can gather, they're sealing off the entire border."

"Shit," Ryder said. "Thanks for finding us, Wilson. The BND warned us that this might happen. *Totale Absperrung*, total shutdown. The refugee flow has picked up since the start of the month, and the Reds are afraid they won't have a labor force if it keeps up. It doesn't help that Senator Fulbright shot his mouth off and said the East Germans had the right to close the border."

Wilson cleared his throat. "Ulbricht has released a statement that it's illegal for East Germans to cross into West Berlin."

"It appears that an informal reconnaissance mission is in order," Ryder said. He swayed slightly when he rose to his feet, righting himself by holding onto the tabletop.

"We'll let you drive, son," Ryder said. "I've had too much firewater tonight."

Outside Doyle's, they climbed into Wilson's Opel Rekord. He drove them up the Ku'damm toward the center of the city. When they reached Pariser Platz, within sight of the Brandenburg Gate, Ryder swore loudly. There was a large group of uniformed men on the Eastern side of the plaza working on a barbed-wire fence under harsh arc lights.

"What the hell," he said. "I think the bastards actually mean to close off the border. We should test that."

"How do you propose doing that?" Hawes asked.

"There are U.S. forces plates on the vehicle, and Wilson and I have diplo credentials. We'll see if they have the balls to try to block access to East Berlin. That's a *casus belli* on the face of it."

At the crossing, the Vopos glared at them, but after Wilson and Ryder held up their credentials to the windows, they reluctantly raised the red-and-white pole that blocked access.

Wilson drove deeper into the Russian sector. They passed a parking lot with ten armor-plated troop carriers. In Marx-Engels-Platz, Hawes counted thirty military trucks.

At the end of one side street, they heard the sound of pneumatic drills at work. Several men were using the drills to break up the cobblestones, and piling the stones high enough to act as a barrier. In the near distance, soldiers were pulling up tracks for the tram.

It was Hawes' turn to curse when he saw two massive T-54 tanks lumbering down the street. "That brings back bad memories," he said. "In Budapest, the Red Army brought in the heavy tanks at the end."

Wilson maneuvered past the tanks and they drove slowly through an intersection. At the end of one of the side streets, there was a pile of stones. Two trucks, unattended, were parked by the side of the road.

"Stop the car," Hawes said.

"What for?" Ryder asked.

"Time to stick a spoke in their wheels," he said.

Hawes left the car and weaved his way down the street until he reached the pile of cobblestones. He picked one of the larger stones and walked over to the first truck. He waved to Ryder and Wilson with his free hand and then turned and smashed the front windshield with the stone.

Then Hawes produced a pocket knife and plunged the blade into the front tires several times until there was a light hissing sound. He did the same for the back tires.

"One down," he announced. "One to go."

Ryder laughed. "Can't let you have all the fun." He opened the trunk of the Opel and rummaged around until he found a tire iron. He walked over to the second truck and swung the tire iron, producing a crack in the front windscreen. His second swing shattered it, sending a shower of glass shards over the front hood and onto the street.

Hawes looked over from the back of the first truck, which was listing to the side, its tires punctured. "Nice work," he said.

"Time to exit," Ryder said.

They climbed back into the Opel, and Wilson reversed the car and headed back to the main boulevard.

"A small gesture, but immensely satisfying," Hawes said.

They drove around the deserted streets for fifteen minutes before returning to the checkpoint by Brandenburg. The Vopos had been reinforced. A few soldiers stood by the barrier, brandishing automatic rifles. Several had large, intimidating dogs on leashes.

After they had crossed back into the British sector, Wilson pulled the car over to the side of the street.

"We need to head back to Dahlem and let Washington know what's happened," Ryder said. "Can we drop you someplace?"

"I'm staying at the Hilton. I'll call London from there. I don't need a secure line for this sorry story. They've taken measure of my prime minister and your president and decided that they'll back down. Neither London nor Washington will take any action. They aren't going to risk a war."

Ryder nodded. "It's the smart play. If we pull down the barriers, what happens? How do you propose we defend West Berlin in the event of hostilities? Assuming we can fight the East Germans and the Russians to a stand-still—which is doubtful—how are we going to resupply? An armored column up the Autobahn?"

"You're right," Hawes said. "Further proof that it's high time for me to retire."

"Is that so?"

"I've done my bit for Queen and country. I need to see more of my wife and son."

"As it happens, I'm also done here," Ryder said. "Back to the States next month. Have you ever been to Oklahoma?"

"Can't say that I have."

"That's my home. McClain County. My plan is to raise quarter horses. Leave city life behind, with all the noise and crowds. I like it when the horizon before you is open and clean." He looked over at Hawes. "You should come visit. Bring your family. Your son can learn how to ride. What's his name?"

"Nigel."

"Well, he'd be the only Nigel in Purcell, Oklahoma. That's for sure."

When they reached Budapesterstrasse, Wilson swung the Opel in front of the Hilton and Hawes climbed out of the car. The lobby was deserted when Hawes walked in—not unusual for just after three o'clock in the morning. He knew it was a mistake to telephone London in his present state of mind, but he didn't really care. He felt the need to tell someone about what he had seen and how angry it made him. Why not the groggy night duty officer back in the Broadway Building? He doubted it would make any difference, but he had decided to speak his mind, no matter the consequences.

* * *

In the morning, after a few hours sleep, Hawes walked over to Pariser Platz. Two cups of coffee had left a bitter taste in his mouth, and what he saw in the large space in front of the Brandenburg Gate didn't improve his mood.

Along the sector boundary, there was an ugly makeshift fence of concertina wire. Three of the five arches of the Brandenburg Gate were already boarded up at street level, and a phalanx of soldiers had massed near the checkpoint for vehicles.

The East Germans were busy strengthening the barrier, rolling out more barbed wire, and Hawes spotted large trucks parked nearby filled with construction materials.

A large crowd had assembled in the square, and a line of West Berlin riot police kept them a good distance from the border. Some of the young people in the crowd began chanting, "KZ, KZ, KZ," suggesting that East Berlin was being turned into a *Konzentrationslager*, a concentration camp. It was clear that the authorities were anxious to avoid any incidents that might provoke violence.

Hawes stood there for another fifteen minutes before he returned to his hotel. He found Jack Ferris of Berlin Station waiting for him in the lobby.

Ferris silently handed him a special edition of *Neues Deutschland*, the East German newspaper, that announced the closing of the border. It was filled with strained excuses for the erection of the "anti-Fascist protection rampart." The lead story reported that the barrier was necessary to guard against the dangers of West German "revanchists and militarists." Hawes wondered how many Berliners remembered Ulbricht assuring a reporter in June that he had no intention of erecting a wall.

"Whitehall is reacting as one might expect," Ferris told him. "No calls for action. We don't have the stomach for a confrontation, and I assume we're taking our lead from the Americans. Our troops are staying in their barracks, on alert, and the French and Americans have done the same."

"What of our access to the East?"

"The East Germans have left thirteen border crossing points open. They're not letting any of their people out. They've stopped anyone trying to take the S-Bahn into the Allied sector."

"Bloody hell. A sad day."

"They want you back in London," Ferris said. "Now. No delay. I gather that your call last night was not well received."

"I imagine that it wasn't," Hawes said. "I was angry and I gave it to them straight. I'm leaving the Service, you know. I've always spoken my mind, and I wasn't about to hold back now."

"I'm sure the duty officer's report made for colorful reading," Ferris said. "Why don't I drive you to Tempelhof?"

"No need to," Hawes said. "I think I can find my way there."

"Sorry, Feliks, but they were quite specific. I'm supposed to accompany you to the airfield, make sure you're on the flight."

"Do they worry I'm going to start World War Three on my own? Precipitate a tank battle at the Brandenburg Gate? Ridiculous."

Ferris didn't say anything, but Hawes knew he hadn't been far off—his angry call to London about the border closing had rattled the Broadway bureaucrats. They wouldn't want to take any chances with a hothead running around Berlin.

"I'll get my bag from my room, and check out," Hawes said. "Drive me to the airport. Why not? There's nothing more to be done here. Nothing that could conceivably matter in the grand scheme of things."

EPILOGUE

Berlin, November 9, 1989

The overseas line to New York wasn't very clear—Caleb immediately noticed an annoying crackling sound as the phone in the art gallery in the Village started ringing—but he had missed calling Meilan the day before, and he didn't like being out of touch.

During the collapse of Caleb's marriage, the couples' therapist had kept stressing the importance of communication in a relationship. While Caleb hadn't cared for the woman's vague New Age pronouncements about the need for "being present," he knew, sadly, that her assessment of his shortcomings as a husband was accurate, and he didn't want to make the same mistakes with Meilan that he had with Madeleine.

On the fourth ring of the gallery phone, the latest intern from NYU, Francesca, answered and agreed to find Meilan. Caleb waited, listening to the static, waiting for his wife to pick up the phone.

"Hey, love," she said.

"How are things?" he asked.

"All goes well. The last of the photographs should arrive tomorrow. We'll hang them, and then we should be ready for the opening." Meilan paused. "Any chance you'll be back by the weekend?"

"Not sure yet. I don't think I'll be here much longer. The demonstrators have made their point, and I think the regime will respond by making some reforms. Not New Hampshire style town hall democracy, but they'll loosen up some. They've already dumped Honecker, which was a huge deal."

Caleb had arrived in Berlin a week earlier in time to witness the massive November 4th demonstration when a million or so East Germans went to the streets to call for a free press, free elections, and the freedom to travel. They had chanted "We are the people. We are staying here," and—as he noted in the piece he filed for the *Monitor*—their message to the ruling kleptocracy had been clear.

"That sounds promising," she said. "As long as it stays peaceful. There's been a lot in the papers that the East Germans might crack down like the Chinese did with Tiananmen Square."

"I wouldn't say it can't happen, but I don't think Gorbachev would allow it. He needs the West for loans to feed his people. And I doubt the East Germans will move against the demonstrators without Moscow's support."

"It must be so exciting. Wish I could be there with you. I miss you, love. You know how I hate sleeping alone."

"No one is more anxious to fix that problem than me," he said. "I'll call again once I have my flight reservations."

"Tim and Katie have invited us for a dinner party at their place a week from Thursday. What should I tell them?"

"Tell them we'll be there," he said. "I'm eager to get back to New York. I miss the hell out of you."

"Great. I'll tell them. And you know I miss you, too, darling. Hurry home."

From his window, Caleb surveyed the street below, Fasanenstrasse, gazing at the pedestrians walking by in their light winter coats. He had chosen the Savoy because he liked staying at hotels with a history—and the Savoy had attracted the Berlin literary and artistic set in its heyday.

He was startled by the sudden ringing of the phone on his desk. It was Derek Pryce, the British freelance photographer who was working with Caleb on assignment. Derek had lived in Berlin in the early 1980's—just after the decadent David Bowie years, he joked—and knew the city and its people well, from the squatters and anarchists in Kreuzberg to the prosperous and well-heeled professionals and government bureaucrats found in Charlottenburg and Wilmersdorf.

Caleb liked and respected Derek—they had worked together covering the Pan-European Picnic in August, an event designed to promote better East-West relations at the border between Austria and Hungary. Several hundred East Germans had rushed across the border that sunny afternoon to seek asylum in the West, and since that day, thousands more had sought refuge in West Germany by passing through Hungary.

"Something strange is going on," Derek said. "Turn on the telly. The spokesman for the SED, Günter Schabowski, announced that East Germany is opening the border for travel."

"Are you sure?"

"I wouldn't have believed it, if I hadn't seen the video on ZDF. Schabowski told a news conference that this policy went into effect immediately, and that it included Berlin."

"Berlin?"

"Amazing, isn't it? I have no idea what they're up to. Part of the power struggle within the Party? Schabowski is part of the group that forced Honecker to step down, so I guess he could be considered a reformer."

"We should head over to one of the checkpoints and see what's happening. Can you meet me outside the Savoy in thirty minutes with the car? We can drive over to Checkpoint Charlie."

"Sure thing." Derek was excited. "Imagine the pics I'll get if this is true. Nothing like being in the right place at the right time."

* * *

Dillon Randolph's first visit to Berlin in three decades had involved a spur-of-the-moment decision. They had been on vacation in London, and when the BBC had shown video footage of the massive demonstrations in East Germany, he had asked Adriana if she wanted to take a side trip to Berlin. He had always wanted to show her the city, and it seemed like a good time to visit.

Since his sharpest Berlin memories centered around Charlottenburg, he had chosen the Savoy for its location—and, if he was honest, for sentimental reasons. He had fond memories of his time at the hotel.

In the Savoy's dining room on their first night in Berlin, Dillon found himself wondering what it would be like if Christa had suddenly appeared—how would he respond? She would be nearing sixty years of age, no doubt matching his gray hair and wrinkles, but he imagined her as an elegant, poised woman, still graceful, still striking. While the Christa of 1959 no longer existed, he couldn't see her ever losing her appeal.

He wondered what her life had been like, and what had happened to her. After he left State, he had lost touch with Feliks Hawes, who was his only source of information about Christa. The last Dillon had heard—some twenty years ago—Christa had started an acting school in Hamburg. She had not married, at least not yet. According to Hawes, her brother had finally been released from prison and allowed to leave East Germany—he had moved to Hamburg to live with her, but had died shortly thereafter, his health ruined.

Dillon hadn't tried to contact her. He had decided to leave the past well enough alone. He had never loved another woman quite the way he had Christa, with the same intensity, the same sense of surrender. It had been the one, and only, true romance of his life, exhilarating and disturbing—and yet, perhaps unequal in its intensity.

His first marriage had been a mistake. Jill had grown to hate Washington, and to despise Dillon for what she saw as his complicity in prosecuting the war in Vietnam. She blamed him, as well, for her persistent unhappiness. When she had moved back to California, to her mother's home in Ventura, with Sandy, their infant daughter, Dillon had been initially relieved. They had called it a trial separation, but they both knew it would most likely end in divorce. When the end of their marriage arrived, Jill had been granted sole custody of Sandy. Dillon hadn't contested it. He regretted that decision later, for it meant he never made much of a connection with his only child.

He was never as guilty on the question of Vietnam as Jill liked to believe, but he couldn't claim to be an innocent. He was part of the bureaucratic machinery that enabled and justified the war. Dillon had waited too long to leave, delaying his day of reckoning, hoping there might be a breakthrough. Negotiations. A ceasefire? A settlement? Of course, he was not the only one at State or in the White House who had accepted the Big Texan's circular logic, the mindless escalation and long-distance violence it had spawned, and the relentless march toward a wider and wider conflict. Dillon could at least claim that he had left the government before '67 and '68, when the hard choices and the sickening consequences for the country became all too clear.

He had gladly left politics behind for teaching, and settled into an academic routine at Emory & Henry, a small private college in southwest Virginia. He had been saved from loneliness by Adriana's arrival on the faculty. Life with Adriana had been different—they had been colleagues and friends before they became lovers, and their relationship had been marked by mutual respect and affection.

He had looked forward to their visit to Berlin. At dinner, he had suggested a tour of the places he remembered best, and she had loved the idea. They skipped dessert and stopped in the Savoy bar for a nightcap. There was a small group clustered around a television set in the corner, watching a newscast. Curious, they walked over to join them, and Dillon watched for a few minutes with growing amazement.

"I can't believe this," he told Adriana. "They're saying that the East Germans are opening the border. Tonight."

"It's true? Not just rumors?"

"It's an announcement by the government." It was a well-dressed younger man, standing next to them. "I'm about to head over to the sector border to see if it's true."

"Are you here in an official capacity?" Dillon asked.

"I'm a journalist," the man said. "Caleb Collins, *Christian Science Monitor*."

Dillon introduced himself, and then Adriana. "I was here as a junior diplomat, a few years before they put up the Wall," he explained. "Ages ago. Then they brought me back to Washington and made me part of what they called the Berlin Task Force. A tense time. Just before Ulbricht had them close the border."

"We were in London on holiday and flew in from Heathrow this morning," Adriana added in her lightly accented English. "Dillon has been very excited about the demonstrations, about what they mean."

"Certainly never thought we'd be here for something like this," Dillon said. "The opening of the border."

"I'll wait until we actually see East Berliners walking down the Ku'damm," Collins said. "First things first—I'm going to check out the activity at the Wall.

"Would you mind if we tag along with you?" Dillon asked.

Collins didn't answer at first, clearly reluctant.

"We'll keep out of the way," Adriana said, smiling at the journalist.

"A tight squeeze in my colleague's Volkswagen," Collins said. "What the hell. Come along and watch history in the making."

* * *

Caleb had hesitated when Dillon Randolph had asked to join him on his visit to the border. He only agreed because he thought he might be able to work Randolph into the story—an American on the scene who remembered what Berlin had been like before the Wall went up.

Caleb guessed that Adriana Randolph was in her late thirties. She was attractive with dark hair and a pert nose. Judging from her accent, she was Italian or Spanish. Her husband had to be twenty years older.

On the drive to Checkpoint Charlie, Randolph and his wife sat in the rear seat. Caleb found RIAS on the radio, and they listened as the announcer reported that massive crowds were gathering at all of the crossing points on both sides of the sector borders. When he mentioned that people were climbing on top of the Wall near the Brandenburg Gate and the border guards seemed unwilling to stop them, Derek turned to Caleb and suggested that they change plans.

"If this is really happening, I'll get the best photos there."

Caleb nodded. "It's Berlin's original heart. Let's go there."

By the time they made their way through the heavy traffic to Pariser Platz, it felt like all of Berlin—or at least everyone under forty—had decided to converge on the center of the city.

When they abandoned the car and approached the plaza on foot, they encountered scenes of jubilation. All around them people were laughing and crying, embracing, exchanging flowers, jumping up and down, dancing with joy. The crowd was drunk on the moment, not really needing the bottles of Sekt and Champagne that were being popped open around them. Some of the revelers were forming conga lines, dancing to the pop music that was blaring from portable tape recorders and car radios.

On the graffiti-covered Wall, Berliners stood waving and cheering in triumph, illuminated by television floodlights. From below the blemished concrete barrier, young men helped newcomers climb the twelve feet to the top. At spots along the Wall, others were busily assaulting the hated symbol of the city's separation with hammers, chisels, and pickaxes. All along the top of the Wall, there were people lighting sparklers and waving them.

Caleb looked over to his left and spotted a television crew—it was Tom Brokaw, the American anchorman, doing a stand-up, front-lit by a portable light.

"The wheel of history turning," Derek said. "Brilliant." He plunged into the crowd with his camera, taking pictures as rapidly as he could.

"The East Germans couldn't stop them," Caleb said. "Not even if they wanted to."

"The world turned upside down," Dillon said. "I never thought I'd see this day."

"Look at the faces," Adriana said. "So beautiful. So happy. They never thought this could happen, either."

"No one did," Caleb said. "Perhaps not even Reagan when he challenged Gorbachev to tear down the Wall. It's finally coming down. Who knows where this will stop? Communism is collapsing in front of us."

"After tonight, the city will be whole again," Dillon said. "Berlin won't be an island any more. Not after tonight."

* * *

There was a young woman swaying and dancing to the music in the crowd near Dillon, her auburn hair partially tucked under a beret. He was immediately reminded of Christa. He caught the woman's eye, and she smiled back at him. Then she was gone, pulled away by her friends as they plunged deeper into the crush of people around them.

Dillon thought again about Christa—was she watching the wild scene in Berlin on television from her home in Hamburg? Did it stir up memories—some bitter, perhaps some sweet? Perhaps he came to mind at that very moment. Did she hold any regrets? Did she wonder what had become of him after all these years? What had been the course of his life?

What might have been if, in their final meeting, they had made different decisions? If Christa had come back to the States with him? Could they have fashioned a life together? Or was she right, that it would never have worked—that, in the light of day, they weren't well suited for each other.

Dillon remembered Kierkegaard's notion that life was lived forward, but understood backward. He felt that was true for him—he believed that he had a better understanding of his past. He had been eager to do his patriotic duty when he arrived in Berlin. Later, as one of the supposed best and the brightest at State, he was ready to "bear the burden of a long twilight struggle." He had learned, sadly, the cost of that commitment. A failed marriage. An estranged daughter. His faith in the virtue of his own government, the wisdom of its leaders, shaken, if not lost.

He had also learned that there were some questions for which he would never find the answers. Had he and Christa and Hawes and Viktor contributed to the jubilant scene in front of him by what they did on May Day, 1959? In some mysterious way, had they altered the course of history, for the better? Had their secret, nasty little skirmish mattered?

There was no way to know, no clear cause and effect. Dillon hoped that Feliks Hawes had been correct on that summer day long ago in Washington—Dillon had done his part, and that counted for something.

He felt Adriana tug at his coat sleeve. "Look," she said, pointing at the young people lining the Wall. "They're so radiant. Isn't it marvelous? It's like a dream."

"Better than a dream. It's real."

"I feel so blessed to be here, to witness tonight. It's something I'll never forget."

"You're so right," he said. "It's something never, ever to forget. Ever."

AUTHOR'S NOTE

The Berlin Crisis of 1958-1961 was effectively resolved by the construction of the Berlin Wall.

The Geneva Conference in May 1959, where diplomats from France, Britain, and the United States met with their Russian counterparts to discuss the status of Berlin, had been a failure. The conference produced little beyond surfacing the possibility of a future summit between Nikita Khrushchev and Dwight Eisenhower in the United States.

In late May, Khrushchev quietly backed away from his Berlin ultimatum. The Soviet leader's visit to the United States was highlighted by visits to New York, the Golden Gate Bridge, and Hollywood (where he met Marilyn Monroe), and a Camp David session with Eisenhower. Their joint statement after their meeting sidestepped the Berlin question.

Hopes of a further thaw in U.S.-Soviet relations were dashed by the downing of an American U-2 spy plane over Russia on May 1, 1960, and the capture of the pilot, Francis Gary Powers. The U-2 incident gave Kremlin hardliners ammunition in demanding a tougher line by Khrushchev. He responded by delivering an insulting tirade over Berlin at the Four Power Summit in Paris, withdrawing his invitation for Eisenhower to visit Russia, and derailing any hopes for progress in East-West relations.

Khrushchev was unimpressed by Jack Kennedy's handling of the Bay of Pigs and rattled the young President at their fateful first meeting in Vienna in June 1961. Fearful that continued migration from East Germany would doom the SED regime, Khrushchev agreed to the construction of the Wall in August 1961. It was to physically divide Berlin for nearly three decades.

The fall of the Berlin Wall in 1989 accelerated the collapse of Communist rule over East Germany. In October 1990, Germany was reunified under the leadership of Helmut Kohl and the Christian Democrats. In less than a year, the status of Berlin and of a divided Germany had been peacefully resolved.

* * *

George Blake not only tipped off his Soviet handlers to the existence of Operation Stopwatch, the tunnel dug in 1955 to intercept Red Army communications, but also betrayed an estimated 400 Western agents working behind the Iron Curtain.

The British did not catch Blake until the spring of 1961 when Polish defector Michael Goleniewski identified him as a penetration agent. Tried at the Old Bailey and convicted of spying for a potential enemy, Blake was sentenced to forty-two years at Wormwood Scrubs prison, the longest sentence in modern times ever imposed on a British traitor.

In October 1966, Blake made a daring escape from the West London prison, assisted by an Irish prisoner, Sean Bourke, and several sympathetic British "peace activists" who smuggled him across the Channel and drove him in a camper van to Germany. He slipped across the border in Berlin, and from there traveled to Moscow, where he joined his fellow British traitors Donald Maclean and Kim Philby.

Blake defended his treachery, even after the fall of the Soviet Union. As late as 2012, when he was ninety years old, he insisted that the agents he betrayed had not been harmed or executed. Blake has never expressed remorse or regret for his crimes. In 2007, former KGB officer Vladimir Putin's Russian government honored Blake on his eighty-fifth birthday by awarding him the Order of Friendship.

To this day, it's unclear whether the full extent of Soviet penetration of British official circles has been exposed. British security was notoriously lax. Without the FBI and CIA, none of the key traitors—Guy Burgess, Maclean, Philby, Blake, the Portland spy ring—would have been caught by the British. John le Carré's George Smiley was indeed a fictional creation—there was no such spy catcher in the British intelligence establishment.

In *An Interlude in Berlin*, Feliks Hawes alerts Sir Dick White to his suspicions about Blake in the spring of 1959, just before Blake returned to England. That's my fabrication; there's no historical evidence that anyone in Berlin or London suspected Blake of passing secrets to the Soviets.

* * *

Berlin in the 21st Century is much different than the pre-Wall city of the late 1950s. Nonetheless, the dramatic changes in the urban landscape that have occurred since 1989 and the reunification of Germany have been greatest in Mitte, the center of the city, and in sections of East Berlin.

The British and American sectors in West Berlin haven't seen the same transformation. Some places are gone: Remde's St. Pauli am Zoo nightclub didn't survive the passage of time, and the Kurbel Kino closed in 2011. But in Charlottenburg, you can still stay in Greta Garbo's suite at the Savoy Hotel, and enjoy bistro food at the nearby Paris Bar. It's still possible to take the elevator to the top of the Funkturm, where you can spy both the Olympic Stadium and the shining new skyscrapers in the center of the city. There haven't been significant alterations in Dahlem, where the U.S. headquarters is now the U.S. consulate.

In East Berlin, Stasi headquarters has been turned into a museum. In 2016, some of the buildings in the complex were used to house Syrian and other migrants. The nearby *Glaubenskirche* (Faith Church) in Roedeliusplatz is now an Orthodox church.

A few historical figures appear in *An Interlude in Berlin*, including Markus Wolf of the Stasi and Dick White, Peter Lunn, and George Blake of the SIS. I have tried to stay true to the historical record, but *An Interlude in Berlin* is, after all, fiction, and I have taken some creative liberties in depicting them.

ACKNOWLEDGEMENTS

For background on the "spy wars" of Berlin, I found helpful *Battleground Berlin: CIA vs. KGB in the Cold War* by David E. Murphy, Sergei A. Kondrashev, and George Bailey; and Paul Maddrell's Cold War International History Project working paper "Exploiting and Securing the Open Border in Berlin: the Western Secret Services, the Stasi, and the Second Berlin Crisis, 1958–1961." For insight into the operations of the Foreign Service and the U.S. Mission in Berlin during the late 1950s, I turned to Brandon Groves' *Behind Embassy Walls: The Life and Times of an American Diplomat* and Marten J. Hillebrand's *Fragments of Our Times: Memoirs of a Diplomat.*

While Florian Henckel von Donnersmarck's marvelous film *The Lives of Others* is set in 1984, more than twenty years after the Berlin Crisis, I found it a constant inspiration when writing *An Interlude in Berlin*.

James Edward Lyons, a director and playwright, was kind enough to share his deep knowledge of German theater and Berlin life. Julie Flanders, a poet and actor, provided first-hand insights into both of those artistic endeavors.

Others who read portions of the novel and offered constructive criticisms include Clayton Flanders, Maria Shapiro, Glenn Speer, Chris von Dehsen, Erinn Whitaker, Stephen Flanders, and Thomas Eng.

Any errors of historical fact or flaws in interpretation are mine alone.

And I'd like to thank my loved ones, especially Maisie, for their support, understanding, and patience.

ABOUT THE AUTHOR

Jefferson Flanders has been a sportswriter, columnist, editor, and publishing executive. He is the author of *Café Carolina and Other Stories*, *The Girl from Recoleta and Other Stories of Love* and of the Cold War First Trumpet trilogy: *Herald Square*, *The North Building*, and *The Hill of Three Borders*.

Made in the USA
Middletown, DE
08 December 2019